Critical acclaim

'An excellent thriller that puts Connelly firmly in the frame as one of the stars of American crime writing'
Sunday Times

'The real thing, and the best of its kind since *Silence of the Lambs* . . . An unputdownable masterclass in thriller writing'
Time Out

'A cracker . . . it fairly coruscates with all that goes to make a good crime thriller'
Irish Times

'Most impressive . . . rich in detail, strong on character, with a fascinating plot that functions on several emotional levels . . . Connelly has, with great skill, given us a detective who inhabits a world filled only with violent, fear and danger'
People Magazine

'Impressive . . . convincing ambience, a mass of procedural detail, authentic dialogue, a speeding plot and a flawed hero'
The Times

'His methods of killing and eluding detection are infernally ingenious, adding an intellectual charge to the visceral kick of the hunt'
New York Times

'One of the most authentic pieces of crime writing I've ever read. It is an extraordinary story, one that engages the reader on the first page and never lets go'
James Lee Burke

'In-depth knowledge informs every turn of a wonderfully Byzantine plot . . . If you are an aspiring crime writer, buy this bravura display of technique'
Sunday Times

'Intensely clever, entirely credible . . . thrilling, suspenseful and securely anchored in procedure and purpose. Not a false note; deeply satisfying stuff'
Literary Review

A former police reporter for the *Los Angeles Times*, Michael Connelly is the author of sixteen acclaimed and bestselling novels. His novels have won an Edgar Award, the Nero Wolfe prize and the Anthony Award. He lives in Florida with his wife and daughter. Visit his website at www.MichaelConnelly.com.

By Michael Connelly

The Lincoln Lawyer
The Closers
The Narrows
Lost Light
Chasing the Dime
City of Bones
A Darkness More Than Night
Void Moon
Angels Flight
Blood Work
Trunk Music
The Poet
The Last Coyote
The Concrete Blonde
The Black Ice
The Black Echo

MICHAEL CONNELLY

THE CONCRETE BLONDE

This is for
Susan, Paul and Jamie,
Bob and Marlen, Ellen,
Jane and Damian

An Orion paperback

First published in Great Britain in 1994
by Orion
This paperback edition published in 1998
by Orion Books Ltd,
Orion House, 5 Upper St Martin's Lane,
London WC2H 9EA

19 20

Reissued 2007

A CIP catalogue record for this book
is available from the British Library.

ISBN-13 978-0-7528-1542-8

Typeset by Deltatype Ltd, Birkenhead, Merseyside
Printed and bound in Great Britain by
Clays Ltd, St Ives plc

The Orion Publishing Group's policy is to use papers
that are natural, renewable and recyclable products and made from
wood grown in sustainable forests. The logging and manufacturing
processes are expected to conform to the environmental
regulations of the country of origin.

www.orionbooks.co.uk

The house in Silverlake was dark, its windows as empty as a dead man's eyes. It was an old California Craftsman with a full front porch and two dormer windows set on the long slope of the roof. But no light shone behind the glass, not even from above the doorway. Instead, the house cast a foreboding darkness about it that not even the glow from the streetlight could penetrate. A man could be standing there on the porch and Bosch knew he probably wouldn't be able to see him.

'You sure this is it?' he asked her.

'Not the house,' she said. 'Behind it. The garage. Pull up so you can see down the drive.'

Bosch tapped the gas pedal and the Caprice moved forward and crossed the entrance to the driveway.

'There,' she said.

Bosch stopped the car. There was a garage behind the house with an apartment above it. Wooden staircase up the side, light over the door. Two windows, lights on inside.

'Okay,' Bosch said.

They stared at the garage for several moments. Bosch didn't know what he expected to see. Maybe nothing. The whore's perfume was filling the car and he rolled his window down. He didn't know whether to trust her claim or not. The one thing he knew he couldn't do was call for backup. He hadn't brought a rover with him and the car was not equipped with a phone.

'What are you going to – there he goes!' she said urgently.

Bosch had seen it, the shadow of a figure crossing behind the smaller window. The bathroom, he guessed.

'He's in the bathroom,' she said. 'That's where I saw all the stuff.'

Bosch looked away from the window and at her.

'What stuff?'

'I, uh, checked the cabinet. You know, when I was in there. Just looking to see what he had. A girl has to be careful. And I saw all the stuff. Makeup shit. You know, mascara, lipsticks, compacts and stuff. That's how I figured it was him. He used all that stuff to paint 'em when he was done, you know, killing them.'

'Why didn't you tell me that on the phone?'

'You didn't ask.'

He saw the figure pass behind the curtains of the other window. Bosch's mind was racing now, his heart jacking up into its overdrive mode.

'How long ago was this that you ran out of there?'

'Shit, I don't know. I hadda walk down to Franklin just to find a fucking ride over to the Boulevard. I was with the ride 'bout ten minutes. So I don't know.'

'Guess. It's important.'

'I don't know. It's been more than an hour.'

Shit, Bosch thought. She stopped to turn a trick before she called the task force number. Showed a lot of genuine concern there. Now there could be a replacement up there and I'm sitting out here watching.

He gunned the car up the street and found a space in front of a hydrant. He turned off the engine but left the keys in the ignition. After he jumped out he stuck his head back in through the open window.

'Listen, I'm going up there. You stay here. If you hear shots, or if I'm not back here in ten minutes, you start knocking on doors and get some cops out here. Tell them an officer needs assistance. There's a clock on the dash. Ten minutes.'

'Ten minutes, baby. You go be the hero now. But I'm getting that reward.'

Bosch pulled his gun as he hurried down the driveway. The stairs up the side of the garage were old and warped. He took them three at a time, as quietly as he could. But still it felt as if he were shouting his arrival to the world. At the top, he raised the gun and broke the bare bulb that was in place over the door. Then, he leaned back into the darkness, against the outside railing. He raised his left leg and put all his weight and momentum into his heel. He struck the door above the knob.

The door swung open with a loud crack. In a crouch, Bosch moved through the threshold in the standard combat stance. Right away he saw the man across the room, standing on the other side of a bed. The man was naked and not only bald but completely hairless. His vision locked on the man's eyes and he saw the look of terror quickly fill them. Bosch yelled, his voice high and taut.

'COPS! DON'T FUCKING MOVE!'

The man froze, but only for a beat, and then began bending down, his right arm reaching for the pillow. He hesitated once and then continued the movement. Bosch couldn't believe it. What the fuck was he doing? Time went into suspension. The adrenaline pounding through his body gave his vision a slow-motion clarity. Bosch knew the man was either reaching for the pillow for something to cover himself with, or he was –

The hand swept under the pillow.

'DON'T DO IT!'

The hand was closing on something beneath the pillow. The man had never taken his eyes off Bosch. Then Bosch realized it wasn't terror in his eyes. It was something else. Anger? Hate? The hand was coming out from beneath the pillow now.

'NO!'

Bosch fired one shot, his gun kicking up in his two-handed grasp. The naked man jerked upright and backward. He hit the wood-paneled wall behind him, then bounced forward and fell across the bed thrashing and gagging. Bosch quickly moved into the room and to the bed.

The man's left hand was reaching again for the pillow. Bosch brought his left leg up and knelt on his back, pinning him to the bed. He pulled the cuffs off his belt and grabbed the groping left hand and cuffed it. Then the right. Behind the back. The naked man was gagging and moaning.

'I can't – I can't,' he said, but his statement was lost in a bloody coughing fit.

'You can't do what I told you,' Bosch said. 'I told you not to move!'

Just die, man, Bosch thought but didn't say. It will be easier for all of us.

He moved around the bed to the pillow. He lifted it, stared at what was beneath it for a few moments and then dropped it. He closed his eyes for a moment.

'Goddammit!' he called at the back of the naked man's head. 'What were you doing? I had a fucking gun and you, you reach – I told you not to move!'

Bosch came around the bed so he could see the man's face. Blood was emptying from his mouth onto the dingy white sheet. Bosch knew his bullet had hit the lungs. The naked man was the dying man now.

'You didn't have to die,' Bosch said to him.

Then the man was dead.

Bosch looked around the room. There was no one else. No replacement for the whore who had run. He had been wrong on that guess. He went into the bathroom and opened the cabinet beneath the sink. The makeup was there, as the whore had said. Bosch recognized some of the brand names. Max Factor, L'Oréal, Cover Girl, Revlon. It all seemed to fit.

He looked back through the bathroom door at the corpse on the bed. There was still the smell of gunpowder in the air. He lit a cigarette and it was so quiet in the place that he could hear the crisp tobacco burn as he dragged the soothing smoke into his lungs.

There was no phone in the apartment. Bosch sat on a chair in the kitchenette and waited. Staring across the room at the body, he realized that his heart was still pounding rapidly and that he felt lightheaded. He also realized that he felt nothing – not sympathy or guilt or sorrow – for the man on the bed. Nothing at all.

Instead, he tried to concentrate on the sound of the siren that was now sounding in the distance and coming closer. After a while, he was able to discern that it was more than one siren. It was many.

ONE

There are no benches in the hallways of the US District Courthouse in downtown Los Angeles. No place to sit. Anybody who slides down the wall to sit on the cold marble floor will get rousted by the first deputy marshal who walks by. And the marshals are always out in the halls, walking by.

The lack of hospitality exists because the federal government does not want its courthouse to give even the appearance that justice may be slow, or nonexistent. It does not want people lining the halls on benches, or on the floor, waiting with weary eyes for the courtroom doors to open and their cases or the cases of their jailed loved ones to be called. There is enough of that going on across Spring Street in the County Criminal Courts building. Every day the benches in the hallways of every floor are clogged with those who wait. Mostly they are women and children, their husbands or fathers or lovers held in lockup. Mostly they are black or brown. Mostly the benches look like crowded life rafts – women and children first – with people pressed together and cast adrift, waiting, always waiting, to be found. Boat people, the courthouse smartasses call them.

Harry Bosch thought about these differences as he smoked a cigarette and stood on the front steps of the federal courthouse. That was another thing. No smoking in the hallways inside. So he had to take the escalator down and come outside during the trial's breaks. Outside there was a sand-filled ash can behind the concrete base of the statue of the blindfolded woman holding up the scales of

6

justice. Bosch looked up at the statue; he could never remember her name. The Lady of Justice. Something Greek, he thought but wasn't sure. He went back to the folded newspaper in his hands and reread the story.

Lately, in the mornings, he would read only the Sports section, concentrating his full attention on the pages in the back where box scores and statistics were carefully charted and updated each day. He somehow found the columns of numbers and percentages comforting. They were clear and concise, an absolute order in a disordered world. Having knowledge of who had hit the most home runs for the Dodgers made him feel that he was still connected in some way to the city, and to his life.

But today he had left the Sports section folded and tucked into his briefcase, which was under his chair in the courtroom. The *Los Angeles Times*'s Metro section was in his hands now. He had carefully folded the section into quarters, the way he had seen drivers on the freeway do it so they could read while they drove, and the story on the trial was on the bottom corner of the section's front page. He once again read the story and once again felt his face grow hot as he read about himself.

TRIAL ON POLICE 'TOUPEE' SHOOTING TO BEGIN
By Joel Bremmer, *Times* Staff Writer

As an unusual civil rights trial gets underway today, a Los Angeles police detective stands accused of having used excessive force four years ago when he shot and killed a purported serial killer he believed was reaching for a gun. The alleged killer was actually reaching for his toupee.

Los Angeles Police Detective Harry Bosch, 43, is being sued in US District Court by the widow of Norman Church, an aerospace worker Bosch shot to death at the climax of the investigation into the so-called Dollmaker killings.

For nearly a year before the shooting, police had sought a serial killer so named by the media because he used

7

makeup to paint the faces of his 11 victims. The highly publicized manhunt was marked by the killer's sending of poems and notes to Bosch and the *Times*.

After Church was killed, police announced they had unequivocal evidence proving that the mechanical engineer was the killer.

Bosch was suspended and later transferred from the homicide special unit of the LAPD Robbery-Homicide Division to the Hollywood Division homicide squad. In making the demotion, police stressed that Bosch was disciplined for procedural errors, such as his failure to call for a backup to the Silverlake apartment where the fatal shooting took place.

Police administrators maintained that the Church killing was a 'good' shooting – department terminology meaning not improper.

Since Church's death precluded a trial, much of the evidence gathered by police has never been provided publicly under oath. That will likely change with the federal trial. A week-long jury selection process is expected to be completed today with the opening statements of the attorneys to follow.

Bosch had to refold the paper to continue reading the story on an inside page. He was momentarily distracted by seeing his own picture, which was on the inside page. It was an old photo and looked not unlike a mug shot. It was the same one that was on his department ID card. Bosch was more annoyed by the photo than the story. It was an invasion of his privacy to put his picture out like that. He tried to concentrate on the story.

Bosch is being defended by the City Attorney's Office because he was acting in the line of duty when the shooting occurred. If any judgment is won by the plaintiff, the city taxpayers, not Bosch, will pay.

Church's wife, Deborah, is being represented by civil rights attorney Honey Chandler, who specializes in police abuse cases. In an interview last week, Chandler said she will seek to prove to the jury that Bosch acted in such a reckless manner that a fatal shooting of Church was inevitable.

'Detective Bosch was cowboying and a man ended up dead,' Chandler said. 'I don't know if he was merely reckless or if there is something more sinister here, but we will find out in the trial.'

That was the line that Bosch had read and reread at least six times since getting the paper during the first break. Sinister. What did she mean by that? He had tried not to let it bother him, knowing that Chandler would not be above using a newspaper interview for a psych-ops outing but, still, it felt like a warning shot. It let him know more was to come.

Chandler said she also plans to question the police evidence that Church was the Dollmaker. She said Church, the father of two daughters, was not the serial killer police sought and that they labeled him as such to cover up Bosch's misdeed.

'Detective Bosch killed an innocent man in cold blood,' Chandler said. 'What we are doing with this civil rights suit is what the police department and the district attorney's office refused to do: bring forward the truth and provide justice for Norman Church's family.'

Bosch and Asst City Atty Rodney Belk, who is defending him, declined comment for this story. Along with Bosch, those expected to testify in the one- to two-week case include –

'Spare change, pal?'

Bosch looked up from the paper into the grimy but familiar face of the homeless man who had staked out the front of the courthouse as his turf. Bosch had seen him out here every day during the week of jury selection, making his change-and-cigarette rounds. The man wore a threadbare tweed jacket over two sweaters and corduroy pants. He carried a plastic bag of belongings and a Big Gulp cup to shake in front of people when he asked for change. He also always carried with him a yellow legal pad with scribbling all over it.

9

Bosch instinctively patted his pockets and shrugged. He had no change.

'I'd take a dollar, you know.'

'Don't have a spare dollar.'

The homeless man dismissed him and looked into the ash can. Yellowed cigarette butts grew from the sand like a crop of cancer. He put his yellow pad under his arm and began to pick through the offerings, taking those that still had a quarter inch or more of tobacco to smoke. Every now and then he would find a nearly whole cigarette and make a clicking sound with his mouth to show his approval. He put the harvest from the ash can in the Big Gulp cup.

Happy with his findings, the man stepped back from the ash can and looked up at the statue. He looked back at Bosch and winked, then began to rock his hips in a lewd mimicry of a sexual act.

'How 'bout my girl here?' he said.

The man then kissed his hand and reached up and patted the statue.

Before Bosch could think of something to say, the pager on his belt began to chirp. The homeless man stepped back another two steps and raised his free hand as if to ward off some unknown evil. Bosch saw the look of deranged panic spread on his face. It was the look of a man whose brain synapses were spread too far apart, the connections dulled. The man turned and scurried away, out toward Spring Street, with his cup of used cigarettes.

Bosch watched him until he was gone and then pulled the pager off his belt. He recognized the number on the display. It was Lieutenant Harvey 'Ninety-eight' Pounds's direct line at the Hollywood station. He put what was left of his cigarette into the sand and went back into the courthouse. There was a bank of pay phones at the top of the escalator, near the second-floor courtrooms.

'Harry, what's happening there?' Pounds asked.

'The usual. Just waiting around. We got a jury, so now the lawyers are in with the judge, talking about openers.

Belk said I didn't have to sit in on that, so I'm just hanging around.'

He looked at his watch. It was ten to twelve.

'They'll be breaking for lunch soon,' he added.

'Good. I need you.'

Bosch didn't reply. Pounds had promised he would be off the case rotation until the trial was over. A week more, maybe two, at the most. It was a promise Pounds had no choice but to make. He knew that Bosch couldn't handle catching a homicide investigation while in federal court four days a week.

'What's going on? I thought I was off the list.'

'You are. But we may have a problem. It concerns you.'

Bosch hesitated again. Dealing with Pounds was like that. Harry would trust a street snitch before he'd trust Pounds. There was always the spoken motive and the hidden motive. It seemed that this time the lieutenant was doing one of his routine dances. Speaking in elliptical phrases, trying to get Bosch to bite on the hook.

'A problem?' Bosch finally asked. A good noncommittal reply.

'Well, I take it you saw the paper today – the *Times* story about your case?'

'Yeah, I was just reading it.'

'Well, we got another note.'

'A note? What are you talking about?'

'I'm talking about somebody dropping a note at the front desk. Addressed to you. And damn if it doesn't sound like those notes you got from the Dollmaker back when all of that was going on.'

Bosch could tell Pounds was enjoying this, the stretching it out.

'If it was addressed to me, how do you know about it?'

'It wasn't mailed. No envelope. It was just one page, folded over. Had your name on the fold. Somebody left it at the front desk. Somebody there read it, you can figure it from there.'

'What does it say?'

'Well, you're not going to like this, Harry, the timing is god-awful, but the note says, it says basically that you got the wrong guy. That the Dollmaker is still out there. The writer says he's the real Dollmaker and that the body count continues. Says you killed the wrong guy.'

'It's bullshit. The Dollmaker's letters were carried in the paper, in Bremmer's book on the case. Anybody could pick up the style and write a note. You –'

'You take me for a moron, Bosch? I know anybody could've written this. But so did the writer know that. So to prove his point he included a little treasure map, I'd guess you'd call it. Directions to another victim's body.'

A long silence filled the line while Bosch thought and Pounds waited.

'And so?' Bosch finally said.

'And so I sent Edgar out to the location this morning. You remember Bing's, on Western?'

'Bing's? Yeah, south of the Boulevard. Bing's. A pool hall. Didn't that place go down in the riots last year?'

'Right,' Pounds said. 'Complete burnout. They looted and torched the place. Just the slab and three walls left standing. There's a city demolition order against it but the owner hasn't acted yet. Anyway, that's the spot, according to this note we got. Note says she was buried under the floor slab. Edgar went out there with a city crew, jackhammers, the works . . .'

Pounds was dragging it out. What a petty asshole, Bosch thought. This time he would wait longer. And when the silence grew nervously long, Pounds finally spoke.

'He found a body. Just like the note said he would. Beneath the concrete. He found a body. That's –'

'How old is it?'

'Don't know yet. But it's old. That's why I'm calling. I need you to go out there during the lunch break and see what you can make of this. You know, is it legit as a Dollmaker victim or is some other wacko jerking us off? You're the expert. You could go out there when the judge breaks for lunch. I'll meet you there. And you'll be back in time for openers.'

Bosch felt numb. He already needed another cigarette. He tried to place all of what Pounds had just said into some semblance of order. The Dollmaker – Norman Church – had been dead four years now. There had been no mistake. Bosch knew that night. He still knew it in his guts today. Church was the Dollmaker.

'So this note just appeared at the desk?'

'Desk sergeant found it on the front counter about four hours ago. Nobody saw anybody leave it. You know, a lot of people come through the front in the mornings. Plus we had change of shift. I had Meehan go up and talk to the desk uniforms. Nobody remembers jack shit about it until they found it.'

'Shit. Read it to me.'

'Can't. SID has it. Doubt there will be any lifts, but we have to go through the motions. I'll get a copy and have it with me at the scene, okay?'

Bosch didn't answer.

'I know what you're thinking,' Pounds said. 'But let's hold our horses till we see what is out there. No reason to worry yet. Might be some stunt cooked up by that lawyer, Chandler. Wouldn't put it past her. She's the type, she'd do anything to nail another LAPD scalp to the wall. Likes seeing her name in the paper.'

'What about the media? They heard about this yet?'

'We've gotten a few calls about a body being found. They must've gotten it off the coroner's dispatch freek. We've been staying off the air. Anyway, nobody knows about the note or the Dollmaker tie-in. They just know there's a body. The idea of it being found under the floor of one of the riot burnouts is sexy, I guess.

'Anyway, we have to keep the Dollmaker part under our hat for the time being. Unless, of course, whoever wrote it also sent copies out to the media. If he did that, we'll hear about it by the end of the day.'

'How could he bury her under the slab of a pool hall?'

'The whole building wasn't a pool hall. There were storage rooms in the back. Before it was Bing's it was a studio prop house. After Bing's took the front, they rented out sections in the back for storage. This is all from Edgar, he got the owner out there. The killer must've had one of the rooms, broke through the existing slab and put this girl's body in there. Anyway, it all got burned down in the riots. But the fire didn't hurt the slab. This poor girl's body has been down in there through all of that. Edgar said it looks like a mummy or something.'

Bosch saw the door to courtroom 4 open and members of the Church family came out followed by their lawyer. They were breaking for lunch. Deborah Church and her two teenaged daughters did not look at him. But Honey Chandler, known by most cops and others in the federal courts building as Money Chandler, stared at him with killer eyes as she passed. They were as dark as burnt mahogany and set against a tanned face with a strong jawline. She was an attractive woman with smooth gold hair. Her figure was hidden in the stiff lines of her blue suit. Bosch could feel the animosity from the group wash over him like a wave.

'Bosch, you still there?' Pounds asked.

'Yeah. It looks like we just broke for lunch.'

'Good. Then head over there and I'll meet you. I can't believe I'm actually saying this, but I hope it's just another wacko. For your sake, it might be best.'

'Right.'

As Bosch was hanging up he heard Pounds's voice and brought the phone back to his ear.

'One more thing. If the media shows up out there, leave them to me. However this turns out, you shouldn't be formally involved in this new case because of the litigation stemming from the old. We are just having you out there as an expert witness, so to speak.'

'Right.'

'See you there.'

TWO

Bosch took Wilshire out of downtown and cut up to Third after he made it through what was left of MacArthur Park. Turning north on Western he could see up on the left the grouping of patrol cars, detective cars and the crime-scene and coroner's vans. In the distance the HOLLYWOOD sign hung over the northern view, its letters barely legible in the smog.

Bing's was three blackened walls cradling a pile of charred debris. No roof, but the uniforms had hung a blue plastic tarp over the top of the rear wall and strung it to the chain-link fence that ran along the front of the property. Bosch knew it hadn't been done because the investigators wanted shade where they worked. He leaned forward and looked up through the windshield. He saw them up there, circling. The city's carrion birds: the media helicopters.

As Bosch pulled to a stop at the curb he saw a couple of city workers standing next to an equipment truck. They had sick looks on their faces and dragged hard and deep on cigarettes. Their jackhammers were on the ground near the back of the truck. They were waiting – hoping – that their work here was done.

On the other side of their truck Pounds was standing next to the coroner's blue van. It looked as though he was composing himself, and Bosch saw that he shared the same sick expression with the civilians. Though Pounds was commander of Hollywood detectives, including the homicide table, he had never actually worked homicide himself. Like many of the department's administrators, his climb up the ladder was based on test scores and brownnosing, not experience. It always pleased Bosch to see someone like Pounds get a dose of what real cops dealt with every day.

Bosch looked at his watch before getting out of his Caprice. He had one hour before he had to be back in court for openers.

'Harry,' Pounds said as he walked up. 'Glad you made it.'

'Always glad to check out another body, Lieutenant.'

Bosch slipped off his suit coat and put it inside his car on the seat. Then he moved to the trunk and got out a baggy blue jumpsuit and put it on over his clothes. It would be hot, but he didn't want to come back into court covered with dirt and dust.

'Good idea,' Pounds said. 'Wish I had brought my stuff.'

But Bosch knew he didn't have any stuff. Pounds ventured to a crime scene only when there was a good chance TV would show up and he could give a sound bite. And it was only TV he was interested in. Not print media. You had to make sense for more than two sentences in a row with a newspaper reporter. And then your words became attached to a piece of paper and were there all the next day and possibly forever to haunt you. It wasn't good department politics to talk to the print media. TV was a more fleeting and less dangerous thrill.

Bosch headed toward the blue tarp. Beneath it he saw the usual gathering of investigators. They stood next to a pile of broken concrete and along the edge of a trench dug into the concrete pad that had been the building's foundation. Bosch looked up as one of the TV helicopters made a low flyover. They wouldn't get much usable video with the tarp hiding the scene. They were probably dispatching ground crews now.

There was still a lot of debris in the building's shell. Charred ceiling beams and timber, broken concrete block and other rubble. Pounds caught up with Bosch and they began carefully stepping through to the gathering beneath the tarp.

'They'll bulldoze this and make another parking lot,' Pounds said. 'That's all the riots gave the city. About a thousand new parking lots. You want to park in South Central these days, no problem. You want a bottle of soda or to put gas in your car, then you got a problem. They burned every place down. You drive through the South Side before Christmas? They got Christmas tree lots every block, all the open space down there. I still don't understand why those people burned their own neighborhoods.'

Bosch knew that the fact people like Pounds didn't understand why 'those people' did what they did was one reason they did it, and would have to do it again someday. Bosch looked at it as a cycle. Every twenty-five years or so the city had its soul torched by the fires of reality. But then it drove on. Quickly, without looking back. Like a hit-and-run.

Suddenly Pounds went down after slipping on the loose rubble. He stopped his fall with his hands and jumped up quickly, embarrassed.

'Damn it!' he cried out, and then, though Bosch hadn't asked, he added, 'I'm okay. I'm okay.'

He quickly used his hand to carefully smooth back the strands of hair that had slipped off his balding cranium. He didn't realize that he was smearing black char from his hand across his forehead as he did this and Bosch didn't tell him.

They finally picked their way to the gathering. Bosch walked toward his former partner, Jerry Edgar, who stood with a couple of investigators Harry knew and two women he didn't. The women wore green jumpsuits, the uniform of the coroner's body movers. Minimum-wage earners who were dispatched from death scene to death scene in the blue van, picking up the bodies and taking them to the ice box.

'Whereyat, Harry?' Edgar said.

'Right here.'

Edgar had just been to New Orleans for the blues festival and had somehow come back with the greeting. He said it so often it had become annoying. Edgar was the only one in the detective bureau who didn't realize this.

Edgar was the standout amidst the group. He was not wearing a jumpsuit like Bosch – in fact, he never did because they wrinkled his Nordstrom suits – and somehow had managed to make his way into the crime scene area without getting so much as a trace of dust on the pants cuffs of his gray double-breasted suit. The real estate market – Edgar's onetime lucrative outside gig – had been in the shithouse for three years but Edgar still managed to be the sharpest dresser in the division. Bosch looked at Edgar's pale blue silk tie, knotted tightly at the black detective's throat, and guessed that it might have cost more than his own shirt and tie combined.

Bosch looked away and nodded to Art Donovan, the SID crime scene tech, but said nothing else to the others. He was following protocol. As at any murder scene a carefully orchestrated and incestuous caste system was in effect. The detectives did most of the talking amongst themselves or to the SID tech. The uniforms didn't speak unless spoken to. The body movers, the lowest on the totem pole, spoke to no one except the coroner's tech. The coroner's tech said little to the cops. He despised them because in his view they were whiners – always needing this or that, the autopsy done, the tox tests done, all of it done by yesterday.

Bosch looked into the trench they stood above. The jackhammer crew had broken through the slab and dug a hole about eight feet long and four feet deep. They had then excavated sideways into a large formation of concrete that extended three feet below the surface of the slab. There was a hollow in the stone. Bosch dropped to a crouch so he could look closer and saw that the concrete hollow was the outline of a woman's body. It was as if it were a mold into which plaster could be poured to make a cast, maybe to manufacture a mannikin. But it was empty inside.

'Where's the body?' Bosch asked.

'They took what was left out already,' Edgar said. 'It's in the bag in the truck. We're trying to figure out how to get this piece of the slab outta here in one piece.'

Bosch looked silently into the hollow for a few moments before standing back up and making his way back out from beneath the tarp. Larry Sakai, the coroner's investigator, followed him to the coroner's van and unlocked and opened the back door. Inside the van it was sweltering and the smell of Sakai's breath was stronger than the odor of industrial disinfectant.

'I figured they'd call you out here,' Sakai said.

'Oh, yeah? Why's that?'

'Cause it looks like the fuckin' Dollmaker, man.'

Bosch said nothing, so as not to give Sakai any indication of confirmation. Sakai had worked some of the Dollmaker cases four years earlier. Bosch suspected he was responsible for the name the media attached to the serial killer. Someone had leaked details of the killer's repeated use of makeup on the bodies to one of the anchors at Channel 4. The anchor christened the killer the Dollmaker. After that, the killer was called that by everybody, even the cops.

But Bosch always hated that name. It said something about the victims as well as the killer. It depersonalized them, made it easier for the Dollmaker stories that were broadcast to be entertaining instead of horrifying.

Bosch looked around the van. There were two gurneys and two bodies. One filled the black bag completely, the unseen corpse having been heavy in life or bloated in death. He turned to the other bag, the remains inside barely filling it. He knew this was the body taken from the concrete.

'Yeah, this one,' Sakai said. 'This other's a stabbing up on Lankershim. North Hollywood's working it. We were coming in when we got the dispatch on this one.'

That explained how the media caught on so quickly, Bosch knew. The coroner's dispatch frequency played in every newsroom in the city.

He studied the smaller body bag a moment and without waiting for Sakai to do it he yanked open the zipper on the heavy black plastic. It unleashed a sharp, musty smell that was not as bad as it could have been had they found the body sooner. Sakai pulled the bag open and Bosch looked at the remains of a human body. The skin was dark and like leather stretched taut over the bones. Bosch was not repulsed because he was used to it and had the ability to become detached from such scenes. He sometimes believed that looking at bodies was his life's work. He had ID'd his mother's body for the cops when he wasn't yet twelve years old, he had seen countless dead in Vietnam, and in nearly twenty years with the cops the bodies had become too many to put a number to. It had left him, most times, as detached from what he saw as a camera. As detached, he knew, as a psychopath.

The woman in the bag had been small, Bosch could tell. But the deterioration of tissue and shrinkage made the body seem even smaller than it had certainly been in life. What was left of the hair was shoulder length and looked as if it had been bleached blonde. Bosch could see the powdery remains of makeup on the skin of the face. His eyes were drawn to the breasts because they were shockingly large in comparison to the rest of the shrunken corpse. They were full and rounded and the skin was stretched taut across them. It somehow seemed to be the most grotesque feature of the corpse because it was not as it should have been.

'Implants,' Sakai said. 'They don't decompose. Could probably take 'em out and resell them to the next stupid chick that wants 'em. We could start a recycling program.'

Bosch didn't say anything. He was suddenly depressed at the thought of the woman – whoever she was – doing that to her body to somehow make herself more appealing, and then to end up this way. Had she only succeeded, he wondered, in making herself appealing to her killer?

Sakai interrupted his thoughts.

'If the Dollmaker did this, that means she's been in the concrete at least four years, right? So if that's the case, decomp isn't that bad for that length of time. Still got the hair, eyes, some internal tissues. We'll be able to work with it. Last week, I picked up a piece of work, a hiker they found out in Soledad Canyon. They figure it was a guy went missing last summer. Now he was nothing but bones. 'Course out in the open like that, you got the animals. You know they come in through the ass. It's the softest entry and the animals –'

'I know, Sakai. Let's stay on this one.'

'Anyway, with this woman, the concrete apparently slowed things down for us. Sure didn't stop it, but slowed it down. It must've been like an airtight tomb in there.'

'You people going to be able to establish just how long she's been dead?'

'Probably not from the body. We get her ID'd, then you people might find out when she went missing. That'll be the way.'

Bosch looked at the fingers. They were dark sticks almost as thin as pencils.

'What about prints?'

'We'll get 'em, but not from those.'

Bosch looked over and saw Sakai smiling.

'What? She left them in the concrete?'

Sakai's glee was smashed like a fly. Bosch had ruined his surprise.

'Yeah, that's right. She left an impression, you could say. We're going to get prints, maybe even a mold of her face, if we can get what's left of that slab out of there. Whoever mixed this concrete used too much water. Made it very fine. That's a break for us. We'll get the prints.'

Bosch leaned over the gurney to study the knotted strip of leather that was wrapped around the corpse's neck. It was thin black leather and he could see the manufacturer's seam along the edges. It was a strap cut away from a purse. Like all the others. He bent closer and the cadaver's smell filled his nose and mouth. The circumference of the leather strap around the neck was small, maybe about the size of a wine bottle. Small enough to be fatal. He could see where it had cut into the now darkened skin and choked away life. He looked at the knot. A slipknot pulled tight on the right side with the left hand. Like all the others. Church had been left-handed.

There was one more thing to check. The signature, as they had called it.

'No clothes? Shoes?'

'Nothing. Like the others, remember?'

'Open it all the way. I want to see the rest.'

Sakai pulled the zipper on the black bag down all the way to the feet. Bosch was unsure if Sakai knew of the signature but was not going to bring it up. He leaned over the corpse and looked down, acting as if he was studying everything when he was only interested in the toenails. The toes were shriveled, black and cracked. The nails were cracked, too, and completely missing from a few toes. But Bosch saw the paint on the toes that were intact. Hot pink dulled by decomposition fluids, dust and age. And on the large toe on the right foot he saw the signature. What was still left of it to be seen. A tiny white cross had been carefully painted on the nail. The Dollmaker's sign. It had been there on all the bodies.

Bosch could feel his heart pounding loudly. He looked around the van's interior and began to feel claustrophobic. The first sense of paranoia was poking into his brain. His mind began churning through the possibilities. If this body matched every known specification of a Dollmaker kill, then Church was the killer. If Church was this woman's killer and is now dead himself, then who left the note at the Hollywood station front desk?

He straightened up and took in the body as a whole for the first time. Naked and shrunken, forgotten. He wondered if there were others out there in the concrete, waiting to be discovered.

'Close it,' he said to Sakai.

'It's him, isn't it? The Dollmaker.'

Bosch didn't answer. He climbed out of the van, pulled the zipper on his jumpsuit down a bit to let in some air.

'Hey, Bosch,' Sakai called from inside the van. 'I'm just

curious. How'd you guys find this? If the Dollmaker is dead, who told you where to look?'

Bosch didn't answer that one either. He walked slowly back underneath the tarp. It looked like the others still hadn't figured out what to do about removing the concrete the body had been found in. Edgar was standing around trying not to get dirty. Bosch signaled to him and Pounds and they gathered together at a spot to the left of the trench, where they could talk without being overheard.

'Well?' Pounds asked. 'What've we got?'

'It looks like Church's work,' Bosch said.

'Shit,' Edgar said.

'How can you be sure?' Pounds asked.

'From what I can see, it matches every detail followed by the Dollmaker. Including the signature. It's there.'

'The signature?' Edgar asked.

'The white cross on the toe. We held that back during the investigation, cut deals with all the reporters not to put it out.'

'What about a copycat?' Edgar offered hopefully.

'Could be. The white cross was never made public until after we closed the case. After that, Bremmer over at the *Times* wrote that book about the case. It was mentioned.'

'So we have a copycat,' Pounds pronounced.

'It all depends on when she died,' Bosch said. 'His book came out a year after Church was dead. If she got killed after that, you probably got a copycat. If she got put in that concrete before, then I don't know . . .'

'Shit,' said Edgar.

Bosch thought a moment before speaking again.

'We could be dealing with one of a lot of different things. There's the copycat. Or maybe Church had a partner and we never saw it. Or maybe . . . I popped the wrong guy. Maybe whoever wrote this note we got is telling the truth.'

That hung out there in the momentary silence like dogshit on the sidewalk. Everybody walks carefully around it without looking too closely at it.

'Where's the note?' Bosch finally said to Pounds.

'In my car. I'll get it. What do you mean, he may have had a partner?'

'I mean, say Church did do this, then where'd the note come from, since he is dead? It would obviously have to be someone who knew he did it and where he had hidden the body. If that's the case, who is this second person? A partner? Did Church have a killing partner we never knew about?'

'Remember the Hillside Strangler?' Edgar asked. 'Turned out it was stranglers. Plural. Two cousins with the same taste for killing young women.'

Pounds took a step back and shook his head as if to ward off a potentially career-threatening case.

'What about Chandler, the lawyer?' Pounds said. 'Say Church's wife knows where he buried bodies, literally. She tells Chandler and Chandler hatches this scheme. She writes a note like the Dollmaker and drops it off at the station. It's guaranteed to fuck up your case.'

Bosch replayed that one in his mind. It seemed to work, then he saw the fault lines. He saw that they ran through all the scenarios.

'But why would Church bury some bodies and not others? The shrink who advised the task force back then said there was a purpose to his displaying of the victims. He was an exhibitionist. Toward the end, after the seventh victim, he started dropping the notes to us and the newspaper. It doesn't make sense that he'd leave some of the bodies to be found and some buried in concrete.'

'True,' Pounds said.

'I like the copycat,' Edgar said.

'But why copy someone's whole profile, right down to the signature, and then bury the body?' Bosch asked.

He wasn't really asking them. It was a question he'd have to answer himself. They stood there in silence for a long moment, each man beginning to see that the most plausible possibility might be that the Dollmaker was still alive.

'Whoever did it, why the note?' Pounds said. He seemed very agitated. 'Why would he drop us the note? He'd gotten away.'

'Because he wants attention,' Bosch said. 'Like the Dollmaker got. Like this trial is going to get.'

The silence came back then for a long moment.

'The key,' Bosch finally said, 'is ID'ing her, finding out how long she's been in the concrete. We'll know then what we've got.'

'So what do we do?' Edgar said.

'I'll tell you what we do,' Pounds said. 'We don't say a damned thing about this to anyone. Not yet. Not until we are absolutely sure of what we've got. We wait on the autopsy and the ID. We find out how long this girl's been dead and what she was doing when she disappeared. We'll make – I'll make a call on which way we go after that.

'Meantime, say nothing. If this is misconstrued, it could be very damaging to the department. I see some of the media is already here, so I'll handle them. No one else is to talk. We clear?'

Bosch and Edgar nodded and Pounds went off, slowly moving through the debris toward a knot of reporters and cameramen who stood behind the yellow tape the uniforms had put up.

Bosch and Edgar stood silent for a few moments, watching him go.

'I hope he knows what the hell he is saying,' Edgar said.

'Does inspire a lot of confidence, doesn't he?' Bosch replied.

'Oh, yeah.'

Bosch walked back over to the trench and Edgar followed.

'What are you going to do about the impression she left in the concrete?'

'The jackhammers don't think it's movable. They said whoever mixed the concrete she was put in didn't follow the directions too well. Used too much water and small-grain sand. It's like plaster of paris. We try to lift the whole thing out in one piece it will crumble under its own weight.'

'So?'

'Donovan's mixing plaster. He's going to make a mold of the face. On the hand – we only got the left, the right side crumbled when we dug in. Donovan's going to try using rubber silicone. He says it's the best chance of pulling out a mold with prints.'

Bosch nodded. For a few moments he watched Pounds talking to the reporters and saw the first thing worth smiling about all day. Pounds was on camera but apparently none of the reporters had told him about the dirt smeared across his forehead. He lit a cigarette and turned his attention back to Edgar.

'So, this area here was all storage rooms for rent?' he asked.

'That's right. The owner of the property was here a little while ago. Said that all this area back in here was partitioned storage. Individual rooms. The Dollmaker – er, the killer, whoever the fuck it was – could've had one of the rooms and had his privacy to do what he wanted. The only problem would be the noise he made breaking up the original flooring. But it could've been night work. Owner said most people didn't come back into the storage area at night. People who rented the rooms got a key to an exterior door off the alley. The perp could've come in and done the whole job in one night.'

The next question was obvious, so Edgar answered before Bosch asked.

'The owner can't give us the name of the renter. Not for sure, at least. The records went up in the fire. His insurance company made settlements with most people that filed claims and we'll get those names. But he said there were a few who never made a claim after the riots. He just never heard from them again. He can't remember all the names, but if one was our guy then it was probably an alias anyway. Leastwise, if I was going to rent a room and dig through the floor to bury a body, you wouldn't find me giving no real name.'

Bosch nodded and looked at his watch. He had to get going soon. He realized that he was hungry but probably wouldn't get the chance to eat. Bosch looked down at the excavation and noticed the delineation of color between the old and newer concrete. The old slab was almost white. The concrete the woman had been encased in was a dark gray. He noticed a small piece of red paper protruding from a gray chunk at the bottom of the trench. He dropped down into the excavation and picked the chunk up. It was about the size of a softball. He pounded it on the old slab until it broke apart in his hand. The paper was part of a crumpled and empty Marlboro cigarette package. Edgar pulled a plastic evidence bag from his suit pocket and held it open for Bosch to drop the discovery in.

'It's got to've been put in with the body,' he said. 'Good catch.'

Bosch climbed out of the trench and looked at his watch again. It was time to go.

'Let me know if you get the ID,' he said to Edgar.

He dumped his jumpsuit back in the trunk and lit a fresh cigarette. He stood next to his Caprice and watched Pounds, who was wrapping up his skillfully planned impromptu press conference. Harry could tell by the cameras and the expensive clothes that most of the reporters were from TV. He saw Bremmer, the *Times* guy, standing at the edge of the pack. Bosch hadn't seen him in a while and noticed he had put on weight and a beard. Bosch knew that Bremmer was standing on the periphery of the circle waiting for the TV questions to end so he could hit Pounds with something solid that would take some thought to answer.

Bosch smoked and waited for five minutes before Pounds was done. He was risking being late for court but he wanted to see the note. When Pounds was finally done with the reporters he signaled Bosch to follow him to his car. Bosch got in the passenger side and Pounds handed him a photocopy.

Harry studied the note for a long time. It was written in the recognizable printed scrawl. The analyst in Suspicious Documents had called the printing Philadelphia block style and had concluded that its right-to-left slant was the result of it's being the work of an untrained hand; possibly a left-handed person printing with his right hand.

Newspaper says the trial's just begun
A verdict to return on the Dollmaker's run
A bullet from Bosch fired straight and true
But the dolls should know me work's not through

On Western is the spot where my heart doth sings
When I think o the dolly laid beneath at Bing's
Too bad, good Bosch, a bullet of bad aim
Years gone past, and I'm still in the game

Bosch knew style could be copied but something about the poem ground into him. It was like the others. The same bad schoolboy rhymes, the same semiliterate attempt at high-flown language. He felt confusion and a tugging in his chest.

It's him, he thought. It's him.

THREE

'Ladies and gentlemen,' US District Judge Alva Keyes intoned as he eyed the jury, 'we begin the trial with what we call opening statements by the attorneys. Mind you, these are not to be construed by you as evidence. These are more or less blueprints – road maps, if you will, of the route each attorney wants to take with his or her case. You do not consider them evidence. They may make some highfalutin allegations, but just because they say it doesn't make it true. After all, they're lawyers.'

This brought a polite titter of laughter from the jury and the rest of courtroom 4. With his southern accent, it sounded as if the judge had said lie-yers, which added to the glee. Even Money Chandler smiled. Bosch looked around from his seat at the defense table and saw that the public seats in the huge wood-paneled courtroom with twenty-foot ceilings were about half full. In the front row on the plaintiff's side were eight people who were Norman Church's family members and friends, not counting his widow, who sat up at the plaintiff's table with Chandler.

There were also about a half dozen courthouse hangers-on, old men with nothing better to do but watch the drama in other people's lives. Plus an assortment of law clerks and students who probably wanted to watch the great Honey Chandler do her thing, and a group of reporters with their pens poised over their pads. Openers always made a story – because, as the judge had said, the lawyers could say anything they wanted. After today, Bosch knew, the reporters would drop in from time to time but there probably wouldn't be many other stories until closing statements and a verdict.

Unless something unusual happened.

Bosch looked directly behind him. There was nobody in the benches back there. He knew Sylvia Moore would not be there. They had agreed on that before. He didn't want her seeing this. He had told her it was just a formality, part of the cop's burden to be sued for doing his job. He knew the real reason he didn't want her here was because he had no control over this situation. He had to sit there at the defense table and let people take their best shots. Anything could come up and probably would. He didn't want her watching that.

He wondered now if the jury would see the empty seats behind him in the spectators gallery and think that maybe he was guilty because no one had come to show support.

When the murmur of laughter died down he looked back at the judge. Judge Keyes was impressive up there on the bench. He was a big man who wore the black robe well, his thick forearms and big hands folded in front of his barrel chest, giving a sense of reserved power. His balding and sun-reddened head was large and seemed perfectly round, trimmed around the edges with gray hair and suggesting the organized storage of a massive amount of legal knowledge and perspective. He was a transplanted southerner who had specialized in civil rights cases as a lawyer and had made a name for himself by suing the LAPD for its disproportionate number of cases in which black citizens died after being put in chokeholds by officers. He had been appointed to the federal bench by President Jimmy Carter, right before he was sent back to Georgia. Judge Keyes had been ruling the roost in courtroom 4 ever since.

Bosch's lawyer, deputy city attorney Rod Belk, had fought like hell during pretrial stages to have the judge disqualified on procedural ground and to get another judge assigned to the case. Preferably a judge without a background as a guardian of civil rights. But he had failed.

However, Bosch was not as upset by this as Belk. He realized that Judge Keyes was cut from the same legal cloth as plaintiff's attorney Honey Chandler — suspicious of police, even hateful at times — but Bosch sensed that beyond that he was ultimately a fair man. And that's all Bosch thought he needed to come out okay. A fair shot at the system. After all, he knew in his heart his actions at the apartment in Silverlake were correct. He had done the right thing.

'It will be up to you,' the judge was saying to the jury, 'to decide if what the lawyers say is proven during trial. Remember that. Now, Ms Chandler, you go first.'

Honey Chandler nodded at him and stood up. She moved to the lectern that stood between the plaintiff's and the defense tables. Judge Keyes had set the strict guidelines earlier. In his courtroom, there was no moving about, no approaching the witness stand or jury box by lawyers. Anything said out loud by a lawyer was said from the lectern between the tables. Knowing the judge's strict demand for compliance to his guidelines, Chandler even asked his permission before turning the heavy mahogany altar at an angle so she would face the jury while speaking. The judge sternly nodded his approval.

'Good afternoon,' she began. 'The judge is quite right when he tells you that this statement is nothing more than a road map.'

Good strategy, Bosch thought from the cellar of cynicism from which he viewed this whole case. Pander to the judge with your first sentence. He watched Chandler as she referred to the yellow legal pad she had put down on the lectern. Bosch noticed that over the top button of her blouse was a large pin with a round black onyx stone set in it. It was flat and as dead as a shark's eye. She had her hair pulled severely back and braided in a no-nonsense style behind her head. But one tress of hair had come loose and it helped affect the image of a woman not preoccupied with her looks but totally focused on the law, on the case, on the heinous miscarriage of justice perpetrated by the defendant. Bosch believed she probably pulled the hair loose on purpose.

As he watched her start, Bosch remembered the thud he had felt in his chest when he heard she was the lawyer for Church's wife. To him, it was far more disturbing than learning Judge Keyes had been assigned the trial. She was that good. That was why they called her Money.

'I would like to take you down the road a piece,' Chandler said and Bosch wondered if she was even developing a southern accent now. 'I just want to highlight what our case is about and what we believe the evidence will prove. It is a civil rights case. It involves the fatal shooting of a man named Norman Church at the hands of the police.'

She paused here. Not to look at her yellow pad but for effect, to gather all attention to what she would say next. Bosch looked over at the jury. Five women and seven men. Three blacks, three Latinos, one Asian and five whites. They were looking at Chandler with rapt attention.

'This case,' Chandler said, 'is about a police officer who wasn't satisfied with his job and the vast powers it gave him. This officer also wanted your job. And he wanted Judge Keyes's job. And he wanted the state's job of administering the verdicts and sentences set down by judges and juries. He wanted it all. This case is about Detective Harry Bosch, who you see sitting at the defendant's table.'

She pointed at Bosch while drawing out the word dee-fend-ant. Belk immediately stood up and objected.

'Miss Chandler does not need to point my client out to the jury or make sarcastic vocalizations. Yes, we are at the defense table. That's because this is a civil case and in this country anybody can sue anybody, even the family of a –'

'Objection, Your Honor,' Chandler shouted. 'He is using his objection to further try to destroy the reputation of Mr Church, who was never convicted of anything because –'

'Enough!' Judge Keyes thundered. 'Objection sustained. Ms Chandler, we don't need to point. We all know who we are. We also do not need inflammatory accent being placed on any words. Words are beautiful and ugly, all on their own. Let them stand for themselves. As for Mr Belk, I find it acutely annoying when opposing counsel interrupts opening statements or closing arguments. You will have your turn, sir. I would suggest that you not object during Ms Chandler's statement unless an egregious trespass on your client has occurred. I do not consider pointing at him worth the objection.'

'Thank you, Your Honor,' Belk and Chandler said in unison.

'Proceed, Ms Chandler. As I said in chambers this morning, I want opening statements done by the end of the day and I have another matter at four.'

'Thank you, Your Honor,' she said again. Then, turning back to the jury, she said, 'Ladies and gentlemen, we all need our police. We all look up to our police. Most of them – the vast majority of them – do a thankless job and do it well. The police department is an indispensable part of our society. What would we do if we could not count on police officers to serve and protect us? But that is not what this trial is about. I want you to remember that as the trial progresses. This is about what we would do if one member of that police force broke away from the rules and regulations, the policies that govern that police force. What we are talking about is called a rogue cop. And the evidence will show that Harry Bosch is a rogue cop, a man who one night four years ago decided to be judge, jury and executioner. He shot a man that he thought was a killer. A heinous serial killer, yes, but at the moment the defendant chose to pull out his gun and fire on Mr Norman Church there was no legal evidence of that.

'Now, you are going to hear from the defense all manner of supposed evidence that police said they found that connected Mr Church to these killings, but remember during the trial where this evidence came from – the police themselves – and when it was found – after Mr Church had been executed. I think we will show that this supposed

33

evidence is questionable at best. Tainted, at best. And, in effect, you will have to decide if Mr Church, a married man with two young children and a well-paying job at an aircraft factory, was indeed this killer, the so-called Dollmaker, or simply was made the fall guy, the scapegoat, by a police department covering up the sin of one of its own. The brutal, unwarranted and unnecessary execution of an unarmed man.'

She continued on, speaking at length about the code of silence known to exist in the department, the force's long history of brutality, the Rodney King beating and the riots. Somehow, according to Honey Chandler, these were all black flowers on a plant grown from a seed that was Harry Bosch's killing of Norman Church. Bosch heard her go on but wasn't really listening anymore. He kept his eyes open and occasionally made eye contact with a juror, but he was off on his own. This was his own defense. The lawyers, the jurors and the judge were going to take a week, maybe longer, to dissect what he had thought and done in less than five seconds. To be able to sit in the courtroom for this he was going to have to be able to go off on his own.

In his private reverie he thought of Church's face. At the end, in the apartment over the garage on Hyperion Street. They had locked eyes. The eyes Bosch had seen were killer's eyes, as dark as the stone at Chandler's throat.

'. . . even if he was reaching for a gun, would that matter?' Chandler was saying. 'A man had kicked the door open. A man with a gun. Who could blame someone for reaching, according to police, for a weapon for protection. The fact that he was reaching for something seemingly as laughable as a hairpiece makes this episode all the more repugnant. He was killed in cold blood. Our society cannot accept that.'

Bosch tuned her out again and thought of the new victim, entombed for what was likely years in a concrete floor. He wondered if a missing-person report was ever taken, if there was a mother or father or husband or child wondering all this time about her. After returning from the scene he had started to tell Belk about the discovery. He asked the lawyer to ask Judge Keyes for a continuance, to delay the trial until the new death could be sorted out. But Belk had cut him off, telling him that the less he knew the better. Belk seemed so frightened of the implications of the new discovery that he determined that the best tack was to do the opposite of what Bosch suggested. He wanted to hurry the trial through before news of the discovery and its possible connection to the Dollmaker became public.

Chandler was now near the end of the one-hour allotment for her opener. She had gone on at length about the police department's shooting policy and Bosch thought she might have lost the grip she had on the jury in the beginning. For a while she had even lost Belk, who sat next to Bosch paging through his own yellow pad and rehearsing his opener in his head.

Belk was a large man – almost eighty pounds overweight, Bosch guessed – and prone to sweating, even in the overly cooled courtroom. Bosch had often wondered during the jury selection if the sweating was Belk's response to the burden of weight he carried or the burden of trying a case against Chandler and before Judge Keyes. Belk couldn't be over thirty, Bosch guessed. Maybe five years max out of a middle-range law school and in over his head going up against Chandler.

The word 'justice' brought Bosch's attention back. He knew that Chandler had turned it up a notch and was coming down the backstretch when she started using the word in almost every sentence. In civil court, justice and money were interchangeable because they meant the same thing.

'Justice for Norman Church was fleeting. It lasted all of a few seconds. Justice was the time it took Detective Bosch to kick open the door, point his satin-finished 9mm Smith & Wesson and pull the trigger. Justice was one shot. The bullet Detective Bosch chose to execute Mr Church with was called an XTP. That is short for extreme terminal performance. It's a bullet that expands to 1.5 times its width on impact and takes out huge portions of tissue and organ in its path. It took out Mr Church's heart. That was justice.'

Bosch noticed that many of the jurors were not looking at Chandler but at the plaintiff's table. By leaning forward slightly he could see past the lectern and saw that the widow, Deborah Church, was dabbing tears on her cheeks with a tissue. She was a bell-shaped woman with short dark hair and small pale blue eyes. She had been the epitome of the suburban housewife and mother until the morning Bosch killed her husband and the cops showed up at her house with their search warrant and the reporters showed up with their questions. Bosch had actually felt sorry for her, even counted her as a victim, until she hired Money Chandler and started calling him a murderer.

'The evidence will show, ladies and gentlemen, that Detective Bosch is a product of his department,' Chandler said. 'A callous, arrogant machine that dispensed justice as he saw it on his own. You will be asked if this is what you want from your police department. You will be asked to right a wrong, to provide justice for a family whose father and husband was taken.

'In closing, I would like to quote to you from a German philosopher named Friedrich Nietzsche, who wrote something a century ago that I think is germane to what we are doing today. He said, "Whoever fights monsters should see to it that in the process he does not become a monster. And when you look into the abyss, the abyss also looks into you . . ."

'Ladies and gentlemen, that is what this case is about. Detective Harry Bosch has not only looked into the abyss, but on the night Norman Church was murdered it looked into him. The darkness engulfed him and Detective Bosch fell. He became that which he served to fight. A monster. I think you will find that the evidence will lead you to no other conclusion. Thank you.'

Chandler sat down and patted her hand in a 'there, there' gesture on Deborah Church's arm. Bosch, of course, knew this was done for the jury's sake, not the widow's.

The judge looked up at the brass hands of the clock built into the mahogany paneling above the courtroom door and declared a fifteen-minute recess before Belk would take the lectern. As he stood for the jury, Bosch noticed one of Church's daughters staring at him from the front row of the spectators section. He guessed she was about thirteen. The older one, Nancy. He quickly looked away and then felt guilty. He wondered if anyone in the jury saw this.

Belk said he needed the break time alone to go over his statement to the jury. Bosch felt like going up to the snack bar on the sixth floor because he still had not eaten, but it was likely a few of the jurors would go there, or worse yet, members of Church's family. Instead, he took the escalator down to the lobby and went out to the ash can in front of the building. He lit a cigarette and leaned back against the base of the statue. He realized that he was clammy with sweat beneath his suit. Chandler's hour-long opener had seemed like an eternity – an eternity with the eyes of the world on him. He knew the suit wouldn't last the week and he would have to make sure his other one was clean. Thinking about such minor details finally helped relax him.

He had already put one butt out in the sand and was on his second smoke when the steel-and-glass door to the courthouse opened. Honey Chandler had used her back to push open the heavy door and therefore hadn't seen him. She turned as she came through the door, her head bent down as she lit a cigarette with a gold lighter. As she straightened and exhaled she saw him. She walked toward the ash can, ready to bury the fresh cigarette.

'It's okay,' Bosch said. 'It's the only one around as far as I know.'

'It is, but I don't think it does either of us good to have to face each other outside of court.'

He shrugged and didn't say anything. It was her move,

she could leave if she wanted to. She took another drag on the cigarette.

'Just a half. I have to get back in anyway.'

He nodded and looked out toward Spring Street. In front of the county courthouse he saw a line of people waiting to go in through the metal detectors. More boat people, he thought. He saw the homeless man coming up the pavement to make his afternoon check of the ash can. The man suddenly turned around and walked back out to Spring and away. He looked back once uneasily over his shoulder as he went.

'He knows me.'

Bosch looked back at Chandler.

'He knows you?'

'He used to be a lawyer. I knew him then. Tom something-or-other. I can't remember at the – Faraday, that's it. I guess he didn't want me to see him that way. But everybody around here knows about him. He's the reminder of what can happen when things go terribly wrong.'

'What happened?'

'It's a long story. Maybe your lawyer will tell you. Can I ask you something?'

Bosch didn't answer.

'Why didn't the city settle this case? Rodney King, the riots. It's the worst time in the world to take a police case to trial. I don't think Bulk – that's what I call him, because I know he calls me Money. I don't think he's got a hold on this one. And you'll be the one hung out to dry.'

Bosch thought a moment before answering.

'It's off the record, Detective Bosch,' she said. 'I'm just making conversation.'

'I told him not to settle. I told him if he wanted to settle, I'd go out and pay for my own lawyer.'

'That sure of yourself, huh?' She paused to inhale on her cigarette. 'Well, we'll see, I guess.'

'I guess.'

'You know it's nothing personal.'

He knew she would get around to saying that. The biggest lie in the game.

'Maybe not for you.'

'Oh, it is for you? You shoot an unarmed man and then you take it personally when his wife objects, when she sues you?'

'Your client's husband used to cut the strap off the purses of his victims, tie it in a slipknot around their neck and then slowly but steadily strangle them while he was raping them. He preferred leather straps. He didn't seem to care about what women he did this to. Just the leather.'

She didn't even flinch. He hadn't expected her to.

'That's *late* husband. My client's late husband. And the only thing that is for sure in this case, that is provable, is that you killed him.'

'Yeah, and I'd do it again.'

'I know, Detective Bosch. That's why we're here.'

She pursed her lips in a frozen kiss which sharply set the line of her jaw. Her hair caught the glint of the afternoon sun. She angrily stubbed her cigarette out in the sand and then went back inside. She swung the door open as if it were made of balsa wood.

FOUR

Bosch pulled into the rear parking lot of the Hollywood station on Wilcox shortly before four. Belk had used only ten minutes of his allotted hour for his opening statement and Judge Keyes had recessed early, saying he wanted to start testimony on a separate day from openers so the jury would not confuse evidentiary testimony with the lawyers' words.

Bosch had felt uneasy with Belk's short discourse in front of the jurors but Belk had told him there was nothing to worry about. He walked in through the back door near the tank and took the rear hallway to the detective bureau. By four the bureau is usually deserted. It was that way when Bosch walked in, except for Jerry Edgar, who was parked in front of one of the IBMs typing on a form Bosch recognized as a 51 – an Investigating Officer's Chronological Record. He looked up and saw Bosch approaching.

'Whereyat, Harry?'

'Right here.'

'Got done early, I see. Don't tell me, directed verdict. The judge threw Money Chandler out on her ass.'

'I wish.'

'Yeah, I know.'

'What do you have so far?'

Edgar said there was nothing so far. No identification yet. Bosch sat down at his desk and loosened his tie. Pounds's office was dark so it was safe to light a cigarette. His mind trailed off into thinking about the trial and Money Chandler. She had captured the jury for most of her

40

argument. She had, in effect, called Bosch a murderer, hitting with a gut-level, emotional charge. Belk had responded with a dissertation on the law and a police officer's right to use deadly force when danger was near. Even if it turned out there was no danger, no gun beneath the pillow, Belk said, Church's own actions created the climate of danger that allowed Bosch to act as he did.

Finally, Belk had countered Chandler's Nietzsche by quoting *The Art of War* by Sun Tzu. Belk said Bosch had entered the 'Dying Ground' when he kicked Church's apartment door open. At that point he had to fight or perish, shoot or be shot. Second-guessing his actions afterward was unjust.

Sitting across from Edgar now, Bosch acknowledged to himself that it hadn't worked. Belk had been boring while Chandler had been interesting, and convincing. They were starting in the hole. He noticed Edgar had stopped talking and Harry had not registered anything he had said.

'What about prints?' he asked.

'Harry, you listening to me? I just said we finished with the rubber silicone about an hour ago. Donovan got prints off the hand. He said they look good, came up in the rubber pretty well. He'll start the DOJ run tonight and probably by morning we'll have the similars. It will probably take him the rest of the morning to go through them. But, at least, they're not letting this one drown in the backup. Pounds gave it a priority status.'

'Good, let me know what comes out. I'll be in and out all week, I guess.'

'Harry, don't worry, I'll let you know what we've got. But try to stay cool. Look, you got the right guy? You got any doubt about that?'

'Not before today.'

'Then don't worry. Might is right. Money Chandler can blow the judge and the whole jury, it's not going to change that.'

'Right is might.'

'What?'

'Nothing.'

Bosch thought about what Edgar had said about Chandler. It was interesting how often a threat from a woman, even a professional woman, was reduced by cops to a sexual threat. He believed that most cops might be like Edgar, thinking there was something about Chandler's sexuality that gave her an edge. They would not admit that she was damn good at her job, whereas the fat city attorney defending Bosch wasn't.

Bosch stood up and went back to the file cabinets. He unlocked one of his drawers and dug into the back to pull out two of the blue binders that were called murder books. Both were heavy, about three inches thick. On the spine of the first it said BIOS. The other was labeled DOCS. They were from the Dollmaker case.

'Who's testifying tomorrow?' Edgar called from across the squad room.

'I don't know the order. The judge wouldn't make her say. But she's got me subpoenaed, also Lloyd and Irving. She's got Amado, the ME coordinator, and even Bremmer. They all gotta show up and then she'll say which ones she'll put on tomorrow and which ones later.'

'The *Times* isn't going to let Bremmer testify. They always fight that shit.'

'Yeah, but he isn't subpoenaed as a *Times* reporter. He wrote that book about the case. So she served paper on him as the author. Judge Keyes already ruled he doesn't have the same reporter's-shield rights. *Times* lawyers may show up to argue but the judge already made the ruling. Bremmer testifies.'

'See what I mean, she's probably already been back in chambers with that old guy. Anyway, it's no matter, Bremmer can't hurt you. That book made you out like the hero who saved the day.'

'I guess.'

'Harry, come here and take a look at this.'

Edgar got up from his typing station and went over to the file cabinets. He gingerly slid a cardboard box off the top and put it down on the homicide table. It was about the size of a hatbox.

'Gotta be careful. Donovan says it should set over night.'

He lifted off the top of the box and there was a woman's face set in white plaster. The face was turned slightly so that its right side was fully sculpted in the plaster. Most of the lower left side, the jawline, was missing. The eyes were closed, the mouth slightly open and irregular. The hairline was almost unnoticeable. The face seemed swollen by the right eye. It was like a classical frieze Bosch had seen in a cemetery or a museum somewhere. But it wasn't beautiful. It was a death mask.

'Looks like the guy popped her on the eye. It swelled up.'

Bosch nodded but didn't speak. There was something unnerving about looking at the face in the box, more so than looking at an actual dead body. He didn't know why. Edgar finally put the top back on the box and carefully put it back on top of the file cabinet.

'What are you going to do with it?'

'Not sure. If we don't get anything from the prints it might be our only way of getting an ID. There's an anthropologist at Cal State Northridge that contracts with the coroner to make facial recreations. Usually, he's working from a skeleton, a skull. I'll take this to him and see if he can maybe finish the face, put a blonde wig on it or something. He can paint the plaster, too, give it a skin color. I don't know, it's probably just pissing in the wind but I figure it's worth a try.'

Edgar returned to the typewriter and Bosch sat down in front of the murder books. He opened the binder marked BIOS but then sat there and watched Edgar for a few moments. He did not know whether he should admire Edgar's hustle on the case or not. They had been partners once and Bosch had essentially spent a year training him to be a homicide investigator. But he was never sure how much of it took. Edgar was always going off to look at real estate, taking two-hour lunches to go to closings. He never seemed to understand that the homicide squad wasn't a job. It was a mission. As surely as murder was an art for some who committed it, homicide investigation was an art for those on the mission. And it chose you, you didn't choose it.

With that in mind it was hard for Bosch to accept that Edgar was busting ass on the case for the right reasons.

'What're you looking at?' Edgar asked without looking up from the IBM or stopping his typing.

'Nothing. I was just thinking about stuff.'

'Harry, don't worry. It's going to work out.'

Bosch dumped his cigarette butt in a Styrofoam cup of dead coffee and lit another.

'Did the priority Pounds put on the case open up the OT?'

'Absolutely,' Edgar said, smiling. 'You're looking at a man who has his head fully in the overtime trough.'

At least he was honest about it, Bosch thought. Content that his original take on Edgar was still intact, Bosch went back to the murder book and ran his fingers along the edge of the thick sheaf of reports on its three rings. There were eleven divider tabs, each marked with a name of one of the Dollmaker's victims. He began leafing from section to section, looking at the crime scene photographs from each killing and the biographical data of each victim.

The women had all come from similar backgrounds; street prostitutes, the higher-class escort outfits, strippers, porno actresses who did outcall work on the side. The Dollmaker had moved comfortably along the underside of the city. He had found his victims with the same ease that they had gone into the darkness with him. There was a pattern in that, Bosch remembered the task force's psychologist had said.

But looking at the frozen faces of death in the photographs, Bosch remembered that the task force had never gotten a fix on common physical aspects of the victims.

There were blondes and brunettes. Heavy-set women and frail drug addicts. There were six white women, two Latinas, two Asians and a black woman. No pattern. The Dollmaker had been indiscriminate in that respect, his only identifiable pattern being that he sought only women on the edge – that place where choices are limited and they go easily with a stranger. The psychologist had said each of the women was like an injured fish, sending off an invisible signal that inevitably drew the shark.

'She was white, right?' he asked Edgar.

Edgar stopped typing.

'Yeah, that's what the coroner said.'

'They already did the cut? Who?'

'No, the autopsy's tomorrow or the next day but Corazón took a look when we brought it in. She guessed that the stiff had been white. Why?'

'Nothing. Blonde?'

'Yeah, at least when she died. Bleached. If you're going to ask if I checked missing persons on a white blonde chick who went into the wind four years ago, fuck you, Harry. I can use the OT but that description wouldn't narrow it down to but three, four hundred. I ain't going to wade into that when I'll probably pull a name on the prints tomorrow. Waste of time.'

'Yeah, I know. I just wish . . .'

'You just wish you had some answers. We all do. But things take time sometimes, my man.'

Edgar started typing again and Harry looked down into the binder. But he couldn't help but think about the face in the box. No name, no occupation. They knew nothing about her. But something about the plaster cast told him she had somehow fit into the Dollmaker's pattern. There was a hardness there that had nothing to do with the plaster. She had come from the edge.

'Anything else found in the concrete after I left?'

Edgar stopped typing, exhaled loudly and shook his head.

'How do you mean, like the cigarette package?'

'With the other ones the Dollmaker left their purses. He'd cut the straps off to strangle them, but when he dumped the bodies we always found the purses and clothes nearby. Only thing missing was their makeup. He always kept their makeup.'

'Not this time – at least in the concrete. Pounds left a uniform on the site while they finished tearing it up. Nothing else was found. That stuff might've been stashed in the storage room and got burned up or looted. Harry, what're you thinking, copycat?'

'I guess.'

'Yeah, me too.'

Bosch nodded and told Edgar he was sorry he kept interrupting. He went back to studying the reports. After a few minutes Edgar rolled the form out of the typewriter and brought it back to the homicide table. He snapped it into a new binder with the thin stack of paperwork from the day's case and put it into a file cabinet behind his chair. He then went through his daily ritual of calling his wife while straightening up the blotter, the message spike and the message pad at his place. He told her he had to make a quick stop on his way home. Listening to the conversation made Bosch think of Sylvia Moore and some of the domestic rituals that had become ingrained for them.

'I'm outta here, Harry,' Edgar said after hanging up.

Bosch nodded.

'So how come you're hanging around?'

'I don't know. I'm just reading through this stuff so I'll know what I'm saying when I testify.'

That was a lie. He didn't need the murder books to refresh his memory of the Dollmaker.

'I hope you tear Money Chandler up.'

'She'll probably rip me. She's good.'

'Well, I gotta hit it. I'll see you.'

'Hey, remember, if you get a name tomorrow, give me a beep or something.'

46

After Edgar was gone Bosch looked at his watch – it was five – and turned on the TV that sat on top of the file cabinet next to the box with the face in it. While he was waiting for the story on the body he picked up his phone and dialed Sylvia's house.

'I'm not going to make it out there tonight.'

'Harry, what's wrong? How did the opening statements go?'

'It's not the trial. It's another case. A body was found today, looks a lot like the Dollmaker did it. We got a note at the station. Basically said I killed the wrong guy. That the Dollmaker, the real one, is still out there.'

'Can it be true?'

'I don't know. There had been no doubt before today.'

'How could –'

'Wait a minute, the story's on the news. Channel 2.'

'I'll put it on.'

They watched on separate TVs but connected by phone as the story was reported on the early news show. The anchor reported nothing about the Dollmaker. There was an aerial shot of the scene and then a sound bite of Pounds saying that little was known, that an anonymous tip had led police to the body. Harry and Sylvia both laughed when they saw Pounds's char-smeared forehead. It felt good to Bosch to laugh. After the report Sylvia turned serious.

'So, he didn't tell the media.'

'Well, we have to make sure. We have to figure out what's going on first. It was either him or a copycat . . . or maybe he had a partner we didn't know about.'

'When will you know which direction to go?'

It was a nice way of asking when he'd know if he had killed an innocent man.

'I don't know, probably tomorrow. Autopsy will tell us some things. But the ID will tell us when she died.'

'Harry, it wasn't the Dollmaker. Don't you worry.'

'Thanks, Sylvia.'

Her unequivocal loyalty was beautiful, he thought. He

then immediately felt guilty because he had never been totally open with her about all the things that concerned them. He had been the one who held back.

'You still haven't said how it went in court today or why you aren't coming out here like you said you would.'

'It's this new case they found today. I am involved . . . and I want to do some thinking on it.'

'You can think anywhere, Harry.'

'You know what I mean.'

'Yes, I do. And court?'

'It went fine, I guess. We only had openers. Testimony starts tomorrow. But this new case . . . It's sort of hanging over everything.'

He switched the channels as he spoke but he had missed reports on the new body discovery on the other channels.

'Well, what's your lawyer say about it?'

'Nothing. He doesn't want to know about it.'

'What a shit.'

'He just wants to get through the case quickly, hope that if the Dollmaker or a partner is still running around out there, that we don't confirm it until the trial is over.'

'But, Harry, that is unethical. Even if it is evidence in the plaintiff's favor, doesn't he have to bring it forward?'

'Yes, if he knows about it. That's just it. He doesn't want to know about it. That makes him safe.'

'When will it be your turn to testify? I want to be there. I can take a personal day and be there.'

'No. Don't worry. It's all a formality. I don't want you to know any more about this story than you do already.'

'Why? It's your story.'

'No it's not. It's his.'

He hung up after telling her he'd call her the next day. Afterward, he looked at the phone on the table in front of him for a long time. He and Sylvia Moore had been spending three or four nights a week together for nearly a year. Though Sylvia had been the one who spoke of changing the arrangement and even had her house for sale,

Bosch had never wanted to touch the question for fear that it might disturb the fragile balance and comfort he felt with her.

He wondered now if he was doing just that, disturbing the balance. He had lied to her. He was involved in the new case to some degree, but he was done for the day and was going home. He had lied because he felt the need to be alone. With his thoughts. With the Dollmaker.

He flipped through the second binder to the back where there were clear plastic Ziploc pouches for holding documentary evidence. In these were copies of the Dollmaker's previous letters. There were three of them. The killer had begun sending them after the media firestorm started and he had been christened with the name Dollmaker. One had gone to Bosch, prior to the eleventh killing – the last. The other two had gone to Bremmer at the *Times* after the seventh and eleventh killings. Harry now studied the photocopy of the envelope that was addressed to him in a printed script of block letters. Then he looked at the poem on the folded page. It also had been printed in the same oddly slanted block script. He read the words he already knew by heart.

> *I feel compelled to forewarn and forsake.*
> *T'night I'm out for a snack – my lust partake.*
> *Another doll for the shelf, as it were't.*
> *She breathes her last – just as I squirt.*

> *A little late mommy and daddy weeple*
> *A fine young miss 'neath my steeple.*
> *As I tight the purse strings 'fore preparing the wash.*
> *I hear the last gasp – a sound like Boschhhhh!*

Bosch closed the binders and put them in his briefcase. He turned off the TV and headed out to the back parking lot. He held the station door for two uniform cops who were

49

wrestling with a handcuffed drunk. The drunk threw a kick out at him but Harry stepped outside of its reach.

He pointed the Caprice north and took Outpost Road up to Mulholland, which he then took to Woodrow Wilson. After pulling into the carport, he sat with his hands on the wheel for a long time. He thought about the letters and the signature the Dollmaker had left on each victim's body, the cross painted on the toenail. After Church was dead they figured out what it had meant. The cross had been the steeple. The steeple of a Church.

FIVE

In the morning, Bosch sat on the rear deck of his house and watched the sun come up over the Cahuenga Pass. It burned away the morning fog and bathed the wildflowers on the hillside that had burned the winter before. He watched and smoked and drank coffee until the sound of traffic on the Hollywood Freeway became one uninterrupted hiss from the pass below.

He dressed in his dark blue suit with a white shirt that had a button-down collar. As he put on a maroon tie dotted with gold gladiator helmets in front of the bedroom mirror, he wondered about how he must appear to the jurors. He had noticed the day before that when he made eye contact with any of the twelve, they were always the first to look away. What did that mean? He would have liked to ask Belk what it meant but he did not like Belk and knew he would feel uncomfortable asking his opinion on anything.

Using the same hole poked through it before, he secured the tie in place with his silver tie tack that said '187' – the California penal code for murder. He used a plastic comb to put his brown-and-gray hair, still wet from the shower, in place and then combed his mustache. He put Visine drops in his eyes and then leaned close to the glass to study them. Red-rimmed from little sleep, the irises as dark as ice on asphalt. Why do they look away from me, he wondered again. He thought about how Chandler had described him the day before. And he knew why.

He was heading to the door, briefcase in hand, when it

opened before he got there. Sylvia stepped in while pulling her key out of the lock.

'Hi,' she said when she saw him. 'I hoped I'd catch you.'

She smiled. She was wearing khaki pants and a pink shirt with a button-down collar. He knew she did not wear dresses on Tuesday and Thursday because those were her assigned days as a schoolyard rover. Sometimes she had to run after students. Sometimes she had to break up fights. The sun coming through the porch door turned her dark blonde hair gold.

'Catch me at what?'

She came to him smiling still and they kissed.

'I know I'm making you late. I'm late, too. But I just wanted to come and say good luck today. Not that you need it.'

He held on to her, smelling her hair. It had been nearly a year since they met, but Bosch still held to her sometimes with the fear that she might abruptly turn and leave, declare her attraction to him a mistake. Perhaps he was still a substitute for the husband she'd lost, a cop like Harry, a narcotics detective whose apparent suicide Bosch had investigated.

Their relationship had progressed to a point of complete comfortableness but in recent weeks he had felt a sense of inertia begin to set in. She had, too, and had even talked about it. She said the problem was he could not drop his guard completely and he knew this was true. Bosch had spent a lifetime alone, but not necessarily lonely. He had secrets, many of them buried too deep to give up to her. Not so soon.

'Thanks for coming by,' he said, pulling back and looking down into her face to see the light still there. She had gotten a fleck of lipstick on one of her front teeth. 'You be careful in the yard today, huh?'

'Yes.' Then she frowned. 'I know what you said, but I want to come and watch court – at least one day. I want to be there for you, Harry.'

'You don't have to be there to be there. Know what I mean?'

She nodded but he knew his answer didn't satisfy her. They dropped it and small-talked for a few minutes more, making plans to get together that night for dinner. Bosch said he would come to her place in Bouquet Canyon. They kissed again and headed out, he to court and she to the high school, both places fraught with danger.

There was always an adrenaline rush at the start of each day as the courtroom fell silent and they waited for the judge to open his door and step up to the bench. It was 9:10 and still no sign of the judge, which was unusual because he had been a stickler for promptness during the week of jury selection. Bosch looked around and saw several reporters, maybe more than the day before. He found this curious since opening arguments were always such a draw.

Belk leaned toward Bosch and whispered, 'Keyes is probably in there reading the *Times* story. Did you see it?'

Running late because of Sylvia, Bosch had had no time to read the paper. He'd left it on the mat at the front door.

'What'd it say?'

The paneled door opened and the judge came out before Belk could answer.

'Hold the jury, Miss Rivera,' the judge said to his clerk. He dropped his girth into his padded chair, surveyed the courtroom and said, 'Counsel, any matters for discussion before we bring the jury in? Ms Chandler?'

'Yes, Your Honor,' Chandler said as she walked to the lectern.

Today she had on the gray suit. She had been alternating among three suits since jury selection began. Belk had told Bosch that this was because she didn't want to give the jurors the idea that she was wealthy. He said women lawyers could lose women jurors over something like that.

'Your Honor, the plaintiff asks for sanctions against Detective Bosch and Mr Belk.'

She held up the folded Metro section of the *Times*. Bosch could see the story had caught the bottom right corner, same as the story the day before. The headline said CONCRETE BLONDE TIED TO DOLLMAKER. Belk stood but did not say anything, for once observing the judge's strict decorum of noninterruption.

'Sanctions for what, Ms Chandler?' the judge asked.

'Your Honor, the discovery of this body yesterday has a tremendous evidentiary impact on this case. As an officer of the court, it was incumbent upon Mr Belk to bring this information forward. Under Rule 11 of discovery, defendant's attorney must —'

'Your Honor,' Belk interrupted, 'I was not informed of this development until last night. My intention was to bring the matter forward this morning. She is —'

'Hold it right there, Mr Belk. One at a time in my courtroom. Seems you need a daily reminder of that. Ms Chandler, I read that story you are referring to and though Detective Bosch was mentioned because of this case, he was not quoted. And Mr Belk has rather rudely pointed out that he knew nothing about this until after court yesterday. Frankly, I don't see a sanctionable offense here. Unless you've got a card you haven't played.'

She did.

'Your Honor, Detective Bosch was well aware of this development, whether quoted or not. He was at the scene during yesterday's lunch break.'

'Your Honor?' Belk tried timidly.

Judge Keyes turned but looked at Bosch, not Belk.

'That right, Detective Bosch, what she says?'

Bosch looked at Belk for a moment and then up at the judge. Fucking Belk, he thought. His lie had left Bosch holding the bag.

'I was there, Your Honor. When I got back here for the afternoon session, there was no time to tell Mr Belk about the discovery. I told him after court last night. I didn't see the paper yet this morning and I don't know what it says, but nothing has been confirmed about this body in regard to the Dollmaker or anyone else. There isn't even an ID yet.'

'Your Honor,' Chandler said, 'Detective Bosch has conveniently forgotten that we had a fifteen-minute break during the afternoon session. I should think that was ample time for the detective to fill in his attorney on such important information.'

The judge looked at Bosch.

'I wanted to tell him during the break but Mr Belk said he needed the time to prepare his opening statement.'

The judge eyed him closely for several seconds without saying anything. Bosch could tell the judge knew he was pushing the edge of the envelope of truth. Judge Keyes seemed to be making some kind of decision.

'Well, Ms Chandler,' he finally said. 'I don't rightly see the conspiracy that you do here. I'm going to let this go with a warning to all parties; withholding evidence is the most heinous crime you can commit in my courtroom. If you do it and I catch ya, you're gonna wish you never took the LSAT. Now, do we want to talk about this new development?'

'Your Honor,' Belk said quickly. He moved to the lectern. 'In light of this discovery less than twenty-four hours ago, I move for a continuance so that this situation can be thoroughly investigated so that it can be determined exactly what it means to this case.'

Now he finally asks, Bosch thought. He knew there was no way he'd get a delay now.

'Uh, huh,' Judge Keyes said. 'What do you think about that, Ms Chandler?'

'No delay, Your Honor. This family has waited four years for this trial. I think any further delay would be perpetuating the crime. Besides, who does Mr Belk propose investigate this matter, Detective Bosch?'

'I am sure the defense counselor would be satisfied with the LAPD handling the investigation,' the judge said.

'But I wouldn't.'

'I know you wouldn't, Ms Chandler, but that's not your concern. You said yourself yesterday that the wide majority of police in this city are good, competent people. You'll just have to live by your own words . . . But I am going to deny the request for a continuation. We've started a trial and we're not going to stop. The police can and should investigate this matter and keep the court informed but I'm not going to stand by. This case will continue until such time that these events need to be addressed again. Anything else? I've got a jury waiting.'

'What about the story in the newspaper?' Belk asked.

'What about it?'

'Your Honor, I'd like the jury to be polled to see if anyone read it. Also, they should be warned again not to read the papers or watch the TV news tonight. All of the channels will likely follow the *Times*.'

'I instructed jurors yesterday not to read the paper or watch the news but I plan to poll them anyway about this very story. Let's see what they say and then, depending on what we hear, we can clear 'em out again if you want to talk about a mistrial.'

'I don't want a mistrial,' Chandler said. 'That's what the defendant wants. That'll just delay this another two months. This family has already waited four years for justice. They –'

'Well, let's just see what the jury says. Sorry to interrupt, Ms Chandler.'

'Your Honor, may I be heard on sanctions?' Belk said.

'I don't think you need to be, Mr Belk. I denied her motion for sanctions. What more's to be said?'

'I know that, Your Honor. I would like to ask for sanctions against Miss Chandler. She has defamed me by alleging this cover-up of the evidence and I –'

'Mr Belk, sit down. I'll tell you both right now; quit with the extracurricular sparring because it doesn't get you anywhere with me. No sanctions either way. One last time, any other matters?'

56

'Yes, Your Honor,' Chandler said.

She had one more card. From beneath her legal pad she pulled out a document and walked it up to the clerk, who handed it to the judge. Chandler then returned to the lectern.

'Your Honor, that is a subpoena I have prepared for the police department that I would like reflected in the record. I am asking that a copy of the note referred to in the *Times* article, the note written by the Dollmaker and received yesterday, be released to me as part of discovery.'

Belk jumped to his feet.

'Hold on, Mr Belk,' the judge admonished. 'Let her finish.'

'Your Honor, it is evidence in this case. It should be turned over immediately.'

Judge Keyes gave Belk the nod and the deputy city attorney lumbered to the lectern, Chandler having to back up to give him room.

'Your Honor, this note is in no way evidence in this case. It has not been verified as having come from anybody. However, it is evidence in a murder case unattached to this proceeding. And it is not the LAPD's practice to parade its evidence out in an open court while there is a suspect still at large. I ask that you deny her request.'

Judge Keyes clasped his hands together and thought a moment.

'Tell you what, Mr Belk. You get a copy of the note and bring it in here. I'll take a look and then decide if it will be entered in evidence. That's all. Ms Rivera, call in the jury please, we're losing the morning.'

After the jury was in the box and everybody in court sat down, Judge Keyes asked who had seen any news stories relating to the case. No one in the box raised a hand. Bosch knew that if any one of them had seen the story, they wouldn't admit to it anyway. To do so would be to invite certain dismissal from the jury – a ticket straight back to the jury assembly room where the minutes tick by like hours.

'Very well,' the judge said. 'Call your first witness, Ms Chandler.'

Terry Lloyd took the witness stand like a man who was as familiar with it as the recliner chair he got drunk in every night in front of the TV set. He even adjusted the microphone in front of him without any help from the clerk. Lloyd had a drinker's badge of a nose and unusually dark brown hair for a man of his age, which was pushing sixty. That was because it was obvious to everyone who looked at him, except maybe himself, that he wore a rug. Chandler went through some preliminary questions, establishing that he was a lieutenant in the LAPD's elite Robbery-Homicide Division.

'During a period beginning four and a half years ago were you placed in charge of a task force of detectives attempting to identify a serial killer?'

'Yes I was.'

'Can you tell the jury how that came about and functioned?'

'It was put together after the same killer was identified as the perpetrator in five killings. We were unofficially known in the department as the Westside Strangler Task Force. After the media got wind of it, the killer became known as the Dollmaker – because he used the victims' own makeup to paint their faces like dolls. I had eighteen detectives assigned to the task force. We broke them up into two squads, A and B. Squad A worked a day shift, B took the nights. We investigated the killings as they occurred and followed the call-in leads. After it hit the media, we were getting maybe a hundred calls a week – people saying this guy or that guy was the Dollmaker. We had to check them all out.'

'The task force, no matter what it was called, was not successful, is that correct?'

'No, ma'am, that is wrong. We were successful. We got the killer.'

'And who was that?'

'Norman Church was the killer.'

'Was he identified as such before or after he was killed?'

'After. He was good for all of them.'

'And good for the department, too?'

'I don't follow.'

'It was good for the department that you were able to connect him to the murders. Otherwise you'd –'

'Ask questions, Ms Chandler,' the judge interrupted.

'Sorry, Your Honor. Lieutenant Lloyd, the man you say was the killer, Norman Church, was not killed himself until there were at least six more murders following the establishment of the task force, is that correct?'

'Correct.'

'Allowing at least six more women to be strangled. How is that considered successful by the department?'

'We didn't allow anything. We did the best we could to track down this perpetrator. We eventually did. That made us successful. Very successful, in my book.'

'In your book. Tell me, Lieutenant Lloyd, had the name Norman Church come up at any time in the investigation before the night he was shot to death while unarmed by Detective Bosch? Any reference at all?'

'No, it hadn't. But we connected –'

'Just answer the question I ask, Lieutenant. Thank you.'

Chandler referred to her yellow pad on the lectern. Bosch noticed that Belk was alternately taking notes on one pad in front of him and writing down questions on another.

'Okay, Lieutenant,' Chandler said, 'your task force did not catch up with a supposed perpetrator, as you call it, until six deaths after you started. Would it be fair to say you and your detectives were under severe pressure to catch him, to close this case?'

'We were under pressure, yes.'

'From who? Who was pressuring you, Lieutenant Lloyd?'

'Well, we had the papers, TV. The department was on me.'

'How so? The department, I mean. Did you have meetings with your supervisors?'

'I had daily meetings with the RHD captain and weeklies – every Monday – with the police chief.'

'What did they tell you about solving the case?'

'They said get the thing solved. People were dying. I didn't need to be told that but they did anyway.'

'And did you communicate that to the task force detectives?'

'Of course. But they didn't need to be told it either. These guys were looking at the bodies every time one showed up. It was hard. They wanted this guy bad. They didn't need to read it in the papers or hear it from the chief or even me, for that matter.'

Lloyd seemed to be getting off on his cop-as-a-lonely-hunter tangent. Bosch could see that he didn't realize he had walked into Chandler's trap. She was going to argue at the end of the trial that Bosch and the cops were under such pressure to find a killer that Bosch killed Church and then they fabricated his ties to the killings. The fall-guy theory. Harry wished he could call time out and tell Lloyd to shut the hell up.

'So everyone on the task force knew there was pressure to find a killer?'

'Not a killer. *The* killer. Yes, there was pressure. It's part of the job.'

'What was Detective Bosch's role on the task force?'

'He was my B squad supervisor. He worked the night shift. He was a detective third grade so he kind of ran things when I wasn't there, which was often. Primarily, I was a floater but I usually worked the day shift with squad A.'

'Do you recall saying to Detective Bosch, "We've gotta get this guy," words to that effect?'

'Not specifically. But I said words to that effect at squad meetings. He was there. But that was our goal, nothing wrong with that. We had to get this guy. Same situation, I'd say it again.'

Bosch began to feel that Lloyd was paying him back for having stolen the show, closing the case without him. His answers no longer appeared to be grounded in congenial stupidity but in malice. Bosch bent close to Belk and whispered, 'He's fucking me because he didn't get to shoot Church himself.'

Belk put his finger to his lips, signaling Harry to be quiet. He then went back to writing on one of his two pads.

'Have you ever heard of the FBI's Behavioral Science Division?' Chandler asked.

'Yes, I have.'

'What do they do?'

'They study serial killers among other things. Come up with psychological profiles, victim profiles, give advice, things like that.'

'You had eleven murders, what advice did the FBI's Behavioral Science Division give you?'

'None.'

'Why was that? Were they stumped?'

'No, we didn't call on them.'

'Ah, and why didn't you call them?'

'Well, ma'am, we believed we had a handle on it. We had worked up profiles ourselves and we didn't think the FBI could help us much. The forensic psychologist helping us, Dr Locke from USC, had once been an adviser to the FBI on sex crimes. We had his experience and the department's staff psychiatrist helping out. We believed we were in good shape in that department.'

'Did the FBI offer their help?'

Lloyd hesitated here. It seemed he was finally understanding where she was headed.

'Uh, yes, somebody called after the case was making a lot of press. They wanted to get in on it. I told them we were fine, that no help was needed.'

'Do you regret that decision now?'

'No. I don't think the FBI could've done any better than

61

us. They usually come in on cases being handled by smaller departments or cases making a big media splash.'

'And you don't think that's fair, correct?'

'What?'

'Bigfooting, I think it's called. You didn't want the FBI coming in and taking over, right?'

'No. It was like I said, we were okay without them.'

'Isn't it true that the LAPD and the FBI have a long-standing history of jealousies and competitiveness that has resulted in the two agencies rarely communicating or working together?'

'No, I don't buy that.'

It didn't matter if he bought it. Bosch knew she was making her points with the jury. Whether *they* bought it was the only thing that mattered.

'Your task force came up with a suspect profile, correct?'

'Yes. I believe I just mentioned that.'

She asked Judge Keyes if she could approach the witness with a document she said was plaintiff's exhibit 1A. She handed it to the clerk, who handed it to Lloyd.

'What is that, Lieutenant?'

'This is a composite drawing and the psychological profile we came up with after, I think, the seventh killing.'

'How did you come up with the drawing of the suspect?'

'Between the seventh and eighth victims, we had an intended victim who managed to survive. She was able to get away from the man and call the police. Working with this survivor, we came up with the drawing.'

'Okay, are you familiar with the facial appearance of Norman Church?'

'Not to a great extent. I saw him after he was dead.'

Chandler asked to approach again and submitted plaintiff's 2A, a collage of several photographs of Church taped to a piece of cardboard. She gave Lloyd a few moments to study them.

'Do you see any resemblance between the composite drawing and the photographs of Mr Church?'

Lloyd hesitated and then said, 'Our killer was known to wear disguises and our witness – the victim who got away – was a drug user. She was a porno actress. She wasn't reliable.'

'Your Honor, can you instruct the witness to answer the questions that are asked?'

The judge did so.

'No,' Lloyd said, his head bowed after being chastised. 'No resemblance.'

'Okay,' Chandler said, 'going back to the profile you have there. Where did that come from?'

'Primarily from Dr Locke at USC and Dr Shafer, an LAPD staff psychiatrist. I think they consulted with some others before writing it up.'

'Can you read that first paragraph?'

'Yes. It says, "Subject is believed to be a white male, twenty-five to thirty-five years old with minimal college education. He is a physically strong man though may not be large in appearance. He lives alone, alienated from family and friends. He is reacting to a deep-rooted hatred of women suggesting an abusive mother or female guardian. His painting of the faces of his victims with makeup is his attempt to remake women into an image that pleases him, that smiles at him. They become dolls, not threats." Do you want me to read the part that outlines the repetitive traits of the killings?'

'No, that is not necessary. You were involved in the investigation of Mr Church after he was killed by Bosch, correct?'

'Correct.'

'List for the jury all of the traits in the suspect profile that your task force found that matched Mr Church.'

Lloyd looked down at the paper in his hands for a long time without speaking.

'I'll help you get started, Lieutenant,' Chandler said. 'He was a white male, correct?'

'Yes.'

'What else is similar? Did he live alone?'

'No.'

'He actually had a wife and two daughters, correct?'

'Yes.'

'Was he between twenty-five and thirty-five years old?'

'No.'

'Actually, he was thirty-nine years old, correct?'

'Yes.'

'Did he have a minimal education?'

'No.'

'Actually, he had a master's degree in mechanical engineering, didn't he?'

'Then what was he doing there in that room?' Lloyd said angrily. 'Why was the makeup from the victims there? Why –'

'Answer the question asked of you, Lieutenant,' Judge Keyes interjected. 'Don't go asking questions. That isn't your job here.'

'Sorry, Your Honor,' Lloyd said. 'Yes, he had a master's degree. I'm not sure exactly what it was for.'

'You mentioned the makeup in your nonresponsive answer a moment ago,' Chandler said. 'What did you mean?'

'In the garage apartment where Church was killed. Makeup that belonged to nine of the victims was found in a cabinet in the bathroom. It tied him directly to those cases. Nine of eleven – it was convincing.'

'Who found the makeup in there?'

'Harry Bosch did.'

'When he went there alone and killed him.'

'Is that a question?'

'No, Lieutenant. I withdraw it.'

She paused to let the jury think about that while she flipped through her yellow pages.

'Lieutenant Lloyd, tell us about that night. What happened?'

Lloyd told the story as it had been described dozens of

times before. On TV, in newspapers, in Bremmer's book. It was midnight, squad B was going off shift when the task force hot line rang and Bosch took the call, the last of the night. A street prostitute named Dixie McQueen said she had just escaped from the Dollmaker. Bosch went alone because the others on squad B had gone home and he figured it might be another dead end. He picked the woman up at Hollywood and Western and followed her directions into Silverlake. On Hyperion she convinced Bosch she had escaped from the Dollmaker and pointed to the lighted windows of an apartment over a garage. Bosch went up alone. A few moments later Norman Church was dead.

'He kicked open the door?' Chandler asked.

'Yes. There was the thought that maybe he had gone and gotten somebody to take the prostitute's place.'

'Did he shout that he was police?'

'Yes.'

'How do you know?'

'He said so.'

'Any witnesses hear it?'

'No.'

'What about Miss McQueen, the prostitute?'

'No. Bosch had kept her in the car parked on the street in case there was trouble.'

'So what you're saying is we have Detective Bosch's word that he feared there might be another victim, that he identified himself and that Mr Church made a threatening move toward the pillow.'

'Yes,' Lloyd said reluctantly.

'I notice, Lieutenant Lloyd, that you wear a toupee yourself.'

There was some muffled laughter from the back. Bosch turned and saw that the media contingent was steadily growing. He saw Bremmer sitting in the gallery now.

'Yes,' Lloyd said. His face had turned red to match his nose.

'Have you ever put your toupee under your pillow? Is that the proper care for it?'

'No.'

'Nothing further, Your Honor.'

Judge Keyes looked at the clock at the wall and then at Belk.

'What do you think, Mr Belk? Break for lunch now so you won't be interrupted?'

'I only have one question.'

'Oh, then by all means, ask it.'

Belk took his pad to the lectern and leaned to the microphone.

'Lieutenant Lloyd, from all of your knowledge about this case, do you have any doubt whatsoever that Norman Church was the Dollmaker?'

'None at all. None . . . at . . . all.'

After the jury filed out, Bosch leaned to Belk's ear and urgently whispered, 'What was that? She tore him up and you asked only one question. What about all the other things that tied Church to the case?'

Belk held up his hand to calm Bosch and then spoke calmly.

'Because you are going to testify about all of that. This case is about you, Harry. We either win it or lose it with you.'

SIX

The Code Seven had closed its dining room during the recession and somebody put a salad and pizza bar in the space to serve the office workers from the civic center. The Seven's barroom was still open but the dining room had been the last place within walking distance of Parker Center that Bosch had liked to eat at. So during the lunch break he got his car out of the lot at Parker and drove over to the garment district to eat at Gorky's. The Russian restaurant served breakfast all day and he ordered the eggs, bacon and potatoes special and took it to a table where someone had left behind a copy of the *Times*.

The concrete blonde story had Bremmer's byline on it. It combined quotes from the opening arguments in the trial with the discovery of the body and its possible connection to the case. The story also reported that police sources revealed that Detective Harry Bosch had received a note from someone claiming to be the real Dollmaker.

There was obviously a leak in Hollywood Division but Bosch knew it would be impossible to trace the person down. The note had been found at the front desk and any number of uniform officers could have known about it and leaked the word to Bremmer. After all, Bremmer was a good friend to have. Bosch had even leaked information to him in the past and on occasion found Bremmer to be quite useful.

Citing the unnamed sources, the story said police investigators had not concluded whether the note was legitimate or if the discovery of the body was connected to the Dollmaker case which ended four years earlier.

The only other point of interest in the story for Bosch was the short history on the Bing's Billiards building. It had been burned on the second night of the riots, no arrests ever made. Arson investigators said the separations between the storage units were not bearing walls, meaning trying to stop the flames was like trying to hold water in a cup made of toilet paper. From ignition to full involvement of flames was only eighteen minutes. Most of the storage units were rented by movie industry people and some valuable studio props were either looted or lost in the fire. The building was a total loss. The investigators traced the origin to the billiard hall. A pool table had been set on fire and it went from there.

Bosch put the paper down and began thinking about Lloyd's testimony. He remembered what Belk had said, that the case rode on himself. Chandler must know this as well. She would be waiting for him, ready to make Lloyd's outing seem like a joy ride in comparison. He grudgingly had to admit to himself that he respected her skill, her toughness. It made him remember something and he got up to use the pay phone out front. He was surprised to find Edgar was at the homicide table and not out eating lunch.

'Any luck on the ID?' Bosch asked.

'No, man, the prints didn't check. No matches at all. She didn't have a record. We're still trying other sources, adult entertainment licenses, stuff like that.'

'Shit.'

'Well, we got something else cooking. Remember that CSUN anthropology professor I was telling you about? Well, he's been here all morning with a student, painting the plaster face and getting it ready. I got the press coming in at three to show it off. Rojas went out to buy a blonde wig we'll stick on it. If we get good play on the tube we might crack loose an ID.'

'Sounds like a plan.'

'Yeah. How's court? The shit hit the fan in the *Times* today. That guy Bremmer has some sources.'

'Court's fine. Let me ask you something. After you left the scene yesterday and went back to the station, where was Pounds?'

'Pounds? He was – we got back at the same time. Why?'

'When did he leave?'

'A little while later. Right before you got here.'

'Was he on the phone in his office?'

'I think he made a few calls. I wasn't really watching. What's going on, you think he's Bremmer's source?'

'One last question. Did he close the door when he was on the phone?'

Bosch knew Pounds was paranoid. He always kept the door to his office open and the blinds on the glass partitions up so he could see and hear what was happening in the squad room. If he ever closed either or both, the troops outside knew something was up.

'Well, now that you mention it, I think he did have the door closed a little while. What is it?'

'Bremmer I'm not worried about. But somebody was talking to Money Chandler. In court this morning she knew I had been called out to the scene yesterday. That wasn't in the *Times*. Somebody told her.'

Edgar was silent a moment before replying.

'Yeah, but why would Pounds talk to her?'

'I don't know.'

'Maybe Bremmer. He could have told her, even though it wasn't in his story.'

'The story says she couldn't be reached for comment. It's got to be somebody else. A leak. Probably the same person talked to Bremmer and Chandler. Somebody who wants to fuck me up.'

Edgar didn't say anything and Bosch let it go for now.

'I better head back to court.'

'Hey, how'd Lloyd do? I heard on KFWB he was the first wit.'

'He did about as expected.'

'Shit. Who's next?'

'I don't know. She has Irving and Locke, the shrink, on subpoena. My guess is, it will be Irving. He'll pick up where Lloyd left off.'

'Well, good luck. By the way, if you're looking for something to do. This press gig I'm holding will hit the TV news tonight. I'll be here waiting by the phones. If you want to answer a few, I could use the help.'

Bosch thought briefly about his plan for dinner with Sylvia. She'd understand.

'Yeah, I'll be there.'

The afternoon testimony was largely uneventful. Chandler's strategy, it seemed to Bosch, was to build a two-part question into the jury's eventual deliberation, giving her clients two shots at the prize. One would be the wrong-man theory, which held that Bosch had flat-out killed an innocent man. The second question would be the use of force. Even if the jury determined that Norman Church, family man, was the Dollmaker, serial killer, they would have to decide whether Bosch's actions were appropriate.

Chandler called her client, Deborah Church, to the witness stand right after lunch. She gave a tearful account of a wonderful life with a wonderful husband who fawned over everybody; his daughters, his wife, his mother and mother-in-law. No misogynistic aberrations here. No sign of childhood abuse. The widow held a box of Kleenex in her hand as she testified, going to a new tissue every other question.

She wore the traditional black dress of a widow. Bosch remembered how appealing Sylvia had been when he saw her at her husband's funeral dressed in black. Deborah Church looked downright scary. It was as if she reveled in her role here. The widow of the fallen innocent. The real victim. Chandler had coached her well.

It was a good show, but it was too good to be true and Chandler knew it. Rather than leave the bad things to be drawn out on cross-examination, she finally got around to asking Deborah Church how, her marriage being so wonderful, her husband was in that garage apartment – which was rented under an alias – when Bosch kicked the door open.

'We had been having some difficulty.' She stopped to dab an eye with a tissue. 'Norman was going through a lot of stress – he had a lot of responsibility in the aircraft design department. He needed to expend it and so he took the apartment. He said it was to be alone. To think. I didn't know about this woman he brought there. I think it was probably his first time doing something like that. He was a naive man. I think she saw this. She took his money and then set him up by calling the police on him and giving the crazy story that he was the Dollmaker. There was a reward, you know.'

Bosch wrote a note on a pad he kept in front of him and slid it over to Belk, who read it and then jotted something down on his own pad.

'What about all of the makeup found there, Mrs Church?' Chandler asked. 'Can you explain that?'

'All I know is that I would have known if my husband was that monster. I would have known. If there was makeup found there, it was put there by somebody else. Maybe after he was already dead.'

Bosch believed he could feel the eyes of the courtroom burning into him as the widow accused him of planting evidence after murdering her husband.

After that, Chandler moved her questioning on to safer topics like Norman Church's relationship with his daughters and then ended her direct examination with a weeper.

'Did he love his daughters?'

'Very much so,' Mrs Church said as a new production of tears rolled down her cheeks. This time she did not wipe them away with a tissue. She let the jury watch them roll down her face into the folds of her double chin.

After giving her a few moments to compose herself, Belk got up and took his place at the lectern.

'Again, Your Honor, I will be brief. Mrs Church, I want to make this very clear to the jury. Did you say in your testimony that you knew about your husband's apartment but didn't know about any women he may or may not have brought there?'

'Yes, that is correct.'

Belk looked at his pad.

'Did you not tell detectives on the night of the shooting that you had never heard of any apartment? Didn't you emphatically deny that your husband even had such an apartment?'

Deborah Church didn't answer.

'I can arrange to have a tape of your first interview played in court if it will help refresh your –'

'Yes, I said that. I lied.'

'You lied? Why would you lie to the police?'

'Because a policeman had just killed my husband. I didn't – I couldn't deal with them.'

'The truth is you told the truth that night, correct, Mrs Church? You never knew about any apartment.'

'No, that's not true. I knew about it.'

'Had you and your husband talked about it?'

'Yes, we discussed it.'

'You approved of it?'

'Yes . . ., reluctantly. It was my hope he would stay at home and we could work this stress out together.'

'Okay, Mrs Church, then if you knew of the apartment, had discussed it and given your approval, reluctantly or not, why then did your husband rent it under a false name?'

She didn't answer. Belk had nailed her. Bosch thought he saw the widow glance in Chandler's direction. He looked at the lawyer but she made no move, no change in facial expression to help her client.

'I guess,' the widow finally said, 'that was one of the questions you could have asked him if Mr Bosch had not murdered him in cold blood.'

Without Belk's prompting, Judge Keyes said, 'The jury will disregard that last characterization. Mrs Church, you know better than that.'

'I'm sorry, Your Honor.'

'Nothing further,' Belk said as he left the lectern.

The judge called a ten-minute recess.

During the break, Bosch went out to the ash can. Money Chandler didn't come out but the homeless man made a pass. Bosch offered him a whole cigarette, which he took and put in his shirt pocket. He was unshaven again and the slight look of dementia was still in his eyes.

'Your name is Faraday,' Bosch said, as if speaking to a child.

'Yeah, what about it, Lieutenant?'

Bosch smiled. He had been made by a bum. All except for the rank.

'Nothing about it. I just heard that's what it was. I also heard you were a lawyer once.'

'I still am. I'm just not practicing.'

He turned and watched a jail bus go by on Spring, heading to the courthouse. It was full of angry faces looking out through the black wire windows. Somebody by one of the back windows made Bosch as a cop, too, and stuck his middle index finger up through the wire. Bosch smiled back at him.

'My name was Thomas Faraday. But now I prefer Tommy Faraway.'

'What happened to make you stop practicing law?'

Tommy looked back at him with milky eyes.

'Justice is what happened. Thanks for the smoke.'

He walked away then, cup in hand, and headed toward City Hall. Maybe that was his turf, too.

After the break, Chandler called a lab analyst from the coroner's office named Victor Amado. He was a very small and bookish-looking man with eyes that shifted from the judge to the jury as he walked to the witness chair. He was balding badly, though he seemed to be no more than twenty-eight. Bosch remembered that four years earlier he had all his hair and members of the task force referred to him as The Kid. He knew Belk was going to call Amado as a witness if Chandler didn't.

Belk leaned over and whispered that Chandler was following a good guy–bad guy pattern by alternating police witnesses with her sympathetic witnesses.

'She'll probably put one of the daughters up there after Amado,' he said. 'As a strategy, it is completely unoriginal.'

Bosch didn't mention that Belk's trust-us-we're-the-cops defense had been around as long as the civil suit.

Amado testified in painstaking detail about how he had been given all of the bottles and compacts containing makeup that were found in Church's Hyperion apartment and had then traced them to specific victims of the Dollmaker. He said he had come up with nine separate lots or groupings of makeup – mascara, blush, eyeliner, lipstick, etc. Each lot was connected through chemical analysis to samples taken from the faces of the victims. This was further corroborated by detectives who interviewed relatives and friends to determine what brands the victims were known to use. It all matched up, Amado said. And in one instance, he added, an eyelash found on a mascara brush in Church's bathroom cabinet was identified as having come from the second victim.

'What about the two victims no matching makeup was found for?' Chandler asked.

'That was a mystery. We never found their makeup.'

'In fact, with the exception of the eyelash that was allegedly found and matched to victim number two, you can't be one hundred percent sure that the makeup police did supposedly find in the apartment came from the victims, correct?'

'This stuff is mass produced and sold around the world. So there is a lot of it out there, but I would guess that the

74

chances of nine different exact combinations of makeup being found like that by mere coincidence are astronomical.'

'I didn't ask you to guess, Mr Amado. Please answer the question I asked.'

After flinching at being dressed down, Amado said, 'The answer is we can't be one hundred percent sure, that is correct.'

'Okay, now tell the jury about the DNA testing you did that connected Norman Church to the eleven killings.'

'There wasn't any done. There —'

'Just answer the question, Mr Amado. What about serology tests, connecting Mr Church to the crimes?'

'There were none.'

'Then it was the makeup comparison that was the clincher — the linchpin in the determination that Mr Church was the Dollmaker?'

'Well, it was for me. I don't know about the detectives. My report said —'

'I'm sure for the detectives it was the bullet that killed him that was the clincher.'

'Objection,' Belk yelled angrily as he stood. 'Your Honor, she can't —'

'Ms Chandler,' Judge Keyes boomed. 'I have warned you both about exactly this sort of thing. Why would you go and say something you know full well is prejudicial and out of order?'

'I apologize, Your Honor.'

'Well, it's a little late for apologies. We'll discuss this matter after the jury goes home for the day.'

The judge then instructed the jurors to disregard her comment. But Bosch knew it had been a carefully thought out gambit by Chandler. The jurors would now see her even more as the underdog. Even the judge was against her — which he really wasn't. And they might be distracted, thinking about what just happened, when Belk stepped up to repair Amado's testimony.

'Nothing further, Your Honor,' Chandler said.

'Mr Belk,' the judge said.

Don't say just a few questions again, Bosch thought as his lawyer moved to the lectern.

'Just a few questions, Mr Amado,' Belk said. 'Plaintiff's counsel mentioned DNA and serology tests and you said they had not been done. Why is that?'

'Well, because there was nothing to test. No semen was ever recovered from any of the bodies. The killer had used a condom. Without samples to attempt to match to Mr Church's DNA or blood, there was not much point in running tests. We would have the victims' but nothing to compare it to.'

Belk drew a line with his pen through a question written on his pad.

'If there was no recovery of semen or sperm, how do you know these women were raped or even had engaged in consensual sexual activity?'

'The autopsies of all eleven of the victims showed vaginal bruising, much more than is considered usual or even possible from consensual sex. On two of the victims there was even tearing in the vaginal wall. The victims were brutally raped, in my estimation.'

'But these women came from walks of life where sexual activity was common and frequent, even "rough sex", if you will. Two of them performed in pornographic videos. How can you be sure they were sexually assaulted against their will?'

'The bruising was such that it would have been very painful, especially for the two with vaginal tears. Hemorrhaging was considered perimortem, meaning at the time of death. The deputy coroners who performed these autopsies unanimously concluded these women were raped.'

Belk drew another line on his pad, flipped the page and came up with a new question. He was doing well with Amado, Bosch thought. Better than Money had. It

76

may have been a mistake for her to have called him as a witness.

'How do you know that the killer used a condom?' Belk asked. 'Couldn't these women have been raped with an object and that account for the lack of semen?'

'That could have happened and it could account for some of the damage. But there was clear evidence in five of the cases that they had had sex with a man wearing a condom.'

'And what was that?'

'We did rape kits. There was –'

'Hold it a second, Mr Amado. What is a rape kit?'

'It's a protocol for collecting evidence from bodies of people that may have been the victims of rape. In the case of a woman, we take vaginal and anal swabs, we comb the pubic area looking for foreign pubic hair, procedures such as that. We also take samples of blood and hair from the victim in case there is a call for comparison to evidence found on a suspect. It's collected together in an evidence kit.'

'Okay. Before I interrupted there, you were going to tell us about the evidence found in five of the victims that was indicative of sex with a man who wore a condom.'

'Yes, we did the rape kits each time we got a Dollmaker victim. And there was a foreign substance found in vaginal samplings in five of the victims. It was the same material in each of the women.'

'What was it, Mr Amado?'

'It was identified as a condom lubricant.'

'Was this material something that could be identified to a specific brand and style of condom?'

Looking at Belk, Bosch could see the heavy man was chomping at the bit. Amado was answering each question slowly and each time Bosch could see that Belk could barely wait for the answer before plowing ahead with a new question. Belk was on a roll.

'Yes,' Amado said. 'We identified the product. It was from a Trojan-Enz lubricated condom with special receptacle end.'

Looking at the court reporter, Amado said, 'That's spelled E-N-Z.'

'And that was the same for all five samples received from the five bodies?' Belk asked.

'Yes it was.'

'I am going to ask you a hypothetical question. Assuming that the attacker of eleven women used the same brand of lubricated condom, how could you account for lubrication being found in the vaginal sampling of only five victims?'

'I believe that a number of factors could be involved. Such as the intensity of the victim's struggle. But essentially it would be just a matter of how much of the lubricant came off the condom and stayed in the vagina.'

'When police officers brought you the various containers of makeup from the Hyperion apartment rented by Norman Church for analysis, did they bring anything else?'

'Yes they did.'

'What was that?'

'A box of Trojan-Enz lubricated condoms with special receptacle ends.'

'How many condoms did the box hold?'

'Twelve separately packaged condoms.'

'How many were still in the box when the police delivered it to you?'

'There were three left.'

'Nothing further.'

Belk returned to the defense table with a triumphant spring in his walk.

'A moment, Your Honor,' Chandler said.

Bosch watched her open a fat file full of police documents. She leafed through the pages and took out a short stack of documents held together with a paper clip. She read the top one quickly and then held it up to leaf through the rest. Bosch could see the top one was the protocol list from a rape kit. She was reading the protocols from all eleven victims.

Belk leaned over to him and whispered, 'She's about to

step into some deep shit. I was going to bring this up later, during your testimony.'

'Ms Chandler?' the judge intoned.

She jumped up.

'Yes, Your Honor, I'm ready. I have a quick redirect of Mr Amado.'

She brought the stack of protocols with her to the lectern, read the last two and then looked at the coroner's analyst.

'Mr Amado, you mentioned that part of the rape kit consisted of combing for foreign pubic hairs, do I have that right?'

'Yes.'

'Can you explain that procedure a little more?'

'Well, basically, the comb is passed through the pubic hair of the victim and it collects unattached hairs. Oftentimes, this unattached hair is from the victim's attacker, or possibly other sexual partners.'

'How's it get there?'

Amado's face flushed to a crimson hue.

'Well, uh, it – uh, during sex . . . there is I guess what you call friction between the bodies?'

'I am asking the questions, Mr Amado. You are answering.'

There was quiet tittering from the gallery seats. Bosch felt embarrassed for Amado and thought that his own face might be turning red.

'Yes, well, there is friction,' Amado said. 'And this causes some transference. Loose pubic hair from one person can be transferred to that of the other.'

'I see,' Chandler said. 'Now, you as coordinator of the Dollmaker evidence from the coroner's office were familiar with the rape kits of all eleven victims, correct?'

'Yes.'

'With how many of the victims did the findings include foreign pubic hair?'

Bosch understood what was happening now and realized that Belk was right. Chandler was walking into the buzz saw.

'All of them,' Amado answered.

Bosch saw Deborah Church raise her head and look sharply at Chandler at the lectern. Then she looked over at Bosch and their eyes met. She quickly looked away but Bosch knew. She, too, knew what was about to happen. Because she, too, knew her late husband the way Bosch had on that last night. She knew what he looked like naked.

'Ah, all of them,' Chandler said. 'Now, can you tell the jury how many of these pubic hairs found on these women were analyzed and identified as having been from the body of Norman Church?'

'None of them were from Norman Church.'

'Thank you.'

Belk was up and moving to the lectern before Chandler had time to remove her pad and the rape kit protocols. Bosch watched her sit down and saw the widow Church lean to her and desperately begin whispering. Bosch saw Chandler's eyes go dead. She held up her hand to tell the widow she had said enough and then leaned back and exhaled.

'Now, let's clear something up first,' Belk said. 'Mr Amado, you said you found pubic hairs on all of the eleven victims. Were these hairs all from the same man?'

'No. We found a multitude of samples. In most cases, what looked like hair from possibly two or three men on each victim.'

'What did you attribute this to?'

'Their lifestyle. We knew these were women with multiple sexual partners.'

'Did you analyze these samples to determine if there were common hairs? In other words, whether hair from one man was found on each of the victims.'

'No, we did not. There was a huge amount of evidence collected in these cases and manpower dictated that we focus on evidence that would help identify a killer. Because we had so many different samples, it was determined that this was evidence that would be held and then used to link or clear a suspect, once that suspect was in custody.'

'I see, well, then once Norman Church had been killed and was identified as the Dollmaker, did you then match any of the hairs from the victims to him?'

'We did not.'

'And why is that?'

'Because Mr. Church had shaved his body hair. There was no pubic hair to match.'

'Why would he have done that?'

Chandler objected on the grounds that Amado could not answer for Church and the judge sustained it. But Bosch knew it didn't matter. Everybody in the courtroom knew why Church had shaved himself – so he wouldn't leave pubic hairs behind as evidence.

Bosch looked at the jury and he saw two of the women writing in the notebooks the marshals had given them to help them keep track of important testimony. He wanted to buy Belk – and Amado – a beer.

SEVEN

It looked like a cake in a box, one of those novelty things custom-made to look like Marilyn Monroe or something. The anthropologist had painted on a beige skin tone and red lipstick to go with blue eyes. It looked like frosting to Bosch. A wavy blonde wig was added. He stood in the squad room looking down at the plaster image, wondering if it really looked like anybody at all.

'Five minutes till show time,' Edgar said.

He was sitting in his chair, which was turned toward the TV on the file cabinets. He was holding the channel changer. His blue suit coat was hung neatly on a hanger, which was hooked on the coatrack at the end of the table. Bosch took his jacket off and hung it on one of the coatrack pegs. He checked his slot in the message box and sat down at his spot at the homicide table. There had been a call from Sylvia, nothing else important. He dialed her number as the Channel 4 news began. He knew enough about the news priorities in this town to know the report on the concrete blonde wouldn't be a lead story.

'Harry, we're gonna need that line clear once they show it,' Edgar said.

'I'll only be a minute. They won't show it for a while. If they show it at all.'

'They'll show it. I made secret deals with all of them. They all think they'll be getting the exclusive if we get an ID. They all want to get a boo hoo story with the parents.'

'You're playing with fire, man. You make a promise like that and then they find out you fucked them around –'

Sylvia picked up the phone.

'Hey, it's me.'

'Hi, where are you?'

'The office. We have to watch the phones a while. They're putting the face of the victim from yesterday's case on TV tonight.'

'How was court?'

'It's the plaintiff's case at the moment. But I think we scored a couple punches.'

'I read the *Times* today at lunch.'

'Yeah, well, they got about half of it right.'

'Are you coming out? Like you said.'

'Well, eventually. Not right now. I've got to help answer phones on this and then it's depending on what we get. If we're skunked I'll be out early.'

He noticed he had lowered his voice so Edgar wouldn't hear his conversation.

'And if you get something good?'

'We'll see.'

An indrawn breath, then silence. Harry waited.

'You've been saying "we'll see" too much, Harry. We've talked about this. Sometimes –'

'I know that.'

' – I think that you just want to be left alone. Stay in your little house on the hill and keep the whole world out. Including me.'

'Not you. You know that.'

'Sometimes, I don't. I don't feel like I know it right now. You push me away just at the time when you need me – somebody – to be close.'

He had no answer. He thought of her there on the other end. She was probably sitting on the stool in the kitchen. She had probably already begun making a dinner for both of them. Or maybe she was getting used to his ways and had waited for the call.

'Look, I'm sorry,' he said. 'You know how it is. What are you doing about dinner?'

'Nothing, and I'm not going to do anything, either.'

Edgar made a low, quick whistle. Harry looked up at the TV and saw it was showing the painted face of the victim. The TV was on Channel 7 now. The camera showed a long close-up of the face. It looked all right on the tube. At least, it didn't look much like a cake. The screen flashed the detective bureau's two public numbers.

'They're showing it now,' Bosch said to Sylvia. 'I need to keep this line clear. Let me call you back later, when I know something.'

'Sure,' she said coldly and hung up.

Edgar had the TV on 4 now and they were showing the face. He then flipped to 2 and caught the last few seconds of their report on it. They had even interviewed the anthropologist.

'Slow news day,' Bosch said.

'Shit,' Edgar replied. 'We're banging on all cylinders now. All we –'

The phone rang and he grabbed it up.

'No, it just went out,' he said after listening for a few moments. 'Yeah, yeah, I will. Okay.'

He hung up and shook his head.

'Pounds?' Bosch asked.

'Yeah. Thinks we're going to have her name ten seconds after the broadcast went out. Christ, whadda nitwit.'

The next three calls were pranks, all testifying to the glaring lack of originality and the mental health of the TV viewing audience. All three callers said 'Your mother!' or words to that effect and hung up laughing. About twenty minutes later Edgar got a call and started taking notes. The phone rang again and Bosch took it.

'This is Detective Bosch, who am I speaking with?'

'Is this being taped?'

'No, it's not. Who is this?'

'Never mind, just thought you'd like to know the girl's name is Maggie. Maggie something or other. It's Latin. I seen her on videos.'

'What videos? MTV?'

'No, Sherlock. Adult videos. She fucked on film. She was good. She could put a rubber on a prick with her mouth.'

The line went dead. Bosch wrote a couple of notes down on the pad he had in front of him. Latin? He didn't think the way the face had been painted gave any indication that the victim was a Latina.

Edgar hung up then and said his caller had said her name was Becky, that she had lived in Studio City a few years back.

'What'd you get?'

'I got a Maggie. No last name. Possibly a Latin last name. He said she was in porno.'

'That would fit, except she don't look Mexican to me.'

'I know.'

The phone rang again. Edgar picked up and listened a few moments and then hung up.

'Another one that recognizes my mom.'

Bosch took the next one.

'I just wanted to tell you that the girl they were showing on TV was in porno,' the voice said.

'How do you know she was in porno?'

'I can tell by that thing they showed on TV. I rented a tape. Only once. She was in it.'

Only once, Bosch thought, but he remembered. Yeah, sure.

'You know her name?'

The other phone rang and Edgar picked it up.

'I don't know names, man,' Bosch's caller said. 'They all use fake ones anyway.'

'What was the name of the tape?'

'Can't remember. I was, uh, intoxicated when I saw it. Like I said, it was the only time.'

'Look, I'm not taking your confession. You got anything else?'

'No, smartass, I don't.'

'Who is this?'

'I don't have to say.'

'Look, we're trying to find a killer here. What was the name of the place you rented it?'

'I'm not telling you, you might be able to get my name from them. Doesn't matter, they have those tapes all over, every adult place.'

'How would you know if you only rented one once?'

The caller hung up.

Bosch stayed another hour. By the end they had five calls saying the painted face belonged to a porno starlet. Only one of the callers said her name was Maggie, the other four men saying they didn't pay much attention to names. There was one call naming her Becky of Studio City, and one saying she was a stripper who had worked for a while at the Booby Trap on La Brea. One man who called said the face belonged to his missing wife, but Bosch learned through further questioning that she had been missing only two months. The concrete blonde had been dead too long. The hope and desperation in the caller's voice seemed genuine to Bosch, and he didn't know whether he was telling the man good news by explaining that it could not be his wife or bad news because he was left in the void again.

There were three callers who gave vague descriptions of a woman they thought might be the concrete blonde, but after a few questions into each conversation Bosch and Edgar identified the callers as cop geeks, people who got a thrill from talking to the police.

The most unusual call was from a Beverly Hills psychic who mentioned that she had placed her hand on the TV screen while it showed the face and felt the dead woman's spirit cry out to her.

'What did it cry?' Bosch asked patiently.

'Praise.'

'Praise for what?'

'Jesus our savior, I would assume but I don't know. That was all I received. I might receive more if I could touch the actual plaster cast of the —'

'Well, did this spirit that was giving praise identify itself? See, that's what we're doing here. We're more interested in a name than cries of praise.'

'Someday you will believe but by then you will be lost.'

She hung up on him.

At seven-thirty Bosch told Edgar he was splitting.

'How 'bout you? You going to hang out for the eleven o'clock news?'

'Yeah, I'll be here but I can handle it. If I get a lot of calls I'll pull one of the dipshits off the desk.'

Stock that O.T., Bosch thought.

'What's next?' he asked.

'I don't know. What do you think?'

'Well, aside from all the calls saying it's your mother, this porno thing seems to be the way to go.'

'Leave my blessed mother out of it. How you think I can check the porno?'

'Administrative Vice. Guy over there, a detective-three, name of Ray Mora, he works porno. He's the best. He also was on the Dollmaker task force. Call him and see if he can come take a look at the face. He might've known her. Tell him we had one call saying her name was Maggie.'

'Will do. It fits with the Dollmaker, doesn't it? The porno, I mean.'

'Yeah, it fits.' He thought about this a moment, then added, 'Two of the other victims were in the business. The one that got away from him was, too.'

'The lucky one – she still in it?'

'Last I heard. But she might be dead now for all I know.'

'Still doesn't mean anything, Harry.'

'What?'

'The porno. Still doesn't mean it was the Dollmaker. The real one, I mean.'

Bosch just nodded. He had an idea about something to do on his way home. He went out to his Caprice and got the Polaroid camera out of the trunk. In the squad room, he took two shots of the face in the box and put them in his coat pocket after they developed.

Edgar watched this and asked, 'What're you going to do?'

'Might stop at that adult supermarket in the Valley on my way up to Sylvia's.'

'Don't get caught in one of those little rooms with your dick out.'

'Thanks for the tip. Let me know what Mora says.'

Bosch worked his way on surface streets up to the Hollywood Freeway. He went north and then exited on Lankershim, which took him into North Hollywood in the San Fernando Valley. He had all four windows down and the air was cool as it buffeted him from all directions. He smoked a cigarette, flicking the ashes into the wind. There was some techno-funk jazz on KAJZ so he turned the radio off and just drove.

The Valley was the city's bedroom community in more ways than the obvious. It was also home to the nation's pornography industry. The commercial-industrial districts of Van Nuys, Canoga Park, Northridge and Chatsworth housed hundreds of porno production outfits, distributors and warehouses. Modeling agencies in Sherman Oaks provided ninety percent of the women and men who performed in front of the cameras. And, consequently, the Valley was also one of the largest retail outlets for the material. It was made here, it was sold here – through video mail-order businesses also nestled in the warehouses with the production outfits, and places like X Marks the Spot on Lankershim Boulevard.

Bosch pulled into the lot in front of the huge store and appraised it for a few moments. It had formerly been a Pic N Pay supermarket, but the front plate-glass windows had been walled up. Under the red neon X Marks the Spot sign, the front wall was whitewashed and painted with black figures of naked and overly buxom female figures, like the metallic silhouettes Bosch saw all the time on the mudflaps of trucks on the freeway. The men who put those on their trucks were probably the same guys this place catered to, Bosch figured.

X Marks the Spot was owned by a man named Harold Barnes, who was a front for the Chicago Outfit. It grossed more than a million dollars a year – on the books. Probably another one under the counter. Bosch knew all of this from Mora of Ad-Vice, whom he had partnered with on some nights while they both were on the task force four years earlier.

Bosch watched a man of about twenty-five get out of his Toyota, walk quickly to the solid wood front door, and slip in like a secret agent. He followed. The front half of the former supermarket was dedicated to retail – the sale and rental of videos, magazines and other assorted adult-oriented and mostly rubber products. The rear was split between private 'encounter' rooms and private video booths. The entry to this area was through a curtained doorway. Bosch could hear heavy-metal rock music coming from back there mixed with the canned-sounding cries of phony passion coming from the video booths.

To his left was a glass counter with two men behind it. One was a big man, there to keep the peace; the other was smaller, older, there to take the money. Bosch knew by the way they looked at him and the skin stretched tight around their eyes that they had made him as soon as he had come in. He walked over and put one of the Polaroids on the counter.

'I am trying to ID her. Heard she worked in video, do you recognize her?'

The small guy leaned forward and looked while the other guy didn't move.

'Looks like a fucking cake, man,' the small guy said. 'I don't know any cakes. I eat cakes.'

He looked back at the big guy and they exchanged clever smiles.

'So you don't recognize her. What about you?'

'I say what he says,' the big guy said. 'I eat cakes, too.'

This time they laughed out loud and probably had to restrain themselves from exchanging a high five. The small guy's eyes sparkled behind rose-tinted glasses.

'Okay,' Bosch said. 'Then I'll just look around. Thanks.'

The big guy stepped forward and said, 'Just keep your gun covered, man, we don't want to excite the patrons.'

The big guy's eyes were dull and he set out a five-foot zone of body odor. A duster, Bosch thought. He wondered why the small guy didn't fire his ass.

'No more excited than they are,' Bosch said.

He turned from the counter to the two walls of shelves that were lined with hundreds of video boxes for sale or rent. There were a dozen men, including the secret agent, looking. Appraising the scene and the number of video boxes, Bosch somehow was reminded of how he once had read all the names on the Vietnam War Memorial wall while on a case. It had taken several hours.

The video wall proved to be less time consuming. Skipping the gay and black performer videos he scanned each box for a face like the concrete blonde's or the name Maggie. The videos were in alphabetical order and it took him nearly an hour to get to the T's. A face on the box of a video called *Tails from the Crypt* caught his eye. There was a nude woman lying in a coffin on the front. She was blonde and had an upturned nose like the plaster face in the box. He turned the box over and there was another photo of the actress, on her hands and knees with a man pressed up behind her. Her mouth was slightly open and her face was turned back toward her sex partner.

It was her, Bosch knew. He looked at the credits and saw that the name fit. He took the empty video box to the counter.

''Bout time,' said the small guy. 'We don't allow loitering here. The cops give us a hard time on that.'

'I want to rent this.'

'Can't, it's already rented. See, the box is empty.'

'She in anything else you know of?'

The small guy took the box and looked at the photographs.

'Magna Cum Loudly, yeah. I don't know. She was just getting started and then dropped out. Probably married a rich guy, lots of them do.'

The big guy stepped over to look at the box and Bosch stepped back, out of his odor zone.

'I'm sure they do,' he said. 'What else was she in?'

'Well,' the small guy said, 'she had just made her way out of the loops and then, pfffft, she's gone. *Tails* was her first top billing. She did a fabulous two-way in *Whore of the Roses* and that's what got her started. Before that it was just the loops.'

Bosch went back to the W's and found the box for *Whore of the Roses*. It also was empty and there were no photos of Magna Cum Loudly on it. Her name was last billing on the credits. He went back to the small guy and pointed to the Tails from the Crypt box.

'What about the box, then? I'll buy it.'

'We can't sell you just the box because then how do we display the video when it comes back? We don't sell many boxes here. Guys want stills, they buy magazines.'

'What's the price of the whole video? I'll buy it. When the renter brings it back you can hold it for me and I'll come pick it up. How much?'

'Well, *Tails* is popular. We're going with a $39.95 price tag but for you, Officer, I'll give our law enforcement discount. Fifty bucks.'

Bosch said nothing to that. He had the cash and paid it.

'I want a receipt.'

After the purchase was completed, the small guy put the video box in a brown paper bag.

'You know,' he said, 'Maggie Cum Loudly is still on a couple of our loops in the back. You might want to check it out.'

He smiled and pointed to a sign on the wall behind him.

'We have a no-exchange policy, by the way.'

Bosch smiled back.

'I'll check it out.'

'Hey, by the way, what name you want us to hold this video under when it comes back in?'

'Carlo Pinzi.'

It was the name of the Outfit's LA capo.

'Very fucking funny, Mr Pinzi, we'll do that.'

Bosch went through the curtain into the back rooms and was almost immediately met by a woman wearing high heels, a black G-string and an ice-cream man's coin changer on a belt, nothing else. Her large silicone-perfected breasts were dotted by unusually small nipples. Her dyed blonde hair was short and she had too much makeup around her glassy brown eyes. She looked like she was either nineteen or thirty-five.

'Do you want a private encounter or change for the video booths?' she asked.

Bosch took out his now thin fold of cash and gave her two dollars for quarters.

'Can I keep a dollar for myself? I don't get paid nothin', just tips.'

Bosch gave her another dollar and took his eight quarters to one of the small curtained booths where the occupied light wasn't on.

'Let me know if you need anything in there,' the woman in the G-string called after him.

She was either too stoned or too stupid or both not to have made him as a cop. Bosch waved her away and pulled the curtain shut behind him. The space he had was about the size of a phone booth. There was a glass viewing window through which he could see a video screen. Displayed on the screen was a directory of twelve different videos he could select from. It was all video now, though they were still called loops, after the 16mm film loops that ran over and over again in the first peep machines.

There was no chair but there was a small shelf with an ashtray and a Kleenex box on it. Used tissues were littered on the floor and the booth smelled like the industrial disinfectant they used in the coroner's vans. He put all eight quarters in the coin slot and the video picture came on.

It was two women on a bed kissing and massaging each other. It took Bosch only a few seconds to eliminate them as possibly being the girl on the video box. He began pushing the channel button and the picture jumped from coupling to coupling – heterosexual, homosexual, bisexual – his eyes lingering only long enough to determine whether the woman he was looking for was there.

She was on the ninth loop. He recognized her from the video box he had bought. Seeing her in motion also helped convince him that the woman who used the name Magna Cum Loudly was the concrete blonde. In the video she lay on a couch on her back, biting one of her fingers while a man knelt between her legs on the floor and rhythmically ground his hips into hers.

Knowing this woman was dead, had died violently, and standing there watching her submit to another kind of violence affected him in a way he was unsure he even understood. Guilt and sorrow welled up as he watched. Like most cops, he had spent a stint in vice. He had also seen some of the films of the two other adult film actresses who were killed by the Dollmaker. But this was the first time this uneasiness had hit him.

On the video, the actress took the finger out of her mouth and began to moan loudly, living up to her billing. Bosch fumbled with the sound knob and turned it down. But he could still hear her, her moans turned into shouts, from videos in other booths. Other men were watching the same show. It made Bosch feel creepy knowing the video had drawn the interest of different men for different reasons.

The curtain behind him rustled and he heard someone move behind him into the booth. At the same moment he felt a hand move up his thigh to his crotch. He reached into his jacket for his gun as he turned but then saw it was the coin changer.

'What can I do for you, darling?' she cooed.

He pushed her arm away from him.

'You can start by getting out of here.'

'C'mon, lover, why look at it on TV when you can be doing it? Twenty bucks. I can't go lower. I have to split it with the management.'

She was pressed against him now and Bosch couldn't tell if it was his breath or hers that was lousy with cigarettes. Her breasts were hard and she was pushing them against his chest. Then suddenly she froze. She had felt the gun. Their eyes held each other for a moment.

'That's right,' Bosch said. 'If you don't want to go for a ride to the cage, get out of here.'

'No problem, Officer,' she said.

She parted the curtain and was gone. Just then the screen went back to the directory. Bosch's two dollars were up.

As he walked out, he heard Magna Cum Loudly yelling in false joy from the other booths.

EIGHT

On the ride on the freeway to the next valley, he tried to imagine that life. He wondered what hope she might still have had and still nurtured and protected like a candle in the rain, even as she lay there on her back with distant eyes turned toward the stranger inside her. Hope must have been the only thing she had left. Bosch knew that hope was the lifeblood of the heart. Without it there was nothing, only darkness.

He wondered how the two lives – killer's and victim's – had crossed. Maybe the seed of lust and murderous desire had been planted by the same loop Bosch had just seen. Maybe the killer had rented the video Bosch had just paid fifty dollars for. Could it have been Church? Or was there another out there? The box, Bosch thought, and pulled off at the next exit, Van Nuys Boulevard in Pacoima.

He pulled to the curb and took the video box out of the brown paper bag the small guy had provided. He turned the light on in the car and studied every surface of the box, reading every word. But there was no copyright date that would have told him when the tape was made, whether it had been made before or after Church's death.

He got back on the Golden State, which took him north into the Santa Clarita Valley. After exiting on Bouquet Canyon Road he wound his way through a series of residential streets, past a seemingly endless line of California custom homes. On Del Prado, he pulled to the curb in front of the house with the Ritenbaugh Realty sign out front.

Sylvia had been trying to sell the house for more than a year, without luck. When he thought about it, Bosch was relieved. It kept him from facing a decision about what he and Sylvia would do next.

Sylvia opened the door before he reached it.

'Hey.'

'Hey.'

'What do you have?'

'Oh, it's something from work. I've gotta make a couple calls in a while. Did you eat?'

He bent down and kissed her and moved inside. She had on the gray T-shirt dress she liked to wear around the house after work. Her hair was loose and down to her shoulders, the blonde highlights catching the light from the living room.

'Had a salad. You?'

'Not yet. I'll fix a sandwich or something. I'm sorry about this. With the trial and now this new case, it's . . . well, you know.'

'It's okay. I just miss you. I'm sorry about how I acted on the phone.'

She kissed him and held him. He felt at home with her. That was the best thing. That feeling. He had never had it before and he would forget it at times when he was away from her. But as soon as he was back with her it was there.

She took him by the hand into the kitchen and told him to sit down while she made him a sandwich. He watched her put a pan on the stove and turn on the gas. Then she put four strips of bacon in the pan. While they cooked, she sliced a tomato and an avocado and laid out a bed of lettuce. He got up, took a beer from the fridge and kissed her on the back of the neck. He stepped back, annoyed that the memory of the woman grabbing him in the booth intruded on the moment. Why had that happened?

'What's the matter?'

'Nothing.'

She put two slices of sunflower bread into the toaster and

took the bacon out of the pan. A few minutes later she put the sandwich in front of him at the table and sat down.

'Who do you have to call?'

'Jerry Edgar, maybe a guy at Ad-Vice.'

'Ad-Vice? She was porno? This new victim?'

Sylvia had once been married to a cop and she made leaps of thought like a cop. Bosch liked that about her.

'Think so. I have a line on her. But I've got court, so I want to give it to them.'

She nodded. He never had to tell her not to ask too much. She always knew just when to stop.

'How was school today?'

'Fine. Eat your sandwich. I want you to hurry up and make your calls because I want us to forget about court and school and your investigation. I want us to open some wine, light some candles and get in bed.'

He smiled at her.

They had fallen into such a relaxed life together. The candles were always her signal, her way of initiating their lovemaking. Sitting there, Bosch realized he had no signals. She initiated it almost every time. He wondered what that meant about him. He worried that maybe theirs was a relationship solely founded on secrets and hidden faces. He hoped not.

'Are you sure nothing's wrong?' she asked. 'You're really spaced.'

'I'm fine. This is good. Thank you.'

'Penny called tonight. She's got two people interested, so she's going to have an open house on Sunday.'

He nodded, still eating.

'Maybe we could go somewhere for the day. I don't want to be here when she brings them through. We could even leave Saturday and go overnight somewhere. You could get away from all of this. Maybe Lone Pine would be good.'

'That sounds good. But let's see what happens.'

After she left the kitchen for the bedroom, Bosch called the bureau and Edgar picked up. Bosch deepened his voice and said, 'Yeah, you know that thing you showed on TV. The one that gots no name?'

'Yes, can you help us?'

'Sure can.'

Bosch covered his mouth with his hand to hold back the laughter. He realized he hadn't thought of a good punch line. His mind raced as he tried to decide what it should be.

'Well, who is it, sir?' Edgar said impatiently.

'It – it's – it's . . .'

'It's who?'

'It's Harve Pounds in drag!'

Bosch burst out laughing and Edgar easily guessed who it was. It was stupid, not even funny, but they both laughed.

'Bosch, what do you want?'

It took him some time to stop laughing. He finally said, 'Just checking in. Did you call Ray Mora?'

'Nah, I called over to Ad-Vice and they said he wasn't working tonight. I was going to talk to him tomorrow. How'd you do?'

'I think I've got a name. I'll give Mora a call at home so he can pull what they have on her first thing.'

He told Edgar the name and heard the other detective laugh.

'Well, at least it's original. How – what makes you think it's her?'

Bosch answered in a low voice in case his voice was carrying to the bedroom.

'I saw a loop and I have a box from a video with her picture on it. It looks like the plaster face you got. A little off on the wig. But I think it's her. I'll drop the box off on your desk on my way into court tomorrow.'

'Cool.'

'Maybe Mora can get an early start on getting her real name and prints over to you. She probably had an adult entertainment license. All right if I call him?'

'That's cool. You know him.'

They hung up. Bosch didn't have a home number for

Mora. He called Detective Services and gave his name and badge number and asked to be put through. It took about five minutes and then Mora answered after three rings. He seemed out of breath.

'It's Bosch, you gotta minute?'

'Bosch, yeah, Bosch, what's up, man?'

'How's business?'

'Still sucks.'

He laughed at what Bosch guessed was an insider's joke.

'Actually, it goes further down all the time – no pun intended. Video ruined it, Bosch. Made it too big. The industry got big, the quality got small. Nobody cares about quality anymore.'

Mora was talking more like a supporter of the porno industry than a watchdog.

'I miss the days when it was in those smoky theaters on Cahuenga and Highland. We had a better handle on things then. At least, I did. So how's court? I hear you guys caught another one that looks like the Dollmaker. What's going on with that? How could –'

'That's why I'm calling. I've got a name – I think she was from your side of the tracks. The victim.'

'Give it to me.'

'Magna Cum Loudly. Maybe known as Maggie, too.'

'Yeah, I've heard that one. She was around a while ago and then, you're right, she disappeared or dropped out.'

Bosch waited for more. He thought he heard a voice in the background – in person or on TV and Mora told him to hold on a minute. He couldn't make out what had been said or whether it was a man or a woman. It made him wonder what Mora had been doing when he called. There were rumors floating around the department about Mora having gotten too close to the subject he was expert in. It was a common cop malady. Still, he knew Mora had successfully fended off any attempts to transfer him in the early years of his assignment. Now, he had so much expertise, it would be ridiculous to move him. It would be like taking Orel

Hershiser off the Dodgers pitching staff and putting him in the outfield. He was good at what he did. He had to be left there.

'Um, Harry, I don't know. I think she was around a couple years ago. What I'm saying is, if it's her, then it couldn't have been Church. You know what I'm saying? I don't know how that plays with what you've got working on this.'

'Don't worry about it, Ray. If Church didn't do her, somebody else did. We still gotta get him.'

'Right. So I'll get on it. By the way, how'd you make her?'

Bosch told him about his visit to X Marks the Spot.

'Yeah, I know them guys. The big one, that's Carlo Pinzi the capo's nephew, Jimmie Pinzi. They call him Jimmie Pins. He may act big and dumb but he's really the little guy Pinkie's boss. Watches over the place for his uncle. The little one's called Pinkie on account of those glasses he wears. Pinkie and Pins. It's all an act. Anyway, they charged you about forty beans too many for that video.'

'That's what I guessed. Oh, and I was going to ask you, there's no copyright on the video box. Would that be on the video or is there any way I can figure out when this was made?'

'Usually they don't put the copyright on the box. Customers want fresh meat. So the players figure the customer sees a copyright on the box that's a couple years old, then they'll buy something else. It's a fast business. Perishable goods. So no dates. Sometimes they're not even on the video cartridge. Anyway, I've got catalogs at the office going back twelve years. I can find a date, no problem.'

'Thanks, Ray. I might not make it by. A guy from the homicide table, Jerry Edgar, might come by to see you. I got court.'

'That's fine, Harry.'

Bosch had nothing else to ask and was about to say good-bye when Mora spoke in the silence.

'You know, I think about it a lot.'

'What?'

'The task force. I wish I hadn't taken off early that night and I was there with you. Who knows, maybe we'd have gotten this guy alive.'

'Yeah.'

'Be no trial then – I mean, for you.'

Bosch was silent as he looked at the picture on the back of video box. The woman's face turned to the side, just like the plaster face. It was her. He felt sure of it.

'Ray, with only this name – Magna Cum Loudly – can you still get a real name, get prints?'

'Sure can. No matter what anybody thinks of the product, there is legit stuff and illegit stuff out there. This girl Maggie looks like she had graduated to the legit world. She was out of loops and that shit and was in mainstream adult video. That means she probably had an agent, had an adult entertainment license. They gotta get 'em to prove they're eighteen. So her license will have her real name on it. I can go through them and find her – they got their pictures on them. Might take me a couple hours but I can find her.'

'Okay, good, will you do that in the morning and, if Edgar doesn't come by, get the prints to him at Hollywood homicide?'

'Jerry Edgar. I'll do it.'

Neither spoke for a few moments as they thought about what they were doing.

'Hey, Harry?'

'Yeah.'

'The paper said that there was a new note, that true?'

'Yeah.'

'Is it legit? Did we fuck up?'

'I don't know yet, Ray, but I appreciate you saying "we". A lot of people just want to point at me.'

'Yeah, listen, I ought to tell you, I got subpoenaed today by that Money bitch.'

It didn't surprise Bosch, since Mora had been on the Dollmaker task force.

'Don't worry about it. She's probably papered everybody who was on the task force.'

'Okay.'

'But try to keep this new stuff under your hat if you can.'

'As long as I can.'

'She's got to know what to ask before she can ask it. I'm just looking for some time to work with this, see what it means.'

'No problem, man. You and I both know the right guy went down. No doubt about that, Harry.'

But saying it out loud like that put a doubt to it, Bosch knew. Mora was wondering the same things Bosch was.

'You need me to drop this video box off tomorrow so you know what she looks like before flipping through the files?'

'No, like I said, we've got all sorts of catalogs. I'll just look up *Tails from the Crypt* and get it from there. If that don't work I'll go through the agency books.'

They hung up and Bosch lit a cigarette, though Sylvia didn't like him doing it in the house. It wasn't that she had a problem with his smoking but she thought potential buyers might be turned off if they thought it had been a smoker's house. He sat there alone for several minutes, peeling the label off the empty beer bottle and thinking about how quickly things could change. Believe something for four years and then find out you might be wrong.

He brought a bottle of Buehler zinfandel and two glasses into the bedroom. Sylvia was in bed with the covers pulled up to her naked shoulders. She had a lamp on and was reading a book called *Never Let Them See You Cry*. Bosch walked to her side of the bed and sat down next to her. He poured out two glasses, they tapped them together and sipped.

'To victory in court,' she said.

'Sounds good to me.'

They kissed.

'Were you smoking out there again?'

'Sorry.'

'Was it bad news? The calls?'

'No. Just bullshit.'

'You want to talk?'

'Not now.'

He went into the bathroom with his glass and took a quick shower. The wine, which had been beautiful, tasted terrible after he brushed his teeth. When he came out, the reading light was out and the book put away. There were candles burning on both night tables and the bureau. They were in silver votive candle holders with crescent moons and stars cut out on the sides. The flickering flames threw blurry, moving patterns on the walls and curtains and in the mirror, like a silent cacophony.

She lay propped on three pillows, the covers off. He stood naked at the foot of the bed for a few moments and they smiled at each other. She was beautiful to him, her body tan and almost girlish. She was thin, with small breasts and a small, flat stomach. Her chest was freckled from too many summer days at the beach while growing up.

He was eight years older and knew he looked it, but he was not ashamed of his physical appearance. At forty-three, he still had a flat stomach and his body was still ropey with muscles – muscles not created on machines but by lifting the day-to-day weight of his life, his mission. His body hair was curiously going to gray at a much faster pace than the hair on his head. Sylvia often would kid him about this, accusing him of having dyed his hair, of having a vanity they both knew he did not have.

When he climbed onto the bed next to her she ran her fingers over his Vietnam tattoo and the scars a bullet had left on his right shoulder a few years earlier. She traced the surgery zipper the way she did every time they were together here.

'I love you, Harry,' she said.

He rolled onto her and kissed her deeply, letting her taste

of red wine and the feel of her warm skin take him away from worry and the images of violent ends. He was in the temple of home, he thought but did not say. I love you, he thought but did not say.

NINE

For everything that had gone well for Bosch on Tuesday, the following morning provided a fresh undoing. The first disaster occurred in Judge Keyes's chambers, where he convened lawyers and clients after studying the note from the alleged Dollmaker in private for a half hour. His private reading had come after Belk had argued for an hour against the inclusion of the note in the trial.

'I have read the note and considered the arguments,' he said. 'I cannot see how this letter, note, poem, whatever, can possibly be withheld from this jury. It is so on point to the thrust of Ms Chandler's case that it is the point. I'm not making any judgment on whether it's for real or from some crackpot, that will be for the jury to figure out. If they can. But because the investigation is still underway is no reason to withhold this. I am granting the subpoena and, Ms Chandler, you can introduce this at the appropriate time, provided you've put down the proper foundation. No pun intended. Mr Belk, your exception to this ruling will be noted for the record.'

'Your Honor?' Belk tried.

'No, we'll have no more argument on it. Let's move on out to court.'

'Your Honor! We don't know who wrote this. How can you allow it into evidence when we don't have the slightest idea where it came from or who sent it?'

'I know the ruling is a disappointment, so I'm allowing you some leeway as far as not coming down on you for that showing of your apparent disrespect for the wishes of this court. I said no more argument, Mr Belk, so I'll go over this only one time. The fact that this note of unknown origin led directly to the discovery of a body bearing all the similarities of a Dollmaker victim is in itself a verification of some authenticity. This is no prank, Mr Belk. No joke. There is something here. And the jury is going to see it. Let's go. Everybody out.'

Court had no sooner been called into session than the next debacle occurred. Belk, perhaps dazed by his defeat in chambers, waltzed into a trap Chandler had deftly set for him.

Her first witness of the day was a man named Wieczorek, who testified that he knew Norman Church quite well and was sure he had not committed the eleven murders attributed to him. Wieczorek and Church had worked together for twelve years in the design lab, he said. Wieczorek was in his fifties, with white hair trimmed so short his pink scalp showed through.

'What makes you so confident in your belief that Norman was not a killer?' Chandler asked.

'Well, for one thing, I know for a fact he didn't kill one of those girls, the eleventh, because he was with me the whole time she was getting . . . whatever. He was with me. Then the police kill him and pin eleven murders on him. Well, I figure, if I know he didn't kill one of those girls, then they are probably lying about the rest. The whole thing is a cover-up for them killing –'

'Thank you, Mr Wieczorek,' Chandler said.

'Just saying what I think.'

Belk stood and objected anyway, going to the lectern and whining that the entire answer was speculation. The judge agreed but the damage was done. Belk strode back to his chair and Bosch watched him leaf through a thick transcript of a deposition taken of Wieczorek a few months earlier.

Chandler asked a few more questions about where the witness and Church were on the night the eleventh victim was murdered and Wieczorek answered that they were at his own apartment with seven other men holding a bachelor party for a fellow employee from the lab.

'How long was Norman Church at your apartment?'

'The whole time of the party. I'd say from nine o'clock on. We finished up after two in the morning. The police said that girl, the eleventh one, went to some hotel at one and got herself killed. Norman was with me at one o'clock in the morning.'

'Could he have slipped away for an hour or so without you realizing it?'

'No way. You're in a room with eight guys and you know if one mysteriously disappears for a half hour.'

Chandler thanked him and sat down. Belk leaned to Bosch and whispered, 'I wonder what he's going to do with the new asshole I'm going to tear him.'

He got up armed with the deposition transcript and lumbered to the lectern as if he were lugging an elephant rifle. Wieczorek, who wore thick glasses that magnified his eyes, watched him suspiciously.

'Mr Wieczorek, do you remember me? Remember the deposition I took of you a few months back?'

Belk held the transcript up, as a reminder.

'I remember you,' Wieczorek said.

'Ninety-five pages, Mr Wieczorek. Nowhere in this transcript is there any mention of any bachelor party. Why is that?'

'I guess because you didn't ask.'

'But you didn't bring it up, did you? The police are saying your best buddy murdered eleven women, you supposedly know that's a lie, but you don't say a thing, is that right?'

'Yeah, that's right.'

'Care to tell us why?'

'Far as I was concerned, you were part of it. I only answered what I was asked. I wasn't volunteering shi – uh, nothing.'

'Let me ask you, did you ever tell the police this? Back

then, back when Church was killed and all the headlines said he killed eleven women? Ever pick up the phone one time and tell them they got the wrong guy?'

'No. At the time I didn't know. It was only when I read a book that came out on the case a couple years ago and there were details in there about when that last girl got killed. Then I knew he was with me during that whole time. I called the police and asked for the task force and they said it was disbanded long ago. I left a message for that fellow the book said was in charge, Lloyd, I think it was, and he never called me.'

Belk exhaled into the lectern's microphone, creating a loud sigh that indicated his weariness in dealing with this moron.

'So, if I can recap, you are telling this jury that two years after the murders, when this book came out, you read it and immediately realized you had an ironclad alibi for your dead friend. Am I missing anything, Mr Wieczorek?'

'Uh, just the part about suddenly realizing. It wasn't sudden.'

'Then what was it?'

'Well, when I read the date – September 28 – it set me to thinking and I just remembered that the bachelor party was on September 28 that year and Norman was there at my house all that time. So then I verified it and called Norman's wife to tell her he wasn't what they said he was.'

'You verified it? With the others at the party?'

'No, didn't have to.'

'Then how, Mr Wieczorek?' Belk asked in an exasperated tone.

'I looked at the video I had of that night. It had the date and time down in the corner of the frame.'

Bosch saw Belk's face turn a lighter shade of pale. The lawyer looked at the judge, then down at his pad, then back up at the judge. Bosch felt his heart sink. Belk had broken the same cardinal rule Chandler had broken the day before. He had asked a question for which he didn't already know the answer.

It didn't take a lawyer to know that since it was Belk who had drawn out mention of the videotape, Chandler was now free to explore it, to move to introduce the videotape as evidence. It had been a clever trap. Because it was new evidence from Wieczorek, not contained in his deposition, Chandler would have had to inform Belk earlier if she planned to draw it out on direct examination. Instead, she had skillfully allowed Belk to blunder in and draw it out. He now stood there defenseless, hearing it for the first time along with the jurors.

'Nothing further,' Belk said and returned to his seat with his head down. He immediately pulled one of the law books on the table onto his lap and began paging through it.

Chandler went to the lectern for redirect.

'Mr Wieczorek, this tape you mentioned to Mr Belk, do you still have it?'

'Sure, brought it with me.'

Chandler then moved to have the tape shown to the jury. Judge Keyes looked at Belk, who lumbered slowly to the lectern.

'Your Honor,' Belk managed to say, 'can defense have a ten-minute recess to research case law?'

The judge glanced at the clock.

'It's a little early, isn't it, Mr Belk? We just started.'

'Your Honor,' Chandler said. 'The plaintiff has no objection. I'll need time to set up the video equipment.'

'Very well,' the judge said. 'Ten minutes for counsel. The jury can take a fifteen-minute break and then report back to the assembly room.'

While they stood for the jury, Belk was flipping pages in the heavy law book. And when it was time to sit down, Bosch pulled his chair close to his lawyer's.

'Not now,' Belk said. 'I've got ten minutes.'

'You fucked up.'

'No, we fucked up. We are a team. Remember that.'

Bosch left his teammate there while he went out to smoke a cigarette. When he got to the statue, Chandler was already there. He lit a smoke anyway and kept his distance. She looked at him and smirked. Bosch spoke.

'You tricked him, didn't you?'

'Tricked him with the truth.'

'Is it?'

'Oh, yeah.'

She put a half-smoked cigarette in the sand of the ash can and said, 'I better get back in there and get the equipment set up.'

She smirked again. Bosch wondered if she was that good or it was Belk who was that bad.

Belk lost his half-hour argument to keep the tape from being introduced. He said that since it was not brought up during deposition, it was new evidence which the plaintiff could not submit at so late a date. Judge Keyes denied his claim, pointing out what everyone knew, that it had been Belk who had brought the tape to light.

After the jury was brought back in, Chandler asked Wieczorek several questions about the tape and where it had been for the last four years. After Judge Keyes dismissed one more objection from Belk, she rolled a TV/VCR combination to a position in front of the jury box and put in the tape, which Wieczorek had retrieved from a friend sitting in the gallery. Bosch and Belk had to stand up and move into the gallery seats to get a view of the TV screen.

As he made the move, Harry saw Bremmer from the *Times* sitting in one of the back rows. He gave a small nod to Bosch. Harry wondered if he was there to cover the trial or because he was subpoenaed.

The tape was long and boring but was not continuous. It was stopped and started during the evening of the bachelor party but the digital readout in the lower right corner kept the time and date. If it was correct, it was true that Church had an alibi for the last killing attributed to him.

It was dizzying for Bosch to watch. There was Church, no toupee, bald as a baby, drinking beer and laughing with his friends. The man Bosch had killed, toasting a friend's marriage, looking like the All American nerd that Bosch knew he had not been.

The tape lasted ninety minutes, climaxing with a visit from a telegram stripper who sang a song to the groom-to-be, dropping lingerie on his head as she removed each piece. In the video, Church seemed embarrassed to be seeing this, his eye more on the groom than on the woman.

Bosch pulled his eyes from the screen to watch the jury and he could see the tape was devastating to his defense. He looked away.

After the tape was finished, Chandler had a few more questions for Wieczorek. They were questions Belk would have asked but she was beating him to the punch.

'How is the date and time set on the video frame?'

'Well, when you buy it, you set it. Then the battery keeps it going. Never had to fiddle with it after I bought it.'

'But if you wanted to, you could put in any date you wanted, anytime you wanted, correct?'

'I s'pose.'

'So, say you were going to take a video of a friend to be used later as an alibi, could you set the date back, say a year, and then take the video?'

'Sure.'

'Could you put a date on an already existing video?'

'No. You can't superimpose a date over an existing video. Doesn't work that way.'

'So, in this case, how could you do it? How could you make a phony alibi for Norman Church?'

Belk stood up and objected on the grounds that Wieczorek's answer would be speculation, but Judge Keyes overruled him, saying the witness had expertise with his own camera.

'Well, you couldn't do that now 'cause Norman's dead,' Wieczorek said.

'So what you are saying is that in order to make a phony

tape you would have to have conspired with Mr Church to make it before he was killed by Mr. Bosch, correct?'

'Yes. We'd have to have known that somewhere down the line he'd need this tape and he'd have to've told me what date to set it on and so on and so forth. It's all pretty farfetched, especially because you can pull the newspapers from that year and find the wedding announcement that says my friend got married September thirtieth. That'll show you that his bachelor party had to have been the twenty-eighth or thereabouts. It's not a phony.'

Judge Keyes agreed with Belk's objection to the last sentence as being nonresponsive to the question and told the jury to disregard it. Bosch knew they didn't need to have heard it. They all knew the tape wasn't a phony. He did, too. He felt clammy and sick. Something had gone wrong but he didn't know what. He wanted to get up and walk out but he knew that to do so would be an admission of guilt so loud the walls would shake as if during an earthquake.

'One last question,' Chandler said. Her face had become flushed as she rode this one to victory. 'Did you ever know Norman Church to wear a hairpiece of any kind?'

'Never. I knew him a lot of years and I never saw or heard of such a thing.'

Judge Keyes turned the witness back over to Belk, who lumbered to the lectern without his yellow pad. He was apparently too flustered by this turnabout to remember to say, 'Just a few questions.' Instead he got right to his meager damage-control effort.

'You say you read a book about the Dollmaker case and then discovered this tape's date matched one of the killings, is that right?'

'That's right.'

'Did you look into finding alibis for the other ten murders?'

'No, I didn't.'

'So. Mr Wieczorek, you have nothing to offer in terms

of defending your longtime friend against these other cases a task force of numerous officers connected to him?'

'The tape put the lie to all of 'em. Your task –'

'You're not answering the question.'

'Yes I am, you show the lie on one of the cases, it puts a lie to the whole shooting match, you ask me.'

'We're not asking you, Mr. Wieczorek. Now, uh, you said you never saw Norman Church wear a hairpiece, correct?'

'That's what I said, yes.'

'Did you know he kept that apartment, using a false name?'

'No, I did not.'

'There was a lot you didn't know about your friend, wasn't there?'

'I suppose.'

'Do you suppose it is possible that just as he had that apartment without you knowing, that he occasionally wore a hairpiece without you knowing?'

'I suppose.'

'Now, if Mr. Church was the killer police claim him to be, and used disguises as police said the killer did, wouldn't it be –'

'Objection,' Chandler said.

' – expected that there would be something such –'

'Objection!'

' – as a toupee in the apartment?'

Judge Keyes sustained Chandler's objection to Belk's question as seeking a speculative answer, and chastised Belk for continuing the question after the objection was lodged. Belk took the berating and said he had no further questions. He sat down, sweat lines gliding out of his hairline and running down his temples.

'Best you could do,' Bosch whispered.

Belk ignored it, took out a handkerchief and wiped his face.

After accepting the videotape as evidence, the judge

broke for lunch. After the jury was out of the courtroom a handful of reporters quickly moved up to Chandler. Bosch watched this and knew it was the final arbiter of how things were going. The media always gravitated to the winners, the perceived winners, the eventual winners. It's always easier to ask them questions.

'Better start thinking of something, Bosch,' Belk said. 'We could have settled this six months ago for fifty grand. Way things are going, that would have been nothing.'

Bosch turned and looked at him. They were at the railing behind the defense table.

'You believe it, don't you? The whole thing. I killed him, then we planted everything that connected him to it.'

'Doesn't matter what I believe, Bosch.'

'Fuck you, Belk.'

'Like I said, you better start thinking of something.'

He pushed his wide girth through the gate and headed out of the courtroom. Bremmer and another reporter approached him but he waved them away. Bosch followed him out a few moments later and also brushed the reporters off. But Bremmer kept stride with him as he took the hallway to the escalator.

'Listen, man, my ass is on the line here, too. I wrote a book about the guy and if it was the wrong guy, I want to know.'

Bosch stopped and Bremmer almost bumped into him. He looked closely at the reporter. He was about thirty-five, overweight, with brown, thinning hair. Like many men, he made up for this by growing a thick beard, which only served to make him look older. Bosch noticed that the reporter's sweat had stained the underarms of his shirt. But body odor wasn't his problem; cigarette breath was.

'Look, you think it's the wrong guy, then write another book and get another hundred thousand advance. What do you care if it's the wrong guy or not?'

'I have a reputation in this town, Harry.'

'So did I. What are you going to write tomorrow?'

'I have to write what's going down in there.'

'And you're also testifying? Is that ethical, Bremmer?'

'I'm not testifying. She released me from the subpoena yesterday. I just had to sign a stipulation.'

'To what?'

'That said that to the best of my knowledge the book I wrote contained true and accurate information. The source of that information was almost wholly from police sources and police and other public records.'

'Speaking of sources, who told you about the note for yesterday's story?'

'Harry, I can't reveal that. Look at how many times I've kept you confidential as a source. You know I can never reveal sources.'

'Yeah, I know that. I also know somebody is setting me up.'

Bosch stepped onto the escalator and went down.

TEN

Administrative Vice is located on the third floor of the
Central Division station in downtown. Bosch got there in
ten minutes and found Ray Mora behind his desk in the
squad room, with the telephone held to his ear. Open on his
desk was a magazine with color photographs of a couple
engaged in sex. The girl in the photos looked very young.
Mora was glancing at the photos and turning the pages
while listening to the caller. He nodded to Bosch and
pointed to a seat in front of his desk.

'Well, that was all I was checking,' Mora said into the
phone. 'Just trying to put a line in the water. Ask around
and let me know what you come up with.'

Then there was more listening. Bosch looked at the vice
cop. He was about Harry's size, with deep bronze skin and
brown eyes. His straight brown hair was trimmed short and
he had no facial hair. Like most vice cops, he affected a
casual appearance. Blue jeans and black polo shirt, open at
the neck. If Bosch could see under the desk he knew he'd
find cowboy boots. Bosch could see a gold medallion
hanging high on his chest. Imprinted on it was a dove, its
wings open, the symbol of the Holy Spirit.

'You think you can get me the shoot location?'

Silence. Mora finished with the magazine, wrote something on the front cover and picked up another and began
paging through it.

Bosch noticed the Adult Film Performers Guild calendar
taped to the side of a vertical file on his desk. There was a
photo of a porn star named Delta Bush lounging nude above

the days of the week. She had become well known in recent years because she was linked romantically in the gossip tabs to a mainline movie star. On the desk below the calendar was a religious statue Bosch identified as the Infant of Prague.

He knew this because one of his foster mothers had given him a similar statue when he was a boy and was being sent back to McClaren. He hadn't been what the fosters had in mind. Giving him the statue and saying good-bye, the woman had explained to him that the infant was known as the Little King, the saint who took special care to hear the prayers of children. Bosch wondered if Mora knew that story, or if the statue was there as some kind of joke.

'All I'm saying is try,' Mora said into the phone. 'Get me the shoot. Then you'll be in line for the snitch fund . . . Yeah, yeah. Later.'

He hung up.

'Hey, Harry, whereyat?'

'Edgar's been here, huh?'

'Just left a little while ago. He talk to you?'

'No.'

Mora noticed Bosch looking at the spread on the page he had the magazine open to. It was two women kneeling in front of a man. He put a yellow Post-it on the page and closed it.

'Lord, I gotta look through all this shit. Got a tip that this publisher is using underage models. You know how I check?'

Bosch shook his head.

'It's not the face or the tits. It's ankles, Harry.'

'Ankles.'

'Yeah, ankles. Something about them. They are just smoother on younger chicks. I can usually tell, over or under eighteen, by the ankles. Then, of course, I go out and confirm with birth certificates, DLs, etc. It's crazy but it works.'

'Good for you. What did you tell Edgar?'

The phone rang. Mora picked up, said his name and listened a few moments.

'I can't talk now. I have to get back to you. Whereyat?'

He hung up after making a note.

'Sorry. I gave Edgar the ID. Maggie Cum Loudly. I had prints, photos, the whole thing. I got some stills of her in action, if you want to see.'

He pushed his chair back toward a file cabinet but Bosch told him never mind with the stills.

'Whatever. Anyway, Edgar has it all. Took prints to the coroner's I think, to confirm the ID. Chick's name was Rebecca Kaminski. Becky Kaminski. Be twenty-three if she were alive today. Formerly of Chicago before she came on out to sin city for fame and fortune. What a waste, huh? She was a fine young piece, God bless her.'

Bosch felt uncomfortable with Mora. But this was not new. When they had worked the task force together, Harry had never had the feeling that the killings meant much to the vice detective. Didn't make much of a dent. Mora was just putting in his time, lending his help where it was needed. He definitely was good in his area of expertise, but it didn't seem to matter to him whether the Dollmaker was stopped or not.

Mora had a strange way of mingling gutter talk and Jesus talk. At first Bosch had thought he was simply playing the born-again line that was popular in the department a few years earlier, but he was never sure. He once saw Mora cross himself and say a silent prayer at one of the Dollmaker murder scenes. Because of the uneasiness Bosch felt, he had had little contact with Mora since the Norman Church shooting and the breakup of the task force. Mora went back to Ad-Vice and Bosch was shipped to Hollywood. Occasionally the two would see each other in the courthouse or at the Seven or the Red Wind. But even at the bars, they were usually with different groups and sat apart, taking turns sending beers back and forth.

'Harry, she was definitely among the living until at least

two years ago. That flick you came across, *Tails from the Crypt,* it was made two years ago. Means Church definitely didn't do her . . . Probably whoever sent the note did. I don't know if that is good or bad news for you.'

'I don't either.'

Church had a rock-solid alibi for the Kaminski killing; he was dead. With that added to the apparent alibi Wieczorek's video-tape provided Church for the eleventh killing, Bosch's sense of paranoia was turning to panic. For four years there had been no doubt for him about what he had done.

'So how's the trial going, anyway?' Mora asked.

'Don't ask. Can I use your phone?'

Bosch dialed Edgar's pager number and then punched in Mora's phone number. After he hung up to wait for the call back, he didn't know what else to say.

'The trial's a trial. You still supposed to testify?'

'I guess. I'm on for tomorrow. I don't know what she wants from me. I wasn't even there the night you took that bastard down.'

'Well, you were on the task force with me. That's good enough to drag you into it.'

'Well, we'll –'

The phone rang and Mora picked it up. He then passed it to Bosch.

'Whereyat, Harry?'

'I'm here with Mora. He filled me in. Anything on the prints?'

'Not yet. I missed my man at SID. Musta gone to lunch. So I left the prints there. Should have a confirmation later today. But I'm not waiting on it.'

'Where are you now?'

'Missing Persons. Trying to see if this girl ever got reported missing, now that I have a name to go with the body.'

'You gonna be there a while?'

'Just started. We're looking through hard copies. They only went to computer eighteen months ago.'

'I'll be over.'

'You got your trial, man.'

'I have some time.'

Bosch felt that he had to keep moving, to keep thinking. It was the only way to keep from examining the horror building in his mind, the possibility he had taken down the wrong man. He drove back to Parker Center and took the stairs down to the first subterranean level. Missing Persons was a small office inside the Fugitives section. Edgar was sitting on a desk, looking through a stack of white forms. Bosch recognized these as cases that were not even investigated after the reports had been made. They would have been in files if there had been any follow-up.

'Nothing so far, Harry,' Edgar said. He then introduced Bosch to Detective Morgan Randolph, who was sitting at a nearby desk. Randolph gave Bosch a stack of reports and he spent the next fifteen minutes looking through the pages, each one an individual story of someone's pain that had fallen on the deaf ears of the department.

'Harry, on the description, look for a tattoo above the ass,' Edgar said.

'How do you know?'

'Mora had some photos of Magna Cum Loudly. In action, as Mora says. And there's a tattoo – it's Yosemite Sam, you know, the cartoon? – to the left of the dimple over the left side of her ass.'

'Well, did you find that on the body?'

'Didn't notice it 'cause of the severe skin discoloration. But I didn't really look at the backside, either.'

'What's going on with that? I thought you said the cut was going to be done yesterday.'

'Yeah, that's what they said, but I called over and they're still backed up from the weekend. They haven't even prepped it yet. I called Sakai a little while ago and he's going to take a look in the freezer after lunch. Check on the tattoo.'

Bosch looked back at his stack. The recurrent theme was

the young ages of the missing people. LA was a drain which drew a steady stream of the nation's runaways. But there were many who disappeared from here as well.

Bosch finished his stack without seeing the name Rebecca Kaminski, her alias, or anyone that matched her description. He looked at his watch and knew he had to get back to court. He took another stack off Randolph's desk anyway and began to wade through it. As he searched, he listened to the banter between Edgar and Randolph. It was clear that they had known each other before this day's meeting. Edgar called him Morg. Bosch figured they might've known each other from the Black Peace Officers Association.

He found nothing in the second stack.

'I gotta go. I'm gonna be late.'

'Okay, man. I'll let you know what we find.'

'And the prints, too, okay?'

'You got it.'

Court was already in session when Bosch got to courtroom 4. He quietly opened the gate, went through and took his seat next to Belk. The judge eyed him disdainfully but said nothing. Bosch looked up to see Assistant Chief Irvin Irving in the witness seat. Money Chandler was at the lectern.

'Good going,' Belk whispered to him. 'Late for your own trial.'

Bosch ignored him and watched as Chandler began asking Irving general questions about his background and years on the force. They were preliminary questions; Bosch knew he couldn't have missed much.

'Look,' Belk whispered next. 'If you don't care about this, at least pretend you do for the jury's sake. I know we are only talking about taxpayers' money here, but act like it's going to be your own money they will be deciding to give.'

'I got tied up. It won't happen again. You know, I'm trying to figure out this case. Maybe that doesn't matter to you, since you've already decided.'

He leaned back in his chair to get away from Belk. He was reminded that he had not eaten lunch by a sharp signal of resentment from his stomach. He tried to concentrate on the testimony.

'As assistant chief, what does your command include?' Chandler asked Irving.

'I am presently the commanding officer of all detective services.'

'At the time of the Dollmaker investigation, you were one rank below. A deputy chief, correct?'

'Yes.'

'As such you were in charge of the Internal Affairs Division, correct?'

'Yes. IAD and Operations Bureau, which basically means I was in charge of managing and allocating the department's personnel.'

'What is the mission of the IAD, as it is known?'

'To police the police. We investigate all citizen complaints, all interior complaints of misconduct.'

'Do you investigate police shootings?'

'Not per se. There is an Officer Involved Shooting team that handles the initial investigation. After that, if there is an allegation of misconduct or any impropriety, it is forwarded to IAD for follow-up.'

'Yes, and what do you recall of the IAD investigation of the shooting of Norman Church by Detective Harry Bosch?'

'I recall all of it.'

'Why was it referred to IAD?'

'The shooting team determined that Detective Bosch had not followed procedures. The shooting itself was within departmental policy but some of his actions prior to the gunfire were not.'

'Can you be more specific?'

'Yes. Basically, he went there alone. He went to this man's apartment without backup, placing himself in danger. It ended in the shooting.'

'It's called cowboying it, isn't it?'

'I've heard the phrase. I don't use it.'

'But does it fit?'

'I wouldn't know.'

'You wouldn't know. Chief, would you know if Mr Church would be alive today if Detective Bosch had not created this situation by playing cow –'

'Objection!' Belk shrieked.

But before he could walk to the lectern to argue, Judge Keyes sustained the objection and told Chandler to avoid speculative questions.

'Yes, Your Honor,' she said pleasantly. 'Chief, basically what you have testified to is that Detective Bosch set in motion a series of events that ultimately ended with an unarmed man being killed, am I right?'

'That is incorrect. The investigation found no substantive indication or evidence that Detective Bosch deliberately set this scenario in motion. It was spur of the moment. He was checking out a lead. When it looked good, he should have called for backup. But he didn't. He went in. He identified himself and Mr Church made the furtive move. And here we are. That is not to say that the outcome would have been different had there been a backup. I mean, anybody who would disobey an order from a police officer holding a gun would probably do it with two officers holding guns.'

Chandler successfully had the last sentence of the answer struck from the record.

'To come to the conclusion that Detective Bosch did not intentionally set the situation into motion, did your investigators study all facets of the shooting?'

'Yes, indeed.'

'How about Detective Bosch, was he studied?'

'Unquestionably. He was rigorously questioned about his actions.'

'And about his motives?'

'His motives?'

'Chief, did you or any of your investigators know that Detective Bosch's mother was slain in Hollywood about thirty years ago by a killer who was never arrested? That prior to that, she had a record for multiple arrests for loitering?'

Bosch felt his skin go hot, as if klieg lights had been turned on him, and that everyone in the courtroom was staring at him. He was sure they were. But he looked only at Irving, who stared silently ahead, a palsied look on his face, the capillaries on either side of his nose flaring. When Irving didn't answer, Chandler prompted him.

'Did you know, Chief? It is referenced in Detective Bosch's personnel file. When he applied to the force, he had to say if he had ever been the victim of a crime. He lost his mother, he wrote.'

Finally, Irving said, 'No, I did not know.'

'I believe that loitering was a euphemism for prostitution in the 1950s, when Los Angeles was engaged in a denial of crime problems such as rampant prostitution on Hollywood Boulevard, is that correct?'

'I don't recall that.'

Chandler asked to approach the witness and handed Irving a thin stack of papers. She gave him nearly a minute to read through them. He furrowed his brow as he read and Bosch could not see his eyes. The muscles of his cheeks bunched together below his temples.

'What is that, Chief Irving?' Chandler asked.

'It is what we call a due diligence report detailing the investigation of a homicide. It is dated November 3, 1962.'

'What is a due diligence report?'

'Every unsolved case is looked at annually – we call it due diligence – until such time that we feel the prognosis for bringing the case to a successful conclusion is hopeless.'

'What is the victim's name and circumstances of her death?'

'Marjorie Phillips Lowe. She was raped and strangled, October 31, 1961. Her body was found in an alley behind Hollywood Boulevard between Vista and Gower.'

'What is the investigator's conclusion, Chief Irving?'

'It says that at this time, which was a year after the crime, there are no workable leads and prognosis for successful conclusion of the case is deemed hopeless.'

'Thank you. Now, one more thing, is there a box on the cover form listing next of kin?'

'Yes, it identifies the next of kin as Hieronymus Bosch. Next to that in brackets it says "Harry". A box marked "son" has been checked off.'

Chandler referred to her yellow pad for a few moments to let this information soak into the jury. It was so quiet Bosch could actually hear Chandler's pen scratching on the pad as she made a notation.

'Now,' she said, 'Chief Irving, would knowing about Detective Bosch's mother have caused you to take a closer look at this shooting?'

After a long moment of silence, he said, 'I can't say.'

'He shot a man suspected of doing almost the exact same thing that had happened to his mother – his mother's slaying being unsolved. Are you saying you don't know if that would have been germane to your investigation?'

'I, yes . . . I don't know at this time.'

Bosch wanted to put his head down on the table. He had noticed that even Belk had stopped scribbling notes and was just watching the interchange between Irving and Chandler. Bosch tried to shake off the anger he felt and concentrate on how Chandler had obtained the information. He realized she had probably gotten the P-file in a discovery motion. But the details of the crime and his mother's background would not be in it. She had most likely procured the due diligence report from the archives warehouse on a Freedom of Information petition.

He realized he had missed several questions to Irving. He began watching and listening again. He wished he had a lawyer like Money Chandler.

'Chief, did you or any IAD detectives go to the scene of the shooting?'

'No, we did not.'

'So your information about what happened came from members of the shooting team, who in turn got their information from the shooter, Detective Bosch, correct?'

'Essentially, yes.'

'You have no personal knowledge of the evidentiary layout: the toupee under the pillow, the cosmetics beneath the sink in the bathroom?'

'Correct. I was not there.'

'Do you believe all of that was there as I just stated?'

'Yes, I do.'

'Why?'

'It was all there in the reports – reports from several different officers.'

'But all originating with the information from Detective Bosch, correct?'

'To a degree. There were investigators swarming that place. Bosch didn't tell them what to write.'

'Before, as you say, they swarmed the place, how long was Bosch there alone?'

'I don't know.'

'Is that piece of information on any report that you know of?'

'I'm not sure.'

'Isn't it true, Chief, that you wanted to fire Bosch and refer this shooting to the district attorney's office for the filing of criminal charges against him?'

'No, that is wrong. The DA looked at it and passed. It's routine. They said it was within policy, too.'

Well, score one for me, Bosch thought. It was the first misstep he had seen her take with Irving.

'What happened to the woman who gave Bosch this tip? Her name was McQueen. I believe she was a prostitute.'

'She died about a year later. Hepatitis.'

'At the time of her death was she part of an ongoing investigation of Detective Bosch and this shooting?'

'Not that I am aware of and I was in charge of IAD at the time.'

'What about the two IAD detectives who investigated the shooting? Lewis and Clarke, I believe their names were. Didn't they continue their investigation of Bosch long after the shooting had been determined officially to be within policy?'

Irving took a while to answer. He was probably leery of being led to slaughter again.

'If they conducted such an ongoing investigation it was without my knowledge or approval.'

'Where are those detectives now?'

'They are also dead. Both killed in the line of duty a couple years ago.'

'As the commander of IAD wasn't it your practice to initiate covert investigations of problem officers that you had marked for dismissal? Wasn't Detective Bosch one of those officers?'

'The answer to both questions is no. Unequivocally, no.'

'And what happened to Detective Bosch for his violation of procedures during the shooting of the unarmed Norman Church?'

'He was suspended for one deployment period and transferred within detective services to Hollywood Division.'

'In English, that means he was suspended for a month and demoted from the elite Robbery-Homicide squad to the Hollywood Division, correct?'

'You could say it that way.'

Chandler flipped a page up on her pad.

'Chief, if there were no cosmetics in the bathroom and no evidence that Norman Church was anything other than a lonely man who had taken a prostitute to his apartment, would Harry Bosch still be on the force? Would he have been prosecuted for killing this man?'

'I'm not sure I understand the question.'

'I'm asking, sir, did the alleged evidence tying Mr

Church to the killings that was allegedly found in his apartment save Detective Bosch? Did it not only save his job but save him from criminal prosecution?'

Belk stood up and objected, then walked to the lectern.

'She is asking him to speculate again, Your Honor. He can't tell what would have happened given an elaborate set of circumstances that didn't exist.'

Judge Keyes clasped his hands together in front of him and leaned back thinking. Then he abruptly leaned forward to the microphone.

'Ms Chandler is laying the groundwork to make a case that the evidence in the apartment was fabricated. I'm not saying whether she has adequately done this or not, but since that is her mission I think the question is answerable. I'm going to allow it.'

After some thought, Irving finally said, 'I can't answer that. I don't know what would have happened.'

ELEVEN

Bosch was able to smoke two cigarettes during the ten-minute recess that followed the end of Irving's testimony. On redirect Belk had asked only a few questions, trying to rebuild a fallen house with a hammer but no nails. The damage was done.

Chandler had so far used the day to skillfully plant the seeds of doubt about both Church and Bosch. The alibi for the eleventh killing opened the door to Church's possible innocence. And now she had subscribed a motive to Bosch's action: revenge for a murder more than thirty years old. By the end of the trial the seeds would be in full bloom.

He thought about what Chandler had said about his mother. Could she have been right? Bosch had never consciously considered it. It was always there – the idea of revenge – flickering in some part of his mind with the distant memories of his mother. But he had never taken it out and examined it. Why had he gone out there alone that night? Why hadn't he called one of the others back in – Mora or any of the investigators in his command?

Bosch had always told himself and others it was because he doubted the whore's story. But now, he knew, it was his own story he was beginning to doubt.

Bosch was so deep in these thoughts that he did not notice Chandler had come through the door until the flare of her lighter caught his eye. He turned and stared at her.

'I won't stay long,' she said. 'Just a half.'

'I don't care.'

He was almost done with the second cigarette.

'Who's next?'

'Locke.'

The USC psychologist. Bosch nodded, though he immediately saw this as a break from her good guy-bad guy pattern. Unless she counted Locke as a good guy.

'Well, you're doing good,' Bosch said. 'But I guess you don't need me to tell you that.'

'No, I don't.'

'You may even win – you probably will win, but ultimately you're wrong about me.'

'Am I? . . . Do you even know?'

'Yeah, I know. I know.'

'I have to go.'

She stubbed the cigarette out. It was less than half smoked. It would be a prize for Tommy Faraway.

Dr John Locke was a gray-bearded, bald and bespectacled man who looked as though he could have used a pipe to complete the picture of university professor and researcher of sexual behavior. He testified that he had offered his expertise to the Dollmaker task force after reading about the killings in the newspapers. He helped an LAPD psychiatrist draw up the first profiles of the suspect.

'Tell the jury about your expertise,' Chandler asked.

'Well, I am the director of the Psychohormonal Research Laboratory at USC. I am founder of that unit as well. I have conducted wide-ranging studies of sexual practice, paraphilia and psychosexual dynamics.'

'What is a paraphilia, doctor? In language we will all understand, please.'

'Well, in layman's terms, paraphilia are what are commonly referred to by the general public as sexual perversions – sexual behavior generally considered un-acceptable by society.'

'Such as strangling your sex partner?'

'Yes, that would be one of them, big time.'

There was a polite murmur of humor in the courtroom

and Locke smiled. He seemed very at ease on the witness stand, Bosch thought.

'Have you written scholarly articles or books about these subjects you mentioned?'

'Yes, I have contributed numerous articles to research publications. I've written seven books on various subjects, sexual development of children, prepubescent paraphilia, studies of sadomasochism – the whole bondage thing, pornography, prostitution. My last book was on childhood development histories of deviant murderers.'

'So you've been around the block.'

'Only as a researcher.'

Locke smiled again and Bosch could see the jury warming to him. All twenty-four eyes were on the sex doctor.

'Your last book, the one on the murderers, what was it called?'

'*Black Hearts: Cracking the Erotic Mold of Murder.*'

Chandler took a moment to look at her notes.

'What do you mean by "erotic mold"?'

'Well, Ms Chandler, if I could digress a moment, I think I should fill in some background.'

She nodded her go-ahead.

'There are generally two fields, or two schools of thought, when it comes to the study of sexual paraphilia. I am what you call a psychoanalyst, and psychoanalysts believe that the root of paraphilia in an individual comes from hostilities nurtured in childhood. In other words, sexual perversions – in fact, even normal erotic interests – are formed in early childhood and then manifest in expressions as the individual becomes an adult.

'On the other hand, behaviorists view paraphilia as learned behaviors. An example being, molestation in the home of a child may trigger similar behavior by him as an adult. The two schools, for lack of a better word, are not that divergent. They are actually quite closer than psychoanalysts and behaviorists usually like to admit.'

He nodded and folded his hands together, seeming to have forgotten the original question.

'You were going to tell us about erotic molds,' Chandler prompted.

'Oh yes, I'm sorry, I lost the train there. Uh, the erotic mold is the description I use to cover the whole shebang of psychosexual desires that go into an individual's ideal erotic scene. You see, everybody has an ideal erotic scene. This could include the ideal physical attributes of a lover, the location, the type of sex act, the smell, taste, touch, music, whatever. Everything, all the ingredients that go into this individual achieving the ultimate erotic scene. A leading authority on this, out of Johns Hopkins University, calls it a "lovemap". It is sort of a guide to the ultimate scene.'

'Okay, now in your book, you applied it to sexual murderers.'

'Yes, with five subjects – all convicted of murder involving a sexual motivation or practice – I attempted to trace each man's erotic mold. To crack it open and trace the parts back to development in childhood. These men had damaged molds, so to speak. I wanted to find where the damage took place.'

'How did you pick your subjects?'

Belk stood up and made an objection and moved to the lectern.

'Your Honor, as fascinating as all of this is, I don't believe it is on point to this case. I will stipulate Dr Locke's expertise in this field. I don't think we have to go through the history of five other murderers. We are here in trial on a case about a murderer who is not even mentioned in Dr Locke's book. I am familiar with the book. Norman Church is not in it.'

'Ms Chandler?' Judge Keyes said.

'Your Honor, Mr Belk is correct about the book. It's about sadistic sex killers. Norman Church is not in it. But its significance to this case will be clear in the next set of questions. I think Mr Belk realizes this and that is the reason for his objection.'

'Well, Mr Belk, I think the time for an objection was probably about ten minutes ago. We are well into this line of questioning and I think we need to see it through now. Besides, you are correct about it being rather fascinating. Go on, Ms Chandler. The objection is overruled.'

Belk dropped back into his chair and whispered to Bosch, 'He's gotta be banging her.' It was said just loud enough that Chandler might have heard him, but not the judge. If she did, she showed nothing.

'Thank you, Your Honor,' she said. 'Dr Locke, Mr Belk and I were correct when we said that Norman Church was not one of the subjects of your study, were we not?'

'Yes, that is correct.'

'When did the book come out?'

'Just last year.'

'That would be three years after the end of the Dollmaker case?'

'Yes.'

'Well, having been part of the Dollmaker task force and obviously becoming familiar with the crimes, why didn't you include Norman Church in your study? It would seem to be an obvious choice.'

'It would seem that way but it wasn't. First of all, Norman Church was dead. I wanted subjects that were alive and cooperative. But incarcerated, of course. I wanted people that I could interview.'

'But of the five subjects you wrote about, only four are alive. What about the fifth, a man named Alan Karps, who was executed in Texas before you even began your book? Why not Norman Church?'

'Because, Ms Chandler, Karps had spent much of his adult life in institutions. There were voluminous public records on his treatment and psychiatric study. With Church there was nothing. He had never been in trouble before. He was an anomaly.'

Chandler looked down at her yellow pad and flipped a page, letting the point she just scored hang in the quiet courtroom like a cloud of cigarette smoke.

'But you did at least make preliminary inquiries about Church, didn't you?'

Locke hesitated before answering.

'Yes, I made a very preliminary inquiry. It amounted to contacting his family and asking his wife if she would grant me an interview. She turned me down. Since the man himself was dead and there were no records about him – other than the actual details of the murders, which I was already familiar with – I didn't pursue it. I went with Karps in Texas.'

Bosch watched Chandler cross several questions off on her legal pad and then flip several pages to a new set. He guessed that she was changing tack.

She said, 'While you were working with the task force you drew up a psychological profile of the killer, correct?'

'Yes,' Locke said slowly. He adjusted himself in the chair, straightening up for what he knew was coming.

'What was that based on?'

'An analysis of the crime scenes and method of homicide filtered through what little we know about the deviant mind. I came up with common attributes that I thought might be part of our suspect's makeup – no pun intended.'

No one in the courtroom laughed. Bosch looked around and saw that the spectator rows were becoming crowded. This must be the best show in the building, he thought. Maybe all of downtown.

'You were not very successful, were you? If Norman Church was the Dollmaker, that is.'

'No, not very successful. But that happens. It's a lot of guesswork. Rather than a testimonial to my failure, it is more a testimonial to how little we know about people. This man's behavior did not make so much as a blip on anybody's radar screen – not counting, of course, the women he killed – until the night he was shot.'

'You speak as if it is a given that Norman Church was the killer, the Dollmaker. Do you know that to be true based on indisputable facts?'

'Well, I know it to be true because it is what the police told me.'

'If you take it backwards, doctor. If you start with what you know about Norman Church now and leave out what the police have told you about the supposed evidence, would you ever believe him capable of what he has been accused of?'

Belk was about to stand up to object but Bosch strongly put his hand on his arm and held him down. Belk turned and looked angrily at him but by then Locke was answering.

'I wouldn't be able to count him in or out as a suspect. We don't know enough about him. We don't know enough about the human mind in general. All I know is, anybody is capable of anything. I could be a sexual killer. Even you, Ms Chandler. We all have an erotic mold and for most of us, it is quite normal. For some it may be a bit unusual but still only playful. For the others, on the extreme, who find they can only reach erotic excitement and fulfillment through administering pain, even killing their partners, it is buried deep and dark.'

Chandler was looking down at her pad and writing when he finished. When she didn't ask another question immediately, he continued unbidden.

'Unfortunately, the black heart is not worn on the sleeve. The victims who see it usually don't live to talk about it.'

'Thank you, Doctor,' Chandler said. 'I have nothing further.'

Belk plowed in without any preliminary soft-ball questions, a look of concentration on his wide florid face that Bosch had not seen previously.

'Doctor, these men with these so-called paraphilia, what do they look like?'

'Like anybody. There is no look that gives them away.'

'Yes, and are they always on the prowl? You know,

looking to indulge their aberrant fantasies by acting them out?'

'No, actually, studies have shown that these people obviously know they have aberrant tastes and they work to keep them in check. Those brave enough to come forward with their problems often lead completely normal lives with the aid of chemical and psychological therapy. Those that don't are periodically overcome by the compulsion to act out, and they may follow these urges and commit a crime.

'Psychosexually motivated serial killers often exhibit patterns that are quite repetitive, so that police tracking them can almost predict within a few days or a week when they will strike. This is because the buildup of stress, the compulsion to act, will follow a pattern. Often, what you have are decreasing intervals – the overpowering urge comes back sooner and sooner each time.'

Belk was leaning over the lectern, his weight firmly against it.

'I see, but between these moments of compulsion when the acts take place, does this man seem to have a normal life or, you know, is he standing in the corner, slobbering? Or whatever?'

'No, nothing like that – at least, until the intervals become so short that they literally don't exist. Then you might have someone out there always on the prowl, as you said. But between the intervals there is normalcy. The aberrant sexual act – rape, strangulation, voyeurism, anything – will provide the subject with the memory to construct fantasy. He will be able to use the act to fantasize and stimulate arousal during masturbation or normal sex.'

'Do you mean that he will sort of replay the murder in his mind so that he can become sexually aroused for having normal sexual intercourse with, say, his wife?'

Chandler objected and Belk had to rephrase the question so it was not leading Locke.

'Yes, he will replay the aberrant act in his mind so that he can accomplish the act that is socially acceptable.'

'So in doing so, a wife, for example, might not even know of her husband's real desires, correct?'

'That is correct. It has happened often.'

'And a person such as this could carry on at work and with friends and not reveal this side of himself, correct?'

'Again, that is correct. There is ample evidence of this in the case histories of sexual sadists who kill. Ted Bundy led a well-documented double life. Randy Kraft, killer of dozens of hitchhikers here in Southern California. I could name many, many more. You see, this is the very reason they kill so many victims before being caught, and then it is usually only because of a small mistake.'

'Like with Norman Church?'

'Yes.'

'As you testified earlier, you could not find or gather enough information about Norman Church's early development and behavior to include him in your book. Does that fact dissuade you from belief that he was the killer police claim him to be?'

'Not in the least. As I said, these desires can be easily cloaked in normal behavior. These people know they have desires that are not accepted by society. Believe me, they take pains to hide them. Mr Church was not the only subject I considered for the book and then discarded for lack of valuable information. I did preliminary studies of at least three other serial killers who were either dead or uncooperative and dropped them as well because of the lack of public record or background on them.'

'You mentioned earlier that the roots of these problems are planted in childhood. How?'

'I should have said "may", the roots may be planted in childhood. It is a difficult science and nothing is known for sure. Getting to your question, if I had a definite answer I guess I wouldn't have a job. But what psychoanalysts such as myself believe is that the paraphilia can come through emotional or physical trauma or both. It basically is a synthesis of these, possibly some biological determinants and social learning. It is hard to pinpoint, but we believe it happens very early, generally five to eight years of age. One of the fellows in my book was molested by an uncle at age three. My thesis, or belief or whatever you want to call it, is that this trauma set him on the trail toward becoming a murderer of homosexuals. In most of these killings he emasculated his victims.'

The courtroom had become so quiet during Locke's testimony that Bosch heard the slight bump of one of the rear doors opening. He glanced back and saw Jerry Edgar taking a seat in the rear row. Edgar nodded at Harry, who looked up at the clock. It was 4:15; the trial would be recessed for the day in fifteen minutes. Bosch figured Edgar was on his way back from the autopsy.

'Would the childhood trauma that's at the root of a person's criminal activities as an adult need to be so overt? In other words, as traumatic as molestation?'

'Not necessarily. It could be rooted in more traditional emotional stress placed on a child. The awesome pressure to succeed in a parent's eyes, coupled with other things. It is hard to discuss this in a hypothetical context because there are so many dimensions of human sexuality.'

Belk followed up with a few more general questions about Locke's studies before ending. Chandler asked a couple more questions on redirect but Bosch had lost interest. He knew that Edgar would not have come to the courtroom unless he had something important. Twice he glanced back at the clock on the wall and twice he looked at his watch. Finally, when Belk said he had nothing further on cross, Judge Keyes called it a day.

Bosch watched Locke step down and head out through the gate and toward the door. A couple of the reporters followed him. Then the jury stood and filed out.

Belk turned to Bosch as they watched and said, 'Better be ready tomorrow. My guess is that it's going to be your turn in the sun.'

*

'What've you got, Jerry?' Bosch asked when he caught up with Edgar in the hallway leading to the escalator.

'Your car over at Parker Center?'

'Yeah.'

'I'm there, too. Let's walk that way.'

They got on the escalator but didn't talk because it was crowded with spectators from the courtroom. Out on the sidewalk, when they were alone, Edgar pulled a folded white form out of his coat pocket and handed it to Bosch.

'All right, we got it confirmed. The prints Mora dug up on Rebecca Kaminski match the hand mold we made on the concrete blonde. I also just came from the autopsy and the tattoo is there, above the ass. Yosemite Sam.'

Bosch unfolded the paper. It was a photocopy of a standard missing person report.

'That's a copy of the report on Rebecca Kaminski, also known as Magna Cum Loudly. Missing twenty-two months and three days.'

Bosch was looking at the report.

'Doesn't look like any doubt to me,' he said.

'Nope, no doubt. It was her. The autopsy also confirms manual strangulation as the cause. The knot pulled tight on the right side. Most likely a lefty.'

They walked without talking for half a block. Bosch was surprised by how warm it was for so late in the day. Finally, Edgar spoke.

'So, obviously, we've got it confirmed; this may look like one of Church's dolls but there's no way in the world he did it unless he came back from the dead . . .

'So I did some checking at the bookstore over by Union Station. Bremmer's book, *The Dollmaker,* with all the details a copycat would need, was published in hardback seventeen months after you put Church in the dirt. Becky Kaminski goes missing about four months after the book came out. So our killer could've bought the book and then used it as a sort of blueprint on what to do to make it look like that Dollmaker.'

Edgar looked over at him and smiled.

'You're in the clear, Harry.'

Bosch nodded, but didn't smile. Edgar didn't know about the videotape.

They walked down Temple to Los Angeles Street. Bosch didn't notice the people around him, the homeless shaking their cups on the corners. He almost crossed Los Angeles in front of traffic until Edgar put a hand on his arm. While waiting for the walk sign, he looked down and scanned the report again. It was bare bones. Rebecca Kaminski had simply gone out on a 'date' and not returned. She was meeting the unnamed man at the Hyatt on Sunset. That was it. No follow-up, no additional information. The report had been made by a man named Tom Cerrone, who was identified in the report as Kaminski's roommate in Studio City. The light changed and they walked across Los Angeles Street and then right toward Parker Center.

'You going to talk to this Cerrone guy, the roommate?' he asked Edgar.

'I don't know. Probably get around to it. I'm more interested in what you think about all of this, Harry. Where do we go from here? Bremmer's book was a fuckin' bestseller. Anybody who read it is a suspect.'

Bosch said nothing until they got to the parking lot and stopped near the entrance booth before separating. Bosch looked down at the report in his hands and then up at Edgar.

'Can I keep this? I might take a run by the guy.'

'Be my guest . . . Another thing you should know, Harry.'

Edgar reached in his inside coat pocket and pulled out another piece of paper. This one was yellow and Bosch knew it was a subpoena.

'I got served at the coroner's office. I don't know how she knew I was there.'

'When d'you have to be in court?'

'Tomorrow at ten. I had nothing to do with the Dollmaker task force so we both know what she's going to ask about. The concrete blonde.'

TWELVE

Bosch threw his cigarette into the fountain that was part of the memorial to officers killed in the line of duty and walked through the glass doors into Parker Center. He badged one of the cops behind the front desk and walked around to the elevators. There was a red line painted on the black tile floor. That was the route visitors were told to take if they were going to the Police Commission hearing room. There was also a yellow line for Internal Affairs and a blue for applicants who wanted to become cops. It was a tradition for cops standing around waiting for elevators to stand on the yellow line, thereby making any citizens who were going to IAD – usually to file complaints – walk around them. This maneuver was usually accompanied by a baleful stare from cop to citizen.

Every time Bosch waited for an elevator he remembered the prank he had been partially responsible for while still in the academy. He and another cadet had come into Parker Center at four one morning, drunk and hiding paint brushes and cans of black and yellow paint in their windbreakers. In a quick and daring operation, his partner had used the black paint to obliterate the yellow line on the tile floor while Bosch painted a new yellow line which went past the elevators, down the hall, into a men's room and right to a urinal. The prank had given them near legendary status in their class, even among the instructors.

He got off the elevator on the third floor and walked back to the Robbery-Homicide Division. The place was empty. Most RHD cops worked a strict seven-to-three shift. That way the job didn't get in the way of all the moonlighting gigs they had lined up. RHD dicks were the cream of the department. They got all the best gigs. Chauffeuring visiting Saudi princes, security work for studio bosses, body-guarding Vegas high rollers – LVPD did not allow its people to moonlight, so the high-paying jobs fell to LAPD.

When Bosch had first been promoted to RHD there were still a few detective-threes around who had worked body-guard duty for Howard Hughes. They had spoken of the experience as if that was what the RHD job was all about, a means to an end, a way to get a job working for some deranged billionaire who didn't need any bodyguards because he never went anywhere.

Bosch walked to the rear of the room and turned on one of the computers. He lit a cigarette while the tube warmed up and took the report Edgar had given him out of his coat pocket. The report was nothing. It had never been looked at, acted on, cared about.

He noticed it was a walk-in – Tom Cerrone had come into the North Hollywood Division station and made the report at the front desk. That meant it had probably been written up by a probationary rookie or a burned-out vet who didn't give a shit. In either case, it was not taken for what it was: a cover-your-ass report.

Cerrone said he was Kaminski's roommate. According to the brief summary, two days before the report was made she had told Cerrone she was going on a blind date, meeting an unnamed man at the Hyatt on the Sunset Strip and that she hoped the guy wasn't a creep. She never came back. Cerrone got worried and went to the cops. The report was taken, passed through North Hollywood detectives where it didn't make a blip on anyone's screen and then sent to Missing Persons in downtown where four detectives are charged with finding the sixty people reported missing on average each week in the city.

In reality, the report was put in a stack of others like it and was not looked at again until Edgar and his pal, Morg, found it. None of this bothered Bosch, though anyone who spent two minutes reading the report should have known that Cerrone wasn't what he said he was. But Bosch figured Kaminski was dead and in the concrete long before the report was made. So there was nothing anyone could have done anyway.

He punched the name Thomas Cerrone into the computer and ran a search on the California Department of Justice information network. As he expected, he got a hit. The computer file on Cerrone, who was forty years old, showed he had been popped nine times in as many years for soliciting for prostitution and twice for pandering.

He was a pimp, Bosch knew. Kaminski's pimp. Harry noticed that Cerrone was on thirty-six months' probation for his last conviction. He got out his black telephone book and rolled his chair over to a desk with a phone. He dialed the after-hours number for the county probation department and gave the clerk who answered Cerrone's name and DOJ number. She gave back Cerrone's current address. The pimp had come down in the world, from Studio City to Van Nuys, since Kaminski had gone to the Hyatt and not come back.

After hanging up, he thought of calling Sylvia and wondered if he should tell her it was likely he would be called by Chandler to testify the next day. He was unsure if he wanted her to be there, to see him cornered on the witness stand by Money Chandler. He decided not to call.

Cerrone's home address was an apartment on Sepulveda Boulevard in an area where prostitutes were not too discreet about how they got their customers. It was still daylight and Bosch counted four young women spread apart over a two-block stretch. They wore halter tops and short shorts. They held their thumb out like hitchhikers when cars went by. But it was clear they were only interested in a ride around the corner to a parking lot where they could take care of business.

Bosch parked at the curb across from the Van-Aire Apartments, where Cerrone had told his probation officer he was living. A couple of the numbers from the address had fallen off the front wall but it was readable because the smog had left the rest of the wall a dingy beige. The place needed new paint, new screens, some plastering to fill in the cracks in the facade and probably new tenants.

Actually, it needed to be knocked down. Start over, Bosch thought as he crossed the street. Cerrone's name was on the residents list next to the front security door but no one answered the buzzer at apartment six. Bosch lit a cigarette and decided to hang around for a while. He counted twenty-four units on the residents list. It was six o'clock. People would be coming home for dinner. Some-one would come along.

He walked away from the door and back out to the curb. There was graffiti on the sidewalk, all of it in black paint. The monikers of the local homeboys. There was also a scrip painted in block letters that asked, R U THE NEX RODDY KING? He wondered how someone could mis-spell a name that had been heard and printed so many times.

A woman and two young children came to the steel-grated door from the other side. Bosch timed his approach so that he was at the door just as she opened it.

'Have you seen Tommy Cerrone around?' he asked as he passed her.

She was too busy with the children to answer. Bosch walked into the courtyard to get his bearings and to look for a door with a six on it – Cerrone's apartment. There was graffiti on the concrete floor of the courtyard, a gang insignia Bosch couldn't make out. He found number six on the first floor toward the back. There was a rusted-out hibachi grill on the ground next to the door. There was also a child's bike with training wheels parked under the front window.

The bike didn't fit. Bosch tried to look in but the curtains were drawn, leaving only a three-inch band of darkness he could not see beyond. He knocked on the door and as was his practice, stepped to the side. A Mexican woman with what looked like an eight-month pregnancy beneath her faded pink bathrobe answered the door. Behind the small woman Bosch could see a young boy sitting on the living room floor in front of a black-and-white TV tuned to a Spanish language channel.

'Hola,' Bosch said. 'Señor Tom Cerrone aqui?'

The woman stared at him with frightened eyes. She seemed to close in on herself, as if to get smaller before him. Her arms moved up from her side and closed over her swollen belly.

'No migra,' Bosch said. 'Policia. Tomás Cerrone. Aqui?'

She shook her head no and began to close the door. Bosch put his hand out to stop it. Struggling with his Spanish he asked if she knew Cerrone and where he was. She said he only came once a week to collect the mail and the rent. She moved back a step and gestured to the card table where there was a small stack of mail. Bosch could see an American Express bill on top. Gold Card.

'Teléfono? Necesidad urgente?'

She looked down from his eyes and her hesitation told him she had a number.

'Por favor?'

She told him to wait and she left the doorway. While she was gone the boy sitting ten feet inside the door turned from the TV – Bosch could see it was some kind of game show – and looked at him. Bosch felt uncomfortable. He looked away, into the courtyard. When he looked back the boy was smiling. He had his hand up and was pointing a finger at Bosch. He made a shooting sound and giggled. Then the mother was back at the door with a piece of paper. There was a local phone number on it, that was all.

Bosch copied it down in a small notebook he carried and then told her he would take the mail. The woman turned and looked at the card table as if the answer to what she should do was sitting on it with the mail. Bosch told her it would be okay and she finally lifted the stack and handed it to him. The frightened look was in her eyes again.

He stepped back and was going to walk away when he stopped and looked back at her. He asked how much the rent was and she told him it was one hundred dollars a week. Bosch nodded and walked away.

Out on the street he walked down to a pay phone that was in front of the next apartment complex. He called the downtown communications center, gave the operator the phone number he had just gotten and said he needed an address. While he waited he thought about the pregnant woman and wondered why she stayed. Could things be worse back in the Mexican town she came from? For some, he knew, the journey here was so difficult that returning was out of the question.

As he was flipping through Cerrone's mail, one of the hitchhikers walked up to him. She wore an orange tank top over her surgically augmented breasts. Her cutoff jeans were cut so high above the thighs that the white pockets hung out below. In one of the pockets he could see the distinctive shape of a condom package. She had the gaunt, tired look of a strawberry – a woman who would do anything, anytime, anywhere to keep crack in her pipe. Factoring in her deteriorated appearance, he put her age at no more than twenty. To Bosch's surprise, she said, 'Hey, darling, looking for a date?'

He smiled and said, 'You're going to have to be more careful than that, you want to stay out of the cage.'

'Oh, shit,' she said and turned to walk away.

'Wait a minute. Wait a minute. Don't I know you? Yeah, I know you. It's . . . what's your name, girl?'

'Look, man, I'm not talking to you and I'm not blowing you, so I gotta go.'

'Wait. Wait. I don't want anything. I just thought, you know, that we'd met. Aren't you one of Tommy Cerrone's girls? Yeah, that's where I met you.'

The name put a slight stutter in her step. Bosch let the phone dangle by its cord and caught up to her. She stopped.

'Look, I'm not with Tommy anymore, okay? I gotta go to work.'

She turned from him and put her thumb out as a wave of southbound traffic started by.

'Wait a minute, just tell me something. Tell me where Tommy is these days. I need to get with him on something.'

'On what? I don't know where he is.'

'A girl. You remember Becky? Couple years ago. Blonde, liked red lipstick, had a set like yours. She mighta used the name Maggie. I want to find her and she was working for Tom. You remember her?'

'I wasn't even around then. And I haven't seen Tommy in four months. And you are full of shit.'

She walked off and Bosch called after her, 'Twenty bucks.'

She stopped and came back.

'For what?'

'An address. I'm not bullshitting. I want to talk to him.'

'Well, give it.'

He took the money out of his wallet and gave it to her. It occurred to him that Van Nuys Vice might be watching him from somewhere around here and wondering why he was giving a hooker a twenty.

'Try the Grandview,' she said. 'I don't know the number or anything but it's on the top floor. You can't tell'm I sent ya. He'll fuck me up.'

She walked away putting the money in one of the flapping pockets. He didn't have to ask her where the Grandview was. He watched her cut in between two apartment buildings and disappear, probably going to get a rock. He wondered if she had told the truth and why he could find it in himself to give her money but not the woman in apartment six. The police operator had hung up by the time he got back to the pay phone.

Bosch redialed and asked for her and she gave him the

address that went with the phone number he'd gotten. Suite P-1, the Grandview Apartments, on Sepulveda in Sherman Oaks. He had just wasted twenty bucks on crack cocaine. He hung up.

In the car, he finished looking through the mail. Half of it was junk mail, the rest credit card bills and mailers from Republican candidates. There was also a post card invitation to an Adult Film Performers Guild awards banquet in Reseda the following week.

Bosch opened the American Express bill. The illegality of this did not concern him in the least. Cerrone was a criminal who was lying to his probation officer. There would be no complaint from him. The pimp owed American Express $1855.05 this month. The bill was two pages, and Bosch noticed two billings for airline flights to Las Vegas and three billings from Victoria's Secret. Bosch was familiar with Victoria's Secret, having studied the mail-order lingerie catalog at Sylvia's on occasion. In one month, Cerrone had ordered nearly $400 in lingerie by mail. The money paid by the poor woman who rented the apartment Cerrone was using as a front for a probation address was basically subsidizing the lingerie bills of Cerrone's whores. It angered Bosch, but it gave him an idea.

The Grandview Apartments were the ultimate California ideal. Built alongside a shopping mall, the building afforded its tenants the ability to walk directly from their apartment into the mall, thereby cutting out the heretofore required middle ground for all Southern California culture and interaction: the car. Bosch parked in the mall's garage and entered the outer lobby through the rear entrance. It was an Italian marble affair with a grand piano in its center that was playing by itself. Bosch recognized the song as a Cab Calloway standard, 'Everybody That Comes to My Place Has to Eat.'

There was a directory and a phone on the wall by the

security door that led to the elevators. The name next to P-1 was Kuntz. Bosch took it to be an inside joke. He lifted the phone and pushed the button. A woman answered and he said, 'UPS. Gotta package.'

'Uh,' she said. 'From who?'

'Um, it says, I can't read the writing – looks like Victor's secretary or something.'

'Oh,' she said and he heard her giggle. 'Do I have to sign?'

'Yes, ma'am, I need a signature.'

Rather than buzz him in, she said she would come down. Bosch stood at the glass door for two minutes waiting before he realized the scam wouldn't work. He was standing there in a suit and had no package in his hand. He turned his back to the elevator just as the polished chrome doors began to part.

He took a step toward the piano and looked down as if he was fascinated by it and didn't notice the elevator's arrival. From behind him he heard the security door start to open and he turned around.

'Are you UPS?'

She was blonde and stunning even in her blue jeans and pale blue Oxford shirt. Their eyes met and right away Bosch knew she knew it was a scam. She immediately tried to close the door but Bosch got there in time and pushed his way through.

'What are you doing? I –'

Bosch clamped a hand over her mouth because he thought she was about to scream. Covering half her face accentuated the fright in her eyes. She didn't seem as stunning to Bosch anymore.

'It's okay. I'm not going to hurt you, I just want to talk to Tommy. Let's go up.'

He slowly pulled his hand back and she didn't scream.

'Tommy's not there,' she said in a whisper, as if to signal her cooperation.

'Then we can wait.'

He gently pushed her toward the elevator and punched the button.

She was right. Cerrone wasn't there. But Bosch didn't have to wait long. He had barely had time to check on the opulent furnishings of the two-bedroom, two-bath and loft apartment with private roof garden when the man arrived.

Cerrone stepped through the front door, *Racing Forum* in hand, just as Bosch stepped into the living room from the balcony that overlooked Sepulveda and the crowded Ventura Freeway.

Cerrone initially smiled at Bosch but then the face became blank. This often happened to Bosch with crooks. He believed it was because the crooks often thought they recognized him. And it was true they probably did. Bosch's picture had been in the paper and on TV several times in the last few years, including once this week. Harry believed that most crooks who read the papers or watched the news looked closely at the pictures of the cops. They probably thought it gave them an added advantage, someone to look out for. But instead it bred familiarity. Cerrone had smiled as though Bosch was a long-lost friend, then he realized it was probably the enemy, a cop.

'That's right,' Bosch said.

'Tommy, he made me bring him up,' the girl said. 'He called on the –'

'Shut up,' Cerrone barked. Then, to Bosch, he said, 'If you had a warrant, you wouldn't be here alone. No warrant, get the fuck out.'

'Very observant,' Bosch said. 'Sit down. I have questions.'

'Fuck you and the questions you rode in on. Get out.'

Bosch sat down on a black leather couch and took out his cigarettes.

'Tom, if I go, it's to go see your PO and see about getting you revoked for this address scam you're playing. The probation department frowns on cons telling them they live one place when they actually live somewhere else. Especially when one's a dump and one's the Grandview.'

Cerrone threw the *Forum* across the room at the girl.

'See?' he said. 'See the shit you got me in?'

She seemed to know better than to say anything. Cerrone folded his arms and stood in the living room but he wasn't going to sit down. He was a well-built guy gone to fat. Too many afternoons at Hollywood or Del Mar, sipping cocktails and watching the ponies.

'Look, what do you want?'

'I want to know about Becky Kaminski.'

Cerrone looked puzzled.

'You remember, Maggie Cum Loudly, the blonde with the tits you probably had her enlarge. You were bringing her up through the video business, doin' some outcall work on the side, and then she disappeared on you.'

'What about her? That was a long time ago.'

'Twenty-two months and three days, I am told.'

'So what? She turned up and is saying some shit about me, it don't matter. Take it to court, man. We'll see –'

Bosch jumped up off the couch and slapped him hard across the face, then pushed him over a black leather chair onto the floor. Cerrone's eyes immediately went to the girl's, which told Bosch that he had complete control of the situation. The power of humiliation sometimes was more awesome than a gun held to the head. Cerrone's face was a bright red all over.

Bosch's hand stung. He bent over the fallen man and said, 'She didn't turn up and you know it. She's dead and you knew it when you made the missing person report. You were just covering your ass. I want to know how you knew.'

'Look, man, I didn't have any –'

'But you knew she wasn't coming back. How?'

'I just had a hunch. She didn't turn up for a couple days.'

'Guys like you don't go to the police on hunches. Guys like you, they get their place broken into, they don't even call the cops. Like I said, you were just covering your ass. You didn't want to get blamed 'cause you knew she wasn't coming back alive.'

'Awright, awright, it was more than a hunch. Okay? It was the guy. I never saw him but his voice and some of the things he said. It was familiar, you know? Then after I sent her and she didn't come back, it dawned on me. I remembered him. I had sent him somebody else once and she ended up dead.'

'Who?'

'Holly Lere. I can't remember her real name.'

Bosch could. Holly Lere was the porno name of Nicole Knapp. The seventh victim of the Dollmaker. He sat back down on the couch and put a cigarette in his mouth.

'Tommy,' the girl said, 'he's smoking.'

'Shut the fuck up,' he said to her.

'Well, you said no smoking in here except on the bal –'

'Shut the fuck up!'

'Nicole Knapp,' Bosch said.

'Yeah, that's it.'

'You knew the cops said the Dollmaker got her?'

'Yeah, and I always thought that until Becky disappeared and I remembered this guy and what he said.'

'But you didn't tell anybody. You didn't call the cops.'

'It's like you said, man, guys like me, we don't call.'

Bosch nodded.

'What did he say? The caller, what was it he said?'

'He said, "I have a special need tonight." Both times. Just like that. He said the same thing both times. And his voice was weird. It was like he was talking through clenched teeth or something.'

'And you sent her to that.'

'I didn't put it together until after she didn't come back. Look, man, I made a report. I told the cops the hotel she went to and they never did nothing. I'm not the only one to blame. Shit, the cops said that guy was caught, that he was dead. I thought it was safe.'

'Safe for you, or the girls you put out on the street?'

'Look, you think I would've sent her if I knew? I had a lot invested in her, man.'

'I'm sure you did.'

Bosch looked over at the blonde and wondered how long it would be before she looked like the one he had given the twenty to on the street. His guess was that Cerrone's girls all ended up used up and on the street with their thumb out, or they ended up dead. He looked back at Cerrone.

'Did Rebecca smoke?'

'What?'

'Smoke. Did she smoke? You lived with her, you should know.'

'No, she didn't smoke. It's a disgusting habit.'

Cerrone looked over at the blonde and glared. Bosch dropped his cigarette on the white rug and ground it out as he stood up. He headed toward the door but stopped after he opened it.

'Cerrone, the woman in that dump your mail goes to?'

'What about her?'

'She doesn't pay rent anymore.'

'What are you talking about?'

He climbed up from the floor, regaining a measure of his pride.

'I'm talking about her not paying you rent anymore. I'm going to check on her from time to time. If she's paying rent, your PO gets a call and your scam gets blown. Probation gets revoked and you do your time. It's tough to run an outcall business from county lockup. Only two phones on each floor and the brothers control who uses them and for how long. I guess you'd have to cut them in.'

Cerrone just stared at him, anger thumping in his temples.

'And she better still be there when I check,' Bosch said. 'If I hear she went back to Mexico, I blame you and make the call. If I hear she bought a fucking condo, I make the call. She just better be there.'

'That's extortion,' Cerrone said.

'No, asshole, that's justice.'

He left the door open. Out in the hallway waiting for the elevator, he once again heard Cerrone yell, 'Shut the fuck up!'

THIRTEEN

The last vestiges of the evening rush hour made it a slow run up to Sylvia's. She was sitting at the dining room table in faded blue jeans and a Grant High T-shirt, reading book reports, when he came in. One of the eleventh-grade English classes she taught down in the Valley at Grant was called Los Angeles in Literature. She had told him she developed the class so the students might come to know their city better. Most of them came from other places, other countries. She had once told him that the students in one of her classes accounted for eleven different native languages.

He put his hand on the back of her neck and bent down to kiss her. He noticed the reports were on Nathanael West's *Day of the Locust*.

'Ever read it?' she asked.

'Long time ago. Some English teacher in high school made us read it. She was crazy.'

She elbowed him in the thigh.

'All right, wise guy. I try to rotate the tough ones with the easy ones. I assigned them *The Big Sleep*.'

'That's probably what they thought this one should've been called.'

'Aren't you the life of the party today. Something good happen?'

'Actually, no. Everything is turning to shit out there. But in here . . . it's different.'

She got up and they embraced. He ran his hand up and down her back the way he knew she liked.

'What's happening on the case?'

'Nothing. Everything. I might be going into the mud puddle. Wonder if I can get a job after this as a private eye. Like Marlowe.'

She pushed away.

'What are you talking about?'

'I'm not sure. Something. I have to work on it tonight. I'll take the kitchen table. You can stay out here with the locusts.'

'It's your turn to cook.'

'Then, I'm going to hire the colonel.'

'Shit.'

'Hey, that's not a good thing for an English teacher to say. What's the matter with the colonel?'

'He's been dead for years. Never mind. It's okay.'

She smiled at him. This ritual occurred often. When it was his turn to cook he usually took her out. He could see she was disappointed by the prospect of fried chicken to go. But there was too much going on, too much to think about.

She had a face that made him want to confess everything bad he had ever done. Yet he knew he could not. She knew it, too.

'I humiliated a man today.'

'What? Why?'

'Because he humiliates women.'

'All men do that, Harry. What did you do to him?'

'Knocked him down in front of his woman.'

'He probably needed it.'

'I don't want you to come to court tomorrow. I'm probably going to be called by Chandler to testify but I don't want you there. It's going to be bad.'

She was silent for a moment.

'Why do you do this, Harry? Tell me all these things that you do but keep the rest a secret? In some ways we are so intimate and in others . . . You tell me about the men you knock down but not about you. What do I know about you, your past? I want us to get to that, Harry. We have to or

155

we'll end up humiliating each other. That's how it ended for me before.'

Bosch nodded and looked down. He didn't know what to say. He was too burdened by other thoughts to get into this now.

'You want the extra crispy?' he finally asked.

'Fine.'

She went back to her book reports and he went out to get dinner.

After they were done eating and she went back to the dining room table, he opened his briefcase on the kitchen table and took out the blue murder books. He had a bottle of Henry Weinhard's on the table but no cigarette. He wouldn't smoke inside. At least not while she was awake.

He unsnapped the first binder and laid out the sections on each of the eleven victims across the table. He stood up with the bottle so he could look down and take them all in at once. Each section was fronted by a photograph of the victim's remains, as they were found. There were eleven of these photos in front of him. He did some thinking on the cases and then went into the bedroom and checked the suit he had worn the day before. The Polaroid of the concrete blonde was still in the pocket.

He brought it back to the kitchen and laid it on the table with the others. Number twelve. It was a horrible gallery of broken, abused bodies, their garish makeup showing false smiles below dead eyes. Their bodies were naked, exposed to the harsh light of the police photographer.

Bosch drained the bottle and kept staring. Reading the names and the dates of the deaths. Looking at the faces. All of them lost angels in the city of night. He didn't notice Sylvia come in until it was too late.

'My God,' she said in a whisper as she saw the photos. She took a step backward. She was holding one of her students' papers in her hand. Her other hand had come up to her mouth.

'I'm sorry, Sylvia,' Bosch said. 'I should've warned you not to come in.'

'Those are the women?'

He nodded.

'What are you doing?'

'I'm not sure. Trying to make something happen, I guess. I thought if I looked at them all again I might get an idea, figure out what's happening.'

'But how can you look at those? You were just standing there looking.'

'Because I have to.'

She looked down at the paper in her hand.

'What is it?' he asked.

'Nothing. Uh, one of my students wrote something. I was going to read it to you.'

'Go ahead.'

He stepped over to the wall and turned off the light that hung over the table. The photos and Bosch became shrouded in darkness. Sylvia stood in the light cast from the dining room through the kitchen entrance.

'Go ahead.'

She held up the paper and said, 'It's a girl. She wrote, "West foreshadowed the end of Los Angeles's halcyon moment. He saw the city of angels becoming a city of despair, a place where hopes get crushed under the weight of the mad crowd. His book was the warning." '

She looked up.

'She goes on but that was the part I wanted to read. She's only a tenth-grader taking advanced classes but she seemed to grasp something so strong there.'

He admired her lack of cynicism. Bosch's first thought was that the kid had plagiarized – where'd she get a word like halcyon? But Sylvia saw past that. She saw the beauty in things. He saw the darkness.

'It's good,' he said.

'She's African-American. She comes up on the bus. She's one of the smartest I have and I worry about her on the bus. She said the trip is seventy-five minutes each way and that is the time when she reads the assignments I give. But I worry about her. She seems so sensitive. Maybe too much so.'

'Give her time and she'll grow a callous on her heart. Everybody does.'

'No, not everybody, Harry. That's what I worry about with her.'

She looked at him there in the darkness for a long moment.

'I'm sorry I intruded.'

'You never intrude on me, Sylvia. I am sorry I brought this home. I can leave if you want, take it to my place.'

'No, Harry, I want you here. You want me to put on some coffee?'

'No, I'm fine.'

She went back to the living room and he turned the light back on. He looked over the gallery again. Though they looked the same in death because of the makeup applied by each one's killer, the women fell into numerous physical categories according to race, size, coloring, and so on.

Locke had told the task force that this meant that the killer was simply an opportunistic predator. Not concerned with body type, only the acquisition of a victim which he could then place into his erotic program. He did not care if they were black or white as long as he could snatch them with as little notice as possible. He was a bottom feeder. He moved on a level where the women he encountered were victims long before he got to them. They were women who had already given up their bodies to the unloving hands and eyes of strangers. They were out there waiting for him. The question, Bosch now knew, was whether the Dollmaker was still out there, too.

He sat down and from the pocket of the binder he pulled a map of West LA. Its creases cracked and split in some sections as he unfolded it and put it down on top of the photos. The round black stickers that represented locations where bodies had been found were still in place. The victim's name and date of discovery were written next to each black dot. Geographically, the task force had found no significance until after Church was dead. The bodies were found in locations stretching from Silverlake to Malibu. The Dollmaker littered the entire Westside. Still, for the most part, the bodies were clustered in Silverlake and Hollywood, with only one found in Malibu and one in West Hollywood.

The concrete blonde was found farther south in Hollywood than any of the previous bodies. She was also the only one that had been buried. Locke had said location of disposal was probably a choice of convenience. After Church was dead this seemed true. Four of the bodies had been dumped within a mile of his Silverlake apartment. Another four were in eastern Hollywood, not a long drive, either.

The dates had done nothing for the investigation. No pattern. Initially there was a decreasing-interval pattern between discoveries of victims, then it began to vary widely. The Dollmaker would go five weeks between strikes, then two weeks, then three. Nothing to make of this; the detectives on the task force simply let it go.

Bosch moved on. He began reading the background packets that had been drawn up on each victim. Most of these were short – two to three pages about their sad lives. One of the women who worked Hollywood Boulevard at night was going to beautician school by day. Another had been sending money to Chihuahua, Mexico, where her parents believed she had a good job as a tour guide at the famous Disneyland. There were odd matches between some of the victims, but nothing that ever amounted to anything.

Three of the Boulevard whores went to the same doctor for weekly clap shots. Members of the task force put him under surveillance for three weeks. But one night while they were watching him, the real Dollmaker picked up a prostitute on Sunset and her body was found in Silverlake the next morning.

Two of the other women also shared a doctor. The same Beverly Hills plastic surgeon had performed breast-implant surgery on them. The task force had rallied on this discovery, for a plastic surgeon remakes images, similarly after a fashion to the way the Dollmaker used makeup. The plastic man, as he was called by the cops, was also placed under surveillance. But he never made a suspicious move and seemed to be the picture of domestic bliss with a wife whose physical features he had sculpted to his own liking. They were still watching him when Bosch took the telephone tip that led to the shooting of Norman Church.

As far as Bosch knew, neither doctor ever knew he had been watched. In the book Bremmer wrote, they were identified by pseudonyms.

Nearly two-thirds through the background packets, as he read about Nicole Knapp, the seventh victim, Bosch saw the pattern within the pattern. He had somehow missed it before. All of them had. The task force, Locke, the media. They had put all the victims into the same classification. A whore is a whore is a whore. But there were differences. Some were streetwalkers, some were higher up the scale as escorts. Within these two groups, some were also dancers; one was a telegram stripper. And two made livings in the pornography trade – as had the latest victim, Becky Kaminski – while taking outcall hooking assignments on the side.

Bosch took the packets and photos of Nicole Knapp, the seventh victim, and Shirleen Kemp, the eleventh victim, off the table. These were the two porn actresses, known on video as Holly Lere and Heather Cumhither, respectively.

He then paged through one of the binders until he found the package on the lone survivor, the woman who had gotten away. She, too, was a porn actress who took outcall sex jobs. Her name was Georgia Stern. Her video name was Velvet Box. She had gone to the Hollywood Star Motel to meet a date arranged through the outcall service she advertised in the local sex tabloids. After she arrived, her client asked her to undress. She turned her back to do this, offering a show of modesty in case that was a turn-on for the client. She then saw the leather strap of her purse come over her head and he began choking her from behind. She fought, as probably all the victims had, but she was able to get free by driving an elbow into her attacker's ribs, then turning and delivering a kick to his genitals.

She ran naked from the room, all thought of modesty long gone. By the time police went back in, the attacker was gone. It was three days before the reports on the incident filtered their way to the task force. By then the hotel room had been used dozens of times – the Hollywood Star offered hourly rates – and it was useless as far as gathering physical evidence went.

Reading the reports on it now, Bosch realized why the composite drawing that Georgia Stern had helped a police artist sketch was so different from the appearance of Norman Church.

It had been a different man.

An hour later, he turned one of the binders to the last page, where he had kept a listing of phone numbers and addresses of the principals involved in the investigation. He went to the wall phone and dialed the home of Dr John Locke. He hoped the psychologist had not changed his number in four years.

Locke picked up after five rings.

'Sorry, Dr Locke, I know it's getting late. It's Harry Bosch.'

'Harry, how are you? I am sorry we didn't get to talk today. It was not the best circumstance for you, I'm sure, but I –'

'Yes, Doctor, listen, something's come up. It's related to the Dollmaker. I have some things I want to show you and talk about. Would it be possible for me to come there?'

There was a lengthy silence before Locke answered.

'Would that be about this new case I've read about in the paper?'

'Yes, that and some other things.'

'Well, let's see, it's nearly ten o'clock. Are you sure this can't wait until tomorrow morning?'

'I am in court tomorrow morning, Doctor. All day. It's important. I'd really appreciate your time. I'll be there before eleven and be out before twelve.'

When Locke didn't say anything, Harry wondered if the soft-spoken doctor was afraid of him or just didn't want a killer cop in his home.

'Besides,' Bosch said into the silence, 'I think you'll find it interesting.'

'Very well,' Locke said.

After getting the address, Harry packed all the paperwork back into the two binders. Sylvia came into the kitchen after hesitating at the doorway until she was sure the photos were packed away.

'I heard you talking. Are you going to his place tonight?'

'Yeah, right now. In Laurel Canyon.'

'What's going on?'

He stopped his hurried movement. He had both binders stacked under his right arm.

'I . . . well, we missed something. The task force. We messed up. I think all along there were two, but I didn't see it until now.'

'Two killers?'

'I think so. I want to ask Locke about it.'

'Are you coming back tonight?'

'I don't know. It will be late. I was thinking about just going to my place. Check my messages, get some fresh clothes.'

'This weekend is not looking good, is it?'

'What – oh, yeah, Lone Pine, yeah. Well, uh, I –'

'Don't worry about it. But I may want to hang out at your place while they have the open house here.'

'Sure.'

She walked him to the door and opened it. She told him to be careful and to call her the next day. He said he would. At the threshold he hesitated. He said, 'You know, you were right.'

'About what?'

'What you said about men.'

FOURTEEN

Laurel Canyon is a winding cut through the Santa Monica Mountains that connects Studio City with Hollywood and the Sunset Strip. On the south side, where the road drops below Mulholland Drive and the fast four lanes thin to two crumbling invitations to a head-on collision, the canyon becomes funky LA, where forty-year-old Hollywood bungalows sit next to multilevel glass contemporaries that sit next to gingerbread houses. Harry Houdini built a castle in here among the steep hillsides. Jim Morrison lived in a clapboard house near the little market that still serves as the canyon's only commercial outpost.

The canyon was a place where the new rich – rock stars, writers, film actors and drug dealers – came to live. They braved the mudslides and the monumental traffic tie-ups just to call Laurel Canyon home. Locke lived on Lookout Mountain Drive, a steep upward grade off Laurel Canyon Boulevard that made Bosch's department-issue Caprice work extra hard. The address he was looking for could not be missed because it blinked in blue neon from the front wall of Locke's house. Harry pulled to the curb behind a multicolor Volkswagen van that was at least twenty-five years old. Laurel Canyon was like that, a time warp.

Bosch got out, dropped his cigarette in the street and stepped on it. It was very quiet and dark. He heard the Caprice's engine ticking away its heat, the smell of burning oil wafting from the undercarriage. He reached in through the open window and grabbed the two binders.

It had taken most of an hour to get to Locke's and during

that time Bosch had been able to refine his thoughts on the discovery of the pattern within a pattern. He also realized along the way that there was a key way of attempting to confirm it.

Locke answered with a glass of red wine in his hand. He was barefoot and wearing blue jeans and a surgeon's green shirt. Hanging from a leather thong around his neck was a large pink crystal.

'Good evening, Detective Bosch. Please come in.'

He led the way through an entry hall to a large living room/dining room area with a wall of French doors that opened onto a brick patio surrounding a lighted blue pool. Bosch noticed the pinkish carpet was dirty and worn but otherwise the place was not bad for a college sex professor and author. He noticed the water of the pool was choppy, as if someone had been swimming recently. He thought he smelled a trace of stale marijuana smoke.

'Beautiful place,' Bosch said. 'You know we're almost neighbors. I live on the other side of the hill. On Woodrow Wilson.'

'Oh, really? How come it took you so long to get here?'

'Well, actually, I didn't come from home. I was at a friend's place up in Bouquet Canyon.'

'Ah, a girlfriend, that explains the forty-five-minute wait.'

'Sorry to hold you up, Doctor. Why don't we get on with this so I don't keep you any longer than necessary.'

'Yes, please.'

He signaled Bosch to put the binders down on the dining room table. He didn't ask if Harry wanted a glass of wine, an ashtray or even a pair of swimming trunks.

'I'm sorry to intrude,' Harry offered. 'I'll be quick.'

'Yes, you said that. I'm sorry this came up now myself. Testifying put me back a day on my research and writing schedule and I was trying to recoup tonight.'

Bosch noticed his hair wasn't wet. Maybe he had been working while someone else had been in the pool.

Locke took a seat at the dining room table and Bosch told the story of the concrete blonde investigation in exact chronological order after starting by showing him the copy of the new note left at the station on Monday.

While telling the details of the latest death, Bosch saw Locke's eyes brighten with interest. When he was done, the psychologist folded his arms and closed his eyes and said, 'Let me think about this before we go on.'

He sat perfectly still. Bosch wasn't sure what to make of it. After twenty seconds went by, he finally said, 'If you're going to think, I'm going to borrow your phone.'

'In the kitchen,' Locke said without opening his eyes.

Bosch got Amado's phone number from the task force list in the binder and called him. He could tell he had awakened the coroner's analyst.

After identifying himself, Bosch said, 'Sorry to wake you. But things are happening very quickly on this new Dollmaker case. Did you read about it in the paper?'

'Yeah. But they said it wasn't known for sure if it was the Dollmaker.'

'Right. That's what I'm working on. I have a question.'

'Go ahead.'

'You testified yesterday about the rape kits taken from each victim. Where are they now? The evidence, I mean.'

There was a long silence before Amado said, 'They're probably still in evidence storage. The coroner's policy is to keep evidence seven years after resolution of a case. You know, in case of appeals or something. Now, since your perp is dead, there would be no reason to keep the stuff even that long. But it takes an order from the medical examiner to clear out an evidence locker. The chances are the ME at the time would not have thought or remembered to do this after you, uh, killed Church. It's too big of a bureaucracy to run that well. My guess is the kits would still be there. The evidence custodian would only request a disposal order after seven years.'

'Okay,' Bosch said, excitement evident in his voice.

'What about the condition? Would it still be usable as evidence? And for analysis?'

'Should be no deterioration, I would think.'

'How full's your plate?'

'It's always full. But you've got me hooked here. What's up?'

'I need someone to pull the kits from victims seven and eleven. That's Nicole Knapp and Shirleen Kemp. Got it? Seven and eleven, like the store.'

'I got it. Seven eleven. Then what?'

'Cross-reference the pubic combs. Look for the same foreign hair in both places, on both women. How long will it take?'

'Three, four days. We have to send that to the DOJ lab. I can put a rush on it, maybe get it sooner. Can I ask you something? Why are we doing this?'

'I think there was someone else besides Church. A copycat. He did seven, eleven and the one this week. And I'm thinking he might not have been smart enough to shave himself like Church. If you find similar hair in the combs, I think that will clinch it.'

'Well, I can tell you something right off that is interesting about those two. Seven and eleven.'

Bosch waited.

'I reviewed everything before I testified, so it's still fresh, you know? Remember I testified that two of the victims had extreme damage, vaginal tears? Well, it was those two, seven and eleven.'

Bosch thought about this for a few moments. From out in the dining room he heard Locke say, 'Harry?'

'Be right there,' he called out. To Amado, he said, 'That's interesting.'

'It means this second guy, whoever he is, he's rougher trade than Church. Those two women were hurt the most.'

Something came together in Bosch's mind then. Something that had not seemed right about Amado's testimony the day before. Now it was clear.

'The condoms,' he said.

'What about them?'

'You testified that it was a box of twelve, only three left.'

'That's right! Nine used. You subtract victims seven and eleven from the list and you have nine victims. It fits, Harry. Okay, first thing tomorrow, I'm on this. Give me three days, max.'

They hung up and Bosch wondered if Amado would get any sleep tonight.

Locke had replenished his wineglass but still did not ask Bosch if he wanted a glass when he returned to the dining room. Bosch sat down across the table from him.

'I'm ready to go on,' Locke said.

'Let's do it.'

'You're saying that the body found this week exhibited every known detail ascribed to the Dollmaker?'

'Right.'

'Except now we have a new method of disposal. A private disposal as opposed to the public challenge of the others. It's all very interesting. What else?'

'Well, from trial testimony I think we can eliminate Church as the perp in the eleventh killing. A wit produced a tape in –'

'A wit?'

'A witness. In court. He was a friend of Church's. He came in with a video that showed Church at a party at the time number eleven got abducted. The tape is convincing.'

Locke nodded his head and was silent. At least he didn't close his eyes, Bosch thought. The psychologist thoughtfully rubbed the graying whiskers on his chin, which made Bosch do the same thing.

'Then there is number seven,' Bosch said.

He told Locke about the information he got from Cerrone, about the voice the pimp had recognized.

'Voice identification wouldn't pass as evidence but say for the sake of argument he is right. That connects the concrete blonde to our seventh victim. The videotape eliminates

168

Church from the eleventh case. Amado, the guy from the coroner's office, I don't know if you remember him, he says numbers seven and eleven had similar injuries, injuries that stood out if compared with those of the others.

'Another thing I just remembered is the makeup. After Church was dead they found the makeup in the Hyperion apartment, remember? They matched it to nine of the victims. The two victims there was no makeup for were –'

'Seven and eleven.'

'Right. So what we have are multiple ties between these two cases – seven and eleven. Then you have a tangential connection to number twelve, this week's victim, based on the pimp recognizing the customer's voice. The connection gets stronger if you look at the lifestyles of the three women. All were in porno, all worked outcall.'

'I see the pattern within the pattern,' Locke said.

'Gets better. Now, we add in our lone survivor, she was also in porno and did outcall work.'

'And she described an attacker who looked nothing like Church.'

'Exactly. That's because I don't think it was Church. I think the three, plus the survivor, make up one set of victims of one killer. The remaining nine are another set with another killer. Church.'

Locke got up and began pacing back and forth on one side of the dining room table. He kept his hand to his chin.

'Anything else?'

Bosch opened one of the binders and took out the map and a folded piece of paper on which he had earlier written a series of dates. He carefully unfolded the map and spread it on the table. He leaned in and over it.

'Okay, look. Let's call the nine Group A and the three Group B. On the map I have circled the locations where Group A victims were found. You see, if you take the Group B victims out of the picture, you have a nice geographic concentration. Group B vics were found in Malibu, West Hollywood, South Hollywood. But the A list was concentrated here in eastern Hollywood and Silverlake.'

Bosch ran his finger in a circle on the map, showing the dumping zone Church had used.

'And here in almost the center of this zone is Hyperion Street – Church's killing pad.'

He straightened up and dropped the folded paper on the map.

'Now here is a list of dates of the eleven killings originally attributed to Church. You see there is an interval pattern at the start – thirty days, thirty-two days, twenty-eight, thirty-one, thirty-one. But then the pattern goes to hell. Remember that? How it confused us back then?

'Yes, I do.'

'We have twelve days, then sixteen, then twenty-seven, thirty and eleven. The pattern disintegrates into no pattern. But now separate the dates of Group A and Group B.'

Bosch unfolded the paper. There were two columns of dates. Locke leaned over the table into the light to study the columns. Bosch could see a thin line, a scar, on the top of his bald and freckled crown.

'On Group A we now have a pattern,' Bosch continued. 'A clearly discernable pattern of intervals. We have thirty days, thirty-two, twenty-eight, thirty-one, thirty-one, twenty-eight, twenty-seven and thirty. On Group B we have eighty-four days between the two killings.'

'Better stress management.'

'What?'

'The intervals between the acting out of these fantasies is dictated by the buildup of stress. I testified about this. The better the actor handles it, the longer the interval between killings. The second killer has better stress management. Or, at least, had it back then.'

Bosch watched him pace the room. He took out a cigarette and lit it. Locke said nothing.

'What I want to know is, is this possible?' Bosch asked. 'I mean, is there any precedent for this that you know of?'

'Of course, it's possible. The black heart does not beat alone. You don't even have to look outside the boundaries of your own jurisdiction to find ample evidence it is possible. Look at the Hillside Stranglers. There was even a book written about them called *Two of a Kind*.

'Look at the similarities in the method of operation employed by the Nightstalker and the Sunset Strip Strangler in the early eighties. The short answer is, yes, it's possible.'

'I know about those cases but this is different. I worked some of those and I know this is different. The Hillside Stranglers worked together. They were cousins. The other two were similar but there were major differences. Here, someone came along and copied the other exactly. So closely that we missed it and he got away.'

'Two killers working independently of each other but using exactly the same methodology.'

'Right.'

'Again, I say anything is possible. Another example: remember in the eighties there was the Freeway Killer in Orange and LA counties?'

Bosch nodded. He had never worked those cases so he knew little about them.

'Well, one day they got lucky and caught a Vietnam vet named William Bonin. They tied him to a handful of the cases and believed he was good for the rest. He went to death row but the killings kept happening. They kept right on happening until a highway patrol officer pulled over a guy named Randy Kraft who was driving down the freeway with a body in his car. Kraft and Bonin didn't know each other but for a while they secretly shared the nom de plume "The Freeway Killer". Each working independently of the other, out there killing. And being mistaken for the same person.'

That sounded close to the theory Bosch was working with. Locke continued talking, no longer bothered by the late-night intrusion.

'Do you know, there is a guard on death row at San Quentin whom I know from doing research up there. He told me there are four serial killers, including Kraft and Bonin, waiting for the gas. And, well, the four of them play cards every day. Bridge. Among them, they've got fifty-nine convictions for murder. And they play bridge. Anyway, the point is, he says Kraft and Bonin think so much alike that as a team they are almost never beaten.'

Bosch started refolding the map. Without looking up, he said, 'Kraft and Bonin, did they kill their victims the same way? The exact same way?'

'Not exactly. But my point is that there could be two. But the follower in this case is smarter. He knew exactly what to do to have all the police go the other way, to put it on Church. Then, when Church was dead and no longer available for use as camouflage, the follower went underground, so to speak.'

Bosch looked up at him and a thought suddenly struck him that spun everything he knew into a new light. It was like the cue ball hitting a rack of eight, colors shooting off in all directions. But he didn't say anything. This new thought was too dangerous to bring up. Instead he asked Locke a question.

'But even when this follower went underground, he kept the same program as the Dollmaker,' Bosch said. 'Why do it, if no one was going to see it? Remember, with the Dollmaker we believed his leaving of the bodies in public locations, their faces painted, was part of the erotic program. Part of his turn-on. But why did the second killer do it – follow the same program – if the body was never intended to be found?'

Locke put both hands on the table to brace his weight and thought a moment. Bosch thought he heard a sound from the patio. He looked through the open French doors and saw only the darkness of the steep hillside rising above the illuminated pool. Its kidney-shaped surface was calm now. He looked at his watch. It was midnight.

'It's a good question,' Locke said. 'I don't know the

answer. Maybe the acolyte knew that eventually the body would be revealed, that he himself might want to reveal it. You see, we probably have to assume now that it was the follower who sent the notes to you and the newspaper four years ago. It shows the exhibitionistic portion of his program. Church apparently didn't find the same need to torment his hunters.'

'The follower got off on tweaking us.'

'Exactly. What he was doing was having his fun, taunting his trackers and all the while the blame for the murders he committed went to the real Dollmaker. Follow?'

'Yes.'

'Okay, so what happened? The real Dollmaker, Mr Church, is killed by you. The follower no longer has a cover. So what he does is, he continues his work – his killing – but now he buries the victim, hides her under concrete.'

'You're saying he still follows the whole erotic program with the makeup and everything but then buries her so no one will see her?'

'So no one will know. Yes, he follows the program because that is what turned him on in the first place. But he can no longer afford to discard the bodies publicly because that would reveal his secret.'

'So then, why the note? Why send a note to the police this week that opens him to exposure?'

Locke paced around the dining room table thinking.

'Confidence,' he finally said. 'The follower has become strong over the past four years. He thinks he is invincible. It is a common trait in the disassembling phase of a psychopath. A state of confidence and invulnerability rises as, in actuality, the psychopath is making more and more mistakes. Disassembling. Becoming vulnerable to discovery.'

'So because he has gotten away with his actions for four years, he thinks he is clear and is so untouchable that he sends another note to tweak us?'

'Exactly, but that is only one factor. Another is pride, authorship. This big trial on the Dollmaker has begun and he wants to steal some of the attention. You must

173

understand, he craves attention for his acts. After all, it was the follower, not Church who sent the letters earlier. So being prideful and feeling above the reach of the police – I guess, godlike is the way to describe his sense of himself – he writes the note this week.'

'Catch me if you can.'

'Yes, one of the oldest games around. . . . And lastly, he might have sent the note because he is still angry with you.'

'Me?'

Bosch was surprised. He had never considered this.

'Yes, you took Church away. You ruined his perfect cover. I don't imagine the note and its mention in the press has helped your court case any, has it?'

'No. It might sink me.'

'Yes, so maybe this is the follower's way of repaying you. His revenge.'

Bosch thought about all of this for a moment. He could almost feel the adrenaline surging through his body. It was after midnight but he wasn't the least bit tired. He had a focus now. He was no longer lost in the void.

'You think there are more out there, don't you?' he asked.

'You mean women in concrete, or similar confinement? Yes, unfortunately, I do. Four years is a long time. Many others are out there, I'm afraid.'

'How do I find him?'

'I'm not sure. My work has usually come at the end. After they're caught. After they're dead.'

Bosch nodded, closed the binders and put them under his arm.

'There is one thing, though,' Locke said. 'Look at his pool of victims. Who are they? How does he get to them? The three who are dead and the survivor, they all were in the porno industry, you said.'

Bosch put the binders back down on the table. He lit another cigarette.

'Yes, they all did outcall work, too,' he said.

'Yes. So while Church was the opportunistic killer,

taking victims of any size, age or race, the follower was more specific in his tastes.'

Bosch recalled the porno victims quickly.

'Right, the follower's victims were white, young, blonde and large-breasted.'

'That is a clear pattern. Did these women advertise their outcall services in the adult-related media?'

'I know two of them did, and the survivor. The latest victim did outcall but I'm not sure how she advertised.'

'Did the three who did advertise include photographs of themselves in the copy?'

Bosch could specifically remember only Holly Lere's ad, and it did not include her photo. Just her stage name, a phone drop and a guarantee of lewd pleasure.

'I don't think so. The one I remember didn't. But her porno name was in the ad. So anyone familiar with her work in video would know her physical appearance and attributes.'

'Very good. We are already creating a profile of the follower. He is someone who uses adult videos to choose the women for his erotic program. He then contacts them through ads in the adult media by seeing either their names or photos in the advertisements. Have I helped you, Detective Bosch?'

'Absolutely. Thanks for the time. And keep this under your hat. I'm not sure we want to go public with this yet.'

Bosch picked up the binders again and headed toward the door but Locke stopped him.

'We haven't finished, you know.'

Bosch turned around.

'How do you mean?' he asked, though he knew.

'You haven't spoken about the aspect of this that is most troubling. The question of how our follower learned the killer's routine. The task force did not divulge every detail of the Dollmaker's program to the media. Not back then. Details were held back so the loonies who confessed would not know exactly what to confess to. It was a safeguard. The task force could quickly eliminate the bogus confessions.'

'So?'

'So the question is, how did the follower know?'

'I don't –'

'Yes, you do. The book Mr Bremmer wrote made those details available to the world. That, of course, could account for the concrete blonde. . . . But not, as I am sure you have realized, for victims seven and eleven.'

Locke was right. It was what Bosch had realized earlier. He avoided thinking about it because he dreaded the implications.

Locke said, 'The answer is that the follower was somehow privy to the details. The details are what triggered his action. You have to remember that what we are dealing with here is someone who very likely was already in the midst of some great internal struggle when he stumbled onto an erotic program that matched his own needs. This man already had problems, whether they had manifested in his committing crimes or not. He was a sick puppy, Harry, and he saw the Dollmaker's erotic mold and realized, That's me. That's what I want, what I need for fulfillment. He then adopted the Dollmaker's program and acted on it, to the very last detail. The question is, how did he stumble onto it? And the answer is, he was given access.'

For a moment they just looked at each other, then Bosch spoke.

'You're talking about a cop. Someone on the task force. That can't be. I was there. We all wanted this guy to go down. Nobody was . . . getting off on this, man.'

'Possibly a member of the task force, Harry, only possibly. But remember, the circle of those who knew about the program was much larger than just the task force. You have medical examiners, investigators, beat cops, photographers, reporters, paramedics, the passersby who found the bodies – many people who had access to details the follower obviously knew about.'

Bosch tried to pull together a quick profile in his mind. Locke read him.

'It would have to be someone in or around the investigation, Harry. Not necessarily a vital part or a continuous part. But someone who intersected with the investigation at a point that would allow him to gain knowledge of the full program. More than what was publicly known at the time.'

Bosch said nothing until Locke prompted him.

'What else, Harry? Narrow it down.'

'Left-handed.'

'Possibly but not necessarily. Church was left-handed. The follower may only have used the left hand to make the perfect copy of Church's crimes.'

'That's right but then there are the notes. Suspicious docs said they believed it was a left-handed writer. They weren't one hundred percent. They never are.'

'Okay, then, possibly left-handed. What else?'

Bosch thought for a moment.

'Maybe a smoker. There was a package found in the concrete. Kaminski, the victim, didn't smoke.'

'Okay, that's good. These are the things you need to think about to narrow it down. It's in the details, Harry, I'm sure of it.'

A cool wind came down the hillside and in through the French doors and chilled Bosch. It was time to go, to be alone with this.

'Thanks again,' he said as he started once more for the door.

'What will you do?' Locke called after him.

'I don't know yet.'

'Harry?'

Bosch stopped at the threshold and looked back at Locke, the pool glowing eerily in the darkness behind him.

'The follower, he may be the smartest to come along in a long time.'

'Because he's a cop?'

'Because he probably knows everything about the case that you know.'

*

It was cold in the Caprice. At night the canyons always carried a dark chill. Bosch turned the car around and it floated quietly down Lookout Mountain to Laurel Canyon. He took a right and drove to the canyon market, where he bought a six-pack of Anchor Steam. Then he took his beer and his questions back up the hill to Mulholland.

He drove to Woodrow Wilson Drive and then down to his small house that stood on cantilevers and looked out across the Cahuenga Pass. He had left no lights on inside because with Sylvia in his life he never knew how long he would go without being here.

He opened the first beer as soon as the Caprice was parked at the curb in front. A car slowly went by and left him in the dark. He watched one of the beams from the spotlights at Universal City cut across the clouds over the house. Another one chased after it a few seconds later. The beer felt and tasted good going down his throat. But it felt heavy in his stomach and Bosch stopped drinking. He put the bottle back in its carton.

But it wasn't the beer, he knew, that was really bothering him. It was Ray Mora. Of all the people who were close enough to the case to know the details of the program, Mora was the one who jabbed at Bosch's gut. The follower's three victims were porno actresses. And that was Mora's gig. He probably knew them all. The question that was now beginning to push its way into Bosch's mind was, did he kill them all? It bothered him to even think about it, but he knew he had to. Mora was a logical starting point when Bosch considered Locke's advice. The vice cop stood out in Bosch's mind as someone who easily intersected both worlds: the porn trade and the Dollmaker's. Was it just coincidence or enough to classify Mora as an actual suspect? Bosch wasn't sure. He knew he had to proceed as cautiously with an innocent man as he would with a guilty man.

Inside, the place smelled musty. He went directly to the rear sliding door and opened it. He stood there for a moment listening to the hissing sound of traffic coming up from the freeway at the bottom of the pass. The sound never died. No matter what time, what day, there was always traffic down there, blood coursing through the veins of the city.

The light on the answering machine was blinking the number three. Bosch hit rewind and lit a cigarette. The first voice was Sylvia's: 'I just want to say good-night, sweetheart. I love you and be careful.'

Jerry Edgar was next: 'Harry, it's Edgar. Wanted to let you know, I'm off it. Irving called me at home and told me to turn everything I've got over to RHD in the morning. To a Lieutenant Rollenberger. Take care, buddy. And watch six.'

Watch six, Bosch thought. Watch your back. He hadn't heard that one since Vietnam. And he knew Edgar had never been there.

'It's Ray,' the last voice on the tape said. 'I've been thinking about this concrete blonde job and have a few ideas you might be interested in. Call me in the morning and we'll talk.'

FIFTEEN

'I want a continuance.'

'What?'

'You have to get the trial delayed. Tell the judge.'

'What the fuck are you talking about, Bosch?'

Bosch and Belk were sitting at the defense table, waiting for the Thursday morning court session to begin. They were speaking in loud whispers and Bosch thought that when Belk cursed, it came off as sounding too contrived as if he were a sixth-grader trying to fit in with the eighth-graders.

'I am talking about that witness yesterday, Wieczorek, he was right.'

'About what?'

'The alibi, Belk. The alibi on the eleventh victim. It's legit. Church didn't –'

'Wait a minute,' Belk yelped. Then in a low whisper he said, 'If you are about to confess to me that you killed the wrong guy, I don't want to hear it, Bosch. Not now. It's too late.'

He turned back to his legal tablet.

'Belk, listen goddammit, I'm not confessing anything. I got the right guy. But we missed something. Another guy. There were two killers. Church is good for nine – the nine we tied up on the makeup comparisons. The other two, and the one we found in the concrete this week, were done by somebody else. You have to stop this thing until we figure out what exactly is going on. If it comes out in court it will tip the second killer, the follower, to how close we are to him.'

Belk threw his pen down on the pad and it bounced off the table. He didn't get up to get it.

'I'm going to tell you what's going on, Bosch. We are not stopping anything. Even if I wanted to, I probably couldn't – the judge is in her pants. All she needs to do is object and no sale, no delay. So I'm not even going to bring it up. You have to understand something, Bosch, this is a trial. This is the controlling factor of your universe right now. You don't control it. You can't expect the trial to recess every time you need to change your story . . .'

'You finished?'

'Yes, I'm finished.'

'Belk, I understand everything you just said. But we have to protect the investigation. There is another guy out there killing people. And if Chandler puts me or Edgar up there and starts asking questions, the killer is going to read about it and know everything we've got. We'll never get him then. You want that?'

'Bosch, my duty is to win this case. If in doing that, it compromises your –'

'Yeah, but don't you want to know the truth, Belk? I think we're close. Delay it until next week and by then we'll have it together. We'll be able to come in here and blow Money Chandler out of the water.'

Bosch leaned back, away from him. He was tired of fighting him.

'Bosch, how long you been a cop?' Belk asked without looking at him. 'Twenty years?'

That was close. But Bosch didn't answer. He knew what was coming.

'And you're going to sit there and talk to me about truth? When was the last time you saw a truthful police report? When was the last time that you put down the un-adulterated truth in a search warrant application? Don't tell me about truth. You want truth, go see a priest or something. I don't know where to go, but don't come in here. After twenty on the job you should know, the truth has got nothing to do with what goes on in here. Neither does justice. Just words in a law book I read in my previous life.'

Belk turned away and took another pen out of his shirt pocket.

'Okay, Belk, you're the man. But I'm going to tell you how it's going to look when it comes out. It's going to come out in bits and pieces and it will look bad. That's Chandler's specialty. It will look like I hit the wrong guy.'

Belk was ignoring him, writing on his yellow pad.

'You fool, she is going to stick it into us so deep it's going to come out the other side. You keep writing her off as having the judge's hand on her ass, but we both know that's how you deal with the fact that you couldn't carry her lunch. For the last time, get a delay.'

Belk stood up and walked around the table to pick up the fallen pen. After straightening up, he adjusted his tie and his cuffs and sat back down. He leaned over his pad and without looking at Bosch said, 'You're just afraid of her, aren't you, Bosch? Don't want to be on the stand with the cunt asking questions. Questions that might expose you for what you are: a cop who likes killing people.'

Now he turned and looked at Bosch.

'Well, it's too late. Your time has come and there is no backing away. No delays. Show time.'

Harry stood up and bent over the fat man.

'Fuck you, Belk. I'm going outside.'

'That's nice,' Belk said. 'You know, you guys are all the same. You blow some guy away and then come in here and think that just because you wear that badge that you have some kind of a divine right to do whatever you want. That badge is the biggest power trip going.'

Bosch went out to the bank of phones and called Edgar. He picked up on the homicide table after one ring.

'I got your message last night.'

'Yeah, well, that's all there is. I'm gone. RHD came up this morning and took my file. Saw them snoopin' around your spot, too, but they didn't take anything.'

'Who came?'

'Sheehan and Opelt. You know 'em?'

'Yeah, they're okay. You coming over here on the subpoena?'

'Yeah, I gotta be there by ten.'

Bosch saw the door to courtroom 4 open and the deputy marshal leaned out and signaled to him.

'I gotta go.'

Back in the courtroom, Chandler was at the lectern and the judge was speaking. The jury was not in the box yet.

'What about the other subpoenas?' the judge asked.

'Your Honor, my office is in the process of notifying those people this morning, releasing them.'

'Very well, then. Mr Belk, ready to proceed?'

As Bosch came through the gate Belk passed him on the way to the lectern without even looking at him.

'Your Honor, since this is unexpected, I would ask for a half-hour recess so I can consult with my client. We would be ready to proceed after that.'

'Very well, we're going to do exactly that. Recess for a half hour. I'll see all parties back here then. And Mr Bosch? I expect you to be in your place there, the next time I come out ready to begin. I don't like sending marshals up and down the halls when the defendant knows where he ought to be and when he ought to be there.'

Bosch said nothing.

'Sorry, Your Honor,' Belk said for him.

They stood as the judge left the bench and Belk said, 'Let's go down the hall to one of the lawyer-client conference rooms.'

'What happened?'

'Let's go down the hall.'

As he was going through the courtroom door, Bremmer was coming in, holding his notebook and pen.

'Hey, what's happening?'

'I don't know,' Bosch said. 'Half-hour recess.'

'Harry, I have to talk to you.'

'Later.'

'It's important.'

At the end of the hall near the lavatories there were several small attorney conference rooms, all about the size of the interrogation rooms at the Hollywood station. Bosch and Belk went into one and took chairs on either side of a gray table.

'What happened?' Bosch asked.

'Your heroine rested.'

'Chandler rested without calling me?'

This seemed to make no sense to Bosch.

'What's she doing?' he asked.

'She's being extremely shrewd. It's a very smart move.'

'Why?'

'Look at the case. She is in very good shape. If it ended today and went to the jury, who would win? She would. See, she knows you have to get on the stand and defend what you did. Like I told you the other day, we win or lose with you. You either take the ball and ram it down her throat or you fumble it. She knows that and if she was to call you, she would ask the questions first, then I would come in with the fungoes – the easy ones that you'd hit out of the park.

'Now she's reversing that. My choice is to not call you and lose the case, or to call you and essentially give her the best shot at you. Very shrewd.'

'So what are we going to do?'

'Call you.'

'What about the delay?'

'What delay?'

Bosch nodded. There was no changing it. There would be no delay. He realized he had handled it badly. He had approached Belk the wrong way. He should have tried to make Belk believe it had been his own idea to go for a delay. Then it would have worked. Instead, Bosch was beginning to feel the jitters – that uneasy feeling that came with approaching the unknown. He felt the way he did before he climbed down into a VC tunnel for the first time in Vietnam. It was fear, he knew, blossoming like a black rose in the pit of his chest.

'We've got twenty-five minutes,' Belk said. 'Let's forget about delays and try to work out how we want your testimony to go. I am going to lead you down the path. The jury will follow. But remember, you have to take it slow or you will lose them. Okay?'

'We got twenty minutes,' Bosch corrected him. 'I need to go out for a smoke before I sit up there on the stand.'

Belk pressed on as if he hadn't heard.

'Remember, Bosch, there could be millions of dollars at stake here. It may not be your money but it may be your career.'

'What career?'

Bremmer was hanging around the door to the conference room when Bosch came out twenty minutes later.

'Get it all?' Harry asked.

He walked by him and headed toward the escalator. Bremmer followed.

'No, man, I wasn't listening. I'm just waiting for you. Listen, what's going on with the new case? Edgar won't tell me shit. Did you get an ID or what?'

'Yeah, we ID'd her.'

'Who was it?'

'Not my case, man. I can't give it out. Besides, I give it to you and you'll run to Money Chandler with it, right?'

Bremmer stopped walking beside him.

'What? What are you talking about?'

Then he scurried up to Bosch's side and whispered.

'Listen, Harry, you're one of my main sources. I wouldn't screw you like that. If she's getting inside shit, look for somebody else.'

Bosch felt bad about accusing the reporter. He'd had no evidence.

'You sure? I'm mistaken about this, right?'

'Absolutely. You're too valuable to me. I wouldn't do it.'

'Okay, then.'

That was as close as he'd come to an apology.

'So what can you tell me about the ID?'

'Nothing. It's still not my case. Try RHD.'

'RHD has it? They took it from Edgar?'

Bosch got on the escalator and looked back at him. He nodded as he went down. Bremmer didn't follow.

Money Chandler was already on the steps smoking when Bosch came out. He lit a cigarette and looked back at her.

'Surprise, surprise,' he said.

'What?'

'Resting.'

'Only a surprise to Bulk,' she said. 'Any other lawyer would have seen it coming. I almost feel sorry for you, Bosch. Almost, but not quite. In a civil rights case, the chances of a win are always a long shot. But going up against the city attorney's office always kind of levels the playing field. These guys like Bulk, they couldn't make it on the outside. . . . If he had to win in order to eat, your lawyer would be a thin man. He needs that steady paycheck from the city coming in, win or lose.'

What she said, of course, was correct. But it was old news. Bosch smiled. He didn't know how to act. A part of himself liked her. She was wrong about him, but somehow he liked her. Maybe it was her tenacity, because her anger – though misdirected – was so pure.

Maybe it was because she wasn't afraid to talk to him outside of court. He had seen how Belk studiously avoided coming in contact with Church's family. Before getting up during recesses, he would sit at the defendant's table until he was sure they were all safely down the hall and on the escalator. But Chandler didn't play that kind of game. She was an up-front player.

Bosch guessed that this was what it was like when two

boxers touched gloves before the bell. He changed the subject.

'I talked to Tommy Faraday out here the other day. He's Tommy Faraway now. I asked him what happened but he didn't say. He just said justice happened, whatever that means.'

She blew a long stream of blue smoke out but didn't say anything for a while. Bosch looked at his watch. They had three minutes.

'You remember the Galton case?' she said. 'It was a civil rights case, an excessive force.'

Bosch thought about it. The name was familiar but it was difficult to place in the blend of excessive force cases he had heard or known about over the years.

'It was a dog case, right?'

'Yes. André Galton. This was before Rodney King, back when the wide majority of people in this city did not believe that their police engaged in horrible abuses as a matter of routine. Galton was black and driving with an expired tag through the hills of Studio City when a cop decided to pull him over.

'He had done nothing wrong, wasn't wanted, just had the tag one month overdue. But he ran. Great mystery of life, he ran. He got all the way up to Mulholland and ditched the car at one of those pull-offs where people look out at the view. Then he jumped out and climbed down the incline. There was nowhere to go down there but he wouldn't come back up and the cops wouldn't go down – too dangerous, they claimed at the trial.'

Bosch remembered the story now but he let her tell it. Her indignation was so pure and stripped of lawyerly pose that he just wanted to hear her tell it.

'So they sent a dog down,' she said. 'Galton lost both testicles and had permanent nerve damage to the right leg. He could walk but he had to kind of drag it behind him. . . .'

'Enter Tommy Faraday,' Bosch prompted.

'Yeah, he took the case. It was dead bang. Galton had done nothing wrong but to run. The response of the police certainly did not meet the offense. Any jury would see this. And the city attorney's office knew this. In fact, I think it was Bulk's case. They offered half a million to settle and Faraday passed. He thought he'd get a minimum three times that in trial, so he passed.

'And like I said, this was in the old days. Civil rights lawyers call it BK, that's short for Before King. A jury listened to four days of evidence and found for the cops in thirty minutes. Galton got nothing but a dead leg and a dead dick out of the whole thing. He came out here afterward and went to that hedge right there. He had hidden a gun – wrapped it in plastic and buried it there. He came over to the statue here and put the gun in his mouth. Faraday was coming through the door just then and saw it happen. Blood all over the statue, everywhere.'

Bosch didn't say anything. He remembered the case very clearly now. He looked up at the City Hall tower and watched the gulls circling above it. He always wondered what drew them there. It was miles from the ocean but there were always seabirds on top of City Hall. Chandler kept talking.

'Two things I've always been curious about,' she said. 'One, why did Galton run? And, two, why did he hide the gun? And I think the answers are both the same. He had no faith in justice, in the system. No hope. He had done nothing wrong but he ran because he was a black man in a white neighborhood and he had heard the stories all his life about what white cops do to black men in that position. His lawyer told him he had a dead-bang case, but he brought a gun to the courthouse because he had heard all his life about what jurors decide when it's a black man's word against the cops.'

Bosch looked at his watch. It was time to go in but he did not want to walk away from her.

'So that's why Tommy said justice happened,' she said.

'That was justice for André Galton. Faraday referred all his cases to other lawyers after that. I took a few. And he never set foot in a courtroom again.'

She stubbed out what was left of her cigarette.

'End of story,' she said.

'I'm sure the civil rights lawyers tell that one a lot,' Bosch said. 'And now you put me and Church into that, is that it? I'm like the guy who sent the dog down the hill after Galton?'

'There are degrees, Detective Bosch. Even if Church was the monster you claim, he didn't have to die. If the system turns away from the abuses inflicted on the guilty, then who can be next but the innocents? You see, that's why I have to do what I'm going to do to you in there. For the innocents.'

'Well, good luck,' he said.

He put his own cigarette out.

'I won't need it,' she said.

Bosch followed her gaze to the statue above the spot where Galton had killed himself. Chandler looked at it as if the blood were still there.

'That's justice,' she said, nodding at the statue. 'She doesn't hear you. She doesn't see you. She can't feel you and won't speak to you. Justice, Detective Bosch, is just a concrete blonde.'

SIXTEEN

The courtroom seemed as silent as a dead man's heart while Bosch walked behind the plaintiff and defendant tables and in front of the jury box to get to the witness stand. After taking the oath he gave his full name and the clerk asked him to spell it.

'H-I-E-R-O-N-Y-M-U-S B-O-S-C-H.'

Then the judge turned it over to Belk.

'Tell us a little bit about yourself, Detective Bosch, about your career.'

'I've been a police officer nearly twenty years. I currently am assigned to the homicide table at Hollywood Division. Before that –'

'Why do they call it a table?'

Jesus, Bosch thought.

'Because it's like a table. It is six small desks pushed together to make a long table, three detectives on each side. It's always called a table.'

'Okay, go on.'

'Before this assignment I spent eight years in Robbery-Homicide Division's Homicide Special squad. Before that I was a detective on the homicide table in North Hollywood and robbery and burglary tables in Van Nuys. I was on patrol about five years, mostly in the Hollywood and Wilshire divisions.'

Belk slowly led him through his career up until the time he was on the Dollmaker task force. The questioning was slow and boring – even to Bosch, and it was his life. Every now and then he would look at the jurors when he answered a question and only a few seemed to be looking at him or paying attention. Bosch felt nervous and his palms were damp. He had testified in court at least a hundred times. But never like this, in his own defense. He felt hot though he knew the courtroom was overly cool.

'Now where was the task force physically located?'

'We used a second-floor storage room at the Hollywood station. It was an evidence and file storage room. We temporarily moved that stuff out into a rented trailer and used the room. We also had a room at Parker Center. The night shift, which I was on, generally worked out of Hollywood.'

'You were closer to the source, correct?'

'We thought so, yes. Most of the victims were taken from Hollywood streets. Many were later found in the area.'

'So you wanted to be able to act quickly on tips and leads and being right there in the center of things helped you do that, correct?'

'Correct.'

'On the night you got the call from the woman named Dixie McQueen, how did you get that call?'

'She called in on nine one one and when the dispatcher realized what she was talking about, the call was transferred out to the task force in Hollywood.'

'Who answered it?'

'I did.'

'Why is that? I thought you testified you were the supervisor of the night shift. Didn't they have people answering phones?'

'Yes, we had people, but this call came in late. Everybody had left for the night. I was only there because I was bringing the Chronological Investigation Record up to date – we had to turn it in at the end of each week. I was the only one there. I answered.'

'When you went to meet this woman, why didn't you call for a backup?'

'She hadn't told me enough over the phone to convince

me there was anything to it. We were getting dozens of calls a day. None of them amounted to anything. I have to admit I went to take her report not believing it would amount to anything.'

'Well, if you thought that, Detective, why did you go to her? Why not just take her information over the phone?'

'The main reason was that she said she didn't know the address she had been to with this man, but could show me the place if I drove her down Hyperion. Also, there seemed to be something genuine about her complaint, you know? It seemed that something had definitely scared her. I was about to head home so I thought I would just check it out on the way.'

'Tell us what happened after you got to Hyperion.'

'When we got there we could see lights on in the apartment over the garage. We even saw a shadow pass across one of the windows. So we knew the guy was still there. That's when Miss McQueen told me about the makeup she saw in the cabinet under the sink.'

'What did that mean to you?'

'A lot. It immediately got my attention because we had never said in the press that the killer was keeping the victims' makeup. It had leaked that he was painting their faces but not that he also kept their makeup. So when she told me she had seen this collection of makeup, it all clicked. It gave what she said some immediate legitimacy.'

Bosch drank some water from a paper cup the marshal had filled for him earlier.

'Okay, what did you do next?' Belk said.

'It occurred to me that in the time it had taken her to call me and for me to pick her up and get back to Hyperion, he could have gone out and gotten another victim. So I knew there was a good chance there was another woman up there in danger. I went up. I ran up.'

'Why didn't you call for backup?'

'First of all, I did not believe there was time to wait even five minutes for backup. If he had another woman in there, five minutes could mean her life. Secondly, I did not have a rover with me. I couldn't make the call even if I wanted to –'

'A rover?'

'A portable radio. Detectives usually take them on assignment. Problem is, there are not enough of them to go around. And since I was going home I didn't want to take one because I wasn't coming back until the next evening shift. That would mean one less rover available during the next day.'

'So you couldn't radio for backup. What about a phone?'

'It was a residential neighborhood. I could drive out and find a pay phone or knock on somebody's door. It was about one A.M. and I didn't think people would open their doors quickly to a single man claiming to be a police officer. Everything was a question of time. I didn't believe I had any. I had to go up by myself.'

'What happened?'

'Believing someone was in imminent danger, I went through the door without knocking. I was holding my gun out.'

'Kicked it open?'

'Yes.'

'What did you see?'

'First of all, I announced myself. I yelled, "Police". I moved a few steps into the room – it was a studio apartment – and I saw the man later identified as Church standing next to the bed. It was a foldout bed from a couch.'

'What was he doing?'

'He was standing there naked, next to the bed.'

'Did you see anyone else?'

'No.'

'What next?'

'I yelled something along the lines of "Freeze" or "Don't move" and took another step into the room. At first he didn't move. Then he suddenly reached down to the bed and his hand swept under the pillow. I yelled, "No," but he continued the movement. I could see his arm move as if his hand had grasped something and he started bringing the hand out. I fired one time. It killed him.'

'How far away from him would you say you were?'

'I was twenty feet away. It was one big room. We were at opposite sides of it.'

'And did he die instantly?'

'Very quickly. He dropped across the bed. The autopsy later showed the bullet entered under the right arm – the one he was reaching under the pillow with – and crossed through the chest. It hit his heart and both lungs.'

'After he was down, what did you do?'

'I went to the bed and checked to see if he was alive. He was still alive at that point, so I handcuffed him. He died a few moments later. I lifted the pillow. There was no gun.'

'What was there?'

Looking directly at Chandler, Bosch said, 'Great mystery of life, he had been reaching for a toupee.'

Chandler had her head down and was busy writing but she stopped and looked up at him and their eyes locked momentarily until she said, 'Objection, Your Honor.'

The judge agreed to strike Bosch's comment about the mystery of life. Belk asked a few more questions about the shooting scene and then moved on to the investigation of Church.

'You were no longer part of that, correct?'

'No, as is routine I was assigned desk duty while my actions in the shooting were investigated.'

'Well, were you made aware of the results of the task force's investigation into Church's background?'

'Generally. Because I had a stake in the outcome, I was kept informed.'

'What did you learn?'

'That the makeup found in the bathroom cabinet was tied to nine of the victims.'

'Did you ever have any doubts yourself or hear of any doubts from other investigators as to whether Norman Church was responsible for the deaths of those women?'

'For those nine? No, no doubts at all. Ever.'

'Well, Detective Bosch, you heard Mr Wieczorek testify about being with Mr Church on the night the eleventh victim, Shirleen Kemp, was killed. You saw the videotape presented as evidence. Didn't that raise any doubts?'

'It does about that case. But Shirleen Kemp was not among the nine whose makeup was found in Church's apartment. There is no doubt in my mind or in anybody's on the task force that Church killed those nine women.'

Chandler objected to Bosch speaking for the rest of the task force and the judge sustained it. Belk changed the subject, not wanting to venture any further into the area of victims seven and eleven. His strategy was to avoid any reference to a second killer, leaving that to Chandler to take a swing at on cross-examination, if she wanted to.

'You were disciplined for not going in with backup. Do you feel the department handled the matter correctly?'

'No.'

'How so?'

'As I explained, I did not believe I had a choice in what I did. If I had to do it again – even knowing I would be transferred as a result – I would do the same thing. I would have to. If there had been another woman in there, another victim, and I had saved her, I probably would have been promoted.'

When Belk didn't immediately ask a follow-up question, Bosch continued.

'I believe the transfer was a political necessity. The bottom line was, I shot an unarmed man. It did not matter that the man I shot was a serial killer, a monster. Besides, I was carrying baggage from –'

'That will be fine –'

'Run-ins with –'

'Detective Bosch.'

Bosch stopped. He had made his point.

'So what you are saying is you don't have any regrets about what happened in the apartment, correct?'

'No, that's not correct.'

This apparently surprised Belk. He looked down at his notes. He had asked a question he expected a different reply to. But he realized he had to follow through.

'What do you regret?'

'That Church made that move. He drew the fire. There was nothing I could do but respond. I wanted to stop the killings. I didn't want to kill him to do that. But that's the way it turned out. It was his play.'

Belk showed his relief by breathing heavily into the microphone before saying he had no further questions.

Judge Keyes said there would be a ten-minute break before cross-examination began. Bosch returned to the defense table, where Belk whispered that he thought they had done well. Bosch didn't respond.

'I think everything is going to ride on her cross. If you can get through it without heavy damage I think we've got it.'

'What about when she brings up the follower, introduces the note?'

'I don't see how she can. If she does, she'll be flying blind.'

'No, she won't. She's got a source in the department. Someone fed her stuff about the note.'

'I'll ask for a sidebar conference if it gets to that point.'

That wasn't very encouraging. Bosch looked at the clock, trying to gauge whether he had time for a smoke. He didn't think so and got up and went back to the witness stand. He passed behind Chandler, who was writing on a legal pad.

'Great mystery of life,' she said without looking up.

'Yeah,' Bosch said without looking back at her.

As he sat and waited, he saw Bremmer come in, followed by the guy from the *Daily News* and a couple of wire service reporters. Somebody had put out the word that the top act was about to begin. Cameras were not allowed in federal court, so one of the stations had sent a sketch artist over.

From the witness seat, Bosch watched Chandler working. He guessed she was writing out questions for him.

Deborah Church sat next to her with her hands folded on the table, her eyes averted from Bosch. A minute later the door to the jury room opened and the jurors filed into the box. Then the judge came out. Bosch took a deep breath and got ready as Chandler walked to the lectern with her yellow pad.

'Mr Bosch,' she began, 'how many people have you killed?'

Belk immediately objected and asked for a sidebar. The attorneys and the court reporter moved to the side of the bench and whispered for five minutes. Bosch only heard bits and pieces, most of it from Belk, who was loudest. At one point he argued that one shooting only was in dispute – the Church slaying – and all others were irrelevant. He heard Chandler say that the information was relevant because it illustrated the mind-set of the defendant. Bosch couldn't hear the judge's response but after the attorneys and reporter were back in place, the judge said, 'The defendant will answer the question.'

'I can't,' Bosch replied.

'Detective Bosch, the court is ordering you to answer.'

'I can't answer it, Judge. I don't know how many people I've killed.'

'You served in combat in Vietnam?' Chandler asked.

'Yes.'

'What were your duties?'

'Tunnel rat. I went into the enemy's tunnels. Sometimes this resulted in direct confrontation. Sometimes I used explosives to destroy tunnel complexes. It's impossible for me to know how many people were in them.'

'Okay, Detective, since you finished your duties with the armed services and became a police officer, how many people have you killed?'

'Three, including Norman Church.'

'Can you tell us about the two incidents not involving Mr Church? In general.'

'Yes, one was before Church, the other after. The first

time I killed someone it was during a murder investigation. I went to question a man I thought was a witness. Turned out he was the killer. When I knocked on the door, he fired a shot through it. Missed me. I kicked the door open and went in. I heard him running toward the rear of the house. I followed him to the yard, where he was climbing over a fence. As he was about to go over, he twisted around to take another shot at me. I fired first and he went down.

'The second time, this was after Church, I was involved in a murder and robbery investigation with the FBI. There was a shoot-out between two suspects and myself and my partner at the time, an FBI agent. I killed one of the suspects.'

'So in those two cases, the men you killed were armed?'

'That is correct.'

'Three shootings involving deaths, that is quite a lot, even for a twenty-year veteran, isn't it?'

Bosch waited a beat for Belk to make an objection but the fat man was too busy writing on his tablet. He had missed it.

'Um, I know twenty-year cops who have never even had to draw their guns, and I know some that have been involved in as many as seven deaths. It's a matter of what kind of cases you draw, it's a matter of luck.'

'Good luck or bad luck?'

This time Belk objected and the judge sustained it. Chandler quickly went on.

'After you killed Mr Church while he was unarmed, did you feel badly about it?'

'Not really. Not until I got sued and heard you were the lawyer.'

There was laughter in the courtroom and even Honey Chandler smiled. After he had quieted the room with a sharp rebuke from his gavel, the judge instructed Bosch to keep his answers on point and to refrain from personal asides.

'No bad feelings,' Bosch said. 'Like I said before, I would rather have taken Church alive than dead. But I wanted to take him off the street, either way.'

'But you set the whole thing up, tactically, so that it had to end in his permanent removal, didn't you?'

'No, I didn't. Nothing was set up. Things just happened.'

Bosch knew better than to show any anger toward her. Rather than make angry denouncements, the rule of thumb was to answer each question as if he was dealing with a person who was simply mistaken.

'You were, however, satisfied that Mr Church had been killed while unarmed, nude, totally defenseless?'

'Satisfaction doesn't enter into it.'

'Your Honor,' Chandler said. 'May I approach the witness with an exhibit? It's marked plaintiff's 3A.'

She handed copies of a piece of paper to Belk and the judge's clerk, who handed it over the bench to the judge. While the judge was reading it, Belk went to the lectern and objected.

'Your Honor, if this is offered as impeachment, I don't see how it is valid. These are the words of a psychiatrist, not my client.'

Chandler moved to the microphone and said, 'Judge, if you look in the section marked Summary, the last paragraph is what I would like to be read by the witness. You will also notice that the defendant signed the statement at the bottom.'

Judge Keyes read some more, wiped his mouth with the back of his hand and said, 'I'll accept it. You may show it to the witness.'

Chandler brought another copy up to Bosch and placed it in front of him without looking at him. Then she walked back to the lectern.

'Can you tell us what that is, Detective Bosch?'

'It's a confidential psychological release form. Supposedly confidential, I guess I should say.'

'Yes, and what does it relate to?'

'My release allowing me to return to duty after the Church shooting. It is routine to be interviewed by the department's psychiatrist after being involved in a shooting. Then he clears you to return to duty.'

'You must know him well.'

'Excuse me?'

'Ms Chandler, that's not necessary,' Judge Keyes said before Belk got up.

'No, Your Honor. Strike that. You were cleared to return to duty – to your new assignment in Hollywood – after the interview, correct?'

'Correct.'

'Isn't it true that this is really nothing more than a rubber-stamp process? The psychiatrist never holds an officer back from returning on psychiatric grounds?'

'No on the first question. I don't know on the second.'

'Well, let me turn it around. Have you ever heard of an officer being held back by the psychiatric interview?'

'No, I haven't. They're supposed to be confidential so I doubt I would hear anything anyway.'

'Will you please read the last paragraph of the summary section on the report in front of you?'

'Yes.'

He picked up the paper and began reading. Silently.

'Out loud, Detective Bosch,' she said in an exasperated tone. 'I thought that was implicit in the question.'

'Sorry. It says: "Through his war and police experiences, most notably including the aforementioned shooting resulting in fatality, the subject has to a high degree become desensitized to violence. He speaks in terms of violence or the aspect of violence being an accepted part of his day-to-day life, for all of his life. Therefore, it is unlikely that what transpired previously will act as a psychological deterrent should he again be placed in circumstances where he must act with deadly force in order to protect himself or others. I believe he will be able to act without delay. He will be able to pull the trigger. In fact, his conversation reveals no ill effects at all from the shooting, unless his sense of satisfaction with the outcome of the incident – the suspect's death – should be deemed inappropriate." '

Bosch put the paper down. He noticed the entire jury was looking at him now. He had no idea whether the report was highly damaging or helpful to his cause.

'The subject of that report is you, correct?' Chandler asked.

'Yes, it's me.'

'You just testified that there was no satisfaction, but the report by the psychiatrist said you did feel a sense of satisfaction with the outcome of the incident. Which is right?'

'Those are his words on the report, not mine. I don't think I would have said that.'

'What would you have said?'

'I don't know. Not that.'

'Then why did you sign the release form?'

'I signed it because I wanted to get back to work. If I was going to argue with him about what words he used, I was never going to get back to work.'

'Tell me, Detective, did the psychiatrist who examined you and made that report know about your mother?'

Bosch hesitated.

'I don't know,' he finally answered. 'I didn't tell him. I don't know if he would have had the information previously.'

He could hardly concentrate on his words, for his mind was scrambling.

'What happened to your mother?'

He looked directly at Chandler for a long moment before answering. She didn't look away.

'As was testified to earlier, she was killed. I was eleven. It happened in Hollywood.'

'And no one was ever arrested, correct?'

'That is correct. Can we go on to something else? This has already been testified about.'

Bosch looked over at Belk who got the point and stood up and objected to Chandler's repetitive line of questioning.

'Detective Bosch, do you want a break?' Judge Keyes asked. 'To sort of calm down a little?'

'No, Judge, I'm fine.'

'Well, I'm sorry. I can't restrict proper cross-examination. The objection is overruled.'

The judge nodded to Chandler.

'I'm sorry to ask such personal questions, but, after she was gone, did your father raise you?'

'You're not sorry. You –'

'Detective Bosch!' the judge boomed. 'We cannot have this. You must answer the questions asked of you. Say nothing else. Just answer the questions.'

'No. I never knew my father. I was put in the youth hall and then foster homes.'

'Any brothers or sisters?'

'No.'

'So the man who strangled your mother not only took the one closest to you, he destroyed much of your life at that point?'

'I'd say so.'

'Did the crime have something to do with your becoming a policeman?'

Bosch found he could no longer look at the jury. He knew his face had turned red. And he felt as if he were dying under a magnifying glass.

'I don't know. I never really analyzed myself to that extent.'

'Did it have something to do with the satisfaction you felt in killing Mr Church?'

'As I said before, if there was any satisfaction – you keep using that word – it was that I was satisfied with closing the case. To use your word, the man was a monster. He was a killer. I was satisfied we stopped him, wouldn't you be?'

'You're answering the questions, Detective Bosch,'

Chandler said. 'The question I now have is, did you stop the killings? All of them?'

Belk jumped up and asked for a sidebar conference. The judge said to the jurors, 'We're going to take that break now after all. We'll call you back when we're ready.'

SEVENTEEN

Belk asked for a discussion of his objection to Chandler's question out of earshot of the press, so the judge convened a hearing in his chambers. The hearing included the judge, Chandler, Belk, Bosch, the court reporter and the court clerk. They had to drag a couple of chairs in from the courtroom, then they all took places around the judge's huge desk. It was dark mahogany and looked like a box a small foreign car could have come in.

The first thing the judge did was light a cigarette. When Bosch saw Chandler follow suit, he did the same. The judge pushed the ashtray on his desk to the corner so they all could get at it.

'So, Mr Belk, it's your party,' the judge said.

'Your Honor, I am concerned with the direction Miss Chandler is taking this.'

'Call her Ms Chandler, Mr Belk. You know she prefers it. As far as which way she's going, how can you tell from one question?'

It was obvious to Bosch that Belk may have objected too soon. It was unclear how much information Chandler had, aside from the note. But Bosch thought Belk's tap-dancing around the problem was a waste of time.

'Judge,' he said. 'If I answer that last question it will compromise an ongoing investigation.'

The judge leaned back in his padded leather chair.

'How so?' he asked.

'We believe there is another killer,' Bosch said. 'The body found this week was identified yesterday and it has been determined that she could not have been killed by Church. She was alive up until two years ago. The –'

'The method used by the killer was identical to that of the real Dollmaker,' Belk interjected. 'The police believe there is a follower, someone who knew how Church killed and followed the same pattern. There is evidence to suggest the follower was responsible for the seventh and eleventh victims previously attributed to Church.'

Bosch said, 'The follower would have to be someone close to the original investigation, someone who knew the details.'

Belk said, 'If you allow her to open this line of questioning, it will be reported by the media and it will tip off the follower. He will know how close he is to being revealed.'

The judge was silent as he considered all of this for a moment.

'That all sounds real interesting and I wish you all the best of luck catching this follower, as you call him,' he finally said. 'But the problem you have, Mr Belk, is that you haven't given me any legal reason to stop your client from answering the question Ms Chandler put to him. No one wants to compromise an investigation. But you put your client on the stand.'

'That's if there is a second killer,' Chandler said. 'It's obvious there was only one killer and it wasn't Church. They've come up with this elaborate –'

'Ms Chandler,' the judge interrupted. 'That's for the jury to decide. Save your argument for them. Mr Belk, the problem is this is your witness. You called him and you've left him open to this line of questioning. I don't know what to tell you. I'm certainly not going to clear the media out of there. Off the record here, Miss Penny.'

The judge watched the court reporter lift her fingers from the keys.

'Mr Belk, you're fucked – 'scuse the language, ladies. He's gonna answer the question and the one after that and the one after that. Okay, we're back on.'

The reporter put her fingers back on the keys.

'Your Honor, this can't –'

'I've made my ruling, Mr Belk. Anything else?'

Belk then surprised Bosch.

'We would like a continuance.'

'What?'

'Your Honor, plaintiff opposes,' Chandler said.

'I know you do,' the judge said. 'What are you talking about, Mr Belk?'

'Your Honor, you have to put the trial on hiatus. Until at least next week. It will give the investigation time to possibly come to some fruition.'

'Some fruition? Forget it, Belk. You're in the middle of a trial, my friend.'

Belk stood and leaned across the great wide desk.

'Your Honor, I request an emergency stay of these proceedings while we take the matter on appeal to the ninth district.'

'You can appeal anything you like, Mr Belk, but there is no stay. We're in trial here.'

There was silence as everyone looked at Belk.

'What if I refuse to answer?' Bosch asked.

Judge Keyes looked at him a long moment and said, 'Then I'll hold you in contempt. Then I'll ask you to answer again and if you refuse again I will put you in jail. Then when your attorney here asks for bail while he appeals, I will say no bail. All of this will take place out there in front of the jury and the media folks. And I will place no restrictions on what Ms Chandler does or doesn't say to the reporters in the hallway. So, what I am saying is, you can try to be some kind of hero and not answer, but the story will get to the media anyway. It's like I said a few minutes ago to Mr Belk when we were off the rec –'

'You can't do this,' Belk suddenly erupted. 'It, it – it's not right. You have to protect this investigation. You –'

'Son, don't you ever tell me what I have to do,' the judge said very slowly and sternly. He seemed to grow in stature while Belk shrank back away from him. 'Only thing I have to do is ensure there is a fair trial on this matter. You are asking me to sit on information that could be vital to the plaintiff's case. You are also trying to intimidate me and that is one thing I don't take to. I'm no county judge that needs your nod every time an election comes 'round. I'm appointed for life. We're off here.'

Miss Penny stopped typing. Bosch almost didn't want to see Belk's slaughter. The deputy city attorney's head was bowed and he had assumed the posture of the doomed. The back of his neck was turned up and ready to receive the axe.

'So my advice here is that you get your fat ass out there and start working on how the hell you're going to salvage this on redirect. Because in five minutes Detective Bosch is going to answer that question or he's going to be handing his gun and his badge and his belt and shoelaces over to a marshal at the federal lockup. We're back on. Hearing adjourned.'

Judge Keyes brought his arm down and ground his cigarette into the ashtray. He never took his eyes off Belk.

As the procession made its way back into the courtroom, Bosch moved up closely behind Chandler. He glanced back to make sure the judge had turned to go to the bench and then said in a low voice, 'If you're getting your information from inside the department, I'm going to burn your source down when I find him.'

She didn't miss a stride. She didn't even turn back when she said, 'You mean, if you're not already ashes.'

Bosch took his place at the witness stand and the jury was brought back in. The judge told Chandler to continue.

'Rather than have the reporter find the last question, let me just rephrase it. After you killed Mr Church, did the so-called Dollmaker killings stop?'

Bosch hesitated, thinking. He looked out into the spectator section and saw that there were more reporters now – or at least people he thought were reporters. They all sat together.

He also saw Sylvia, sitting in the back row by herself. She offered a small smile to him which he did not return. He wondered how long she had been out there.

'Detective Bosch?' the judge prompted.

'I can't answer the question without compromising an ongoing investigation,' Bosch finally said.

'Detective Bosch, we just went over this,' the judge said angrily. 'Answer the question.'

Bosch knew that his refusal and jailing would not stop the story from getting out. Chandler would tell all the reporters as the judge had given her the okay to do. So putting himself in jail, he knew, only stopped him from chasing the follower. He decided to answer. He carefully composed a statement while stalling by taking a long, slow drink of water from the paper cup.

'Norman Church obviously stopped killing people after he was dead. But there was somebody – there is somebody else still out there. A killer who uses the same methods as Norman Church.'

'Thank you, Mr Bosch. And when did you come to that conclusion?'

'This week, when another body was found.'

'Who was that victim?'

'A woman named Rebecca Kaminski. She had been missing two years.'

'The details of her death matched the murders of the other Dollmaker victims?'

'Exactly, except for one thing.'

'And that was what?'

'She had been entombed in concrete. Hidden. Norman Church always discarded his victims in public places.'

'No other differences?'

'Not that I know of at the moment.'

'Yet, because she died two years after Norman Church was killed by you, there is no way possible that he is responsible.'

'Correct.'

'Because he was dead he has the perfect alibi, doesn't he?'

'Correct.'

'How was the body found?'

'As I said, it had been buried in concrete.'

'And what led police to the spot where it was buried?'

'We received a note with directions.'

Chandler then offered a copy of the note as plaintiff's exhibit 4A and Judge Keyes accepted it after overruling an objection by Belk. Chandler then handed a copy to Bosch to identify and read.

'Out loud this time,' she said before he could start. 'For the jury.'

Bosch felt eerie reading the words of the follower out loud in the quiet courtroom. After a beat of silence when he was done, Chandler began again.

' "I'm still in the game," he writes. What does that mean?'

'It means he is trying to take credit for all of the killings. He wants attention.'

'Could that be because he committed all of the murders?'

'No, because Norman Church committed nine of them. The evidence found in Church's apartment irrefutably links him to those nine. There is no doubt.'

'Who found this evidence?'

Bosch said, 'Me.'

'So, then, isn't there a lot of doubt, Detective Bosch? Isn't this idea of a second killer who uses the exact same method preposterous?'

'No, it's not preposterous. It is happening. I did not kill the wrong man.'

'Isn't it the truth that this talk of a copycat killer, a follower, is all an elaborate charade for covering up the fact that you did exactly that, killed the wrong man? An innocent, unarmed man who had done nothing worse than hire a prostitute with his wife's tacit approval?'

'No, it's not. Norman Church killed –'

'Thank you, Mr Bosch.'

'– a lot of women. He was a monster.'

'Like the one who killed your mother?'

He unconsciously looked out into the audience, saw Sylvia and then looked away. He tried to compose himself, slow his breathing. He was not going to let Chandler tear him open.

'I would say yes. They were probably similar. Both monsters.'

'That's why you killed him, wasn't it? The toupee wasn't under the pillow. You killed him in cold blood because you saw your mother's killer.'

'No. You are wrong. Don't you think if I was going to make up a story I could come up with something better than a toupee? There was a kitchenette, knives in the drawer. Why would I plant –'

'Hold it, hold it, hold it,' Judge Keyes barked. 'Now, we've gone off the tracks here. Ms Chandler, you started making statements instead of asking questions and, Detective Bosch, you did the same thing instead of answering. Let's start over.'

'Yes, Your Honor,' Chandler said. 'Isn't it true, Detective Bosch, that the whole thing – this pinning all the murders on Norman Church – was an elaborate cover-up that is now unraveling with the discovery of the woman in the concrete this week?'

'No, it is not true. Nothing is unraveling. Church was a killer and he deserved what he got.'

Bosch mentally flinched and closed his eyes as soon as the words were out of his mouth. She had done it. He opened his eyes and looked at Chandler. Her eyes seemed flat and blank, emotionless.

Softly, she said, 'You say he deserved what he got. When were you appointed judge, jury and executioner?'

Bosch drank more water from the cup.

'What I meant was that it was his play. Whatever happened to him, he was ultimately responsible. You put something in play like that and you have to accept the consequences.'

'Like Rodney King deserved what he got?'

'Objection!' Belk shouted.

'Like André Galton deserved what he got?'

'Objection!'

'Sustained, sustained,' the judge said. 'All right now, Ms Chandler, you –'

'They're not the same.'

'Detective Bosch, I sustained the objections. That means don't answer.'

'No further questions at this time, Your Honor,' Chandler said.

Bosch watched her walk to the plaintiff's table and drop her tablet onto the wooden surface. The loose strand of hair was there at the back of her neck. He was sure now that even that detail was part of her carefully planned and orchestrated performance during the trial. After she sat down, Deborah Church reached over and squeezed her arm. Chandler didn't smile or make any gesture in return.

Belk did what he could to repair the damage on redirect examination, asking more details about the heinous nature of the crimes, and the shooting and investigation of Church. But it seemed as if no one was listening. The courtroom had been sucked into a vacuum created by Chandler's cross-examination.

Belk was apparently so ineffective that Chandler didn't bother to ask anything on recross and Bosch was excused from the witness seat. He felt as if the walk back to the defense table covered at least a mile.

'Next witness, Mr Belk?' the judge asked.

'Your Honor, can I have a few minutes?'

'Surely.'

Belk turned to Bosch and whispered, 'We're going to rest, you have a problem with that?'

'I don't know.'

'There is no one else to call, unless you want to get other members of the task force over here. They'll say the same thing you did and get the same treatment from Chandler. I'd rather leave that alone.'

'What about bringing Locke back? He'll back me up on everything I said about the follower.'

'Too risky. He is a psychologist, for everything we get him to say is a possibility, she'll also get him to concede it is possibly not. He hasn't been deposed on this matter and we won't know for sure what he would say. Besides, I think we need to stay off the second killer. It's confusing the jury and we –'

'Mr Belk,' the judge said. 'We're waiting.'

Belk stood up and said, 'Your Honor, the defense rests.'

The judge stared a long moment at Belk before turning to the jury and telling them they were excused for the day because the lawyers would need the afternoon to prepare closing arguments and he would need time to prepare jury instructions.

After the jury filed out, Chandler went to the lectern. She asked for a directed verdict in favor of the plaintiff, which the judge denied. Belk did the same thing, asking for a verdict in favor of the defendant. In a seemingly sarcastic tone, the judge told him to sit down.

Bosch met Sylvia in the hallway outside after the crowded courtroom took several minutes to empty. There was a large gathering of reporters around the two lawyers and Bosch took her arm and moved her down the hall.

'I told you not to come here, Sylvia.'

'I know, but I felt I had to come. I wanted you to know that I support you no matter what. Harry, I know things about you the jury will never know. No matter how she tries to portray you, I know you. Don't forget that.'

She was wearing a black dress with a silvery-white pattern that Bosch liked. She looked very beautiful.

'I, uh, I – how long were you here?'

'For most of it. I'm glad I came. I know it was rough, but I saw the goodness of what you are come through all the harshness of what you sometimes have to do.'

He just looked at her a moment.

'Be optimistic, Harry.'

'The stuff about my mother . . .'

'Yes, I heard it. It hurt me that this is where I learned about it. Harry, where are we if there are those kinds of secrets between us? How many times do I have to tell you that it is endangering what we have?'

'Look,' he said, 'I can't do this right now. Deal with this and you, us – it's too much for right now. It's not the right place. Let's talk about it later. You're right, Sylvia, but I, uh, I just can't . . . talk. I –'

She reached up and straightened his tie and then smoothed it on his chest.

'It's okay,' she said. 'What will you do now?'

'Follow the case. Whether officially or not, I have to follow this. I have to find the second man, the second killer.'

She just looked at him for a few moments and he knew she had probably hoped for a different answer.

'I'm sorry. It's not something I can put off. Things are happening.'

'I'm going to go in to school then. So I don't lose the whole day. Will you be up to the house tonight?'

'I'll try.'

'Okay, see you, Harry. Be optimistic.'

He smiled and she leaned into him and kissed him on the cheek. Then she walked off toward the escalator.

Bosch was watching her go when Bremmer came up.

'You want to talk about this? That was some interesting testimony in there.'

'I said all I'm saying on the stand.'

'Nothing else?'

'Nope.'

'What about what she says? That the second killer is really the first and that Church didn't kill anybody.'

'What do you expect her to say? It's bullshit. Just remember, what I said in the courtroom was under oath.

What she says out here isn't. It's bullshit, Bremmer. Don't fall for it.'

'Look, Harry, I have to write this. You know? It's my job. You going to understand that? No hard feelings?'

'No hard feelings, Bremmer. Everybody has got their job to do. Now I'm going to go do mine, okay?'

He walked off toward the escalator. Outside at the statue, he lit a cigarette and gave one to Tommy Faraway, who had been sifting through the ash can.

'What's happening, Lieutenant?' the homeless man asked.

'Justice is happening.'

EIGHTEEN

Bosch drove over to Central Division and found an open parking space at the front curb. For a while, he sat in his car looking at two trustees from the lockup washing the painted enamel mural that stretched along the front wall of the bunkerlike station. It was a depiction of a nirvana where black and white and brown children played together and smiled at friendly police officers. It was a depiction of a place where the children still had hope. In angry black spray paint along the bottom of the mural someone had written, 'This is a damnable lie!'

Bosch wondered whether someone from the neighborhood or a cop had done it. He smoked two cigarettes and tried to clear his mind of what had happened in the courtroom. He felt strangely at peace with the idea that some of his secrets had been revealed. But he held little hope for the outcome of the trial. He had moved into a feeling of resignation, an acceptance that the jury would find against him, that the twisted delivery of evidence in the case would convince them that he had acted, if not like the monster Chandler had described, then at least in an undesirable and reckless manner. They would never know what it was like to have to make such decisions as he had made in so fleeting a moment.

It was the same old story that every cop knew. The citizens want their police to protect them, to keep the plague from their eyes, from their doors. But those same John Q.'s are the first to stare wide-eyed and point the finger of outrage when they see close up exactly what the job they've given the cops entails. Bosch wasn't a hardliner. He didn't condone the actions taken by police in the André Galton cases and the Rodney King cases. But he understood those actions and knew that his own actions ultimately shared a common root.

Through political opportunism and ineptitude, the city had allowed the department to languish for years as an understaffed and underequipped paramilitary organization. Infected with political bacteria itself, the department was top-heavy with managers while the ranks below were so thin that the dog soldiers on the street rarely had the time or inclination to step out of their protective machines, their cars, to meet the people they served. They only ventured out to deal with the dirtbags and, consequently, Bosch knew, it had created a police culture in which everybody not in blue was seen as a dirtbag and was treated as such. Everybody. You ended up with your André Galtons and your Rodney Kings. You ended up with a riot the dog soldiers couldn't control. You ended up with a mural on a station house wall that was a damnable lie.

He badged his way past the front desk and took the stairs up to the Administrative Vice offices. At the door to the squad room he stood for a half minute and watched Ray Mora sitting at his desk on the other side of the room. It looked as if Mora was writing a report, rather than typing it. That probably meant it was a Daily Activity Report, which required little attention – just a few lines – and wasn't worth the time it took to get up and find a working typewriter.

Bosch noticed that Mora wrote with his right hand. But he knew this did not eliminate the vice cop as possibly being the follower. The follower knew the details and would have known about pulling the ligature around his victim's neck from the left side, thereby emulating the Dollmaker. Just as he knew about painting the white cross on the toe.

Mora looked up and saw him.

'What're you doing over there, Harry?'

'Didn't want to interrupt.'

Bosch walked over.

'What, interrupt a day report? Are you kidding?'

'Thought it might be something important.'

'It's important for me to get my paycheck. That's about it.'

Bosch dragged a chair away from an empty desk and pulled it up and sat down. He noticed the statue of the Infant of Prague had been moved. Turned, actually. Its face was no longer looking at the nakedness of the actress on the porn calendar. Bosch looked at Mora and realized he was not sure how to proceed here.

'You left a message last night.'

'Yeah, I was thinking . . .'

'About what?'

'Well, we know Church didn't kill Maggie Cum Loudly because of the timing, right? He was already dead when she got her ass dropped in the concrete.'

'That's right.'

'So, we've gotta copycat.'

'Right again.'

'So I was thinking: what if the copycat who did her started earlier?'

Bosch felt his throat start to tighten. He tried not to show Mora anything. Just gave him the deadpan look.

'Earlier?'

'Yeah. What if the two other porno chicks who were killed were actually done by the copycat? Who says he had to start after Church was dead?'

Bosch felt the full chill now. If Mora was the follower, was he so confident that he would risk laying the whole pattern out for Bosch? Or could his hunch – after all, that's all it was, a guess – be completely out of line? Regardless, it felt creepy sitting with Mora, his desk covered by magazines with sex acts depicted on the covers, the calendar girl leering from the vertical file. The statue's clay face turned away. Bosch realized that Delta Bush, the actress on the calendar Mora had displayed, was blonde-haired and buxom. She fit the pattern. Was that why Mora had put up the calendar?

'You know, Ray,' he said, after composing his voice into a monotone, 'I've been thinking the same thing. It fits better that way, all the evidence, I mean, if the follower did all three of them . . . What made you think of it?'

Mora put the report he was working on away in a desk drawer and leaned onto his desk. Subconsciously he brought his left hand up and pulled the Holy Spirit medal from his open collar. He rubbed it between his thumb and forefinger as he leaned back in his seat again, elbows on the arm rests.

He dropped the medal and said, 'Well, I remembered something is what I did. It was a tip that I got right before you nailed Church. See, I dropped it when you dropped Church.'

'You're talking about four years ago.'

'Yeah. We all thought that was it, end of case, when you got Church.'

'Get to it, Ray, what'd you remember?'

'Yeah, right, well, I remember a couple days, maybe a week before you got Church, I was given one of the call-in tips. It was given to me 'cause I was the resident expert on porno and it was a porno chick who called it in. She used the name Gallery. That's it, just Gallery. She was in the bottom-line stuff. Loops, live shows, peep booths, nine hundred phone call stuff. And she was just beginning to move up, get her name on some video boxes.

'Anyway, she called the task force – this was right before you nailed Church – and said there was a Tom that'd been making the rounds of the sets up in the Valley. You know, watching the action, hanging out with the producers, but he wasn't like the other Toms.'

'I don't know what you mean. Toms?'

'That's short for Peeping Tom. That's what the girls call these guys who hang out on the sets. Usually they're friendly with the producer or they've kicked in part of the budget. They throw a grand to the producer and he lets the guy hang around and watch 'em shoot. It's pretty common. These shoots draw a lot of people for whom seeing it on video isn't enough. They want to be right up there and see it live.'

'All right, so what about this guy?'

'Well, Harry, look, there's really only one reason these people hang around the sets. They're hitting on the chicks between takes. I mean, these guys wanna get laid. Or they want to make flicks themselves. They want to break in. And that was the thing with this guy. He wasn't hitting on anybody. He was just hanging around. She – this is Gallery – said she never saw this dude make the move on anybody. He talked to some of the girls but never left with any of them.'

'And that's what made him weird? He didn't want to get laid?'

Mora raised his hands and shrugged like he knew it sounded weak.

'Yeah, basically. But listen, Gallery worked shoots with both Heather Cumhither and Holly Lere, the two Dollmaker victims, and she said it was on those shoots that she saw this Tom. That's why she called.'

Now the story had Bosch's attention. But he didn't know what to make of it. Mora could be simply trying to deflect attention, to send Bosch down the wrong trail.

'She didn't have a name on the guy?'

'No, that was the problem. That was why I didn't jump all over it. I had a backlog of tips I was assigned and she calls in with this one without a name. I would have gotten to it eventually, but a few days later you put Church's dick in the dirt and that was that.'

'You let it go.'

'Yeah, dropped it like a bag of shit.'

Bosch waited. He knew Mora would go on. He had more to say. There had to be more.

'So the thing is, when I looked up the card on Magna Cum Loudly for you yesterday, I recognized some of her early titles. She worked with Gallery in some of her early work. That's what made me remember the tip. So just stringing along on a hunch, I try to look Gallery up, ask around with some people in the business I know, and it turns out Gallery dropped out of the scene three years ago. Just like that. I mean, I know a top producer with the Adult Film Association and he told me she dropped out right in the middle of one of his shoots. Never said a word to anyone. And no one ever heard from her again. The producer, he remembered it pretty clearly 'cause it cost him a lot of money to reshoot the flick. There would've been no continuity if he just dumped in another actress to take her place.'

Bosch was surprised that continuity was even a factor in such films. He and Mora were both silent a moment, thinking about the story, before Bosch finally spoke.

'So, you're thinking she might be in the ground somewhere? Gallery, I'm talking about. In concrete like the one we found this week.'

'Yeah, that's exactly what I'm thinking. People in the industry – I mean, they are not your mainstream people, so there are plenty of disappearing acts. I remember this one broad, she dropped out, next thing I know I see her in *People* magazine. One of those stories about some celebrity fund-raiser and she's on the arm of what's his name, guy has his own TV show about the guy in charge of a kennel. Noah's Bark. I can't think of –'

'Ray, I don't give –'

'Okay, okay, anyway the point is, these chicks drop in and out of the biz all the time. Not unusual. They aren't the smartest people in the first place. They just get it in their mind to do something else. Maybe they meet a guy who they think is going to keep them in cocaine and caviar, be their sugar daddy, like that Noah's Bark asshole, and they never show up for work again – until they find out they were wrong. As a group, they don't look much past the next line of blow.

'Y'ask me, what they're all looking for is Daddy. They all got knocked around when they were a kid and this is some fucked-up way of showing they're worth something to Daddy. Least I read that somewhere. Prob'ly bullshit like everything else.'

Bosch didn't need the psychology lesson.

'C'mon Ray, I'm in court and I'm trying to run down this case. Get to the point. What about Gallery?'

'What I'm saying is that with Gallery the situation's unusual 'cause it's been almost three years and she never came back. See, they always come back. Even if they've fucked over a producer so bad he had to do reshoots, they always come back. They start at the bottom – loops, fluffing – and work their way back up.'

'Fluffing?'

'A fluff is off-camera talent, you could say. Girls who keep the acts up and ready to perform while they're getting cameras ready, moving lights, changing angles. Things like that, if you know what I mean.'

'Yeah, I know what you mean.'

Bosch was depressed after hearing about the business for ten minutes. He looked at Mora, who had been in Ad-Vice for as long as Bosch could remember.

'What about the survivor? You ever check with her on this tip?'

'Never got around to it. Like I said, I dropped it when you dropped Church. Thought we were done with the whole thing.'

'Yeah, so did I.'

Bosch took out a small pocket notebook and wrote down a few notes from the conversation.

'Did you save any notes from this? From back then?'

'Nope, they're gone. The original tip sheet is probably in the main task force files. But it won't say more than I just told you.'

Bosch nodded. Mora was probably right.

'What did this Gallery look like?'

'Blonde, nice set – definitely Beverly Hills plastic. I think I got a picture here.'

He rolled his chair to the file cabinets behind him and dug through one of the drawers, then rolled back with a file. From it he pulled an 8 × 10 color publicity shot. It was a blonde woman posed at the edge of the ocean. She was nude. She had shaved her pubic area. Bosch handed the photo back to Mora and felt embarrassed, as if they were two boys in the schoolyard telling secrets about one of the girls. He thought he saw a slight smile on Mora's face and wondered if the vice cop found humor in his discomfort or it was something else.

'Hell of a job you've got.'

'Yeah, well, somebody's gotta do it.'

Bosch studied him a moment. He decided to take a chance, to try to figure out what made Mora hang on to the job.

'Yeah, but why you, Ray? You've been doing this a long time.'

'I guess I'm a watchdog, Bosch. The Supreme Court says this stuff is legal to a point. That makes me one of the pointmen. It's gotta be monitored. It's gotta be kept clean, no joke intended. That means these people've gotta be licensed, of legal age, and nobody's forced to do something they don't want to do. I spend a lot of days looking through this trash, looking for the stuff even the Supreme Court couldn't take. Trouble is, community standards. LA doesn't have any, Bosch. Hasn't been a successful obscenity prosecution here in years. I've made some underage cases. But I'm still looking for my first obscenity jacket.'

He stopped a moment before saying, 'Most cops do a year in Ad-Vice and then transfer out. That's all they can take. This is my seventh year, man. I can't tell you why. I guess because there's no shortage of surprises.'

'Yeah, but year after year of this shit. How can you take it?'

Mora's eyes dropped to the statue on the desk.

'I'm provided for. Don't worry about me.' He waited another beat and said, 'I've got no family. No wife anymore. Who's going to complain about what I do, anyway?'

Bosch knew from their work on the task force that Mora had volunteered for the B squad, to work nights, because his wife had just left him. He had told Bosch that he found it hardest to get through the nights. Bosch now wondered if Mora's ex-wife was blonde and, if she was, what it would mean.

'Look, Ray, I've been thinking the same things, about this follower. And she fits, you know? Gallery. The three vics and the survivor were all blondes. Church wasn't choosey but the follower apparently is.'

'Hey, you're right,' Mora said, looking at the photo of Gallery. 'I hadn't thought about that.'

'Anyway, this four-year-old tip is as good a place to start as any. There also might be other women, other victims. What've you got going?'

Mora smiled and said, 'Harry, doesn't matter what I got going. It's dogshit compared to this. I gotta vacation next week but I don't leave till Monday. Till then, I'm on it.'

'You mentioned the adult association. Is that –'

'Adult Film Association, yeah. It's run out of a lawyer's office in Sherman Oaks.'

'Yeah, you tight with anybody there?'

'I know the chief counsel. He's interested in keeping the biz clean, so he's a cooperative individual.'

'Can you talk to him, ask around, try to find out if anybody else dropped out like Gallery? They'd have to be blonde and built.'

'You want to know how many other victims we might have.'

'That's right.'

'I'll get on it.'

'What about the agents and the performers guild?'

Bosch nodded at the calendar with Delta Bush on it.

'I'll hit them, too. Two agents handle ninety percent of the casting in this business. They'd be the place to start.'

'What about outcall? Do all of the women do it?'

'Not the top ranks of performers. But the ones below that, yeah, they pretty much go the outcall route. See, the top performers, they spend ten percent of the time making movies and the rest out on the road dancing. They go from strip club to strip club, make a lot of money. They can make a hundred grand a year dancing. Most people think they're getting a bundle to do the nasty on video. That's wrong. It's the dancing. Then if you go below that level, to the performers either going up or coming down, they're the ones you find doing outcall work in addition to the movies and the dancing. A lot of money there, too. These chicks will pull down a grand a night for outcall work.'

'Do they work with pimps, what?'

'Yeah, some got management but it's not a requirement. It's not like the street, where a girl needs her pimp to protect her from the bad johns and other whores. In outcall, all you need is an answering service. Chick puts her ad and her picture in the X press and the calls come in. Most have rules. They won't go to anybody's house, strictly hotel work. They can control the class of clientele they keep by the expense of the hotel. Good way to keep the riff-raff out.'

Bosch thought about Rebecca Kaminski and how she had gone to the Hyatt on Sunset. A nice place, but the riff-raff got in.

Apparently thinking the same thing, Mora said, 'It doesn't always work, though.'

'Obviously.'

'So, I'll see what I can come up with, okay? But off the top of my head, I don't think there will be many. If there was a bunch of women doing the sudden and permanent disappearing act like Gallery did, I think I would've gotten wind of it.'

'You got my beeper number?'

Mora wrote it down and Bosch headed out of the office.

He was heading across the lobby past the front desk when the pager on his belt sounded. He checked the number and saw it was a 485 exchange. He assumed Mora had forgotten to tell him something. He took the stairs back up to the second floor and ducked back into the Ad-Vice squad room.

Mora was there, holding the photo of Gallery and staring at it in a contemplative manner. He looked up then and saw Bosch.

'Did you just beep me?'

'Me? No.'

'Oh, I just thought you were trying to catch me before I left. I'm gonna use one of the phones.'

'You're welcome to 'em, Harry.'

Bosch walked to an empty desk and dialed the number from the pager. He saw Mora slide the photo into the file. He put the file into a briefcase that was on the floor next to his chair.

A male voice answered the call after two rings.

'Chief Irvin Irving's office, this is Lieutenant Felder, how can I help you?'

NINETEEN

As with all three of the department's assistant chiefs, Irving had his own private conference room at Parker Center. It was furnished with a large, round, Formica-topped table and six chairs, a potted plant and a counter that ran along the rear wall. There were no windows. The room could be entered through a door from Irving's adjutant's office or from the sixth floor's main hallway. Bosch was the last one to arrive at the summit meeting called by Irving, taking the last chair. In the others sat the assistant chief, followed counterclockwise by Edgar and three men from Robbery-Homicide Division. Two of them Bosch knew, detectives Frankie Sheehan and Mike Opelt. They had also been attached to the Dollmaker task force four years earlier.

The third man from RHD Bosch knew by name and reputation only. Lieutenant Hans Rollenberger. He had been promoted to RHD sometime after Bosch had been demoted out of it. But friends like Sheehan kept Bosch informed. They told him Rollenberger was another cookie-cutter bureaucrat who avoided controversial and career-threatening decisions the way people avoid pan-handlers on the sidewalk, pretending not to see or hear them. He was a climber and, therefore, he couldn't be trusted. In RHD, the troops already referred to him as 'Hans Off', because that was the kind of commander he was. Morale in RHD, the unit every detective in the police department aspired to, was probably the lowest since the day the Rodney King video hit the TV.

'Sit down, Detective Bosch,' Irving said cordially. 'I think you know everybody.'

Before Bosch could answer, Rollenberger sprang from his chair and offered his hand.

'Lieutenant Hans Rollenberger.'

Bosch shook it, then they both sat down. Bosch noticed a large stack of files at the center of the table and immediately recognized them as the Dollmaker task force case files. The murder books Bosch had were his own personal files. What was piled on the table was the entire main file, probably pulled out of the archives warehouse.

'We're sitting down to see what we can do about this problem that's come up with the Dollmaker case,' Irving said. 'I have – as Detective Edgar has probably told you, I am swinging this case over to RHD. I am prepared to have Lieutenant Rollenberger put as many people on it as needed. I have also arranged for the loan of Detective Edgar to the case and you, as soon as you are free from the trial. I want results quickly. This is already turning into a public relations nightmare with what I understand was revealed during testimony today in your trial.'

'Yeah, well, sorry about that. I was under oath.'

'I understand that. The problem was you were testifying to things only you knew about. I had my adjutant sit in and he informed us of your, uh, theory on what has happened with this new case. Last night, I made the decision to have RHD handle the matter. After hearing the sense of your testimony today, I want to task-force this and get it going.

'Now, I want you to bring us up to speed on exactly what is going on, what you think, what you know. Then, we will plan from there.'

They all looked at Bosch for a moment and he was unsure where to begin. Sheehan stepped in with a question. It was a signal that he believed Irving was playing on the level on this one, that Bosch could feel safe.

'Edgar says it's a copycat. That there is no problem with Church?'

'That's right,' Bosch answered. 'Church was the man. But he was good for nine of the victims, not eleven. He spawned a follower halfway through his run and we didn't see it.'

'Tell it,' Irving said.

He did. It took Bosch forty-five minutes to tell it. Sheehan and Opelt asked several questions as he went. The only thing or person he did not mention was Mora.

At the end, Irving said, 'When you ran this follower theory by Locke, did he say it's possible?'

'Yes. With him I think he thinks anything is possible. But he was useful. He made it pretty clear for me. I want to keep him informed. He's good to bounce stuff off of.'

'I understand there's a leak. Could it be Locke?'

Shaking his head, Bosch said, 'I didn't go to him until last night and Chandler has known things from the start. She knew I was out at the scene the first day. Today she seemed to know the direction we are going, that there is a follower. She's got a good source keeping her informed. And Bremmer over at the *Times,* who knows. He's got a lot of sources.'

'Okay,' Irving said. 'Well, aside from Dr Locke being the exception, nothing in this room leaves this room. No one talks to anyone. You two' – he looked at Bosch and Edgar – 'don't even tell your supervisors at Hollywood what you're doing.'

Without naming Pounds, Irving was postulating his suspicion that Pounds could be a leak. Edgar and Bosch nodded in agreement.

'Now' – Irving looked at Bosch – 'where do we go from here?'

Without hesitation, Bosch said, 'We have to retrace the investigation. Like I told you, Locke said it was someone who had intimate access to the case. Who knew every detail and then copied them. It was a perfect cover. For a while, at least.'

'You're talking about a cop,' Rollenberger said, his first words since the briefing began.

'Maybe. But there are other possibilities. The suspect pool is actually pretty large. You got the cops, people who found the bodies, the coroner's staff, passersby at the crime scenes, reporters, lot of people.'

'Shit,' Opelt said. 'We're going to need more people.'

'Don't worry about that,' Irving said. 'I'll get more. How do we narrow it down?'

Bosch said, 'When we look at the victims we learn things about the killer. The victims and the survivor generally fall into the same archetype. Blonde, well built, worked in porno and did outcall work on the side. Locke thinks that is how the follower picked his victims. He saw them in videos, then found the means of contacting them in the outcall ads in the local adult newspapers.'

'It's like he went shopping for victims,' Sheehan said.

'Yeah.'

'What else?' Irving said.

'Not a lot. Locke said the follower is very smart, much more so than Church was. But that he could be disassembling, as he calls it. Coming apart. That's why he sent the note. Nobody would've ever known but then he sent the note. He's moved into a phase where he wants the attention that the Dollmaker had. He got jealous that this trial threw attention on Church.'

'What about other victims?' Sheehan asked. 'Ones we don't know about yet? It's been four years.'

'Yeah, I'm working on that. Locke says there's gotta be others.'

'Shit,' Opelt said. 'We need more people.'

Everyone was quiet while they thought about this.

'What about the FBI, shouldn't we contact their behavioral science people?' Rollenberger asked.

Everyone looked at Hans Off as if he were the kid who came to the sandlot football game wearing white pants.

'Fuck them,' Sheehan said.

'We seem to have a handle on this – initially, at least,' Irving said.

'What else do we know about the follower?' Rollenberger said, hoping to immediately deflect attention from his miscue. 'Do we have any physical evidence that can give us any insight into him?'

'Well, we need to track down the survivor,' Bosch said. 'She gave a composite drawing that everyone dismissed after I nailed Church. But now we know her drawing was probably of the follower. We need to find her and see if there is anything else that she has, that she can still remember, that will help.'

As he said this Sheehan dug through the stack of files on the table and found the composite. It was very generic and didn't look like anyone Bosch recognized, least of all Mora.

'We have to assume he wore disguises, same as Church, so the composite might not help. But she might remember something else, something about the suspect's manners that might let us know if it was a cop.

'Also, I'm having Amado at the coroner's office compare the rape kits between the two victims we now attribute to the follower. There's a good chance the follower may have made a mistake here.'

'Explain,' Irving said.

'The follower did everything the Dollmaker did, right?'

'Right,' Rollenberger said.

'Wrong. He only did what was known at the time about the Dollmaker. What we knew. What we didn't know was that Church had been smart. He had shaved his body so he would not leave trace hair evidence behind. We didn't know that until after he was dead, so neither did the follower. And by then he had already done two of the victims.'

'So there is a chance those two rape kits hold physical evidence to our guy,' Irving said.

'Right. I'm having Amado cross-check between the two kits. He should know something by Monday.'

'That's very good, Detective Bosch.'

Irving looked at Bosch and their eyes met. It was as if the

assistant chief was sending him a message and taking one at the same time.

'We'll see,' Bosch said.

'Other than that, that's all we've got, right?' Rollenberger said.

'Right.'

'No.'

It was Edgar, who up until now had been silent. Everyone looked at him.

'In the concrete we found – actually, Harry found it – a cigarette pack. It went in when the concrete was wet. So there's a good chance they were the follower's. Marlboro regulars. Soft pack.'

'They also could have been the vic's, right?' Rollenberger asked.

'No,' Bosch said. 'I talked to her manager last night. He said she didn't smoke. The smokes were in all likelihood the follower's.'

Sheehan smiled at Bosch and Bosch smiled back. Sheehan held his hands together as if waiting for handcuffs.

'Here I am boys,' he said. 'That's my brand.'

'Mine, too,' Bosch said. 'But I've got you beat. I'm left-handed, too. I better get an alibi working.'

The men at the table smiled. Bosch dropped his smile when he suddenly thought of something but knew he could not say anything yet. He looked at the files stacked at the center of the table.

'Shit, every cop smokes Marlboros or Camels,' Opelt said.

'It's a dirty habit,' Irving said.

'I agree,' said Rollenberger, a little too quickly.

It brought silence back to the table.

'Who's your suspect?'

It was Irving who asked it. He was looking at Bosch again with those eyes Harry couldn't decipher. The question shocked Bosch. Irving knew. Somehow he knew. Harry didn't answer.

'Detective, it is clear you've had a handle on what's going on for a day. You've also been on this case from the start. I think you've got someone in mind. Tell us. We need to start somewhere.'

Bosch hesitated again but finally said, 'I'm not sure . . . and I don't want . . .'

'To ruin someone's career if you're wrong? To set the dogs on a possibly innocent man? That's understood. But we can't have you pursuing this on your own. Haven't you learned anything from this trial? I believe "cowboying" was the term Money Chandler used to describe it.'

They were all looking at him. He was thinking of Mora. The vice cop was strange but was he that strange? Over the years Bosch had often been investigated by the department and did not want to bring that kind of weight down on the wrong person.

'Detective?' Irving prompted. 'Even if all you have is a hunch, then you must tell us. Investigations start with hunches. You want to protect one person but what are we going to do? We are about to go out and investigate cops. What difference is it if we start with this person or come to him in time? Either way we will get to him. Give us the name.'

Bosch thought about everything Irving had said. He wondered what his own motive was. Was he protecting Mora or simply keeping him for himself? He thought a few more moments and finally said, 'Give me five minutes alone in here with the files. If there is something there that I think is there, then I'll tell you.'

'Gentlemen,' Irving said, 'let's go get some coffee.'

After the room was cleared, Bosch looked at the files for nearly a minute without moving. He felt confused. He wasn't sure whether he wanted to find something that would convince him Mora was the follower or convince him he was not. He thought about what Chandler had said to the jury about monsters and the black abyss where they dwell.

Whoever fights monsters, he thought, should not think too hard about it.

He lit a cigarette and pulled the stack close to him and began looking for two files. The chronologies file was near the top. It was thin. It was basically a quick guide to important dates in the investigation. He found the task force personnel file at the bottom of the stack. It was thicker than the first he pulled out because it contained the weekly shifts schedule for the detectives assigned to the task force and the overtime approval forms. As the detective-three in charge of the B squad, Bosch had been in charge of keeping the personnel file up to date.

From the chronologies file, Bosch quickly looked up the times and dates that the first two porno actresses were murdered and other pertinent information about the way they were lured to their death. Then he looked up the same information about the lone survivor. He wrote it all down in order on a page of his pocket notebook.

- June 17, 11 P.M.
  Georgia Stern aka Velvet Box
  survivor

- July 6, 11:30 P.M.
  Nicole Knapp aka Holly Lere
  W. Hollywood

- Sept 28, 4 A.M.
  Shirleen Kemp aka Heather Cumhither
  Malibu

Bosch opened the personnel file and pulled the shift schedules for the weeks the women were attacked or murdered. June seventeenth, the night Georgia Stern was attacked, was a Sunday, which was the B squad's night off. Mora could've done it, but so could anyone else who was on the squad.

On the Knapp case, Bosch got a hit and his fingers trembled a little as he held the schedule for the week of July 1. His adrenaline was moving faster now. July sixth, the day Knapp was sent on an outcall request at 9 P.M., and was found dead on the sidewalk on Sweetzer in West Hollywood at 11:30 P.M., was a Friday. Mora was on the schedule to be working the three-to-midnight shift with the B squad, but there next to his name in Bosch's own writing was the word 'sick'.

Bosch quickly pulled out the schedule for the week of September twenty-second. The nude body of Shirleen Kemp had been found at the side of the Pacific Coast Highway in Malibu at four in the morning on Friday, September twenty-eighth. He realized that wasn't enough information and looked for the file that contained the investigation of her death.

He quickly read through the file and learned that Kemp had a phone service that had logged a call for her services at the Malibu Inn at 12:55 A.M. When detectives went there they learned from phone records that at 12:55 A.M. a call had been placed by the occupant of room 311. The front desk staff could not provide a good description of the man in 311 and the identification he gave proved to be false. He had paid in cash. The one thing the desk people could say with absolute accuracy was that he checked in at 12:35 A.M. Each registration card was punched with the time. The man had called for Heather Cumhither twenty minutes after he checked in.

Bosch referred back to the work schedule. On the Thursday night before Kemp was murdered, Mora had worked. But he had apparently come in and left early. He had signed in at 2:40 P.M. and out at 11:45 P.M.

That gave him fifty minutes to get from the Hollywood station to the Malibu Inn and checked into room 311 at 12:35 A.M., Friday. Bosch knew that it could be done. Traffic would be light on the PCH that late at night.

It could be Mora.

He noticed that the cigarette he had set on the edge of the table had burned down to the butt and it had discolored the Formica edge. He quickly dropped the cigarette into a pot containing a ficus plant in the corner of the room and turned the table around so the burn mark was positioned at the spot where Rollenberger had been sitting. He waved one of the files in the air to disperse the smoke and then opened the door to Irving's office.

'Raymond Mora.'

Irving had said the name out loud apparently to see how it sounded. He said nothing else when Bosch was finished telling what he knew. Bosch watched him and waited for more but the assistant chief only sniffed at the air, identified the cigarette smoke and frowned.

'Another thing,' Bosch said. 'Locke wasn't the only one I talked to about the follower. Mora knows just about everything I just told you. He was on the task force and we went to him this week for help on the ID of the concrete blonde. I was over at Ad-Vice when you paged me. He had called me last night.'

'What did he want?' Irving asked.

'He wanted to let me know that he thought the follower might've done the two porno queens from the original eleven. He said it had just come to him, that maybe the follower had started way back then.'

'Shit,' Sheehan said, 'this guy is playing with us. If he —'

'What did you tell him?' Irving interrupted.

'I told him I was thinking that, too. And I asked him to check with his sources to see if he could find out if there were other women who disappeared or dropped out of the business like Becky Kaminski did.'

'You asked him to go to work on this?' Rollenberger said, his eyebrows arched in astonishment and outrage.

'I had to. It was the obvious thing for me to ask him. If I didn't, he'd know I was suspicious.'

'He's right,' Irving said.

Rollenberger's chest seemed to deflate a little bit. He couldn't get anything right.

'Yes, now I see,' he dutifully responded. 'Good work.'

'We're going to need more people,' Opelt said, since everybody was being so agreeable.

'I want to begin surveillance on him by tomorrow morning,' Irving said. 'We're going to need at least three teams. Sheehan and Opelt will be one. Bosch, you're involved in court and Edgar, I want you working on tracking down the survivor, so you two are out. Lieutenant Rollenberger, who else can you spare?'

'Well, Yde is sitting around since Buchert is on vacation. And Mayfield and Rutherford are in court on the same case. I can shake one of them loose to pair with Yde. That's all I've got, unless you want to pull back on some ongoing –'

'No, I don't want that. Get Yde and Mayfield in on this. I'll go to Lieutenant Hilliard and see what she can spare from the Valley. She's had three teams on the catering truck case for a month and they're at the wall. I'll take a team off of that.'

'Very good, sir,' Rollenberger said.

Sheehan looked at Harry and made a face like he was going to puke with this guy in charge. Bosch held back his smile. There was always this giddiness that detectives felt when they received their marching orders and were about to go out into the hunt.

'Opelt, Sheehan, I want you on Mora tomorrow morning at eight,' Irving said. 'Lieutenant, I want you to set up a meeting with the new people tomorrow morning. Bring them up to date on what we have and have one team take over surveillance from Opelt and Sheehan at four P.M. They stay with Mora until lights out. If overtime is needed, I'm authorizing it. The other pair will take the surveillance at eight A.M. Saturday and Opelt and Sheehan will take it back at four. Rotate like that. The night-shift watchers have to stay with him until they are sure he is in his home in bed for the night. I want no mistakes. If this guy pulls off something while we're watching him, we can all kiss our careers good-bye.'

'Chief?'

'Yes, Bosch.'

'There is no guarantee that he is going to do something. Locke said he thinks the follower has a lot of control. He doesn't think he is out there hunting every night. He thinks he controls the urge and lives pretty normally, then strikes at irregular intervals.'

'There is no guarantee that we'll even be watching the right man, Detective Bosch, but I want to watch him anyway. I am sitting here hoping we are dreadfully wrong about Detective Mora. But the things you have said here are convincing in a circumstantial way. Nothing near being usable in court. So we watch him and hope if it's him we'll see the sign before he hurts anybody else. My –'

'I agree, sir,' Rollenberger said.

'Don't interrupt me, Lieutenant. My forte is neither detective work nor psychoanalysis, but something tells me that whoever the follower is, he's feeling the pressure. Sure, he brought it on himself with that note. And he may think this is a cat-and-mouse game he can master. Nevertheless, he is feeling the pressure. And one thing I know, just from being a cop, when the pressure is on these people, the edge-dwellers I call them, then they react. Sometimes they crack, sometimes they act out. So what I am saying is, knowing what I know about this case, I want Mora covered if he even walks outside to get the mail.'

They sat there in silence. Even Rollenberger, who seemed cowed by his misstep in interrupting Irving.

'Okay, then, we have our assignments. Sheehan, Opelt, surveillance. Bosch, you are freelancing until you get done with the trial. Edgar, you have the survivor and when you have the time do some checking on Mora. Nothing that will get back to him.'

'He's divorced,' Bosch offered. 'Got divorced right before the Dollmaker task force was put together.'

'All right, there's your start. Go to court, pull his divorce. Who knows, we might get lucky. Maybe his wife dropped him because he liked making her up like a doll. Things have been hard enough on this case, we could use a break like that.'

Irving looked around the table at each man's face.

'The potential for embarrassment to the department on this case is huge. But I don't want anybody holding back. Let the stones fall where they will. . . . Okay, then, everybody has their assignments. Go to it. Everyone is excused with the exception of Detective Bosch.'

As the others filed out of the room, Bosch thought Rollenberger's face showed his disappointment at not getting a chance for a private ass-kissing conference with Irving.

After the door closed, Irving was quiet for a few moments as he composed what he wanted to say. Throughout most of Bosch's career as a detective, Irving had been a nemesis of sorts, always trying to control him and bring him into the fold. Bosch had always resisted. Nothing personal, it just wasn't Bosch's gig.

But now Bosch sensed a softening in Irving. In the way he had treated Bosch during the meeting, in the way he testified earlier in the week. He could have hung Bosch out to dry but didn't. Yet, it wasn't something Bosch could or would acknowledge. So he sat there silently and waited.

'Good work on this, Detective. Especially with the trial and everything going on.'

Bosch nodded but knew that wasn't what this was about.

'Uh, that's why I held you here. The trial. I wanted to – let's see, how do I say this . . . I wanted to tell you, and excuse the language, but I don't give a flying fuck what that jury decides or how much money they give those people. That jury has no idea what it's like to be out there on the edge. To have to make the decisions that may cost or save lives. You can't take a week to accurately examine and judge the decision you had to make in a second.'

Bosch was trying to think of something to say and the silence seemed to drag on too long.

'Anyway,' Irving finally said, 'I guess it's taken me four years to come to that conclusion. But better late than never.'

'Hey, I could use you for closing arguments tomorrow.'

Irving's face cringed, the muscular jaws flexing as if he had just taken a mouthful of cold sauerkraut.

'Don't get me started on that, either. I mean, what is this city doing? The city attorney's office is nothing but a school. A law school for trial lawyers. And the taxpayers pay the tuition. We get these greenhorn, uh, uh, preppies, who don't know the first thing about trial law. They learn from the mistakes they make in court when it counts – for us. And when they finally get good and know what the hell they're doing, they quit and then they're the lawyers suing us!'

Bosch had never seen Irving so animated. It was as if he had taken off the starched public persona he always wore like a uniform. Harry was entranced.

'Sorry about that,' Irving said. 'I get carried away. Anyway, good luck with this jury but don't let it worry you.'

Bosch said nothing.

'You know, Bosch, it only takes a half-hour meeting with Lieutenant Rollenberger in the room for me to want to take a good look at myself and this department and where it's headed. He's not the LAPD I joined or you joined. He's a good manager, yes, and so am I, at least I think so. But we can't forget we're cops . . .'

Bosch didn't know what to say, or if he should say anything. It seemed that Irving was almost rambling now. As if there was something he wanted to say, but was looking for anything else to say instead.

'Hans Rollenberger. What a name, huh? I can guess, the detectives in his crew must call him "Hans Off", am I right?'

'Sometimes.'

'Yes, well, I guess that's expected. He – uh, you know, Harry, I've got thirty-eight years in the department.'

Bosch just nodded. This was getting weird. Irving had never even called him by his first name before.

'And, uh, I worked Hollywood patrol for a lot of years right out of the academy. . . . That question Money Chandler asked me about your mother. That really came out of the blue and I'm sorry about that, Harry, sorry for your loss.'

'It was a long time ago.' Bosch waited a beat. Irving was looking down at his hands, which were clasped on the table. 'If that's it, I think I'll –'

'Yes, that's basically it, but, you know, what I wanted to tell you is that I was there that day.'

'What day?'

'That day that your mother – I was the RO.'

'The reporting officer?'

'Yes, I was the one that found her. I was walking a foot beat on the Boulevard and I ducked into that alley off of Gower. I usually hit it once a day and, uh, I found her. . . . When Chandler showed me those reports I recognized the case right away. She didn't know my badge number – it was there on the report – or she would've known I was the one who found her. Chandler would've had some kind of a field day with that, I guess . . .'

This was hard for Bosch to sit through. Now he was glad Irving wasn't looking at him. He knew, or thought he knew, what it was that Irving wasn't saying. If he had worked the Boulevard foot beat, then he had known Bosch's mother before she was dead.

Irving glanced up at him and then looked away, toward the corner of the room. His eyes fell on the ficus plant.

'Somebody put a cigarette butt in my pot,' he said. 'That yours, Harry?'

TWENTY

Bosch was lighting a cigarette as he used his shoulder to push through one of the glass doors at the entrance to Parker Center. Irving had jolted him with his small-world story. Bosch had always figured he'd run into somebody in the department who knew her or knew the case. Never did Irving fit into that scenario.

As he walked through the south lot to the Caprice he noticed Jerry Edgar standing at the corner of Los Angeles and First waiting for the cross light. Bosch looked at his watch and saw it was 5:10, quitting time. He thought Edgar was probably walking up to the Code Seven or the Red Wind for a draft before fighting the freeway. He thought that wasn't a bad idea. Sheehan and Opelt were probably already sitting on stools at one of the bars.

By the time Bosch got to the corner, Edgar had a block and a half lead on him and was walking up First toward the Seven. Bosch picked up the pace. For the first time in a long time, he felt the actual mental craving for alcohol. For just a while he wanted to forget Church and Mora and Chandler and his own secrets and what Irving had told him in the conference room.

But then Edgar walked right on by the billy club that served as the door handle at the Seven without even giving it a glance. He crossed Spring and walked alongside the *Times* building toward Broadway. Then it's the Red Wind, Bosch thought.

The Wind was okay as far as a watering hole went. They had Weinhard's by the bottle instead of on draft, so the place lost points there. Another minus was that the yuppies from the *Times* newsroom favored the place and it often was more crowded with reporters than cops. The big plus, however, was that on Thursdays and Fridays they had a quartet come in and play sets from six to ten. They were mostly retired club men who weren't too tight, but it was as good a way as any to miss the rush hour.

He watched Edgar cross Broadway and stay on First instead of taking a left to go down to the Wind. Bosch slowed his pace a bit so Edgar could renew his block-and-a-half lead. He lit another cigarette and felt uneasy about the prospect of following the other detective but did it anyway. There was a bad feeling beginning to nag at him.

Edgar turned left on Hill and ducked into the first door on the east side, across from the new subway entrance. The door he went through was to the Hung Jury, a bar that was off the lobby of the Fuentes Legal Center, an eight-story office building solely occupied by attorney offices. Mostly, the tenants were defense and litigation attorneys who had chosen the nondescript if not ugly building because of its main selling point; it was only a half block from the county courts building, a block from the criminal courts building and a block and a half from the federal building.

Bosch knew all of this because Belk had told him all about it on the day the two of them had come to the Fuentes Legal Center to find Honey Chandler's office. Bosch had been subpoenaed to give a deposition in the Norman Church case.

The uneasy feeling turned into a hollow in his gut as he passed the door to the Hung Jury and went into the main lobby of the Fuentes Center. He knew the layout of the bar, having dropped in for a beer and a shot after the deposition with Chandler, and he knew there was an entrance off the building's lobby. He pushed through the lobby entrance door now and stepped into an alcove where there were two pay phones and the doors to the restrooms. He moved up to the corner and carefully looked into the bar area.

A juke box Bosch couldn't see was playing Sinatra's 'Summer Wind', a barmaid with a puffy wig and bills wrapped through her fingers – tens, fives, ones – was delivering a batch of martinis to a four top of lawyers sitting near the front entrance and the bartender was leaning over the dimly lit bar smoking a cigarette and reading the *Hollywood Reporter*. Probably an actor or a screenwriter when he wasn't tending bar, Bosch thought. Maybe a talent scout. Who in this town wasn't?

When the bartender leaned forward to stub out his smoke in an ashtray, Bosch saw Edgar sitting at the far end of the bar with a draft beer in front of him. A match flared in the darkness next to him and Bosch watched Honey Chandler light a smoke and then drop her match into an ashtray next to what looked like a Bloody Mary.

Bosch moved back into the alcove, out of sight.

He waited next to an old plywood shack that was built on the sidewalk at Hill and First and served as a news and magazine stand. It had been closed and boarded for the night. As it grew dark and the streetlights came on, Bosch spent his time fending off panhandlers and passing prostitutes looking for one last businessman's special before heading from downtown into Hollywood for the evening – and the rougher – trade.

By the time he saw Edgar come out of the Hung Jury, Bosch had a nice little pile of cigarette butts on the sidewalk at his feet. He flicked the one he had going into the street and stepped back alongside the news stand so Edgar wouldn't notice him. Bosch saw no sign of Chandler and assumed that she had left the bar through the other door and gone down to the garage and her car. Edgar probably had wisely declined a ride over to the Parker Center lot.

As Edgar passed the stand Bosch stepped out behind him.

'Jerry, whereyat?'

Edgar jumped as if an ice cube had been pressed against his neck and whipped around.

'Harry? What're you – hey, you wanna grab a drink? That's what I was looking to do.'

Bosch let him stand there and squirm for a few seconds before saying, 'You already had your drink.'

'What do you mean?'

Bosch took a step toward him. Edgar looked genuinely scared.

'You know what I mean. A beer for you, right? Bloody Mary for the lady.'

'Listen, Harry, look, I –'

'Don't call me that. Don't ever call me Harry again. Understand? You want to talk to me, call me Bosch. That's what the people who aren't my friends call me, the people I don't trust. Just call me that.'

'Can I explain? Har – uh, I'd like the chance to explain.'

'What's to explain? You fucked me over. Nothing to explain about that. What'd you tell her tonight? You just run down everything we just talked about in Irving's office? I don't think she needs it, pal. The damage is already done.'

'No. She left a long time ago. I was in there most of the time alone thinking about how to get out of this. I didn't tell her shit about today's meeting. Harry, I didn't –'

Bosch took one more step and in a quick motion brought his hand up, palm out, and hit Edgar in the chest, knocking him backward.

'I said don't call me that!' he yelled. 'You fuck! You – we worked together, man. I taught you . . . I'm in that courtroom getting fucked in the ass and I find out you're the guy, you're the goddamn leak.'

'I'm sorry. I –'

'What about Bremmer? You the one who told him about the note? Is that where you're going for a drink now? Going to meet Bremmer? Well, don't let me stop you.'

'No, man, I haven't talked to Bremmer. Look, I made a mistake, okay? I'm sorry. She screwed me, too. It was like blackmail. I couldn't – I tried to get out of it but she had me by the shorthairs. You gotta believe me, man.'

Bosch looked at him for a long moment. It was fully dark now but he thought he saw that Edgar's eyes were shiny in the glow of the streetlights. Maybe he was holding back tears. But what were they tears for, Bosch wondered. For the loss of the relationship they had? Or were they tears of fear? Bosch felt the surge of his power over Edgar. And Edgar knew he had it.

In a low and very even voice Bosch said, 'I want to know everything. You are going to tell me what you did.'

The quartet at the Wind was on a break. They sat at a table in the back. It was a dark, wood-paneled room like hundreds of others in the city. A red leatherette pad ran along the edge of the cigarette-scarred bar and the barmaids wore black uniforms and white aprons and they all had too much red lipstick on their thin lips. Bosch ordered a double shot of Jack Black straight up and a bottle of Weinhard's. He also gave the barmaid money for a pack of cigarettes. Edgar, who now wore the face of a man whose life had run out on him, ordered Jack Black, water back.

'It's the damn recession,' Edgar began before Bosch asked a question. 'Real estate is in the toilet. I had to drop that gig and we had the mortgage and, you know how it is, man, Brenda had gotten used to a cert –'

'Fuck that. You think I want to hear about how you sell me out because your wife has to drive a Chevy instead of a BMW? Fuck you. You –'

'It's not like that. I –'

'Shut up. I'm talking. You're going to –'

They both shut up while the barmaid put the drinks and cigarettes down. Bosch put a twenty on her tray. He never took his dark, angry eyes off Edgar.

'Now, skip the bullshit and tell me what you did.'

Edgar threw back his shot and washed it down with water before starting.

'Uh, you see, uh, it was late Monday afternoon, this was after we'd been out to the scene at Bing's and I was back at the office. And I got a call at the office and it was Chandler. She knew something was up. I don't know how but she knew, but she knew about the note we got and the body being found. She musta gotten tipped by Bremmer or something. She started asking questions, you know, "Was it confirmed as the Dollmaker?" Things like that. I put her off. No comment . . .'

'And then?'

'Then, well, she offered me something. I'm two back on the mortgage and Brenda doesn't even know.'

'What'd I tell you? I don't want to hear your sad story, Edgar. I'm telling you, I don't have any sympathy for that. You tell it and it will only make me madder.'

'All right, all right. She offered me money. I said I'd think about it. She said if I wanted to deal to meet her at the Hung Jury that night. . . . You won't let me say why, but I had reasons and so I went. Yeah, I went.'

'Yeah, and you fucked yourself up,' Bosch said, hoping to knock down the defiant tone that had crept into Edgar's voice.

He had finished the last of his Jack Black and signaled the barmaid but she didn't see him. The musicians were taking their places behind their instruments. The front man was a saxophone player and Bosch wished he was here under other circumstances.

'What did you give her?'

'Just what we knew that day. But she already had just about everything already. I told her you said it looked like the Dollmaker. It wasn't a lot, Ha – and most of it was in the paper the next day, anyway. And I wasn't Bremmer's source on that. You have to believe me.'

'You told her I came out there? To the scene?'

'Yeah, I told her. What was the big secret about that?'

Bosch thought about all of this for a few minutes. He watched the band start up with a Billy Strayhorn number called 'Lush Life'. Their table was far enough away from the quartet that it wasn't too loud. Harry's eyes scanned the rest of the bar to see if anyone else was into it and he saw Bremmer sitting at the bar nursing a beer. He was with a group of what looked like reporter types. One of the other men even had one of those long, skinny notebooks that reporters always carry sticking out of his back pocket.

'Speaking of Bremmer, there he is. Maybe he wants to check a detail or two with you after we're done.'

'Harry, it's not me.'

Bosch let him get away with the Harry that time. He was getting tired and depressed with this scene. He wanted to get it over with and get out of there, go see Sylvia.

'How many times did you talk to her?'

'Every night.'

'She turned it on you, didn't she? You had to go see her.'

'I was stupid. I needed the money. Once I met her the first night she had me by the balls. She said she wanted updates on the investigation or she'd tell you I was the leak, she'd inform IAD. Fuck, she never even paid me.'

'What happened tonight to make her split early?'

'She said the case was over, going to closing arguments tomorrow, so it didn't matter what was happening in the case. She cut me loose.'

'But it won't end there. You know that, don't you? Whenever she needs a plate run, an address from DMV, a witness's unlisted number, she's going to call you. She's got you, man.'

'I know. I'll have to deal with it.'

'All for what? What was the price, that first night?'

'I wanted one goddamn mortgage payment. . . . Can't sell the fuckin' house, can't make the mortgage, I don't know what I'm going to do.'

'What about me? Aren't you worried about what I'm going to do?'

'Yes. Yes, I am.'

Bosch looked back at the quartet. They were staying with

a Strayhorn set and were on to 'Blood Count'. There was a journeyman quality to the sax man's work. He stayed on point and his phrasing was clean.

'What are you going to do?' Edgar asked.

Bosch didn't have to think, he already knew. He didn't take his eyes from the sax man as he spoke.

'Nothing.'

'Nothing?'

'It's what you are going to do. I can't work with you anymore, man. I know we got this thing with Irving but that's it, that's the end. After this is over you go to Pounds and tell him you want to transfer out of Hollywood.'

'But there aren't openings in homicide anywhere else. I looked at the board, you know how rarely they come.'

'I didn't say anything about homicide. I just said you're going to ask for a transfer. You ask for the first thing open, understand? I don't care if you end up on autos in the Seventy-seventh, you take the first thing you can get.'

Now he looked at Edgar, whose mouth was slightly open, and said, 'That's the price you pay.'

'But homicide is what I do, you know that. It's where it's at.'

'And you're not where it's at anymore. This isn't negotiable. Unless you want to take your chances with IAD. But either you go to Pounds or I go to them. I can't work with you anymore. That's it.'

He looked back at the band. Edgar was silent and after a few moments Bosch told him to leave.

'You go first. I can't walk with you back to Parker.'

Edgar stood up and hovered near the table for a few moments before saying, 'Someday, you're going to need all the friends you can get. That's the day you'll remember doing this to me.'

Without looking at him, Bosch said, 'I know.'

After Edgar had gone Bosch got the barmaid's attention and ordered another round. The quartet played 'Rain Check' with some improvisational riffs that Bosch liked. The whiskey was beginning to warm his gut and he sat back and smoked and listened, trying not to think about anything to do with cops and killers.

But soon he felt a presence nearby and turned to see Bremmer standing there with his bottle of beer in hand.

'I take it by the look on Edgar's face when he left that he won't be coming back. Can I join you?'

'No, he won't be back and you can do whatever you want, but I'm off duty, off the record and off the road.'

'In other words, you ain't saying shit.'

'You got it.'

The reporter sat down and lit a cigarette. His small but sharp green eyes squinted through the smoke.

'It's okay, 'cause I'm not working either.'

'Bremmer, you're always working. Even now, I say the wrong word and you aren't going to forget about it.'

'I suppose. But you forget the times we worked together. The stories that helped you, Harry. I write one story that doesn't go the way you want and all of that is forgotten. Now I'm just "that damn reporter" who –'

'I haven't forgotten shit. You're sitting here, right? I remember what you did for me and I'll remember what you did against me. It all evens out in the end.'

They sat in silence for a while and listened to the music. The set ended just as the barmaid was putting Bosch's third double Jack Black on the table.

'I'm not saying I would ever reveal it,' Bremmer said, 'but how come my source on the note story was so important?'

'It's not that important anymore. At the time I just wanted to know who was trying to nail me.'

'You said that before. That someone was setting you up. You really think that?'

'It doesn't matter. What kind of story did you write for tomorrow?'

The reporter straightened up and and his eyes brightened.

'You'll see it. Pretty much a straight court story. Your testimony about someone else continuing the killings. It's going out front. It's a big story. That why I'm here. I always come in for a pop after I hit the front page.'

'Party time, huh? What about my mother? Did you put that stuff in?'

'Harry, if that's what you are worried about, forget it. I didn't even mention that in the story. To be honest, it's of course vitally interesting to you, but as far as a newspaper story goes, I thought it was too much inside baseball. I left it out.'

'Inside baseball?'

'Too arcane, like the stats those sports guys on TV throw around. You know, like how many fastballs Lefty So and So threw during the third inning of the fifth game of the 1956 World Series. I thought the stuff with your mother – Chandler's attempt to use it as your motivation for dropping this guy – was going too far inside.'

Bosch just nodded. He was glad that part of his life would not be in the hands of a million newspaper buyers tomorrow, but he acted nonchalant about it.

'But,' Bremmer said, 'I gotta tell you, if we get a verdict back on this that goes against you and the jurors start saying they thought you did it to avenge your mother's death, then that is usable and I won't have a choice.'

Bosch nodded again. It seemed fair enough. He looked at his watch and saw it was nearly ten. He knew he should call Sylvia and he knew he should get out of there before the next set started and he became entranced by the music again.

He finished his drink and said, 'I'm gonna hit it.'

'Yeah, me, too,' Bremmer said. 'I'll walk out with you.'

Outside, the chilled night air cut through Bosch's whiskey daze. He said good-bye to Bremmer and put his hands in his pockets as he started down the sidewalk.

'Harry, you walking all the way back to Parker Center? Hop in. My car is right here.'

Bosch watched Bremmer unlock the passenger door to his Le Sabre, which was parked right at the curb in front of the Wind. Bosch got in without a word of thanks and leaned over and unlocked the other side. When he was drunk he went through a stage where he said almost nothing, just vegetated in his own juices and listened.

Bremmer started the conversation during the four blocks to Parker Center.

'That Money Chandler is something else, isn't she? She really knows how to play a jury.'

'You think she's got it, don't you?'

'It's going to be close, Harry. I think. But even if it's one of those statement verdicts that are popular these days against the LAPD, she'll get rich.'

'Whaddaya mean?'

'You haven't been in federal court before have you?'

'No. I try not to make it a habit.'

'Well, in a civil rights case, if the plaintiff wins – in this case, Chandler – then the defendant – in this case the city is paying your tab – has to pay the lawyer's fees. I guarantee you, Harry, that in her closing argument tomorrow Money will tell those jurors that all they need to do is make a statement that you acted wrongly. And even damages of a dollar make that statement. The jury will see that as the easy way out. They can say you were wrong and only give a dollar in damages. They won't know, because Belk is not allowed to tell them, that even if the plaintiff wins a dollar, Chandler bills the city. And that won't be a dollar. More like a couple hundred thousand of them. It's a scam.'

'Shit.'

'Yeah, that's the justice system.'

Bremmer pulled into the lot and Bosch pointed out his Caprice in one of the front rows.

'You going to be all right to drive?' Bremmer asked.

'No problem.'

Bosch was about to close the door when Bremmer stopped him.

'Hey, Harry, we both know I can't reveal my source. But I can tell you who it isn't. And I'll tell you it is not someone you'd expect. You know? Edgar and Pounds, if that's who you think it is, forget it. You'd never guess who it was, so don't bother. Okay?'

Bosch just nodded and shut the door.

TWENTY-ONE

After fumbling to find the right one, Bosch put the key in the ignition but didn't turn it. He briefly considered whether he should try to drive or whether he should go get coffee from the cafeteria first. He looked up through the windshield at the gray monolith that was Parker Center. Most of the lights were on but he knew the offices had emptied. The lights of the squad rooms were always left on to give the appearance that the fight against crime never sleeps. It was a lie.

He thought of the couch that was kept in one of the RHD interrogation rooms. That was also an alternative to driving. Unless, of course, it was already taken. But then he thought of Sylvia and how she had come to court despite what he had said about not wanting her there. He wanted to get home to her. Yes, he thought, home.

He put his hand on the key but then dropped it away again. He rubbed his eyes. They were tired and there were so many thoughts swimming in the whiskey. There was the sound of the tenor sax floating there, too. His own improvisational riff.

He tried to think of what Bremmer had just said, that Bosch would never guess who the source was. Why had he said it that way? He found that more tantalizing than wondering who his source actually was.

It didn't matter, he told himself. All would be over soon. He leaned his head against the side window, thinking about the trial and his testimony. He wondered how he had looked up there, all eyes on him. He never wanted to be in that position again. Ever. To have Honey Chandler cornering him with words.

Whoever fights monsters, he thought. What had she told the jury? About the abyss? Yes, where monsters dwell. Is that where I dwell? In the black place? The black heart, he remembered then. Locke had called it that. The black heart does not beat alone. In his mind he replayed the vision of Norman Church being knocked upright by the bullet and then flopping helplessly naked on the bed. The look in the dying man's eyes stayed with him. Four years later and the vision was as clear as yesterday. Why was that, he wanted to know. Why did he remember Norman Church's face and not his own mother's? Do I have the black heart, Bosch asked himself. Do I?

The darkness came up on him then like a wave and pulled him down. He was there with the monsters.

There was a sharp rap on the glass. Bosch abruptly opened his eyes and saw the patrolman next to the car holding his baton and flashlight. Harry quickly looked around and grabbed the wheel and put his foot on the brake. He didn't think he had been driving that badly, then he realized he hadn't been driving at all. He was still in the Parker Center lot. He reached over and rolled the window down.

The kid in the uniform was the lot cop. The lowest-rated cadet in each academy class was first assigned to watch the Parker Center lot during P.M. watch. It was a tradition but it also served a purpose. If the cops couldn't prevent car break-ins and other crime in the parking lot of their own headquarters, then it begged the question, where could they stop crime?

'Detective, are you all right?' he said as he slid his baton back into the ring on his belt. 'I saw you get dropped off and get in your car. Then when you didn't leave I wanted to check.'

'Yes,' Bosch managed to say. 'I'm, uh, fine. Thanks. I musta dozed off there. Been a long day.'

'Yes, they all are. Be careful now.'

'Yes.'

'Are you okay driving?'

'Fine. Thank you.'

'You sure?'

'I'm sure.'

He waited until the cop walked away before starting the car. Bosch looked at his watch and figured he had slept for no more than thirty minutes. But the nap, and the sudden waking, had refreshed him. He lit a cigarette and pulled the car out onto Los Angeles Street and took it to the Hollywood Freeway entrance.

As he drove north on the freeway he rolled the window down so the cool air would keep him alert. It was a clear night. Ahead of him, the lights of the Hollywood Hills ascended into the sky where spotlights from two different locations behind the mountains cut through the darkness. He thought it was a beautiful scene, yet it made him feel melancholy.

Los Angeles had changed in the last few years, but then there was nothing new about that. It was always changing and that was why he loved it. But riot and recession had left a particularly harsh mark on the landscape, the landscape of memory. Bosch believed he would never forget the pall of smoke that hung over the city like some kind of supersmog that could not be lifted by the evening winds. The TV pictures of burning buildings and looters unchecked by the police. It had been the department's darkest hour and it still had not recovered.

And neither had the city. Many of the ills that led to such volcanic rage were still left untended. The city offered so much beauty and yet it offered so much danger and hate. It was a city of shaken confidence, living solely on its stores of hope. In Bosch's mind he saw the polarization of the haves and have-nots as a scene in which a ferry was leaving the dock. An overloaded ferry leaving an overloaded dock, with some people with a foot on the boat and a foot on the dock.

The boat was pulling further away and it would only be so long before those in the middle would fall in. Meanwhile, the ferry was still too crowded and it would capsize at the first wave. Those left on the dock would certainly cheer this. They prayed for the wave.

He thought of Edgar and what he had done. He was one of those about to fall in. Nothing could be done about it. He and his wife, whom Edgar could not bring himself to tell about their precarious position. Bosch wondered if he had done the right thing. Edgar had spoken of the time that would come when Bosch would need every friend he could get. Would it have been wiser to bank this one, to let Edgar go, no harm no foul? He didn't know, but there was still time. He would have to decide.

As he drove through the Cahuenga Pass he rolled the window back up. It was getting cold. He looked up into the hills to the west and tried to spot the unlighted area where his dark house sat. He felt glad that he wasn't going up there tonight, that he was going to Sylvia.

He got there at 11:30 and used his own key to get in. There was a light on in the kitchen but the rest of the place was dark. Sylvia was asleep. It was too late for the news and the late-night talk shows never held his interest. He took his shoes off in the living room so as to not make any noise and went down the hall to her bedroom.

He stood still in the complete darkness, letting his eyes adjust.

'Hi,' she said from the bed, though he could not yet see her.

' 'Lo.'

'Where have you been, Harry?'

She said it sweetly and with sleep still in her voice. It was not a challenge or a demand.

'I had to do a few things, then I had a few drinks.'

'Hear any good music?'

'Yeah, they had a quartet. Not bad. Played a lot of Billy Strayhorn.'

'Do you want me to fix you something?'

'Nah, go to sleep. You have school tomorrow. I'm not that hungry anyway and I can get something if I want it.'

'C'mere.'

He made his way to the bed and crawled across the down quilt. Her hand came up and around his neck and she pulled him down into a kiss.

'Yes, you did have a few drinks.'

He laughed and then so did she.

'Let me go brush my teeth.'

'Wait a minute.'

She pulled him down again and he kissed her mouth and neck. She had a milky sweet smell of sleep and perfume about her that he liked. He noticed that she was not wearing a nightgown, though she usually did. He put his hand under the covers and traced the flatness of her stomach. He brought it up and caressed her breasts and then her neck. He kissed her again and then pushed his face into her hair and neck.

'Sylvia, thank you,' he whispered.

'For what?'

'For coming today and being there. I know what I said before but it meant something to see you when I looked out there. It meant a lot.'

That was all he could say about it. He got up then and went into the bathroom. He stripped off his clothes and carefully hung them on hooks on the back of the door. He would have to wear them again in the morning.

He took a quick shower, then shaved and brushed his teeth with the second set of toiletries he kept in her bathroom. He looked in the mirror as he brushed his damp hair back with his hands. And he smiled. It might have been the residue of the whiskey and beer, he knew. But he doubted it. It was because he felt lucky. He felt that he was neither on the ferry with the mad crowd nor left behind on the dock with the angry crowd. He was in his own boat. With just Sylvia.

They made love the way lonely people do, silently, with each trying too hard in the dark to please the other until they were almost clumsy about it. Still, there was a healing sense about it for Bosch. Afterward, she lay next to him, her finger tracing the outline of his tattoo.

'What are you thinking about?' she asked.

'Nothing. Just stuff.'

'Tell me.'

He waited a few moments before answering.

'Tonight I found out somebody betrayed me. Somebody close. And, well, I was just thinking that maybe I'd had it wrong. That it really wasn't me who was betrayed. It was himself. He had betrayed himself. And maybe living with that is punishment enough. I don't think I need to add to it.'

He thought about what he had said to Edgar at the Red Wind and decided he would have to stop him from going to Pounds for the transfer.

'Betrayed how?'

'Uh, consorting with the enemy, I guess you'd call it.'

'Honey Chandler?'

'Yeah.'

'How bad is it?'

'Not too bad, I guess. It's just that he did it that matters. It hurts, I guess.'

'Is there anything you can do? Not to him, I mean. I mean to limit the damage.'

'No. Whatever damage there is, it's already done. I only figured out it was him tonight. It was by accident, otherwise I probably would have never even thought of him. Anyway, don't worry about it.'

She caressed his chest with the tips of her fingernails.

'If you're not worried, I'm not.'

He loved her knowing the boundaries of how much she could ask him, and that she didn't even think to ask him who it was he was talking about. He felt totally comfortable with her. No worries, no anxieties. It was home to him.

He was just beginning to fall off when she spoke again.

'Harry?'

'Uh huh.'

'Are you worried about the trial, how the closing arguments will go?'

'Not really. I don't like being in the fishbowl, sitting at that table while everybody gets their chance to explain why they think I did what I did. But I'm not worried about the outcome, if that's what you mean. It doesn't mean anything. I just want it to be over and I don't really care anymore what they do. No jury can sanction what I did or didn't do. No jury can tell me I was right or wrong. You know? This trial could last a year and it wouldn't tell them everything about that night.'

'What about the department? Will they care?'

He told her what Irving had told him that afternoon about what effect the trial's outcome would have. He didn't say anything about what the assistant chief had said about knowing his mother. But Irving's story crossed through his mind and for the first time since he had been in bed he felt the need for a cigarette.

But he didn't get up. He put the urge out of his mind and they lay quietly for a while after that. Bosch kept his eyes open in the dark. His thoughts were now about Edgar and then they segued to Mora. He wondered what the vice cop was doing at the same moment. Was he alone in the dark? Was he out looking?

'I meant what I said earlier today, Harry,' Sylvia said.

'What's that?'

'That I want to know all about you, your past, the good and the bad. And I want you to know about me. . . . Don't ignore this. It could hurt us.'

Her voice had lost some of its sleepy sweetness. He was silent and closed his eyes. He knew this one thing was more important to her than anything. She had been the loser in a past relationship where the stories of the past were not used as the building blocks of the future. He brought his hand up and rubbed his thumb along the back of her neck. She always smelled powdery after sex, he thought, yet she had not even gotten up to go into the bathroom. This was a mystery to him. It took him a while to answer her.

'You have to take me without a past. . . . I've let it go and don't want to go back to examine it, to tell it, to even think about it. I've spent my whole life getting away from my past. You understand? Just because a lawyer can throw it at me in a courtroom doesn't mean I have to . . .'

'What, tell me?'

He didn't answer. He turned his body into her and kissed and embraced her. He just wanted to hold her, to pull back away from this cliff.

'I love you,' she said.

'I love you,' he said.

She pulled herself closer to him and put her face in the crook of his neck. Her arms held him tightly, as if maybe she was scared.

It was the first time he had said it to her. It was the first time he had said it to anyone as far back as he could remember. Maybe he had never said it. It felt good to him, almost like a palpable presence, a warm flower of deep red opening in his chest. And he realized he was the one who was a little bit scared. As if by simply saying the words he had taken on a great responsibility. It was scary yet exciting. He thought of himself in the mirror, smiling.

She held herself pressed against him and he could feel her breath against his neck. In a short while her breathing became more measured as she fell asleep.

Lying awake, Bosch held her like that until well into the night. Now sleep would not come to him and with the insomnia came realities that robbed him of the good feelings he had only minutes before. He had thought about what she had said about betrayal and trust. And he knew that the pledges they spoke to each other this night would founder if built on deception. He knew what she had said was true. He would have to tell her who he was, what he was, if the words he had spoken were ever to be more than words. He thought about what Judge Keyes had said about words being beautiful and ugly on their own. Bosch had spoken the word love. He knew now that he must make it either ugly or beautiful.

The bedroom's windows were on the east side of the house and the light of dawn was just beginning to cling to the edges of the blinds when Bosch finally closed his eyes and slept.

TWENTY-TWO

Bosch looked rumpled and worn-out when he entered the courtroom Friday morning. Belk was already there, scribbling on his yellow pad. He looked up and appraised him as Bosch sat down.

'You look like shit and smell like an ashtray. And the jury will know that's the same suit and tie you wore yesterday.'

'A clear sign I'm guilty.'

'Don't be such a smartass. You never know what may turn a juror one way or the other.'

'I don't really care. Besides, you're the one who has to look good today, right, Belk?'

This was not an encouraging thing to say to a man at least eighty pounds overweight who broke out in flop sweat every time the judge looked at him.

'What the hell do you mean you don't care? Everything is on the line today and you waltz in looking like you slept in your car and say you don't care.'

'I'm relaxed, Belk. I call it Zen and the art of not giving a shit.'

'Why now, Bosch, when I could have settled this for five figures two weeks ago?'

'Because I realize now that there are things more important than what twelve of my so-called peers think. Even if, as peers, they wouldn't give me the time of day on the street.'

Belk looked at his watch and said, 'Leave me alone, Bosch. We start in ten minutes and I want to be ready. I'm still working on my argument. I'm going to go shorter than even Keyes demanded.'

Earlier in the trial, the judge had determined that closing arguments would be no longer than a half hour for each side. This was to be divided, with the plaintiff – in the person of Chandler – arguing for twenty minutes followed by the defendant's lawyer – Belk – delivering his entire thirty-minute argument. The plaintiff would then be allowed the last ten minutes. Chandler would have first and last word, another sign, Bosch believed, that the system was stacked against him.

Bosch looked over at the plaintiff's table and saw Deborah Church sitting there by herself, eyes focused straight ahead. The two daughters were in the first row of the gallery behind her. Chandler was not there but there were files and yellow pads laid out on the table. She was around.

'You work on your speech,' he said to Belk. 'I'll leave you alone.'

'Don't be late coming back. Not again, please.'

As he had hoped, Chandler was outside smoking by the statue. She gave him a cold glance, said nothing and then took a few steps away from the ash can in order to ignore him. She had on her blue suit – it was probably her lucky suit – and the one tress of blonde hair was loose from the braid at the back of her neck.

'Rehearsing?' Bosch asked.

'I don't need to rehearse. This is the easy part.'

'I suppose.'

'What's that mean?'

'I don't know. I suppose you're freer from the constraints of law during the arguments. Not as many rules of what you can and can't say. I think that's when you'd be in your element.'

'Very perceptive.'

That was all she said. There was no indication that she knew her arrangement with Edgar had been discovered. Bosch had been counting on that when he rehearsed what

263

he was going to say to her. After waking from his brief sleep, he had looked at the events of the night before with a fresh mind and eyes and had seen something that was missed before. It was now his intention to play her. He had thrown her the soft pitch. Now he had a curve.

'When this is over,' he said, 'I'd like the note.'

'What note?'

'The note the follower sent you.'

A look of shock hit her face but was then quickly erased with the indifferent look she normally gave him. But she had not been quick enough. He had seen the look in her eyes, she sensed danger. He knew then he had her.

'It's evidence,' he said.

'I don't know what you're talking about, Detective Bosch. I need to get back inside.'

She stubbed a half-smoked cigarette with a lipstick print on the butt into the ash can, then took two steps toward the door.

'I know about Edgar. I saw you with him last night.'

That stopped her. She turned around and looked at him.

'The Hung Jury. A Bloody Mary at the bar.'

She weighed her response and then said, 'Whatever he told you, I'm sure it was designed to place him in the best light. I would be careful if you are planning to go public with it.'

'I'm not going public with anything . . . unless you don't give me the note. Withholding evidence of a crime is a crime in itself. But I don't need to tell you that.'

'Whatever Edgar told you about a note is a lie. I told him noth –'

'And he told me nothing about a note. He didn't need to. I figured it out. You called him Monday after the body was found because you already knew about it and knew it was connected to the Dollmaker. I wondered how, and then it was clear. We got a note but that was secret until the next day. The only one who found out was Bremmer but his story said you couldn't be reached for comment. That was

264

because you were out meeting Edgar. He said you called that afternoon asking about the body. You asked if we got a note. That was because you got a note, Counselor. And I need to see it. If it is different from the one we got, it could be helpful.'

She looked at her watch and quickly lit another cigarette.

'I can get a warrant,' he said.

She laughed a fake sort of laugh.

'I'd like to see you get a warrant. I'd like to see the judge in this town who would sign a warrant allowing the LAPD to search my house with this case in the papers every day. Judges are political animals, Detective, nobody's going to sign a warrant and then possibly come out on the wrong end of this.'

'I was thinking more along the lines of your office. But thanks for at least telling me where it is.'

The look came back into her face for a split second. She had slipped and maybe that was as big a shock to her as anything he had said. She put the cigarette into the sand after two puffs. Tommy Faraway would cherish it when he found it later.

'We convene in one minute. Detective, I don't know anything about a note. Understand? Nothing at all. There is no note. If you try to make any trouble over this, I will make even more for you.'

'I haven't told Belk and I'm not going to. I just want the note. It's got nothing to do with the case at trial.'

'That's easy for . . .'

'For me to say because I haven't read it? You're slipping, Counselor. Better be more careful than that.'

She ignored that and went on to other business.

'Another thing, if you think my . . . uh, arrangement with Edgar is grounds for a mistrial motion or a misconduct complaint, you will find that you are dead wrong. Edgar agreed to our relationship without any provocation. He suggested it, in fact. If you make any complaint I will sue you for slander and send out press releases when I do it.'

He doubted anything that happened was at Edgar's suggestion but let it go. She gave him her best dead-eyed, killer look, then opened the door and disappeared through it.

Bosch finished his smoke, hoping his play might at least knock her off speed a little bit during her closing argument. But most of all he was pleased that he had gotten tacit confirmation of his theory. The follower had sent her a note.

The silence that descended over the courtroom as Chandler walked to the lectern was the kind of tension-filled quiet that accompanies the moment before a verdict is read. Bosch felt that this was because the verdict was a foregone conclusion in many of the minds in the courtroom and Chandler's words here would serve as his coup de grâce. The final, deadly blow.

She began with the perfunctory thank-yous to the jury for their patience and close attention to the case. She said she was fully confident that they would fairly deliberate a verdict.

In the trials Bosch had attended as an investigator, this was always stated by both lawyers to the jury, and he always thought it was a crock. Most juries have members who are there simply to avoid going to work at the factory or office. But once there, the issues are either too complicated or scary or boring and they spend their days in the box just trying to stay awake between the breaks, when they can fortify themselves with sugar, caffeine and nicotine.

After that opening salutation, Chandler quickly got to the heart of the matter. She said, 'You will recall that on Monday I stood before you and gave you the road map. I told you what I would set out to prove, what I needed to prove and now it is your job to decide if I have done that. I think when you consider the week's testimony, you will have no doubt that I have.

'And speaking of doubt, the judge will instruct you but I

would like to take a moment to explain to you once again that this is a civil matter. It is not a criminal case. It is not like Perry Mason or like anything else you have seen on TV or at the movies. In a civil trial, in order for you to find for the plaintiff, it requires only that a preponderance of the evidence be in favor of the plaintiff's case. A preponderance, what does that mean? It means the evidence for the plaintiff's case outweighs the evidence against it. A majority. It can be a simple majority, just fifty percent, plus one.'

She spent a lot of time on this subject because this would be where the case was won or lost. She had to take twelve legally inept people – this was guaranteed by the juror selection process – and relieve them of media-conditioned beliefs or perceptions that cases were decided by reasonable doubts or beyond the shadow of doubt. That was for criminal cases. This was civil. In civil, the defendant lost the edge he got in criminal.

'Think of it as a set of scales. The scales of justice. And each piece of evidence or testimony introduced has a certain weight, depending on the validity you give it. One side of the scales is the plaintiff's case and the other, the defendant's. I think that when you have gone into the jury room to deliberate and have properly weighed the evidence of the case, there will be no doubt that the scales are tipped in the plaintiff's favor. If you find that is indeed the case, then you must find for Mrs Church.'

With the preliminaries out of the way, Bosch knew that she now had to finesse the rest, because the plaintiff was essentially presenting a two-part case, hoping to win at least one of them. One being that maybe Norman Church was the Dollmaker, a monstrous serial killer, but even if so, Bosch's actions behind the badge were equally heinous and should not be forgiven. The second part, the one that would surely bring untold riches if the jury bought it, was that Norman Church was an innocent and that Bosch had cut him down in cold blood, depriving his family of a loving husband and father.

'The evidence presented this week points to two possible findings by you,' Chandler told the jury. 'And this will be the most difficult task you have, to determine the level of Detective Bosch's culpability. Without a doubt it is clear that he acted rashly, recklessly and with wanton disregard for life and safety on the night Norman Church was killed. His actions were inexcusable and a man paid for it with his life. A family paid for it with its husband and father.

'But you must look beyond that at the man who was killed. The evidence – from the videotape that is a clear alibi for one killing attributed to Norman Church, if not all of them, to the testimony of loved ones – should convince you that the police had the wrong man. If not, then Detective Bosch's own acknowledgments on the witness stand make it clear that the killings did not stop, that he killed the wrong man.'

Bosch saw that Belk was scribbling on his pad. Hopefully, he was making note of all the things about Bosch's testimony and others that Chandler was conveniently leaving out of her argument.

'Lastly,' she was saying, 'you must look beyond the man who was killed and look at the killer.'

Killer, Bosch thought. It sounded so awful when applied to him. He said the word over and over in his mind. Yes, he had killed. He had killed before and after Church, yet being called simply a killer without the explanations attached somehow seemed horrible. In that moment he realized that he did care after all. Despite what he had said earlier to Belk, he wanted the jury to sanction what he had done. He needed to be told he had done the right thing.

'You have a man,' she said, 'who has repeatedly shown the taste for blood. A cowboy who killed before and since the episode with the unarmed Mr Church. A man who shoots first and looks for evidence later. You have a man with a deep-seated motive for killing a man who he thought might be a serial killer of women, of women from the street . . . like his own mother.'

She let that float out there for a while as she pretended to be checking a point or two in the notes on her pad.

'When you go back into that room, you will have to decide if this is the kind of police officer you want in your city. The police force is supposed to mirror the society it protects. Its officers should exemplify the best in us. Ask yourself while you deliberate, who does Harry Bosch exemplify? What segment of our society does he present the mirror image of? If the answers to those questions don't trouble you, then return with a verdict in the defendant's favor. If they do trouble you, if you think our society deserves better than the cold-blooded killing of a potential suspect, then you have no choice but to return a verdict finding for the plaintiff.'

Chandler paused here to go to the plaintiff's table and pour a glass of water. Belk leaned close to Bosch and whispered, 'Not bad but I've seen her do better. . . . I've also seen her do worse.'

'The time she did worse,' Bosch whispered back, 'did she win?'

Belk looked down at his pad, making the answer clear. As Chandler was returning to the lectern he leaned back to Bosch.

'This is her routine. Now she'll talk about money. After getting the water, Money always talks about money.'

Chandler cleared her throat and began again.

'You twelve people are in a rare position. You have the ability to make societal change. Not many people ever get that chance. If you feel Detective Bosch was wrong, to whatever degree, and find for the plaintiff, you will be making change because you will be sending a clear signal, a message to every police officer in this city. From the chief and the administrators inside Parker Center two blocks from here to every rookie patrol officer on the street, the message will be that we do not want you to act this way. We will not accept it. Now, if you return such a verdict you must also set monetary damages. This is not a complicated task. The complicated part is the first part, deciding whether Detective Bosch was right or wrong. The damages can be anything, from one dollar to one million dollars or more. It doesn't matter. What is important is the message. For with the message, you will bring justice for Norman Church. You will bring justice to his family.'

Bosch looked around behind himself and saw Bremmer in the gallery with the other reporters. Bremmer smiled slyly and Bosch turned back around. The reporter had been right on the money about Money.

Chandler walked back to the plaintiff's table, picked up a book and took it back to the lectern. It was old and without a dust jacket, its green cloth binding cracking. Bosch thought he could see a mark, probably a library stamp, on the top edge of its pages.

'In closing now,' she said, 'I would like to address a concern you might have. I know it is one I might have if I were in your place. And that is, how is it that we have come to have men like Detective Bosch as our police? Well, I don't think we can hope to answer that and it is not at point in this case. But if you recall, I quoted to you the philosopher Nietzsche at the beginning of the week. I read his words about the black place he called the abyss. To paraphrase him, he said we must take care that whoever fights monsters for us does not also become a monster. In today's society it is not hard to accept that there are monsters out there, many of them. And so it is not hard, then, to believe that a police officer could become a monster himself.

'After we finished here yesterday, I spent the evening at the library.'

She glanced over at Bosch as she said this, flaunting the lie. He stared back at her and refused the impulse to look away.

'And I'd like to finish by reading something I found that Nathaniel Hawthorne wrote about the same subject we are dealing with today. That chasm of darkness where it can be easy for a person to cross over to the wrong side. In his book *The Marble Faun,* Hawthorne wrote, "The chasm was merely one of the orifices of that pit of blackness that lies beneath us . . . everywhere."

'Ladies and gentlemen, be careful in your deliberations and be true to yourselves. Thank you.'

It was so quiet that Bosch could hear her heels on the rug as she walked back to her seat.

'Folks,' Judge Keyes said, 'we're gonna take a fifteen-minute break and then Mr Belk gets his turn.'

As they were standing for the jury, Belk whispered, 'I can't believe she used the word orifice in her closing argument.'

Bosch looked at him. Belk seemed gleeful but Bosch recognized that he was just latching on to something, anything, so that he could pump himself up and get ready for his own turn behind the lectern. For Bosch knew that whatever words Chandler had used, she had been awfully good. Appraising the sweating fat man next to him, he felt not one bit of confidence.

Bosch went out to the justice statue and smoked two cigarettes during the break but Honey Chandler never came out. Tommy Faraway swung by, however, and clicked his tongue approvingly when he found the nearly whole cigarette she had put in the ash can before. He moved on without saying anything else. It occurred to Bosch that he had never seen Tommy Faraway smoke one of the stubs he culled from the sand.

Belk surprised Bosch with his closing. It wasn't half bad. It was just that he wasn't in the same league as Chandler. His closing was more a reaction to Chandler's than a stand-alone treatise on Bosch's innocence and the unfairness of the accusations against him. He said things like, 'In all of Ms Chandler's talk about the two possible findings you can come up with, she completely forgot about a third, that being that Detective Bosch acted properly and wisely. Correctly.'

It scored points for the defense but it was also a backhanded confirmation by the defense that there were two possible findings for the plaintiff. Belk did not see this but Bosch did. The assistant city attorney was giving the jury three choices now, instead of two, and still only one choice absolved Bosch. At times he wanted to pull Belk back to the table and rewrite his script. But he couldn't. He had to hunker down as he had in the tunnels of Vietnam when the bombs would be hitting above ground, and hope that there were no cave-ins.

The middle of Belk's argument was largely centered on the evidence linking Church to the nine murders. He repeatedly hammered home that Church was the monster in this story, not Bosch, and the evidence clearly backed that up. He warned the jurors that the fact that similar murders apparently continued was unrelated to what Church had done and how Bosch reacted in the apartment on Hyperion.

He finally hit what Bosch figured to be his stride near the end. An inflection of true anger entered his voice when he criticized Chandler's description of Bosch as having acted recklessly and with wanton disregard for life.

'The truth is that life was all Detective Bosch had on his mind when he went through that door. His actions were predicated on the belief that another woman, another victim, was there. Detective Bosch had only one choice. That was to go through that door, secure the situation and deal with the consequences. Norman Church was killed when he refused repeated orders from a police officer and made the move to the pillow. It was a hand he dealt, not Bosch, and he paid the ultimate price.

'But think of Bosch in that situation. Can you imagine being there? Alone? Afraid? It is a unique individual who faces that kind of situation without flinching. It is what our society calls a hero. I think when you return to the jury room and carefully weigh the facts, not the accusations, of this case you will come to that same conclusion. Thank you very much.'

Bosch couldn't believe Belk had used the word hero in a closing argument but decided not to bring that up with the portly lawyer as he returned to the defense table.

Instead, he whispered, 'You did good. Thanks.'

Chandler went to the lectern for her last shot and promised to be brief. She was.

'You can easily see the disparity of the beliefs the lawyers have in this case. The same disparity between the meanings of the words hero and monster. I suspect, as we all probably do, that the truth of this case and Detective Bosch is somewhere in between.

'Two last things before you begin deliberations. First, I want you to remember that both sides had the opportunity here to present full and complete cases. In Norman Church's behalf, we had a wife, a coworker, a friend, stand up and testify to his character, to what kind of man he was. Yet, the defense chose to have only one witness testify before you. Detective Bosch. No one else stood up for Detective –'

'Objection!' Belk yelled.

'– Bosch.'

'Hold it right there, Ms Chandler,' Judge Keyes boomed.

The judge's face became very red as he thought about how to proceed.

'I should clear the jury out of here to do what I am going to do but I think if you're going to play with fire you have to accept the burns. Ms Chandler, I'm holding you in contempt of this court for that grievous display of poor judgment. We'll talk about sanctions at a later date. But I guarantee that it won't be a pleasant date to look forward to.'

The judge then swiveled in his chair toward the jury and leaned forward.

'Folks, this lady should never have said that. You see, the defense is not obligated to put anybody up as a witness and whether they do or don't, that cannot be seen as a reflection on their guilt or innocence on the matter before you. Ms Chandler darn well knew this. She's an experienced trial lawyer and you better believe she knew this. The fact that she went and said it anyway, knowing Mr Belk over there and myself would practically hit the ceiling, I think shows a cunning on her behalf that I find very distasteful and troubling in a court of law. I'm going to complain about that to the state law board but –'

'Your Honor,' Chandler cut in. 'I object to you tell –'

'Don't interrupt, Counselor. You stand there and keep quiet until I am through.'

'Yes, Your Honor.'

'I said keep quiet.' He turned back to the jury. 'As I was saying, what happens to Ms Chandler is not for you to worry about. See, she's taking a gamble that no matter what I say to you now, you will still think about what she said about Detective Bosch not bringing any supporters to testify. I tell you now with the sternest admonition I can offer, do not think about that. What she said means nothing. In fact, I suspect that if he wanted to, Detective Bosch and Mr Belk could muster a line of police officers ready to testify that would stretch out that door all the way to Parker Center if they thought they wanted it. But they don't. That's the strategy they chose and it is not your duty to question it in any way. Any way at all. Any questions?'

No one in the jury box even moved. The judge turned his chair back and looked at Belk.

'Anything you want to say, Mr Belk?'

'One moment, Your Honor.'

Belk turned to Bosch and whispered, 'What do you think? He's primed to grant a mistrial. I've never seen him so mad. We'd get a new trial, maybe by then this copycat thing will be wrapped up.'

Bosch thought a moment. He wanted this over and did not like the prospect of going through another trial with Chandler.

'Mr Belk?' the judge said.

'I think we go with what we've got,' Bosch whispered. 'What do you think?'

Belk nodded and said, 'I think he might have just given us the verdict.'

Then he stood in his place and said, 'Nothing at this time, Your Honor.'

'You sure now?'

'Yes, Your Honor.'

'Okay, Ms Chandler, like I said, we'll deal with this at a later time but we will deal with it. You can proceed now, but be very careful.'

'Your Honor, thank you. I want to say before going on that I apologize for my line of argument. I meant no disrespect to you. I, uh, was speaking extemporaneously and got carried away.'

'You did. Apology accepted, but we will still deal with the contempt order later. Let's proceed. I want the jury to begin their work right after lunch.'

Chandler adjusted her position at the lectern so that she was looking at the jury.

'Ladies and gentlemen, you heard Detective Bosch on the stand yourself. I ask you, lastly, to remember what he said. He said Norman Church got what he deserved. Think about that statement coming from a police officer and what it means. "Norman Church got what he deserved." We have seen in this courtroom how the justice system works. The checks and balances. The judge to referee, the jury to decide. By his own admission, Detective Bosch decided that was not necessary. He decided there was no need for a judge. No need for a jury. He robbed Norman Church of his chance for justice. And so, ultimately, he robbed you. Think about that.'

She picked her yellow pad up off the lectern and sat down.

TWENTY-THREE

The jury began its deliberations at 11:15 and Judge Keyes ordered the federal marshals to arrange for lunch to be sent in. He said the twelve would not be interrupted until 4:30, unless they came up with a verdict first.

After the jury had filed out, the judge ordered that all parties be able to appear for a reading of the verdict within fifteen minutes of notification by the clerk. That meant Chandler and Belk could go back to their respective offices to wait. Norman Church's family was from Burbank so the wife and two daughters opted to go to Chandler's office. For Bosch, the Hollywood station would have been more than a fifteen-minute commute, but Parker Center was a five-minute walk. He gave the clerk his pager number and told her he'd be there.

The last piece of business the judge brought up was the contempt order against Chandler. He set a hearing for it to be discussed for two weeks later and then banged his gavel down.

Before leaving the courtroom, Belk took Bosch aside and said, 'I think we're in pretty good shape but I'm nervous. You want to spin the dice?'

'What are you talking about?'

'I could try to low-ball Chandler one last time.'

'Offer to settle?'

'Yeah. I have carte blanche from the office for anything up to fifty. After that, I'd have to get approval. But I could throw the fifty at her and see if they'd take it to walk away now.'

'What about legal fees?'

'On a settlement, she'd have to take the cut from the fifty. Someone like her, she's probably going forty percent. That'd be twenty grand for a week in trial and a week picking a jury. Not bad.'

'You think we're going to lose?'

'I don't know. I'm just thinking of all the angles. You never know what a jury will do. Fifty grand would be a cheap way out. She might take it, the way the judge came down on her there at the end. She's the one who's probably scared of losing now.'

Belk didn't get it, Bosch knew. Maybe it had been too subtle for him. The whole contempt thing had been Chandler's last scam. She had purposely committed the infraction so the jury would see her being slapped down by the judge. She was showing them the justice system at work: a bad deed met with stern enforcement and punishment. She was saying to them, do you see? This is what Bosch escaped. This is what Norman Church faced, but Bosch decided to take the judge and jury's role instead.

It was clever, maybe too clever. The more Bosch thought about it, the more he wondered how much the judge had been a willing and knowing player in it. He looked at Belk and saw the young assistant city attorney apparently suspected none of this. Instead, he thought of it as a stroke on his side of the page. Probably in two weeks, when Keyes lets her go with a hundred-dollar fine and a lecture during the contempt hearing, he'll get it.

'You can do whatever you want,' he told Belk. 'But she isn't going to take it. She's in on this one until the end.'

At Parker Center Bosch went into Irving's conference room through the door that opened directly off the hallway. Irving had decided the day before that the now-called Follower Task Force would work out of the conference room so the assistant chief could be kept up on developments to the minute. What wasn't said about the move but was known was that keeping the group out of one of the squad rooms improved the chance that word of what was happening would remain secure – for at least a few days.

When Bosch walked in only Rollenberger and Edgar were in the room. Bosch noticed that four phones had been installed and were on the round meeting table. There were also six rovers – Motorola two-way radios – and a main communications console on the table, ready to be used as needed. When Edgar looked up and saw Bosch he immediately looked away and picked up a phone to make a call.

'Bosch,' Rollenberger said. 'Welcome to our operations center. Are you free from the trial? No smoking in here, by the way.'

'I'm free until a verdict but I've got a fifteen-minute leash on me. Anything going on? What's Mora doing?'

'Not much is happening. Been quiet. Mora spent the morning in the Valley. Went to an attorney's office in Sherman Oaks and then to a couple of casting agencies, also in Sherman Oaks.'

Rollenberger was looking at a logbook in front of him on the table.

'After that he went to a couple houses in Studio City. There were vans outside of these houses and Sheehan and Opelt said they thought they might be making movies at these locations. He didn't stay long at either place. Anyway, he's back over at Ad-Vice now. Sheehan called in a couple minutes ago.'

'Did we get the extra people?'

'Yeah, Mayfield and Yde will take the watch at four from the first team. Then we've got two other teams after that.'

'Two?'

'Chief Irving changed his mind and wants an around-the-clock watch. So we'll be on him through the night, even if he just stays at home and sleeps. Personally, I think it's a good idea that we go 'round the clock.'

Yeah, especially since Irving decided to do it, Bosch thought but didn't say. He looked at the radios on the table.

'What's our freek?'

'Uh, we're on . . . frequency, frequency – oh, yeah, we're on five. Symplex five. It's a DWP communications freek that they only use during a public emergency. Earthquake, flooding, stuff like that. Chief thought it be best to keep off our own freeks. If Mora is our man, then he might be keeping an ear to the radio.'

Bosch thought Rollenberger probably thought it was a good idea, but didn't ask him.

'I think it's a good idea to play it safe this way,' the lieutenant said.

'Right. Anything else I should know?' He looked at Edgar, who was still on the phone. 'What's Edgar got?'

'Still trying to locate the survivor from four years ago. He already pulled a copy of Mora's divorce file. It was uncontested.'

Edgar hung up, finished writing something in a notebook and then stood up without looking at Bosch. He said, 'I'm going down to get a cup.'

'Okay,' Rollenberger said. 'We should have our own coffeemaker in here by this afternoon. I talked it over with the chief and he was going to requisition one.'

Bosch said, 'Good idea. I think I'm going down with Edgar.'

Edgar walked quickly down the hallway so that he could stay ahead of Bosch. At the elevator he pushed the button but then without breaking stride walked past the elevator and into the stairwell to go down. Bosch followed and after they had gone down one floor, Edgar stopped and whipped around.

'What are you following me for?'

'Coffee.'

'Oh, bullshit.'

'Did –'

'No, I didn't talk to Pounds yet. I've been busy, remember?'

'Good, then don't.'

'What are you talking about?'

'If you haven't talked to Pounds about it, then don't. Forget about it.'

'Serious?'

'Yeah.'

He stood there looking at Bosch, still skeptical.

'Learn from it. So will I. I already have. Okay?'

'Thanks, Harry.'

'No, don't "Thanks, Harry" me. Just say "okay".'

'Okay.'

They walked down to the next floor and to the cafeteria. Rather than sit in front of Rollenberger and talk, Bosch suggested they take their coffee to one of the tables.

'Hans Off, what a trip, man,' Edgar said. 'I keep picturing this cuckoo clock, only it's him that comes out and says, "Great idea, Chief! Great idea, Chief!" '

Bosch smiled and Edgar laughed. Harry could tell a great burden had been lifted off the man and so he was heartened by what he had done. He felt good about it.

'So, nothing on the survivor yet?' he said.

'She's out there somewhere. But the four years since she escaped from the Follower have not been good to Georgia Stern.'

'What happened?'

'Well, by reading her sheet and talking to some guys in street vice, it looks like she got on the needle. After that, she probably got too skaggy-looking to make movies. I mean, who wants to watch a film like that and the girl's got track marks up her arms or her thighs or her neck. That's the problem with the porno business if you're a hype. You're naked, man, you can't hide that shit.

'Anyway, I talked to Mora, just to make a routine contact and to tell him I was looking for her. He kinda gave me that rundown on how needle marks are the quickest way out of the business. But he had nothing else. You think that was cool, talking to him?'

Bosch considered it a few moments and then said, 'Yeah,

I do. Best way to keep him from being suspicious is to act like he knows as much as we do. If you hadn't asked him and then he heard from a source or somebody else in vice that you were looking for her, then he'd probably tumble to us.'

'Yeah, that's the way I figured it, so I called him this morning and asked a few questions and then went on. Far as he knows, you and me are the only ones working this new case. He doesn't know anything about our task force. So far.'

'Only problem with asking him about the survivor is that if he knows you're looking, he may go looking for her. We'll have to be careful about that. Let the surveillance teams know.'

'Yeah, I will. Maybe Hans Off can tell 'em. You ought to hear this guy on the rovers, sounds like a fuckin' Eagle Scout.'

Bosch smiled. He imagined Hans Off cut no slack in the use of radio code designations.

'Anyway, so that's why she isn't in the porno biz anymore,' Edgar said, getting back to the survivor. 'In the last three years, we got check charges, a couple of possessions, a couple prostitution rousts and many, many under-the-influence beefs. She's been in and out. Always time served, never anything serious. Two, three days at a time. Not enough to help her kick, either.'

'So where's she work?'

'The Valley. I've been on the phone with Valley Vice all morning. They say she usually works the Sepulveda corridor with the other street pros.'

Bosch remembered the young women he had seen the other afternoon while tracing down Cerrone, Rebecca Kaminski's manager/pimp. He wondered if he had seen or even talked to Georgia Stern and not known it.

'What is it?'

'Nothing. I was out there the other day and was wondering if I'd seen her. You know, not knowing who she was. Did the vice guys say whether she had protection?'

'Nah, no pimp that they know of. I got the idea she's bottom drawer stuff. Most pimps have better ponies.'

'So, is Vice up there looking for her?'

'Not yet,' Edgar said. 'They have training today, but they'll be out on Sepulveda tomorrow night.'

'Any recent photos?'

'Yeah.'

Edgar reached into his sport coat and pulled out a stack of photos. They were copies of a booking photo. Georgia Stern certainly looked used up. Her bleached-blonde hair showed at least an inch of dark roots. There were circles under her eyes so deep they looked as though they had been cut into her face with a knife. Her cheeks were gaunt and she was glassy-eyed. Lucky for her she had fixed before she was busted. It meant less time in the cage hurting, waiting and craving the next fix.

'This is three months old. Under the influence. She did two in Sybil and out.'

Sybil Brand Institute was the county's holding jail for women. Half of it was equipped to handle narcotics addicts.

'Get this,' Edgar said. 'I forgot about this. This guy Dean up in Valley Vice says he was the one who made this bust on her and when he was booking her he found a bottle of powder and was just about ready to run her ticket up to possession when he realized the bottle was a legit scrip. He said the powder was AZT. You know, for AIDS. She's got the virus, man, and she's out there on the street. On Sepulveda. He asked her if she makes 'em use rubbers and her answer was, "Not if they don't want to." '

Bosch just nodded. The story was not unusual. It had been Bosch's experience that most prostitutes despised the men they waved down and serviced for money. Those who became sick got it either from their customers or from dirty needles, which also sometimes came from customers. Either way, he believed it was part of the psychology to not care about passing it on to the population that may have given it to you. It was the belief that what goes around comes around.

'Not if they don't want to,' Edgar said again, shaking his head. 'I mean, man, that's cold.'

Bosch finished his coffee and pushed his chair back. There was no smoking in the cafeteria so he wanted to go down to the lobby and out by the fallen-officers memorial to smoke. As long as Rollenberger was camped out in the conference room, smoking there was out.

'So –'

Bosch's pager went off and he visibly flinched. He had always subscribed to the theory that a quick verdict was a bad verdict was a stupid verdict. Hadn't they given the evidence careful consideration? He pulled it off his belt and looked at the number on the display. He breathed easier. It was an LAPD exchange.

'I think Mora is calling me.'

'Better be careful. What were you going to say?'

'Uh, oh, yeah, I was just wondering if Stern will be any good to us if we find her. It's been four years. She's on the spike and sick. I wonder if she'll even remember the Follower.'

'Yeah, I was thinking that, too. But my only alternatives are to go back to Hollywood and report to Pounds or volunteer for one of the surveillance shifts on Mora. I'm sticking on this. I'm going up there to Sepulveda tonight.'

Bosch nodded.

'Hans Off said you pulled the divorce. Nothing there?'

'Not really. She filed but then Mora didn't contest it. File's about ten pages, that's it. Only one thing of note in it, and I don't know if it means anything or not.'

'What?'

'She filed on the usual grounds. Irreconcilable dif-ferences, mental cruelty. But in the records, she also mentions the loss of consortium. You know what that is?'

'No sex.'

'Yeah. What do you think that means?'

Bosch thought for a few moments and said, 'I don't know. They split just before the Dollmaker stuff. Maybe he was into some strange stuff, building up to the killings. I can ask Locke.'

'Yeah, that's what I was thinking. Anyway, I had DMV run the wife and she's still alive. But I was thinking we shouldn't approach her. Too dangerous. She might tip him.'

'Yeah, don't go near her. Did DMV fax her DL?'

'Yeah. She's blonde. Five-foot-four, hundred and ten. It was only a face shot on the driver's license but I'd say she fits.'

Bosch nodded and stood up.

After taking one of the rovers from the conference room, Bosch drove over to Central Division and parked in the back lot. He was still within the fifteen-minute radius of the federal courthouse. He left the rover in the car and walked out to the sidewalk and around front to the public entrance. He did this so he could see if he could spot Sheehan and Opelt. He assumed they would have to be parked within sight of the lot's exit so they would see Mora leaving, but he did not see them or any car that looked suspicious.

A pair of headlights briefly flashed from a parking lot behind an old gas station that was now a taco stand, featuring a sign that said HOME OF THE KOSHER BURRITO – PASTRAMI! He saw two figures in the car, which was a gray Eldorado, and just looked away.

Mora was at his desk eating a burrito that looked disgusting to Bosch because he could see it was filled with pastrami. It looked unnatural.

'Harry,' he said with his mouth full.

'How is it?'

'It's okay. I'll go back to plain beef after this. I just tried it 'cause I saw a couple guys from RHD over across the street. One of 'em said they come all the way over from Parker to get these kosher things there. Thought I'd give it a try.'

'Yeah, I think I've heard of that place.'

'Well, you ask me, it ain't worth coming over from Parker Center for.'

He wrapped what was left in the oil-stained paper it came in and then got up and walked out of the squad room. Bosch heard the package hit the bottom of a trash can in the hallway and then Mora was back.

'Don't want it to stink up my trash can.'

'So, you buzzed?'

'Yeah, that was me. How's the trial?'

'Waiting on a verdict.'

'Shit, that's scary.'

Bosch knew from experience that if Mora wanted to tell you something, he would tell you in his own time. It would do him no good to keep asking the vice cop why he beeped him.

Back in his chair, Mora swiveled around to the filing cabinets behind him and began opening drawers. Over his shoulder, he said, 'Hang on, Harry. I gotta get some stuff together for you here.'

It took him two minutes during which Bosch saw him open several different files, take out photos and create a short stack. Then he turned back around.

'Four,' he said. 'I've come up with four more actresses that dropped out under what might be termed suspicious circumstances.'

'Only four.'

'Yeah. Actually, there were more than four chicks that people mentioned. But only four fit that profile we talked about. Blonde and built. There is also Gallery, who we already knew about, and your concrete blonde. So we've got six all together. Here are the new ones.'

He handed the group of photos across the desk to Bosch. Harry slowly looked through them. They were color publicity glossies with each woman's name printed in the white border at the bottom of the photo. Two of the women were naked and posing indoors on chairs, their legs apart.

The other two were photographed at the beach and were wearing bikinis that would probably be illegal on most public beaches. To Bosch, the women in the photos almost looked interchangeable. Their bodies were similar. Their faces had the same fake pouts that were intended to show mystery and sexual abandonment at the same time. Each of the women had hair so blonde it was nearly white.

'All Snow Whites,' Mora said, an unneeded commentary that made Bosch look up from the photos to look at him. The vice cop just stared back and said, 'You know, the hair. That's what a producer calls them when he's casting movies. He says he wants a Snow White for this part 'cause he already has a red or whatever. Snow White. It's like the model name. These chicks are all interchangeable.'

Bosch looked back down at the photos, not trusting that his eyes would not give his suspicions away.

He realized, though, that much of what Mora had just said was true. The main physical differences between the women in the photos were the tattoos and their locations on each body. Each woman had a small tattoo of a heart or a rose or a cartoon character. Candi Cummings had a heart just to the left of her carefully trimmed triangle of pubic hair. Mood Indigo had some kind of cartoon just above her left ankle but Bosch couldn't make it out because of the angle the photograph had been taken from. Dee Anne Dozit had a heart wrapped in a vine of barbed wire about six inches above the left nipple, which was pierced with a gold ring. And TeXXXas Rose had a red rose on the soft part of her right hand between the thumb and first finger.

Bosch realized they might all be dead now.

'No one's heard from them?'

'No one in the biz, at least.'

'You're right. Physically, they fit.'

'Yeah.'

'They did outcall?'

'I assume they did, but I'm not sure yet. The people I talked to dealt with them in the film biz so they didn't know what these girls did when the cameras stopped rolling, so to speak. Or, so they said. My next step was to get some back issues of the sex rags and look for ads.'

'Any dates? You know, when they disappeared, stuff like that?'

'Just generally speaking. These people, the agents and the moviemakers, they don't have minds for dates. We're dealing with memories, so I've only got a general picture. If I find out they ran outcall ads, I'll narrow it down pretty close to exact dates when I find out when they last ran. Anyway, let me give you what I got. You got your notebook?'

Mora told him what he had. No specific dates, just months and years. Adding in the approximate dates when Rebecca Kaminski, the concrete blonde, Constance Calvin, who became Gallery on film, and the seventh and eleventh victims originally attributed to Church had disappeared, there was a rough pattern of disappearances of the porno starlets about every six to seven months. The last disappearance was Mood Indigo, eight months earlier.

'See the pattern? He's due. He's out there hunting.'

Bosch nodded and looked up from his notebook at Mora and thought he saw a gleam in his dark eyes. He thought he could see through them into a black emptiness inside. In that one chilling moment Bosch thought he saw the confirmation of evil in the other man. It was as if Mora was challenging him to come farther into the dark with him.

TWENTY-FOUR

Bosch knew he was stretching his leash by going down to USC, but it was two o'clock and his choice was to hang around the conference room with Rollenberger and wait for a verdict or do something useful with his time. He decided on the latter and got on the Harbor Freeway going south. Depending on how northbound traffic on the freeway was, he could conceivably get back to downtown in fifteen minutes if a verdict came in. Getting a parking space at Parker Center and walking over to the courthouse would be another matter.

The University of Southern California was located in the tough neighborhoods that surround the Coliseum. But once through the gate and into the general campus, it seemed as bucolic as Catalina, though Bosch knew this peace had been interrupted with a quickening frequency in recent years, to the point that even Trojan football practice could be dangerous. A couple of seasons back a stray bullet from one of the daily drive-by shootings in the nearby neighborhoods had struck a gifted freshman linebacker while he stood with teammates on the practice field. It was incidents like that that had administrators complaining on a routine basis to the LAPD and students longingly thinking about UCLA, which was cheaper and located in the relatively crime-free suburban milieu of Westwood.

Bosch easily found the psychology building with a map given to him at the entry gate, but once he was inside the four-story brick building there was no directory to help him find Dr John Locke or the psychohormonal studies lab. He walked down one lengthy hallway and then took stairs to the second floor. The first female student he asked for directions to the lab laughed, apparently believing his question was a come-on, and walked away without answering. He finally was directed to the basement of the building.

He read the signs on the doors as he walked along the dimly lit corridor and finally found the lab at the second-to-last doorway at the end of the hall. A blonde student sat behind a desk in the entry. She was reading a thick textbook. She looked up and smiled and Bosch asked for Locke.

'I'll call. Does he expect you?'

'You never know with a shrink.'

He smiled but she didn't get it, then he wondered if it was even a joke.

'No, I didn't say I was coming.'

'Well, Dr Locke has student labs running all day. I shouldn't disturb him if –'

She finally looked up and saw the badge he was holding.

'I'll call right away.'

'Just tell him it's Bosch and I need a few minutes if he can spare them.'

She spoke briefly on the phone to someone, reiterating what Bosch had just said. She then waited silently for a few moments, said 'Okay' and hung up.

'The grad assistant said Dr Locke said he will come get you. It should only be a few minutes.'

He thanked her and sat in one of the chairs by the door. He looked around the entry room. There was a bulletin board with handprinted announcements pinned to the cork. Mostly they were the roommate-wanted type of posting. There was an announcement of a party for psych undergrads this coming Saturday.

There was one other desk in the room in addition to the one the student occupied. But this one was empty at the moment.

'This part of the curriculum?' he asked. 'You have to put in time here as the receptionist?'

She looked up from the textbook.

'No, it's just a job. I'm in child psych but jobs in the lab there are hard to come by. Nobody likes working down here in the basement. So this was open.'

'How come?'

'All the creepy psychology is down here. Psychohormonal at this end. There is –'

The door opened on the other side of the room and Locke stepped through. He was wearing blue jeans and a tie-dyed T-shirt. He stuck his hand out to Bosch and Harry noticed the leather thong tied around his wrist.

'Harry, how goes it?'

'Fine. I'm fine. How're you? I'm sorry to barge in on you like this but I was wondering if you have a few minutes. I have some new information on that thing I bothered you with the other night.'

'No bother at all. Believe me, it's great to get my fingers on a real case. Student labs can be boring.'

He told Bosch to follow him and they went back through the door, down a hallway and into a suite of offices. Locke led him to the room in the back which was his office. Rows of textbooks and what Bosch guessed were collected theses lined shelves on the wall behind his desk. Locke dropped into a padded chair and put a foot up on the desk. A green banker's light on the table was lit, and the only other light came from a small casement window set high on the wall to the right. Every now and then the light from the window would flicker as someone up on the ground level walked by and briefly blocked its path, a human eclipse.

Looking up at the window, Locke said, 'Sometimes I feel like I'm working in a dungeon down here.'

'I think the student out front thinks so, too.'

'Melissa? Well, what do you expect? She's chosen child psychology as her major and I can't seem to convince her to cross to my side of the road. Anyway, I doubt you came to campus to hear stories about pretty young students, though I don't suppose it could hurt.'

'Maybe some other time.'

Bosch could smell that someone had smoked in the room, though he saw no ashtray. He took his cigarettes out without asking.

'You know, Harry, I could hypnotize you and alleviate that problem for you.'

'No thanks, Doc, I hypnotized myself once and it didn't work.'

'Really, are you one of the last of the dying breed of LAPD hypnotists? I heard about that experiment. Courts shot it down, right?'

'Yeah, wouldn't accept hypnotized witnesses in court. I'm the last one they taught who's still in the department. I think.'

'Interesting.'

'Anyway, there've been some developments since we last talked and I thought it would be good to touch base with you, see what you think. I think you steered us right with that porno angle and maybe you'll come up with something now.'

'What have you got?'

'We have —'

'First off, do you want some coffee?'

'Are you having any?'

'Never touch it.'

'Then I'm fine. We've come up with a suspect.'

'Really?'

He dropped his foot off the desk and leaned forward. He seemed genuinely interested.

'And he had a foot in both camps, like you said. He was on the task force and his beat, uh, his area of expertise is the pornography business. I don't think I should identify him at this time because —'

'Of course not. I understand. He's a suspect, hasn't been charged with anything. Detective, don't worry, this entire conversation is off the record. Speak freely.'

Bosch used a trash can next to Locke's desk as an ashtray.

'I appreciate it. So, we are watching him, seeing what he is doing. But it gets tricky here. See, because he is probably the department's top man on the porno industry, it is natural we go to him for advice and information.'

'Naturally, if you didn't, he would most assuredly become suspicious of the fact that you are suspicious of him. Oh what a wonderful web we weave, Harry.'

'Tangled.'

'What?'

'Nothing.'

Locke got up and started pacing around the room. He put his hands in his pockets and then took them out. He was staring at nothing, just thinking the whole time.

'Go on, this is great. What'd I tell you? Two independent actors playing the same role. The black heart does not beat alone. Go on.'

'Well, like I said, it was natural to go to him and we did. We suspected that, with the discovery of the body this week and what you said, that there might be others. Other women who disappeared who were in that business.'

'So you asked him to check it out? Excellent.'

'Yes, I asked him yesterday. And today he gave me four more names. We already had the name of the concrete blonde found this week and one other that the suspect provided the other day. So you add the first two – Dollmaker victims seven and eleven – and now we have a total of eight. The suspect was under surveillance all day so we know he did the legwork needed to come up with these new names. He didn't just give me four names. He went through the motions.'

'Of course he would do that. He would keep up the appearance of normal routine life whether he knew he was being followed or not. He would already know these names, you understand, but he would still go out and get them by doing the routine legwork. It's one of the signs of how smart he –'

He stopped, put his hands in his pocket and frowned while seemingly staring at the floor between his feet.

'You said six new names plus the first two?'

'Right.'

'Eight kills in almost five years. Any chance there are others?'

'I was going to ask you that. This information comes from the suspect. Would he lie? Would he tell us less, give us fewer names than there actually were to screw with us, to mess up the investigation?'

'Ah.' He continued pacing but didn't continue speaking for a half minute. 'My gut instinct is to say no. No, he would not screw with you, as you say. He would do his job in earnest. I think if all he has given you are five new names, then that's all there are. You have to remember that this man thinks he is superior to you, the police, in every aspect. It would not be unusual for him to be perfectly honest with you about some aspects of the case.'

'We have a rough idea of the times. The times of the killings. What it looks like is that he slowed his pace after the Dollmaker was killed. When he started hiding them, burying them, because he couldn't blend in any longer with the Dollmaker, the intervals lengthened. It looks like he went from less than two months between kills during the Dollmaker period to seven months. Maybe even longer. The last disappearance was almost eight months ago.'

Locke looked up from the floor at Bosch.

'And all this recent activity,' he said. 'The trial in the papers. His sending the note. His involvement as a detective in the case. The high activity will speed the end of the cycle. Don't lose him, Harry. It could be time.'

He turned and looked at the calendar that hung on the wall next to the door. There was some kind of maze-like design above the chart of the month's days. Locke started laughing. Bosch didn't get it.

'What?' he asked.

'Jeez, this weekend is a full moon, too.' He spun around to look at Bosch. 'Can you take me on the surveillance?'

'What?'

'Take me along. It would be the rarest of opportunities in the field of psychosexual studies. To observe the stalking pattern of a sexual sadist as it is actually taking place. Unbelievable. Harry, this could get me a grant from Hopkins. It could . . . it could' – his eyes lit up as he looked at the casement window – 'get me out of this fucking dungeon!'

Bosch stood up. He was thinking he had made a mistake. Locke's vision of his own future was obscuring everything else. He had come for help, not to make Locke shrink of the year.

'Look, we're talking about a killer here. Real people. Real blood. I'm not going to do anything that might compromise the investigation. A surveillance is a delicate operation. When you add that it is a cop we are watching, then it makes it even harder. I can't bring you along. Don't even ask. I can tell you things here and fill you in whenever I can but there is no way I or my commander on this would approve bringing a civilian along for the ride.'

Locke's eyes dropped and he looked like a chastised boy. He took a quick glance at the window again and walked around behind the desk. He sat down and his shoulders dropped.

'Yes, of course,' he said quietly. 'I completely understand, Harry. I got carried away there. The important thing is that we stop this man. We'll worry about studying him later. Now, a seven-month cycle. Wow, that's impressive.'

Bosch flicked his ashes and sat back down.

'Well, we don't know for sure, considering the source. There still could be others.'

'I doubt it.'

Locke pinched the bridge of his nose and leaned back in his chair. He closed his eyes. He did not move for several seconds.

'Harry, I'm not sleeping. Just concentrating. Just thinking.'

Bosch watched him for a few moments. It was weird. He then noticed that lined on a shelf just above Locke's head were the books the psychologist had written. There were several, all with his name on the spine. There were several duplicates, too. Maybe, Bosch thought, so he could give them away. He saw five copies of *Black Hearts,* the book Locke had mentioned during his testimony, and three copies of a book called, *The Private Sex Life of the Public Porn Princess*.

'You wrote about the porno business?'

He opened his eyes.

'Why, yes. That was the book I did before *Black Hearts*. Did you read it?'

'Uh, no.'

He closed his eyes again.

'Of course not. Despite the sexy title it really is a textbook. Used at the university level. Last I checked with my publisher, it was being sold in the bookstores at a hundred and forty-six universities, including Hopkins. It's been out two years, fourth printing, still haven't seen a royalty check. Would you like to read it?'

'I would.'

'Well, if you go by the student union on your way out of here, they sell it there. It's steep, I should warn you. Thirty bucks. But I'm sure you can expense it. I should also warn you, it's quite explicit.'

Bosch was annoyed that Locke didn't give him one of the extra copies on the shelf. Perhaps, it was Locke's childlike way of getting back at him for nixing the surveillance ride-along. He wondered what Melissa, the child-psych major, would make of such behavior.

'There is something else about this suspect. I don't know what it means.'

Locke opened his eyes but didn't move.

'He was divorced about a year before the Dollmaker

killings began. In the divorce record there's mention by the wife that there was a loss of consortium. Would that still fit?'

'They stopped doing it, huh?'

'I guess. It was in the court file.'

'It could fit. But to be honest, we shrinks could find a way to make any activity fit into any prognosis we make. That's the field for you. But it could be a case where your suspect simply became impotent with his wife. He was moving toward the erotic mold, and she had no part in it. In effect, he was leaving her behind.'

'So it is not seen by you to be a cause for rethinking our suspicions of this man?'

'On the contrary. My view is that it is more evidence that he has gone through major psychological changes. His sexual persona is evolving.'

Bosch gave this some thought while trying to envision Mora. The vice cop spent every day in the tawdry milieu of pornography. After a while, he couldn't get it up for his own wife.

'Is there anything else you can tell me? Anything about this suspect that might help us? We don't have anything on him. No probable cause. We can't arrest him. All we can do is watch. And that gets dangerous. If we lose him –'

'He could kill.'

'Right.'

'And then you are still left with no probable cause, no evidence.'

'What about trophies? What do I look for?'

'Where?'

'In his home.'

'Ah, I see. You plan to continue your professional interaction with him, to visit him at home. On a ruse, perhaps. But you won't be able to move about freely.'

'I might be able to, if someone else keeps him occupied. I'll go with somebody else.'

Locke leaned forward in his chair, his eyes wide. It was starting again, his excitement.

'What if you kept him busy and I had a look around? I am the expert on this, Harry. You would be better at keeping him busy. You could talk detective talk, I'd ask to use the bathroom. I would have a better grasp of —'

'Forget it, Dr Locke. Listen to me, there is no way it's going to happen that way. Okay? It's too dangerous. Now, do you want to help me here or not?'

'Okay, okay. Again, I'm sorry. The reason I am so exited by the prospect of being inside this man's house and mind is that I think that this man, who is on a killing cycle of seven months plus, would almost certainly have trophies that would help him feed into his fantasy and recreate his kills; thereby dulling urges to physically act out.'

'I understand.'

'You've got a man with an unusually long cycle. Believe me, during those seven months the impulses to act out, to go out and kill, do not lie dormant. They are there. They are always there. Remember, the erotic mold? I testified about it?'

'I remember.'

'Okay, well, he is going to need to satisfy that erotic mold. To fulfill it. How does he do it? How does he last six or seven or eight months? The answer is, he has trophies. These are reminders of past conquests. By conquests I mean kills. He has things that remind him and help bring the fantasy alive. It's not the real thing by a long shot but he can still use the reminders to widen the cycle, to stave off the impulse to act. He knows the less he kills, the less chance there is that he will be caught.

'If you're right about him, he is now nearly eight months into a cycle. It means he is pushing the edge of the envelope, all the while trying to maintain his control. Yet at the same time we have this note and his strange compulsion to not be overlooked. To stand up and say, I'm better than the Dollmaker. I go on! And if you don't believe me, check out what I left in the concrete at such and such a place. The note shows severe disassembling at the same time he is locked in this tremendous battle to control the impulses. He has gone seven months plus!'

Bosch pressed his cigarette against the side of the trash can and dropped it in. He took out his notebook. He said, 'The clothing of the victims, both the Dollmaker's and the Follower's, was never found. These could be the trophies he uses?'

'They could be, but put the notebook away, Harry. It's easier than that. Remember, what you have here is a man who chose his victims after seeing them in videos? So what better way to keep his fantasies alive than through videos. If you get free of him in the house, look for videos, Harry. And a camera.'

'He videotaped the killings,' Bosch said.

It wasn't a question. He was just repeating Locke, preparing himself for what was ahead with Mora.

'Of course, we can't say for sure,' Locke said. 'Who knows? But I'd put my money on it. You remember Westley Dodd?'

Bosch shook his head no.

'He was the one they executed a couple of years ago in Washington. Hanged him – a perfect example of what goes around comes around. He was a child-killer. Liked to hang kids in his closet, on coat hangers. And he also had a Polaroid camera he liked to use. After his arrest the police found a carefully kept photo album, complete with Polaroids of the little boys he killed – hanging in the closet. He had taken the time to carefully label each picture with a caption. Very sick stuff. But as sick as it was, I guarantee you that that photo album saved the lives of other little boys. Absolutely. Because he could use it to indulge his fantasy and not act it out.'

Bosch nodded his understanding. Somewhere in Mora's house he would find a video or maybe a photographic gallery that would turn most people's stomachs. But for Mora it was what kept him out of the black place for as long as eight months at a time.

'What about Jeffrey Dahmer?' Locke said. 'Remember him, in Milwaukee? He was a cameraman, too. Liked taking pictures of corpses, parts of corpses. Helped him go undetected by the police for years and years. Then he started keeping the corpses. That was his mistake.'

They were silent for a few moments after that. Bosch's head filled with horrible images of the dead he had seen. He rubbed his eyes as if that might erase them.

'What's that they say about photos?' Locke asked then. 'On the TV commercials? Something like "the gift that keeps on giving". Then what's that make videotape to a serial killer?'

Before leaving campus, Bosch dropped by the student union and went into the bookstore. He found a stack of copies of Locke's book on the porno business in the section on psychology and social studies. The top one on the stack was well worn around the edges from being thumbed through. Bosch took the one below it.

When the girl at the register opened the book to get the price it flopped open to a black-and-white photo of a woman performing fellatio on a man. The girl's face turned red but not as scarlet as Bosch's.

'Sorry,' was all he could think to say.

'That's okay, I've seen it before. The book, I mean.'

'Yeah.'

'Are you teaching a class with it next semester?'

Bosch realized that since he was too old to look like a student, seemingly the only valid reason for him to be buying the book was if he was a teacher. He thought that explaining that his interest was as a police officer would sound phony and get him more attention than he wanted.

'Yes,' he lied.

'Really, what's it called? Maybe I'll take it.'

'Uh, well, I haven't decided yet. I'm still formulating a –'

'Well, what's your name? I'll look for it in the catalog.'

'Uh . . . Locke. Dr John Locke, psychology.'

'Oh, you wrote the book. Yeah, I've heard of you. I'll look the class up. Thanks and have a good day.'

She gave him his change. He thanked him and left with the book in a bag.

TWENTY-FIVE

Bosch was back in the federal courthouse shortly after four. While they waited for Judge Keyes to come out and dismiss the jury for the weekend, Belk whispered that he had called Chandler's office during the afternoon and offered the plaintiff fifty grand to walk away from the case.

'She told you to shove it.'

'She wasn't that polite, actually.'

Bosch smiled and looked over at Chandler. She was whispering something to Church's wife but must have felt Bosch's stare. She stopped speaking and looked over at him. For nearly half a minute they engaged in an adolescent stare-down contest, with neither backing down until the door to the judge's chambers opened and Judge Keyes bounded out and up to his place on the bench.

He had the clerk buzz in the jury. He asked if there was anything anybody needed to talk about and, when there wasn't, he instructed the jurors to avoid reading newspaper accounts of the case or watching the local TV news. He then ordered the jurors and all other parties to the case to be back by 9:30 A.M., Monday, when deliberations would begin again.

Bosch stepped on the escalator to go down to the lobby exit right behind Chandler. She was standing about two steps up from Deborah Church.

'Counselor?' he said in a low voice so the widow would not hear. Chandler turned around on the step, grabbing the handrail for balance.

'The jury is out, there is nothing that can change the case

now,' he said. 'Norman Church himself could be waiting for us in the lobby and we wouldn't be able to tell the jury. So, why don't you give me the note? This case might be over, but there is still an investigation.'

Chandler said nothing the rest of the way down. But in the lobby she told Deborah Church to go on out to the sidewalk and she'd be along soon. Then she turned to Bosch.

'Again, I deny there is a note, okay?'

Bosch smiled.

'We're already past that, remember? You slipped up yesterday. You said –'

'I don't care what I said or you said. Look, if the guy sent me a note, it would've just been a copy of what you already got. He wouldn't waste his time writing a new one.'

'I appreciate you at least telling me that, but even a copy could be helpful. There could be fingerprints. The copy paper might be traceable.'

'Detective Bosch, how many times did you pull prints from the other letters he sent?'

Bosch didn't answer.

'That's what I figured,' she said. 'Have a good weekend.'

She turned and pushed her way through the exit door. Bosch waited a few seconds, put a cigarette in his mouth and went out himself.

Sheehan and Opelt were in the conference room filling in Rollenberger on their surveillance shift. Edgar was also sitting at the round table listening. Bosch saw he had a photo of Mora on the table in front of him. It was a face shot, like the one the department takes of every cop every year when they reissue ID cards.

'If it happens, it's not going to happen during the day anyway,' Sheehan was saying. 'So maybe tonight they'll have good luck.'

'All right,' Rollenberger said. 'Just type something up for the chron log and you guys can call it a day. I'll need it because I have a briefing with Chief Irving at five. But remember, you're both on call tonight. It's going to be all hands. If Mora starts acting hinky I want you to get back out there with Mayfield and Yde.'

'Right,' Opelt said.

While Opelt sat down at the lone typewriter Rollenberger had requisitioned, Sheehan poured them cups of coffee from the Mr Coffee that had appeared on the counter behind the round table sometime during the afternoon. Hans Off wasn't much of a cop but he could sure set up an Ops Center, Bosch thought. He poured himself a cup and joined Sheehan and Edgar at the table.

'I missed most of that,' he said to Sheehan. 'Sounds like nothing happened.'

'Right. After you dropped by, he went back out to the Valley in the afternoon and stopped by a bunch of different offices and warehouses in Canoga Park and Northridge. We've got the addresses if you want 'em. They were all porno distributors. Never stayed more than a half hour at any of them but we don't know what he was doing. Then he came back, did a little office work and went home.'

Bosch assumed Mora was checking with other producers, trying to hunt down more victims, maybe asking about the mystery man Gallery had described four years ago. He asked Sheehan where Mora lived and wrote down the Sierra Bonita Avenue address in his notebook. He wanted to warn Sheehan about how close he had come to blowing the operation at the taco stand but didn't want to do so in front of Rollenberger. He'd mention it later.

'Anything new?' he asked Edgar.

'Nothing on the survivor, yet,' Edgar answered. 'I'm leaving in five minutes to go up to Sepulveda. The girls do a lot of rush-hour work up there, maybe I'll see her, pick her up.'

Having gotten the updates from everyone else, Bosch told the detectives in the room about the information he had gotten from Mora and what Locke thought of it. At the end,

Rollenberger whistled at the information as if it were a beautiful woman.

'Man, the chief should know this pronto. He might want to double up on the surveillance.'

'Mora's a cop,' Bosch said. 'The more bodies you put on the watch, the better chance he has of making them. If he knows we're watching him, you can forget the whole thing.'

Rollenberger thought about this and nodded, but said, 'Well, we still have to let the man know what's developing. Tell you what, nobody go anywhere for a few minutes. I'll see if I can get with him a little early and we'll see where we go from there.'

He stood up with some papers in his hand and knocked on the door leading to Irving's office. He then opened it and disappeared through.

'Dipshit,' Sheehan said after the door was closed. 'Goin' in for a little mouth-to-ass resuscitation.'

Everybody laughed.

'Hey, you two,' Bosch said to Sheehan and Opelt. 'Mora mentioned your little meeting at the taco stand.'

'Shit!' Opelt exclaimed.

'I think he bought the kosher burrito line,' Bosch said and started laughing. 'Until he tasted one! He couldn't get why you guys'd come all the way over from Parker for one of those shitty things. He threw half of his out. So if he sees you again out there, he'll put it together. Watch your ass.'

'We will,' Sheehan said. 'That was Opelt's idea, that kosher burrito shit. He –'

'What? What'd you want me to say? The guy we're watching suddenly walks up to the car and says, "What's happening, boys?" I had to think of –'

The door opened and Rollenberger came back in. He went to his place but didn't sit down. Instead, he put both hands on the table and sternly leaned forward as if he had just been given orders from God.

'I've brought the chief up to date. He's very pleased with everything we've come up with in just twenty-four hours.

He is concerned about losing Mora, especially with the shrink saying we are at the end of the cycle, but he doesn't want to change the surveillance. Adding another team doubles the chance Mora will see something. I think he's right. It's a very good idea to maintain status quo. We –'

Edgar tried to hold back a laugh but couldn't. It sounded more like a sneeze.

'Detective Edgar, something funny?'

'No, I think I'm getting a cold or something. Go on, please.'

'Well, that's it. Proceed as planned. I will inform the other surveillance teams of what Bosch has come up with. We have Rector and Heikes taking the midnight shift, then the presidents tomorrow morning at eight.'

The presidents were a pair of RHD partners named Johnson and Nixon. They didn't like being called the presidents, especially Nixon.

'Sheehan, Opelt, you are back on tomorrow at four. You've got Saturday night, so be bright. Bosch, Edgar, still freelancing. See what you can come up with. Keep your pagers on and the rovers handy. We might need to pull everybody together on short notice.'

'OT approved?' Edgar asked.

'All weekend. But if you're on the clock, I want to see the work. Only humps on this job, no freeloading. All right, that's it.'

Rollenberger sat down then and pulled his chair close to the table. Bosch figured it was to cover up an erection, he seemed to get off so much on being the taskmaster here. All of them but Hans Off pushed into the hallway then and headed to the elevator.

'Who's drinking tonight?' Sheehan asked.

'More like, who isn't,' Opelt answered.

Bosch got to his house by seven, after having only one beer at the Code Seven and finding that the alcohol was a turn-off after the overindulgence of the night before. He called

Sylvia and told her there was no verdict yet. He said he was going to shower and change clothes and he would be up to see her by eight.

His hair was still damp when she opened her door. She grabbed him as soon as he stepped in and they held each other and kissed in the entry of her house for a long time. It was only when she stepped back that he saw she was wearing a black dress with a neckline that cut deeply between her breasts and a hemline about four inches over her knees.

'How'd it go today, the closing arguments and all?'

'Fine. What are you all dressed up for?'

'Because I am taking you out to dinner. I made reservations.'

She leaned into him and kissed him on the mouth.

'Harry, last night was the best night we've ever had together. It was the best night I can remember with anyone. And not because of the sex. Actually, you and I have done better.'

'Always room for improvement. How 'bout a little practice before dinner?'

She smiled and told him there was no time.

They drove down through the Valley and into Malibu Canyon to the Saddle Peak Lodge. It was an old hunting lodge and the menu featured a vegetarian's nightmare. It was all meat, from venison to buffalo. They each had a steak and Sylvia ordered a bottle of Merlot. Bosch sipped his slowly. He thought the meal and the evening were wonderful. They talked little about the case or anything else. They did a lot of looking at each other.

When they returned to her house, Sylvia turned down the air-conditioner thermostat and built a fire in the living room fireplace. He just watched her; he had never been good at building fires that lasted. Even with the AC on sixty it got very warm. They made love on a blanket she spread out in front of the fireplace. They were perfectly relaxed and moved smoothly together.

Afterward, he watched the fire reflect on the light sheen of sweat on her chest. He kissed her there and put his head down to listen to her heart. The rhythm was strong and it beat counterpoint to his own. He closed his eyes and started thinking of ways to guard against ever losing this woman.

The fire was nothing but a few glowing embers when he woke up in the darkness. There was a shrill sound and he was very cold.

'Your beeper,' Sylvia said.

He crawled to the pile of clothes near the couch, traced the sound and cut it off.

'God, what time is it?' she said.

'I don't know.'

'That's scary. I remember when –'

She stopped herself. Bosch knew it was a story about her husband that she was about to tell. She must have decided not to let his memory intrude here. But it was too late. Bosch found himself wondering if Sylvia and her husband had ever turned down the thermostat on a summer night and made love in front of the fireplace on that same blanket.

'Aren't you going to call?'

'Huh? Oh. Yeah. I'm, uh, just trying to wake up.'

He pulled his pants on and went into the kitchen. He slid the door closed so the light would not bother her. After flicking the switch he looked at the clock on the wall. It was a plate and where the numbers should be were different vegetables. It was half past the carrot, meaning one-thirty. He realized he and Sylvia had been asleep only about an hour. It had seemed like days.

The number had an 818 area code and he didn't recognize it. Jerry Edgar picked up after a half ring.

'Harry?'

'Yeah.'

'Sorry to bother you, man, especially since you're not home.'

'It's okay. What's up?'

'I'm on Sepulveda just south of Roscoe. I got her, man.'

Bosch knew he was talking about the survivor.

'What'd she say? She look at Mora's picture?'

'No. No, man, I don't really have her. I'm watching her. She's on the stroll here.'

'Well, why don't you pick her up?'

'Because I'm alone. I think I could use some backup. I try to take her alone she might bite or something. You know, she's got AIDS.'

Bosch was silent. Through the phone he could hear cars passing Edgar.

'Hey, man, I'm sorry. I shouldn't've called. I thought you might want to get in on this. I'll call the Van Nuys watch commander and get a couple uniforms out here. Have a good –'

'Forget it, I'll be there. Give me half an hour. You been out there all night?'

'Yeah. Went home for dinner. I've been looking all over. Didn't see her till now.'

Bosch hung up wondering if Edgar had really missed her until now or if he was just filling his overtime envelope. He walked back into the living room. The light was on and Sylvia was not on the blanket.

She was in her bed, under the covers.

'I gotta go out,' he said.

'I thought that's what it sounded like, so I decided to come in here. Nothing romantic about sleeping on the floor in front of a dead fireplace by yourself.'

'Are you mad?'

'Of course not, Harry.'

He leaned over the bed and kissed her and she put her hand on the back of his neck.

'I'll try to get back.'

'Okay. Can you turn the thermostat back up on your way out? I forgot.'

Edgar was parked in front of a Winchell's Donuts store,

apparently not realizing the comic implications of this.
Bosch parked behind him and then got in his car.

'Whereyat, Harry?'

'Where's she at?'

Edgar pointed across the street and up a block and a half.
At the intersection of Roscoe and Sepulveda there was a bus
bench with two women sitting on it and three standing
nearby.

'She's the one in red shorts.'

'You sure?'

'Yeah, I drove up to the light and eyeballed her. It's her.
Problem is, we might have a cat fight if we go over there and
try to take her. All them girls are working. The Sepulveda
bus line stops running at one.'

Bosch saw the one in the red shorts and tank top lift her
shirt as a car drove by on Sepulveda. The car braked but
then, after a moment of driver hesitation, went on.

'She had any business?'

'A few hours ago she had one guy. Walked him into that
alley behind the mini mall, did him there. Other than that
it's been dry. She's too skaggy for your discerning john.'

Edgar laughed. Bosch thought about how Edgar had just
slipped up by saying he had been watching her for a few
hours. Well, he thought, at least he didn't beep me while
the fire was going.

'So if you don't want a cat fight, what's the plan?'

'I was thinking you'd drive up to Roscoe and take a left.
Then come into the alley from the back way. You wait there
and get down low. I'll walk over and tell her I want the nasty
and she'll walk me back. Then we take her. But watch her
mouth. She might be a spitter, too.'

'Okay, let's get it over with.'

Ten minutes later Bosch was slouched behind the wheel
and parked in the alley, when Edgar came walking in from
the street. Alone.

'What?'

'She made me.'

'Well, shit, why didn't you just take her? If she made you there's nothing else we can do, she'll know I'm a cop if I try her again five minutes later.'

'All right, she didn't make me.'

'What's going on?'

'She wouldn't go with me. She asked if I had some brown sugar to trade and when I said no, no drugs, she said she doesn't do colored dick. You believe that shit? I haven't been called colored since I grew up in Chicago.'

'Don't worry about it. Wait here and I'll go.'

'Goddam whore.'

Bosch got out of the car and over the roof said, 'Edgar, cool it. She's a whore and a hype, for Chrissake. You care about that?'

'Harry, you have no idea what it's like. You see the way Rollenberger looks at me? I bet he counts the rovers every time I walk out of the room. German fuck.'

'Hey, you're right, I don't know what it's like.'

He took his jacket off and threw it in the car. Then he unbuttoned the top three buttons of his shirt and walked off toward the street.

'Be right back. You better hide. If she sees a colored guy she might not come into the alley with me.'

They borrowed an interview room in the Van Nuys detective bureau. Bosch knew his way around the place because he had worked on the robbery table here after first getting his detective's badge.

What became immediately clear from the start was that the man Edgar had seen Georgia Stern go into the alley with earlier was not a john. He was a dealer and she had probably fixed in the alley. She might have paid for the shot with sex, but that still didn't make the dealer a john.

Regardless of who he was and what she did, she was on the nod when Bosch and Edgar brought her in and, therefore, was almost totally useless. Her eyes were droopy and dilated and would become fixed on objects in the distance. Even in the ten-by-ten interview room she looked as though she was staring at something a mile away.

Her hair was rumpled and the black roots were longer than in the photo Edgar had. She had a sore on the skin below her left ear, the kind of sore addicts get from nervously rubbing the same spot over and over. Her upper arms were as thin as the legs of the chair she sat on. Her deteriorated state was heightened by the T-shirt, which was several sizes too big. The neckline drooped to expose her upper chest and Bosch could see that she used the veins in her neck when she was banging heroin from a needle. Bosch could also see that despite her emaciated condition, she still had large, full breasts. Implants, he guessed, and for a moment a vision of the concrete blonde's desiccated body flashed to him.

'Miss Stern?' Bosch began. 'Georgia? Do you know why you're here? Do you remember what I told you in the car?'

'I mem'er.'

'Now, do you remember the night the man tried to kill you? More than four years ago? A night like this? June seventeenth. Remember?'

She nodded dreamily and Bosch wondered if she knew what he was talking about.

'The Dollmaker, remember?'

'He's dead.'

'That's right, but we need to ask you some questions about the man anyway. You helped us draw this picture, remember?'

Bosch unfolded the composite drawing he had taken from the Dollmaker files. The drawing looked like neither Church nor Mora, but the Dollmaker was known to wear disguises so it was reasonable to believe the Follower did as well. Even so, there was always the chance a physical feature, like maybe Mora's penetrating eyes, would poke through the memory.

She looked at the composite for a long time.

'He was killed by the cops,' she said. 'He deserved it.'

Even coming from her, it felt reassuring to Bosch to hear someone say the Dollmaker got what he deserved. But he knew what she didn't, that they weren't dealing with the Dollmaker here.

'We're going to show you some pictures. You got the six-pack, Jerry?'

She looked up abruptly and Bosch realized his mistake. She thought he was referring to beer, but a six-pack in cop terminology was a package of six mugshots which are shown to victims and witnesses. They usually contain photos of five cops and one suspect with the hope that the wit will point to the suspect and say that's the one. This time the six-pack contained photos of six cops. Mora's was the second one.

Bosch lined them up on the table in front of her and she looked for a long time. She laughed.

'What?' Bosch asked.

She pointed to the fourth photo.

'I think I fucked him once. But I thought he was a cop.'

Bosch saw Edgar shake his head. The photo she had pointed to was of an undercover Hollywood Division narcotics officer named Arb Danforth. If her memory was correct, then Danforth was probably venturing off his beat into the Valley to extort sex from prostitutes. Bosch guessed that he was probably paying them with heroin stolen from evidence envelopes or suspects. What she had just said should be forwarded in a report to Internal Affairs, but both Edgar and Bosch knew without saying a word that neither of them would do that. It would be like committing suicide in the department. No street cop would ever trust them again. Still, Bosch knew Danforth was married and that the prostitute carried the AIDS virus. He decided he would drop Danforth an anonymous note telling him to get a blood test.

'What about the others, Georgia?' Bosch said. 'Look at their eyes. Eyes don't change when somebody's in a disguise. Look at the eyes.'

While she bent down to look closer at the pictures Bosch looked at Edgar, who shook his head. This was going nowhere, he was saying, and Bosch nodded that he knew. After a minute or so, her head jerked as she stopped herself from nodding off.

'Okay, Georgia, nothing there, right?'

'No.'

'You don't see him?'

'No. He's dead.'

'Okay, he's dead. You stay here. We're going out into the hall to talk for a minute. We'll be right back.'

Outside, they decided it might be worth booking her on an under-the-influence charge into Sybil Brand and trying her again when she came off the high. Bosch noted that Edgar was eager to do this and volunteered to drive her downtown to Sybil. Bosch knew this was because it would make Edgar's OT envelope thicker, not because he wanted to get the woman into the narco unit at Sybil and get her straightened out for a while. Compassion had nothing to do with it.

TWENTY-SIX

Sylvia had pulled the bedroom's heavy curtains across the blinds and the room stayed dark until well after the sun was up on Saturday morning. When Bosch awoke alone in her bed, he pulled his watch off the nightstand and saw it was already eleven. He had dreamed but when he woke the dream receded into the darkness and he couldn't reach back to grasp it. He lay there for nearly fifteen minutes trying to bring it back, but it was gone.

Every few minutes he would hear Sylvia make some kind of household noise. Sweeping the kitchen floor, emptying the dishwasher. He could tell she was trying to be quiet but he heard it anyway. There was the back door being opened and the splashing of water in the potted plants that lined the porch. It hadn't rained in at least seven weeks.

At 11:20 the phone rang and Sylvia got to it after one ring. But Bosch knew it was for him. His muscles tensed as he waited for the bedroom door to open and for her to summon him to the call. He had given Sylvia's phone number to Edgar when they were leaving the Van Nuys Division seven hours earlier.

But Sylvia never came and when he relaxed again he could hear parts of her conversation on the phone. It sounded like maybe she was counseling a student. After a while it sounded like she was crying.

Bosch got up, pulled on his clothes and walked out of the bedroom while trying to smooth his hair. She was at the table in the kitchen, holding the cordless phone to her ear.

She was drawing circles on the tabletop with her finger and he had been right, she was crying.

'What?' he whispered.

She held her hand up, signaling him not to interrupt. He didn't. He just watched her on the phone.

'I'll be there, Mrs Fontenot, just call me with the time and address . . . yes . . . yes, I will. Once again, I am so very sorry. Beatrice was such a fine young woman and student. I was very proud of her. Oh, my gosh . . .'

A strong gush of tears came as she hung up. Bosch came to her and put his hand on her neck.

'A student?'

'Beatrice Fontenot.'

'What happened?'

'She's dead.'

He leaned down and held her. She cried.

'This city. . . ,' she began but didn't finish. 'She's the one who wrote what I read to you the other night about *Day of the Locust*.'

Bosch remembered. Sylvia had said she worried about the girl. He wanted to say something but he knew there was nothing to say. This city. It seemed to say it all.

They spent the day around the house, doing odd jobs, cleaning up. Bosch cleared the charred logs out of the fireplace and then joined Sylvia in the backyard, where she was working in the garden, pulling weeds and cutting flowers for a bouquet she was going to take to Mrs Fontenot.

They worked side by side but Sylvia spoke very little. Every now and then she would offer a sentence. She said it had been a drive-by shooting on Normandie. She said it happened the night before and that the girl was taken to Martin Luther King, Jr, Hospital, where she was determined to be brain-dead. They turned the machine off in the morning and harvested the organs for donating.

'That's weird, that they call it harvesting,' she said.

'Sounds like a farm or people growing on trees or something.'

In the midafternoon she went into the kitchen and made an egg salad sandwich and a tuna fish sandwich. She cut them in half and they each had a half of both sandwiches. He made iced tea with slices of orange in the glass. She said that after the huge steaks they'd eaten the night before, she never wanted beef again. It was the day's only attempt at humor, but nobody smiled. She put the dishes in the sink afterward but didn't bother to rinse them. She turned and leaned on the counter and stared down at the floor.

'Mrs Fontenot said the funeral would be sometime next week, probably Wednesday. I think I'm going to bring the class down. Get a bus.'

'I think that'd be nice. Her family would appreciate it.'

'Her two older brothers are dealers. She told me they sell crack.'

He didn't say anything. He knew that was probably the reason the girl was dead. Since the Bloods-Crips gang truce, the street dealing in South Central had lost its command structure. There was a lot of infringement of turfs. A lot of drive-bys, a lot of innocents left dead.

'I think I'll ask her mother if I could read her book report. At the service. Or after. Maybe they'd know then what a loss this was.'

'They probably know already.'

'Yes.'

'You want to take a nap, try to sleep?'

'Yes, I think I will. What are you going to do?'

'I have some stuff to do. Make some calls. Sylvia, I'm going to have to go out tonight. Hopefully, not for long. I'll get back as soon as I can.'

'I'll be all right, Harry.'

'Good.'

Bosch looked in on her at about four and she was sleeping

soundly. He could see where the pillow was wet from her crying.

He went down the hall to a bedroom that was used as a study. There was a desk with a phone on it. He closed the door so as not to disturb her.

The first call he made was to Seventy-seventh Street Division detectives. He asked for the homicide table and got a detective named Hanks. He didn't give a first name and Bosch didn't know him. Bosch identified himself and asked about the Fontenot case.

'What's your angle, Bosch? Hollywood, you said?'

'Yeah, Hollywood, but there's no angle. It's private. Mrs Fontenot called the girl's teacher this morning. The teacher's a friend of mine. She's upset and I was, you know, just trying to find out what happened.'

'Look, I don't have time to be holding people's hands. I'm working a case.'

'In other words, you've got nothing.'

'You've never worked the seven-seven, have you?'

'No. This the part where you tell me how tough it is?'

'Hey, fuck you, Bosch. What I'm gonna tell you is that there is no such thing as a witness south of Pico. Only way we clear a case is we get lucky and pull some prints, or we get luckier and the dude walks in and says, "I's sorry, I did it." You wanna guess how many times that happens?'

Bosch didn't say anything.

'Look, the teacher ain't the only one upset, okay? This is a bad one. They're all bad but some are bad on bad. This is one of those. Sixteen-year-old girl home reading a book, babysittin' her younger brother.'

'Drive-by?'

'Yeah, you got it. Twelve holes in the walls. It was an AK. Twelve holes in the walls and one round in the back of her head.'

'She never knew, did she?'

'No, she never knew what hit her. She must've caught the first one. She never ducked.'

'It was a round meant for one of the older brothers, right?'

Hanks was quiet for a couple of seconds. Bosch could hear a radio squawking in the background of the squad room.

'How you know that, the teacher?'

'The girl told her the brothers sell crack.'

'Yeah? They were walking around MLK this morning boo-hooing like they was altar boys. I'll check it out, Bosch. Anything else I can do you for?'

'Yeah. The book. What was she reading?'

'The book?'

'Yeah.'

'It was called *The Big Sleep*. And that's what she got, man.'

'You can do me a favor, Hanks.'

'What's that?'

'If you talk to any reporters about this, leave the part about the book out.'

'What do you mean?'

'Just leave it out.'

Bosch hung up. He sat at the desk and felt ashamed that when Sylvia had first talked of the girl, he had been suspicious of her fine school work.

After a few minutes thinking about that, he picked the phone up again and called Irving's office. The phone was picked up on half a ring.

'Hello, this is Los Angeles Police Department Assistant Chief Irvin Irving's office, Lieutenant Hans Rollenberger speaking, how can I help you?'

Bosch figured Hans Off must be expecting Irving himself to call in and therefore trotted out the full-count official telephone greeting that was in the officer's manual but was roundly ignored by most of the people who answered phones in the department.

Bosch hung up without saying anything and redialed so the lieutenant could go through the whole spiel again.

'It's Bosch. I'm just checking in.'

'Bosch, did you just call a few moments ago?'

'No, why?'

'Nothing. I'm here with Nixon and Johnson. They just came in and Sheehan and Opelt are with Mora now.'

Bosch noticed how Rollenberger didn't dare call them the presidents when they were in the same room with him.

'Anything happen today?'

'No. The subject spent the morning at home, then a little while ago he went up to the Valley, visited a few more warehouses. Nothing suspicious.'

'Where is he now?'

'At home.'

'What about Edgar?' ·

'Edgar was here. He went over to Sybil to interview the survivor. He found her last night but she apparently was too dopey to talk to. He's giving it another try, now.'

Then in a lower voice, he said, 'If she confirms an ID of Mora, do we move?'

'I don't think it would be a good idea. It's not enough. And we'd tip our hand.'

'My thoughts exactly,' he said louder now, so the presidents would know he was clearly in command here. 'We stick to him like glue and we'll be there when he makes his move.'

'Hopefully. How're you working this with the surveillance teams? They giving you blow by blow?'

'Absolutely. They're on rovers and I'm listening here. I know every move the subject makes. I'm staying on late tonight. I have a feeling.'

'About what?'

'I think t'night's the night, Bosch.'

Bosch woke Sylvia at five but then sat on the bed and rubbed her back and neck for a half hour. After that, she got up and took a shower. Her eyes still looked sleepy when she came out to the living room. She wore her gray cotton

T-shirt dress. Her blonde hair was tied in a tail behind her head.

'When do you have to go?'

'A little while.'

She didn't ask where he was going or what for. He didn't offer to tell her.

'You want me to make you some soup or something?' he asked.

'No, I'm fine. I don't think I'm going to be hungry tonight.'

The phone rang and Harry answered it in the kitchen. It was a reporter from the *Times* who had gotten the number from Mrs Fontenot. The reporter wanted to speak with Sylvia about Beatrice.

'About what?' Bosch asked.

'Well, Mrs Fontenot said Mrs Moore said several nice things about her daughter. We are doing a major story on this because Beatrice was such a good kid. I thought Mrs Moore would want to say something.'

Bosch told her to hold on and went to find Sylvia. He told her about the reporter and Sylvia quickly said she wanted to talk about the girl.

She stayed on the phone fifteen minutes. While she was talking, Bosch went out to his car, turned on the rover and switched it to Symplex five, the DWP frequency. He heard nothing.

He pressed the transmit button and said, 'Team One?'

A few seconds passed and he was about to try again when Sheehan's voice came back on the rover.

'Who's that?'

'Bosch.'

'What it be?'

'How's our subject?'

The next voice was Rollenberger's coming in over Sheehan.

'This is Team Leader, please use your code designations when on the air.'

Bosch smirked. The guy was an ass.

'Leader of the team, what's my designation?'

'You are Team Six, this is Team Leader, out.'

'Rrrrrogaaahhhh that, dream leader.'

'Say again?'

'Say again?'

'Your last transmission, Team Five, what was that?'

Rollenberger's voice had a frustrated quality to it. Bosch was smiling. He could hear a clicking sound over the radio and he knew it was Sheehan punching his transmit button, showing his approval.

'I asked who was on my team.'

'Team Six, you are solo at this time.'

'Then should I have another code, Team Leader? Perhaps, Solo Six?'

'Bo – uh, Team Six, please keep off the air unless you need or are giving information.'

'Rrrogaahhh!'

Bosch put the radio down for a moment and laughed. He had tears in his eyes and he realized he was laughing too hard at something that was mildly humorous at best. He figured it was the release of some of the tension of the day. He picked up the radio again and called Sheehan back.

'Team One, is the subject moving?'

'That's affirmative, Solo – I mean, Team Six.'

'Where is he?'

'He is code seven at the Ling's Wings at Hollywood and Cherokee.'

Mora was eating at a fast-food restaurant. Bosch knew that would not give him enough time to do what he planned, especially since he was a half hour's drive from Hollywood.

'Team One, how's he look? Is he staying out tonight?'

'Looking good. Looks like he is going cruising.'

'Talk to you later.'

'Rrrrrogah!'

He could tell Sylvia had been crying again when he came

inside but her spirits seemed improved. Maybe it was past her, he thought, the initial pain and anger. She was sitting in the kitchen drinking a cup of hot tea.

'Do you want a cup, Harry?'

'No, I'm fine. I'm going to have to go.'

'Okay.'

'What'd you tell her, the reporter?'

'I told her everything I could think of. I hope she does a good story.'

'They usually do.'

It appeared that Hanks hadn't told the reporter about the book the girl had been reading. If he had, the reporter would definitely have told Sylvia to get her reaction. He realized that Sylvia's returning strength was due to her having talked about the girl. He had always marveled about how women wanted to talk, to maybe set the record straight about someone they knew or loved who had died. It had happened to him countless times while making next-of-kin notifications. The women were hurt, yes, but they wanted to talk. Standing in Sylvia's kitchen, he realized that the first time he had met her was on such a mission. He had told her about her husband's death and they had stood in the same room they were in now, and she had talked. Almost from the start, Bosch had been hooked deeply in the heart by her.

'You going to be all right while I'm gone?'

'I'll be fine, Harry. I'm feeling better.'

'I'll try to get back as soon as I can, but I can't be sure when that will be. Get something to eat.'

'Okay.'

At the door, they hugged and kissed and Bosch had an overwhelming urge not to go, to stay with her and hold her. He finally broke away.

'You are a good woman, Sylvia. Better than I deserve.'

She reached up and put her hand on his mouth.

'Don't say that, Harry.'

TWENTY-SEVEN

Mora's house was on Sierra Linda, near Sunset. Bosch pulled to the curb a half block away and watched the house as it grew dark outside. The street was mostly lined with Craftsman bungalows with full porches and dormer windows projecting from the sloping roofs. Bosch guessed it had been at least a decade since the street was as pretty as its name sounded. Many of the houses on the block were in disrepair. The one next to Mora's was abandoned and boarded. On other properties it was clear the owners had opted for chain-link fences instead of paint the last time they had the money to make a choice. Almost all had bars over their windows, even the dormers up top. There was a car sitting on cinderblocks in one of the driveways. It was the kind of neighborhood where you could find at least one yard sale every weekend.

Bosch had the rover on low on the seat next to him. The last report he had heard was that Mora was in a bar near the Boulevard called the Bullet. Bosch had been there before and pictured it in his mind, with Mora sitting at the bar. It was a dark place with a couple of neon beer signs, two pool tables and a TV bolted to the ceiling over the bar. It wasn't a place to go for a quick one. There was no such thing as one drink at the Bullet. Bosch figured Mora was digging in for the evening.

As the sky turned deep purple, he watched the windows of Mora's house but no light came on behind any of them. Bosch knew Mora was divorced but he didn't know if he now had a roommate. Looking at the dark place from the Caprice, he doubted it.

'Team One?' Bosch said into the rover.

'Team One.'

'This is Six, how's our boy?'

'Still bending the elbow. What are you up to tonight, Six?'

'Just hanging around the house. Let me know if you need anything, or if he starts to move.'

'Will do.'

He wondered if Sheehan and Opelt understood what he was saying and he hoped Rollenberger did not. He leaned over to the glove compartment and got his bag of picks out. He reached inside his blue plastic raid jacket and put them in the left pocket. Then he turned the rover's volume control knob to its lowest setting and put it inside the windbreaker in the other pocket. Because it said LAPD in bright yellow letters across the back of the jacket, he wore it inside out.

He got out, locked the car and was ready to cross the street when he heard a transmission from the radio. He got his keys back out, unlocked the car and got back in. He turned the radio up.

'What's that, One? I missed it.'

'Subject is moving. Westbound on Hollywood.'

'On foot?'

'Negative.'

Shit, Bosch thought. He sat in the car for another forty-five minutes while Sheehan radioed reports of Mora's seemingly aimless cruising up and down Hollywood Boulevard. He wondered what Mora was doing. The cruising was not part of the profile of the second killer. The Follower, as far as they knew, worked exclusively out of hotels. That's where he lured his victims. The cruising didn't fit.

The radio was quiet for ten minutes and then Sheehan came up on the air again.

'He's dropping down to the strip.'

The Sunset Strip was another problem altogether. The

strip was in LA but directly south of it was West Hollywood, sheriff's department jurisdiction. If Mora dropped down south and started to make some kind of move, it could result in jurisdictional problems. A guy like Hans Off was completely frightened of jurisdictional problems.

'He's down to Santa Monica Boulevard now.'

That was West Hollywood. Bosch expected Rollenberger to come up soon on the radio. He wasn't wrong.

'Team One, this is Team Leader. What is the subject doing?'

'If I didn't know what this guy was into, I'd say he was cruising Boystown.'

'All right, Team One, keep an eye on him but we don't want any contact. We're out of bounds here. I'll contact the sheriff's watch office and inform.'

'We're not planning any contact.'

Five minutes passed. Bosch watched a man walking his guard dog down Sierra Linda. He stopped to let the animal relieve itself on the burned-out lawn in front of the abandoned house.

'We're cool,' Sheehan's voice said. 'We're back in the country.'

Meaning back inside the boundaries of Los Angeles.

'One, what's your twenty?' Bosch asked.

'Still Santa Monica, going east. Past La Brea – no, he's northbound now on La Brea. He might be going home.'

Bosch slid low in his seat in case Mora came down the street. He listened as Sheehan reported that the vice cop was now eastbound on Sunset.

'Just passed Sierra Linda.'

Mora was staying out. Bosch sat back up. He listened to five minutes of silence.

'He's going to the Dome,' Sheehan finally said.

'The Dome?' Bosch responded.

'Movie theater on Sunset just past Wilcox. He's parked. He's paying for a ticket and is going in. Musta just been driving around till showtime.'

Bosch tried to picture the area in his mind. The huge geodesic dome was one of Hollywood's landmark theaters.

'Team One, this is Team Leader. I want to split you up here. One of you goes in with the subject, one stays on the car, out.'

'Roger that. Team One, out.'

The Dome was ten minutes away from Sierra Linda. Bosch figured that meant that at maximum he had an hour and a half inside the house unless Mora left the movie early.

He quickly got out of the car again, crossed the street and moved up the block to Mora's house. The wide porch completely cloaked the front door in shadows. Bosch knocked on it and while he waited he turned to look at the house across the street. There were lights on downstairs and he could see the bluish glow of a TV on the curtains behind one of the upstairs rooms.

Nobody answered. He stepped back and appraised the front windows. He saw no warnings about security systems, no alarm tape on the glass. He looked between the bars and through the glass into what he believed was the living room. He looked up into the corners of the ceiling, searching for the dull glow of a motion detector. As he expected, there was nothing. Every cop knew the best defense was a good lock or a mean dog. Or both.

He went back to the door, opened the pouch and took out the penlight. There was black electrical tape over the end so that when he switched it on only a narrow beam of light was emitted. He knelt down and looked at the locks on the door. Mora had a dead bolt and a common key-entry knob. Bosch put the penlight in his mouth and aimed the beam at the dead bolt. With two picks, a tension wrench and a hook, he began working. It was a good lock with twelve teeth, not a Medeco but a cheaper knockoff. It took Bosch ten minutes to turn it. By then sweat had come down out of his hair and was stinging his eyes.

He pulled his shirt out of his pants and wiped his face. He also wiped the picks, which had become slippery with sweat, and took a quick look at the house across the street. Nothing seemed changed, nothing seemed amiss. The TV was still on upstairs. He turned back and put the beam on the knob. Then he heard a car coming. He cut the light and crawled behind the porch riser until it had passed.

Back at the door he palmed the knob and was working the hook in when he realized there was no pressure on the knob. He turned it and the door opened. The knob hadn't been locked. It made sense, Bosch knew. The dead bolt was the deterrent. If a burglar got by that, the knob lock was a gimme. Why bother locking it?

He stood in the darkness of the entrance without moving, letting his eyes adjust. When he was in Vietnam he could drop into one of Charlie's tunnels and he would have night eyes in fifteen seconds. Now it took him longer. Out of practice, he guessed. Or getting old. He stood in the entry for nearly a minute. When the shapes and shadows filled in, he called out, 'Hey, Ray? You here? You left your door unlocked. Hello?'

There was no answer. He knew Mora wouldn't have a dog, not living alone and working a cop's hours.

Bosch took a few steps farther into the house and looked at the dark shapes of the furniture in the living room. He had creeped places before, even a cop's house, but the feeling always seemed new, that feeling of exhilaration, jagged fear and panic, all in one. It felt as though his center of gravity had dropped into his balls. He felt a strange power that he knew he could never describe to anyone.

For a brief moment the panic rose and threatened the delicate balance of his thoughts and feelings. The headline flashed in his mind – COP ON TRIAL CAUGHT IN BREAK-IN – but he quickly dismissed it. To think about failure was to invite failure. He saw the stairs and immediately moved toward them. His thought was that Mora would keep his trophies either in his bedroom or near a TV, which also could mean both. Rather than work his way toward the bedroom, he would start there.

The second floor was divided into two bedrooms with a bathroom in between them. The bedroom to the right had been converted to a carpeted gym. There was an assortment of chrome-plated equipment, a rowing machine, a stationary bike and a contraption Bosch didn't recognize. There was a rack of free weights and a bench press with a chest bar across it. On one wall of the room was a floor-to-ceiling mirror. It was spidered by a shatter point about face high in the center. For a moment Bosch looked at himself and studied his shattered reflection. He thought of Mora studying his own face there.

Bosch looked at his watch. It had already been thirty minutes since Mora had gone into the theater. He took out the radio.

'One, how's he doin'?'

'He's still inside. How're you doing?'

'Just hanging around. Call if you need me.'

'Anything interesting on TV?'

'Not yet.'

Then Rollenberger's voice came up.

'Teams One and Six, let's drop the banter and use the radio for pertinent transmissions only. Team Leader, out.'

Neither Bosch nor Sheehan acknowledged him.

Bosch moved across the hallway into the other bedroom. This was where Mora slept. The bed was unmade and clothing was draped over a chair by the window. Bosch peeled some of the tape off his light to give him a wider swath of vision.

On the wall over the bed he saw a portrait of Jesus, his eyes cast downward, his sacred heart visible in his chest. Bosch moved to the bed table and held the light briefly on a framed photo that stood next to the alarm clock. It was a young blonde woman and Mora. His ex-wife, he assumed. Her hair was bleached and Bosch recognized that she fit into the physical archetype of the victims. Was Mora killing his ex-wife over and over? he wondered again. That would be one for Locke and the other headshrinkers to decide. On the table behind the photo was a religious holy card. Bosch picked it up and put the light on it. It was a picture of the Infant of Prague, a golden halo shooting up from behind the little king's head.

The night table's drawer contained mostly innocuous junk: playing cards, aspirin bottles, reading glasses, condoms – not the brand favored by the Dollmaker – and a small telephone book. Bosch sat on the bed and leafed through the phone book. There were several women listed by first names but he was not surprised to find none of the names of the women associated with the Follower or Dollmaker cases listed.

He closed the drawer and put the light on the shelf beneath it. There he found a foot-high stack of explicit pornography magazines. Bosch guessed there were more than fifty, their covers featuring glossy photos of couplings of all equations: male-female, male-male, female-female, male-female-male, and so on. He flipped through a handful of them and saw a check mark made with a Magic Marker on the top right corner of each cover, as he had seen Mora do with the magazines at his office. Mora was taking his work home. Or had he brought the magazines here for another reason?

Looking at the magazines, Bosch felt a tightening in his crotch and some strange feeling of guilt descended on him. What about me? he wondered. Am I doing more than my job here? Am I the voyeur? He put the stack back in place. He knew there were too many magazines for him to go through to try to find victims of the Follower. And if he found any, what would that prove?

There was a tall oak armoire against the wall opposite the bed. Bosch opened its doors and found a television and videocassette recorder inside. There were three videotape cassettes stacked on top of the TV. They were 120-minute tapes. He opened the two drawers in the cabinet and found one more cassette in the top drawer. The bottom drawer contained a collection of store-bought porno tapes. He slid a couple of these tapes out, but again there were too many of them and not enough time. His attention was drawn to the four tapes used for home recording.

He turned on the TV and VCR and checked to see if there was another tape already inserted. There wasn't. He put in one of the tapes that had been stacked on top of the TV. It only showed static. He hit the fast-forward play button and watched as the static continued until the end of the tape. It took him fifteen minutes to run through the three tapes that had been on top of the television. Each was blank.

A curious thing, Bosch thought. He had to assume that the tapes had been used at one time because they were no longer in the cardboard jackets and plastic wrap they came from in the store in. Though he did not own a VCR, he was familiar with them and it occurred to him that people usually did not erase their home tapes. They just taped new programs over the old ones. Why had Mora taken the time to erase what had been on these tapes? He was tempted to take one of the blank tapes to have it analyzed but decided it would be too risky. It would probably be missed by Mora.

The last home tape, the one from the top drawer, wasn't blank. It contained scenes of an interior of a house. A child was playing with a stuffed animal on the floor. Through the window behind the girl Bosch could see a snow-covered yard. Then a man entered the video frame and hugged the girl. At first Bosch thought it was Mora. Then the man said, 'Gabrielle, show Uncle Ray how much you like the horsie.'

The girl hugged the stuffed horse and yelled, 'Fankoo Uggle Way.'

Bosch turned the tape off, returned it to the armoire's top drawer once again and then pulled both drawers out and looked below them. Nothing else. He stepped up onto the bed so he could see on top of the armoire and there was nothing there, either. He turned the equipment off and returned the armoire to the condition it was in when he opened it. He looked at his watch. Nearly an hour had gone by now.

The walk-in closet was neatly lined on both sides with clothes on hangers. The floor had eight pairs of shoes parked toe-in against the back wall. He found nothing else of interest and retreated into the bedroom. He took a quick look under the bed and through the drawers of the bureau but found nothing of interest. He moved back down the stairs and quickly looked into the living room but there was no TV. There was none in the kitchen or dining room either.

Bosch followed a hallway off the kitchen into the back of the house. There were three doors off the hallway and this area appeared to be either a converted garage or an addition that was constructed in recent years. There were air-conditioning vents in the ceiling of the hallway and the white pine flooring was much newer than the scarred and browned oak floors throughout the rest of the first floor.

The first door opened into a laundry room. Bosch quickly opened the cabinets above the washer and dryer and found nothing of interest. The next door was to a bathroom with newer fixtures than those he had seen in the bathroom upstairs.

The last door opened into a bedroom with a four-poster bed as its centerpiece. The coverlet was pink and it had the feel of a woman's room. It was the perfume, Bosch realized. But, still, the room did not have a lived-in feeling. It seemed more like a room waiting for its occupant's return. Bosch wondered if Mora might have a daughter away at college, or was this the room his ex-wife used before she finally ended the marriage and left?

There was a TV and VCR on a cart in the corner. He went to it and opened the video storage drawer below the VCR but it was empty except for a round metal object the size of a hockey puck. Bosch picked it up and looked at it but could not tell what it was. He thought it might be from the weight set upstairs. He put it back and closed the drawer.

He opened the drawers of the white dresser but found nothing but women's underwear in the top drawer. The second drawer held a box containing a palette of varying colors of eye makeup and several brushes. There was also a round plastic container of beige facial powder. The makeup containers were for home use, too large to carry in a purse and therefore could not have come from any of the Follower's victims. They belonged to whoever used this room.

There was nothing at all in the bottom three drawers. He looked at himself in the mirror above the bureau and saw he was sweating again. He knew he was using too much time. He looked at his watch; sixty minutes had gone by now.

Bosch opened the closet door and immediately launched himself backward as a jolt of fear punched into his chest. He took cover to the side of the door while drawing his gun.

'Ray! That you?'

No one answered. He realized he was leaning against the light switch for the deep, walk-in closet. He flicked it on and swung into the doorway in a low crouch, his gun pointing at the man he had seen when he opened the door.

He quickly reached outside the door and killed the light. On the shelf above the clothes bar was a round Styrofoam ball on which sat a wig of long black hair. Bosch caught his breath and stepped all the way into the closet. He studied the wig without touching it. How does this fit? he wondered. He turned to his right and found more pieces of women's sheer lingerie and a few thin silk dresses on hangers. On the floor beneath them, parked toe-in to the wall, was a pair of red shoes with stiletto heels.

On the other side of the closet, behind some clothes in dry-cleaner bags, stood a camera tripod. Bosch's adrenaline began flowing again at a quicker pace. He quickly raised his eyes and began looking among the boxes on the shelves above the clothing bar. One box was marked with Japanese writing and he carefully pulled it down, finding it surprisingly heavy. Opening it, he found a video camera and cassette recorder.

The camera was large and he recognized that it was not a

department store-bought piece of equipment. It was more like the kind of camera Bosch had seen used by TV news crews. It had a detachable industrial battery and a strobe. It was connected by an eight-foot coaxial cable to the recorder. The recorder had a playback screen and editing controls.

He thought that Mora's having such obviously expensive equipment was curious but he did not know what to make of it. He wondered if the vice cop had seized it from a porno producer and never turned it in to the evidence lockup. He pressed a button that opened the cassette housing on the recorder but it was empty. He repacked the equipment in the box and replaced it on the shelf, all the while wondering why a man with such a camera would have only blank tapes. He realized, as he took another quick look around the closet, that the tapes he had found so far might have recently been erased. He knew if that was the case, Mora might have tumbled to the surveillance.

He looked at his watch. Seventy minutes. He was pushing the envelope.

As he closed the closet door and turned around, he caught his own image in the mirror over the bureau. He quickly turned to the door to go. That was when he saw the rack of lights on a track running high on the wall above the bedroom door. There were five lights and he did not need to turn them on to be able to tell they focused on the bed.

He focused on the bed himself for a moment as he began to put it together. He took another glance at his watch, though he already knew it was time to go, and headed for the door.

As he crossed the room he looked at the TV and VCR again and realized that he had forgotten something. He quickly dropped to his knees in front of the machines and turned the VCR on. He hit the eject button and a videocassette popped out. He pushed it back in and hit the rewind button. He turned the TV on and pulled out the rover.

'One, how we doing?'

'Movie's getting out now. I'm watching for him.'

That wasn't right, Bosch knew. No general release movie was that short. And he knew the Dome was a single theater. One movie shown at a time. So Mora had gone into the theater after the movie had started. If he had really gone in. An adrenaline-charged alert swept over him.

'You sure it's over, One? He's barely been in there an hour.'

'We're going in!'

There was panic in Sheehan's voice. Then Bosch understood. We're going in. Opelt had not followed Mora into the theater. They had clicked off on Rollenberger's order to split up but they hadn't followed the order. They couldn't. Mora had seen Sheehan and Opelt the day before at the burrito stand by Central Division. There was no way one of them could go into a dark theater looking for Mora and risk being seen by the vice cop first. If that happened, Mora would instantly tumble to the setup. He would know. Sheehan had rogered the order from Rollenberger because the alternative was to tell the lieutenant that they had fucked up the day before.

The VCR rewind clicked off. Bosch sat there motionless, his finger poised in front of the VCR. He knew they had been made. Mora was a cop. He had made the tail. The theater stop had been a scam.

He hit the play button.

This tape had not been erased. The quality of the image on it was better than Bosch had seen in the video booth at X Marks the Spot four nights earlier. The tape had all the production values of a feature-length porno tape. Framed in the TV picture was the four-poster bed on which two men were engaged in sex with a woman. Bosch watched for a moment and hit the fast forward button while the picture was still on the screen. The players in the video began a quick jerking motion that was almost comedic. Bosch watched as they changed couplings over and over. Every conceivable coupling in fast speed. Finally, he returned it to normal speed and studied the players.

The woman did not fit the Follower's mold. She wore the black wig. She was also rail-thin and young. In fact, she wasn't a woman – legally, at least. Bosch doubted she was more than sixteen years old. One of her partners was young, too, perhaps he was her age or less. Bosch couldn't be sure. He was sure, however, that the third participant was Ray Mora. His face was turned away from the camera but Bosch could tell. And he could see the gold medal, the Holy Spirit, bouncing on his chest. He turned the tape off.

'I forgot about that tape, didn't I?'

Still on his knees in front of the television, Bosch turned. Ray Mora was standing there with a gun pointed at his face.

'Hey, Ray.'

'Thanks for reminding me.'

'Don't worry about it. Look, Ray, why don't you put –'

'Don't look at me.'

'What?'

'I don't want you to look at me! Turn around, look at the screen.'

Bosch obediently looked at the blank screen.

'You're a leftie, right? With your right hand take out your gun and slide it across the floor this way.'

Bosch carefully followed the orders. He thought he heard Mora pick the gun up off the floor.

'You fucks think I'm the Follower.'

'Look, I'm not going to lie to you, Ray, we were checking you out, that's all. . . . I know now, I know we're wrong. You –'

'The kosher burrito boys. Somebody ought to teach them how to follow a fucking suspect. They don't know shit . . . took me a while but I figured something was going down after I saw them.'

'So we're wrong about you, right, Ray?'

'You have to ask, Bosch? After what you just saw? The

335

answer is, yeah, you got your head up your ass. Whose idea was it to check me out? Eyman? Leiby?'

Eyman and Leiby were the co-commanders of Administrative Vice.

'No. It came from me. It was my call.'

A long moment of silence followed this confession.

'Then maybe I ought to just blow your head off right here. Be within my rights, wouldn't it?'

'Look, Ray —'

'Don't!'

Bosch stopped from turning all the way and looked back at the television.

'You do that, Ray, and your life unalterably changes. You know that.'

'It did that as soon as you broke in, Bosch. Why shouldn't I just take it to the logical conclusion? Cap you and just disappear.'

' 'Cause you're a cop, Ray.'

'Am I? Am I still going to be a cop if I let you go? You going to kneel there and tell me you'll make it right for me?'

'Ray, I don't know what to tell you. Those kids on the video are underage. But I only know that because of an illegal search. You end this now and put away the gun, we can work something out.'

'Yeah, Harry? Can everything go back to the way it was? The badge is all I've got. I can't give —'

'Ray. I —'

'Shut up! Just shut up! I'm trying to think.'

Bosch felt the anger hitting him in the back like rain.

'You know my secret, Bosch. How the fuck does that make you feel?'

Bosch had no answer. His mind was tumbling, trying to come up with the next move, the next sentence, when he flinched at the sound of Sheehan's voice coming over the rover in his pocket.

'We lost him. He's not in the theater.'

There was a sharp degree of urgency in Sheehan's voice.

336

Bosch and Mora were silent, listening.

'What do you mean, Team One?' Rollenberger's voice said.

'Who's that?' Mora asked.

'Rollenberger, RHD,' Bosch answered.

Sheehan's voice said, 'The movie got out ten minutes ago. People came out but he didn't. I went in, he's gone. His car is still here but he's gone.'

'I thought one of you went in?' Rollenberger barked, his own voice tightening with panic.

'We did, but we lost him,' Sheehan said.

'Liar,' Mora said. A long moment of silence followed before he said, 'Now, they'll probably start hitting the hotels, looking for me. Because to them, I'm the Follower.'

'Yes,' Bosch said. 'But they know I'm here, Ray. I should call in.'

As if on cue, Sheehan's voice came from the rover.

'Team Six?'

'That's Sheehan, Ray. I'm Six.'

'Call him. Be careful, Harry.'

Bosch slowly took the radio out of his pocket with his right hand and held it up to his mouth. He pressed the transmitter.

'One, did you find him?'

'Negative. In the wind. What's on TV?'

'Nothing. There's nothing on tonight.'

'Then you ought to leave the house and help us out.'

'Already on the way,' Bosch said quickly. 'Where are you at?'

'Bo – uh, Team Six, this is Team Leader, we need you to come in. We're bringing in the task force to help locate the suspect. All units will meet at the Dome parking lot.'

'Be there in ten. Out.'

He dropped his arm back to his side.

'A whole task force, huh?' Mora asked.

Bosch looked down and nodded.

'Look, Ray, that was all code. They know I went to your

house. If I don't show up at the Dome in ten minutes they'll come looking for me here. What do you want to do?'

'I don't know . . . but I guess that gives me at least fifteen minutes to decide, doesn't it?'

'Sure, Ray. Take your time. Don't make a mistake.'

'Too late for that,' he said, almost wistfully. Then he added, 'Tell you what. Take out the tape.'

Bosch ejected the tape and held it up over his left shoulder to Mora.

'No, no, I want you to do this for me, Harry. Open the bottom drawer and take out the magnet.'

That's what the hockey puck was. Bosch put the tape on top of the stand next to the TV and reached down for the magnet. Feeling its heaviness as he lifted it, he wondered if he'd have a chance, if he could maybe turn and hurl it at Mora before the vice cop got off a shot.

'You'd be dead before you tried,' Mora said, knowing his thoughts. 'You know what to do with it.'

Bosch ran the magnet over the top side of the tape.

'Let's put it in and see how we did,' Mora instructed.

'Okay, Ray. Whatever you say.'

Bosch put the tape into the VCR and pushed the play button. The screen filled with the static of a dead channel. It cast a grayish shroud of dull light over Bosch. He hit the fast forward button and the static continued. The tape had been wiped clean.

'Good,' Mora said. 'That ought to do it. That was the last tape.'

'No evidence, Ray. You're in the clear.'

'But you'll always know. And you'll tell them, won't you, Harry? You'll tell IAD. You'll tell the world. I'll never be clear, so don't fuckin' say I'll be clear. Everyone will know.'

Bosch didn't answer. After a moment, he thought he heard the creaking of the wood floor. When Mora spoke, he was very close behind.

'Let me give you a tip, Harry. . . . Nobody in this world is who they say they are. Nobody. Not when they're in their

338

own room with the door shut and locked. And nobody knows anybody, no matter what they think. . . . The best you can hope for is to know yourself. And sometimes when you do, when you see your true self, you have to turn away.'

Bosch heard nothing for several seconds. He kept his eyes on the television screen and thought he could see ghosts forming and disintegrating in the static. He felt the grayish-blue glow burning behind his eyes and the start of a headache. He hoped he was going to live long enough to get it.

'You were always a good guy to me, Harry. I –'

There was a sound from the hallway, then a shout.

'Mora!'

It was Sheehan's voice. Immediately it was followed by light that flooded the room. Bosch heard the pounding of several feet on the wood floor, then there was a shout from Mora and the sound of impact as he was tackled. Bosch took his thumb off the rover's transmit button and began to throw himself to the right, out of harm's way. And in that moment, a gunshot cracked across the room, echoing, it seemed, as loudly as anything he had ever heard.

·

TWENTY-EIGHT

Once Bosch had cleared the rover channel, Rollenberger came up almost immediately.

'Bosch! Sheehan – Team One! What is happening there. What is – report immediately.'

After a long moment went by, Bosch answered calmly.

'This is Six. Team Leader, be advised you should proceed to the subject's twenty.'

'His home? What – did we have shots fired?'

'Team Leader, be advised to keep the channel open. And all task force units, disregard the call out. All units are ten-seven until further notice. Unit Five, are you up?'

'Five,' Edgar responded.

'Five, could you meet me at our subject's twenty?'

'On my way.'

'Six out.'

Bosch turned off the rover before Rollenberger could get back on the channel.

It took the lieutenant a half hour to get from the Parker Center operations post to the house on Sierra Linda. By the time he arrived, Edgar was already there and a plan was in place. Bosch opened the front door just as Rollenberger reached it. The lieutenant strode through the entrance with a face turned red with equal parts of anger and befuddlement.

'Okay, Bosch, what the hell is going on here? You had no authority to cancel the call out, to countermand my order.'

'I thought the less people that know, the better,

Lieutenant. I called out Edgar. I thought that would be enough to handle it and that way not too many would –'

'Know what, Bosch? Handle what? What is going on here?'

Bosch looked at him a moment before answering, then in an even voice said, 'One of the men in your command conducted an illegal search of the suspect's residence. He was caught in the act when the suspect eluded the surveillance you were supervising. That's what happened.'

Rollenberger reacted as if he had been slapped.

'Are you crazy, Bosch? Where's the phone? I want –'

'You call Chief Irving and you can forget about ever running a task force again. You can forget about a lot of things.'

'Bullshit! I had nothing to do with this. You went freelancing on your own and got your fingers caught in the jar. Where's Mora?'

'He's upstairs in the room to the right, handcuffed to the Nautilus machine.'

Rollenberger looked around at the others standing in the living room. Sheehan, Opelt, Edgar. They all gave him deadpan looks. Bosch said, 'If you knew nothing about it, *Lieutenant,* you'll have to prove that. Everything said on Symplex five tonight is on the reel-to-reel down at the city com center. I said I was in the house, you were listening. You even spoke to me a few times.'

'Bosch, you were talking in codes, I didn't – I knew nuh –'

Rollenberger suddenly sprang wildly at Bosch, his hands up and going for his neck. Bosch was ready and reacted more aggressively. He pounded both palms into the other man's chest and slammed him back against a hallway wall. A picture two feet to his side slid off the wall and clattered to the floor.

'Bosch, you fool, the bust is ruined now,' he said while slumped against the wall. 'It was all il –'

'There's no bust. He's the wrong man. I think. But we

341

have to be sure. You want to help us search the place and think about how to contain this, or do you want to call out the chief and explain how badly you handled your command?'

Bosch stepped away, adding, 'The phone's in the kitchen.'

The search of the house took more than four hours. The five of them, working methodically and silently, searched every room, every drawer, every cabinet. What little evidence they gathered of Detective Ray Mora's secret life they put on the dining room table. All the while, their host remained in the upstairs gym room, cuffed to one of the chrome bars of the weight machine. He was accorded fewer rights than a murderer would have received had he been arrested in his home. No phone call. No lawyer. No rights. This was always the case when cops investigated cops. Every cop knew the most flagrant abuses of police power occurred when cops turned on their own.

Occasionally, as they began the initial work, they would hear Mora call out. He called for Bosch most often, sometimes Rollenberger. But no one came to him until finally Sheehan and Opelt – concerned that the neighbors would hear and maybe call the police – went into the room and gagged him with a bathroom towel and black electrical tape.

The silence of the searchers was not in deference to the neighbors, however. The detectives worked quietly because of the tensions among them. Though Rollenberger was visibly angry with Bosch, most of the tension was derived from Sheehan and Opelt having blown the surveillance, which directly led to Mora's discovery of Bosch inside his house. No one except Rollenberger was upset by Bosch's illegal entry of the house. Bosch's own home had been similarly violated at least twice that he knew about during times when he had been the focus of internal investigations. Just like the badge, it came with the job.

When they completed the search the dining room table was stacked with the porno magazines and store-bought tapes, the video equipment, the wig, the women's clothing and Mora's personal phone book. The television that had been hit by Mora's stray shot was also there. By then Rollenberger had cooled somewhat, having apparently used the hours to consider his situation as well as to search.

'All right,' he said as the other four convened around the table and surveyed its contents. 'What have we got? Number one, are we confident Mora is not our man?'

Rollenberger looked around the room and his eyes stopped on Bosch.

'What do you think, Bosch?'

'You heard my story. He denied it and what was on the last tape before he made me erase it doesn't fit with the Follower.' Looked completely consensual, though the boy and girl with him were obviously underage. He isn't the Follower.'

'Then what is he?'

'Somebody with problems. I think he got bent by staying too long in vice and started making his own flicks.'

'Was he selling them?'

'I don't know. I doubt it. No evidence of that here. He didn't go very far in hiding himself in the tape I saw. I think it was just his own stuff. He wasn't in it for money. It was something deeper.'

No one said anything, so Bosch continued.

'My guess is that he made our tail sometime after we set up on him and began getting rid of the evidence. Tonight he was probably playing around with the tail, trying to figure what we were on him for. He got rid of most of the evidence, but if you put somebody on that phone book, my bet is you'll put it together. Some of those listings with only a first name. You track them and you'll probably find some of the kids he used in his videos.'

Sheehan made a move to pick up the phone book.

'Leave it,' Rollenberger said. 'If anybody continues this it will be Internal Affairs.'

'How they going to do that?' Bosch asked.

'What do you mean?'

'It's all fruit of the poison tree. The search, everything. All of it's illegal. We can't move against Mora.'

'And we can't let him carry a badge, either,' Rollenberger said testily. 'The man should be in jail.'

The following silence was broken by the sound of Mora's hoarse but loud voice from upstairs. He had somehow slipped the gag.

'Bosch! Bosch! I wanna deal, Bosch. I'll give –' he began coughing ' – I'll give him to you, Bosch. You hear me! You hear me!'

Sheehan headed toward the stairs, which began in the alcove outside the dining room. He said, 'This time I'll make it so tight the fuck will strangle.'

'Wait a minute,' Rollenberger ordered.

Sheehan stopped at the archway leading to the alcove.

'What's he saying?' Rollenberger said. 'Who will he give?'

He looked at Bosch, who shrugged his shoulders. They waited, Rollenberger looking up at the ceiling, but Mora was silent.

Bosch stepped over to the table and picked up the phone book. He said, 'I think I've got an idea.'

The odor of Mora's sweat filled the room. He sat on the floor, his hands cuffed behind him and to the work-out machine. The towel that had been wrapped around his mouth and taped had slipped down to his neck so that it looked like a cervical collar. The front of it was damp with spittle and Bosch guessed that Mora had loosened it by working his jaw up and down.

'Bosch, unhook me.'

'Not yet.'

Rollenberger stepped forward.

'Detective Mora, you have problems. You've –'

'You've got problems. You're the one. All of this is

344

illegal. How you going to explain this? Know what I'm going to do? I'm going to hire that bitch Money Chandler and sue the department for a million dollars. Yeah, I'll –'

'Can't spend a million dollars in jail, Ray,' Bosch said.

He held up Mora's phone book so that the vice cop could see it.

'This gets dropped off at Internal Affairs and they'll make a case. All those names and numbers, there's gotta be somebody that would talk about you. Somebody underage probably. Think we're giving you a hard time? Wait until IAD takes over. They'll make a case, Ray. And they'll make it without tonight's search. That will just be your word against ours.'

Bosch saw a quick movement in Mora's eyes and he knew he had struck bone. Mora was afraid of the names in the book.

'So,' Bosch said, 'what deal did you have in mind, Ray?'

Mora looked away from the book, first to Rollenberger and then to Bosch and then back to Rollenberger.

'You can make a deal?'

'I have to hear it first,' Rollenberger said.

'Okay, this is the deal. I walk and I give you the Follower. I know who it is.'

Bosch was immediately skeptical but said nothing. Rollenberger looked at him and Bosch shook his head once.

'I know,' Mora said. 'The Peeping Tom I told you about. That was no bullshit. I got the ID today. It fits. I know who it is.'

Now Bosch took him more seriously. He folded his arms in front of his body, threw a quick glance at Rollenberger.

'Who?' Rollenberger said.

'What's the deal first?'

Rollenberger stepped to the window and parted the curtains. He was turning it over to Bosch, who took a step forward and squatted like a baseball catcher in front of Mora.

'This is the deal. It is offered only this one time. Take it or let the chips fall where they may. You give the name to me and your badge to Lieutenant Rollenberger. You resign immediately from the department. You agree not to sue the department or any of us individually. In exchange, you walk.'

'How do I know you'll –'

'You don't. And how do we know that you'll keep your end? I hang on to the phone book, Ray. You try to fuck us and it goes to IAD. Do we have a deal?'

Mora stared at him without speaking a long moment. Finally, Bosch got up and turned to the door. Rollenberger headed that way, too, and said, 'Unhook him, Bosch. Take him to Parker and book him on assault on a police officer, unlawful sex with a minor, pandering, anything you can think –'

'We gotta deal,' Mora blurted. 'But I've got no insurance.'

Bosch turned back to look at him.

'That's right, you don't. The name?'

Mora looked from Bosch to Rollenberger.

'Unhook me.'

'The name, Mora,' Rollenberger said. 'This is it.'

'It's Locke. The fucking shrink. You assholes, you put the finger on me and the whole time he's the one pushing the buttons.'

Bosch was jolted but in that same moment he began immediately to see how it could be. Locke knew the Dollmaker's program, he fit the Follower's profile.

'He was the Tom?'

'Yeah, it was him. Got'm ID'd by a producer today. He went around saying he was writin' a book so he could get close to the girls. Then he killed them, Bosch. The whole time he's been playing doctor with you, Bosch, he's been out there . . . killing.'

Rollenberger turned to Bosch and said, 'What do you think?'

Bosch left the room without answering. He went down

the stairs and trotted out the door to his car. Locke's book was on the back seat where Bosch had left it the day he bought it. As he headed back into the house with it he noticed that the first etchings of dawn's light were in the sky.

On Mora's dining room table, Bosch opened the book and began leafing through it until he came to a page marked Author's Note. In the second paragraph, Locke wrote, 'The material for this book was gathered over the course of three years from interviews with countless adult film performers, many of whom requested that they remain anonymous or be identified only by their stage names. The author wishes to thank them and the film producers who granted him access to the sets and production offices at which these interviews were conducted.'

The mystery man. Bosch realized Mora could be right that Locke was the man whom the video performer Gallery had reported as a suspect when she called the original task force tip number four years earlier. Bosch next flipped to the index of the book and ran his fingers down the names. Velvet Box was listed. So were Holly Lere and Magna Cum Loudly.

Bosch quickly reviewed in his mind Locke's involvement in the case. He would definitely fit as a suspect for the same reasons Mora had fit. He had had a foot in both camps, as Locke himself had described it. He had access to all information about the Dollmaker deaths and, at the same time, was conducting research for a book on the psychology of female performers in the pornography industry.

Bosch became excited, but more so he was angry. Mora had been right. Locke had punched his buttons, to the point that he had helped set the cops on the path to the wrong man. If Locke was the Follower, he had played Bosch perfectly.

Rollenberger dispatched Sheehan and Opelt to Locke's house to put him under immediate surveillance. 'This time don't fuck it up,' he said as he recovered some of his command presence.

Next he announced there would be a meeting of the task force at noon Sunday, little more than six hours away. He said they would then discuss seeking a search warrant for Locke's home and office and decide what moves to make. As he headed to the door, Rollenberger looked at Bosch and said, 'Go cut him loose. Then, Bosch, you better go get some sleep. You're going to need it.'

'What about you? How're you going to handle Irving on this?'

Rollenberger was looking down at the gold detective's shield he held in his hand. It was Mora's. He closed his hand over it and put it in his sport coat pocket. Then he looked at Bosch.

'That's my business, isn't it, Bosch? Don't worry about it.'

After the others had left, Bosch and Edgar went up the stairs to the gym room. Mora was silent and refused to look at them as they removed the handcuffs. They said nothing and left him there, the towel still around his neck like a noose, staring at his fractured image in the wall mirror.

Bosch lit a cigarette and looked at his watch when he got to his car. It was 6:20 and he was too wired to go home to sleep. He got in the car and pulled the rover from his pocket.

'Frankie, you up?'

'Yo,' Sheehan responded.

'Anything?'

'Just got here. No life showing. Don't know whether he's here or not. Garage door is down.'

'Okay, then.'

Bosch thought of an idea. He picked up Locke's book and took the cover off it. He folded it and put it in his pocket, then he started the car.

After stopping for coffee at a Winchell's, Bosch got to the

Sybil Brand Institute by seven. Because of the early hour, he had to get the watch commander's approval to interview Georgia Stern.

He could see she was sick as soon as she was brought into the interview room. She sat hunched over with her arms folded in front of her, as if she were carrying a bag of groceries that had broken and was guarding against losing anything.

'Remember me?' he asked.

'Man, you gotta get me out.'

'Can't do that. But I can get them to take you into the clinic. You can get methadone in your orange juice.'

'I wanna get out.'

'I'll get you in the clinic.'

She dropped her head in defeat. She started a slight rocking motion, back and forth. She seemed pitiful to Bosch. But he knew he had to let it go. There were more important things, and she couldn't be saved.

'You remember me?' he asked again. 'From the other night?'

She nodded.

'We showed you pictures? I've got another.'

He put the dust jacket from the book on the table. She looked at Locke's photo for a long while.

'Well?'

'What? I seen him. He talked to me once.'

'About what?'

'Making movies. He was – I think he's an interviewer.'

'Interviewer?'

'I mean like a writer. He said it was for a book. I told him don't use any of my names but I never checked.'

'Georgia, think back. Hard. This is very important. Could he also be the one who attacked you?'

'You mean the Dollmaker? The Dollmaker's dead.'

'I know that. I think it was someone else who attacked you. Look at the photo. Was it him?'

She looked at the photo and shook her head.

'I don't know. They told me it was the Dollmaker, so I forgot what he looked like after he was killed.'

Bosch leaned back in his chair. It was useless.

'You still going to get me in the clinic?' she asked timidly after seeing his change in mood.

'Yeah. You want for me to tell them you've got the virus?'

'What virus?'

'AIDS.'

'What for?'

'To get you whatever medicine you need.'

'I don't have AIDS.'

'Look, I know the last time Van Nuys Vice put the bust on you you had AZT in your purse.'

'That's for protection. I got that from a friend-a-mine who's sick. He gave me the bottle and I put cornstarch in it.'

'Protection?'

'I don't want to work for no pimp. Some asshole comes up and says he's now your man, I show 'em the shit and say I got the virus, you know, and he splits. They don't want girls with AIDS. Bad for their business.'

She smiled slyly and Bosch changed his mind about her. She might be saved after all. She had the instincts of a survivor.

The Hollywood Station detective bureau was completely deserted, which was not unusual for nine on a Sunday morning. After stealing a cup of coffee from the watch office while the sergeant was busy at the wall map, Bosch went to the homicide table and called Sylvia but got no answer. He wondered if she was gardening out back and hadn't heard the phone or had gone out, maybe to get the Sunday paper to read the story about Beatrice Fontenot.

Bosch leaned back in his chair. He didn't know what his next move was. He used the rover to check with Sheehan and once again was told that there had been no movement at Locke's house.

'Think we should go up and knock?' Sheehan asked.

He wasn't expecting an answer and Bosch didn't give one. But he started thinking about it. It gave him another idea. He decided he would go to Locke's house to finesse him. To run the story about Mora by him and see how Locke reacted and if he would say the vice cop was probably the Follower.

He threw the empty coffee cup in the trash can and looked over at his slot in the memo and mail box on the wall. He saw he had something in there. He got up and took three pink phone message forms and a white envelope back to his desk. He looked at the messages and one by one dismissed them as unimportant and put them on his message spike to be considered later. Two were from TV reporters and one was from a prosecutor asking about evidence in one of his other cases. All the calls had come in Friday.

Then he looked at the envelope and felt a chill, like a cold steel ball rolling down the back of his neck. It had only his name on the outside but the distinctive printing style could mean it was from nobody else. He dropped the envelope on the table, opened his drawer and dug around in the notebooks, pens and paper clips until he found a pair of rubber gloves. Then he carefully opened the Follower's message.

Long aft' the body stops stinking
Of me you'll be thinking
For taking your precious blonde
Oft' your bloody hands

I'll make her my dolly
Aft' I've had my sweet jolly
And maybe to leave then
For other soft lands

No air for her to swallow
Aft' me dare you not follow
Her last word, my gosh!
A sound like Boschhhhhh

As he left the station, he ran through the watch commander's office, almost knocked down the startled duty sergeant and yelled: 'Get hold of Detective Jerry Edgar! Tell'm to come up on the rover. He'll know what I mean.'

TWENTY-NINE

Getting to the freeway was so frustrating that Bosch believed he could actually feel his blood pressure rising. His skin began to feel tight around his eyes, his face grew warm. There was some kind of Sunday morning performance at the Hollywood Bowl and traffic on Highland was backed up to Fountain. Bosch tried taking some side streets but so were many of the people going to the Bowl. He was deep into this quagmire before he cursed himself for not remembering that he had the bubble and siren. Working homicide, it had been so long since he had to race to get anywhere that he had forgotten.

After he slid the bubble onto the roof and hit the siren, the cars began to part in front of him and he remembered how easy it could be. He had just gotten onto the Hollywood Freeway and was speeding north through the Cahuenga Pass when Jerry Edgar's voice came up on the rover on the seat next to him.

'Harry Bosch?'

'Yeah, Edgar, listen. I want you to call the sheriff's department, Valencia station, and tell them to get a car to Sylvia's house code three. Tell them to make sure she's okay.'

Code three meant lights and siren, an emergency. He gave Edgar her address.

'Make the call now and then come back up.'

'Okay, Harry. What's going on?'

'Make the call now!'

Three minutes later Edgar was back on the radio.

'They're on the way. What've you got?'

'I'm on my way, too. What I want you to do is go in to the division. I left a note on my desk. It's from the Follower. Secure it and then call Rollenberger and Irving and tell 'em what's happening.'

'What is happening?'

Bosch had to swerve into the median to avoid hitting a car that pulled into the lane in front of him. The driver hadn't seen Bosch coming and Bosch knew he was going too fast – a steady ninety-three – for the siren to give much of a warning to the cars ahead of him.

'The note's another poem. He says he is going to take the blonde off my hands. Sylvia. There's no answer at her house but there still may be time. I don't think I was supposed to find the note until Monday, when I came in for work.'

'On my way. Be careful, buddy. Stay cool.'

Stay cool, Bosch thought. Right. He thought of what Locke had told him about the Follower being angry, wanting to get back at him for putting down the Dollmaker. Not Sylvia, he hoped. He wouldn't be able to live with it.

He picked the radio back up.

'Team One?'

'Yo,' Sheehan replied.

'Go get him. If he's there, bring him in.'

'You sure?'

'Bring him in.'

There was a lone sheriff's car in front of Sylvia's house. When Bosch pulled to a stop, he saw a uniform deputy standing on the front step, back to the door. It looked as if he was guarding the place. As if he was protecting a crime scene.

As he started to get out, Bosch felt a sharp stabbing pain on the left side of his chest. He held still for a moment and it eased. He ran around the car and across the lawn, working his badge out of his pocket as he went.

'LAPD, what've you got?'

'It's locked. I walked around, all windows and doors secured. No answer. Looks like nobody's –'

Bosch pushed past him and used his key to open the door. He ran from room to room, making a quick search for obvious signs of foul play. There were none. The deputy had been right. Nobody was home. Bosch looked in the garage and Sylvia's Cherokee was not there.

Still, Bosch made a second sweep of the house, opening closets, looking under beds, looking for any indication that something was amiss. The deputy was standing in the living room when Bosch finally came out of the bedroom wing.

'Can I go now? I was pulled off a call that seems a little more important than this.'

Bosch noted the annoyance in the deputy's voice and nodded for him to go. He followed him out and got the rover out of the Caprice.

'Edgar, you up?'

'What do you have there, Harry?'

There was the sound of genuine dread in his voice.

'Nothing here. No sign of her or anything else.'

'I'm at the station, you want me to put a BOLO out?'

Bosch described Sylvia and her Cherokee for the Be On Look Out dispatch that would go out to all patrol cars.

'I'll put it out. We got the task force coming in. Irving, too. We'll be meeting here. There's nothing else to do but wait.'

'I'm going to wait here a while. Keep me posted. . . . Team One, you up?'

'Team One,' Sheehan said. 'We went up to the door. Nobody home. We're standing by. If he shows, we'll bring him in.'

Bosch sat in the living room, his arms folded in front of him, for more than an hour. He now knew why Georgia Stern had held herself this way at Sybil Brand. There was comfort in it. Still, the silence of the house was nerve-racking. He was staring at the portable phone he had put on the coffee table, waiting for it to ring, when he heard a key hit the lock on the front door. He jumped up and was moving toward the entry when the door opened and a man stepped in. It wasn't Locke. It wasn't anyone Bosch knew, but he had a key.

Without hesitating Bosch moved into the entrance and slammed the man up against the door as he turned to close it.

'Where is she?' he shouted.

'What? What?' the man cried out.

'Where is she?'

'She couldn't come. I'm going to watch it for her. She's got another open in Newhall. Please!'

Bosch realized what was happening just as the pager on his belt sounded its shrill tone. He stepped away from the man.

'You're the realtor?'

'I work for her. What are you doing? Nobody's supposed to be here.'

Bosch pulled the pager off his belt and saw the readout was his home phone number.

'I have to make a call.'

He went back to the living room. Over his shoulder he heard the real estate man say, 'Yeah, you do that! What the hell is going on here?'

Bosch punched the number into the phone and Sylvia picked up after one ring.

'Are you okay?'

'Yes, Harry, where are you?'

'At your place. Where have you been?'

'I picked up a pie at Marie Callendar's and took it and the flowers I cut to the Fontenots. I just felt like doing –'

'Sylvia, listen to me. Is the door locked?'

'What? I don't know.'

'Put the phone down and go make sure. Make sure the sliding door to the porch is locked, too. And the door to the carport. I'll wait.'

356

'Harry, what is –'

'Go do it now!'

She was back in a minute. Her voice sounded very timid.

'Okay, everything's locked.'

'Okay, good. Now listen, I'm coming there right now and it will only take me half an hour. In the meantime, no matter who comes to the door, don't answer it and don't make any sound. Understand?'

'You're scaring me, Harry.'

'I know that. Do you understand what I said?'

'Yes.'

'Good.'

Bosch thought for a moment. What else could he tell her?

'Sylvia, after we are done here. I want you to go to the closet near the front door. On the shelf there is a white box. Take it down and take out the gun. There are bullets in the red box in the cabinet over the sink. The red box, not the blue. Load the gun.'

'I can't do – what are you telling me?'

'Yes, you can, Sylvia. Load the gun. Then wait for me. If anybody comes through the door and it's not me, protect yourself.'

She didn't say anything.

'I'm on my way. I love you.'

While Bosch was on the freeway going south, Edgar came up on the radio and told him Sheehan and Opelt still had made no sighting of Locke. The presidents had been dispatched to USC but Locke was not at his office, either.

'They're going to sit on both locations. I'm working on a warrant for the house now. But I don't think the PC is there.'

Bosch knew he was probably right. Mora's identification of Locke as the man hanging around porno sets and the names of three of the victims in his book were not probable cause to search his house.

He told Edgar that he had located Sylvia and was headed

to her now. After signing off, he realized that her trip to the Fontenot house might have saved her life. He saw a symbiotic grace in that. A life taken, a life saved.

Before opening the door to his house he loudly announced he was there, then turned the key and walked into Sylvia's trembling arms. He held her to his chest and said into the radio, 'We're all safe here,' then turned it off.

They sat down on the couch and Bosch told her everything that had happened since they had last been together. He could tell by her eyes that it scared her more knowing what was going on than not.

She, in turn, explained that she had to get out of the house because the realtor was holding an open house. That was why she had gone to Bosch's house after visiting the Fontenots. He explained that he had forgotten about the open house.

'You might need to get a new realtor after today,' he said.

They laughed together to let some of the tension go.

'I'm sorry,' he said. 'This should never have involved you.'

They sat in silence for a while after that. She leaned against him as if she was weary of everything.

'Why do you do this, Harry? You deal with so much – the most awful people and the things they do. Why do you keep going?'

He thought about that but knew there was no real answer and that she wasn't expecting one.

'I don't want to stay here,' he said after a while.

'We can go back to my house at four.'

'No, let's just get out of here.'

The two-room suite at the Loews Hotel in Santa Monica gave them a sweeping view of the ocean across a wide beach. It was the kind of room that came with two full-length terrycloth robes and gold foil-wrapped chocolates left on the pillow. The suite's front door was off the fourth landing of a five-story atrium with a wall of glass that faced the ocean and would capture the entire arc of the sunset.

There was a porch with two chaise lounges and a table and they had lunch delivered by room service there. Bosch had brought the rover in with him but it was turned off. He would keep in touch as the search for Locke went on, but he was out of it for the day.

He had called in and talked to Edgar and then Irving. He told them he would stay with Sylvia, though it seemed unlikely that the Follower would make a move now. He was not needed anyway because the task force was in a holding pattern, waiting for Locke to turn up or something else to break.

Irving had said the presidents had contacted the dean of the psychology department at USC who, in turn, contacted one of Locke's graduate assistants. She reported that Locke had mentioned on Friday that he would be in Las Vegas for the weekend, staying at the Stardust. He taught no classes on Mondays, so he would not be back at the school until Tuesday.

'But we checked the Stardust,' Irving said. 'Locke had a reservation but never checked in.'

'What about the warrant?'

'We've had three turn-downs from three judges. You know it's pretty weak when a judge won't rubber-stamp a search warrant for us. We're going to have to let that jell for a while. In the meantime, we'll be watching his house and his office. I'd like to leave it that way until he surfaces and we can talk to him.'

Bosch heard the doubt in Irving's voice. He wondered how Rollenberger had explained the leap in the investigation from Mora to Locke as the suspect.

'You think we're wrong?'

He realized there was a quiver of doubt in his own voice.

'I don't know. We traced the note. Partially. It was left at the front desk sometime Saturday night. The deskman went back for coffee about nine, got sidetracked by the

359

watch commander and when he came back out it was there on the counter. He had an Explorer put it in your slot. The only thing it means for sure is that we were wrong about Mora. Anyway, the point is, we could be wrong again. Right now all we have are hunches. Good hunches, mind you, but that's all. I want to proceed a little more carefully this time.'

The translation was, you screwed us up with your hunch on Mora. We are going to be more skeptical this time. Bosch understood this.

'What if the Vegas trip was a cover? The note says something about moving on. Maybe Locke's running.'

'Maybe.'

'Should we put out a BOLO, get an arrest warrant?'

'I think we're going to wait until at least Tuesday, Detective. Give him a chance to come back. Just two more days.'

It was clear Irving wanted to sit tight. He was going to wait for events to control what he would do next.

'Okay, I'll check in later.'

They napped in the king-size bed until it was dark and then Bosch turned on the news to see if any of what had happened in the last twenty-four hours had leaked.

It hadn't, but midway through the newscast on 2, Bosch stopped flipping through the channels with the selector. The story that stopped him was an update on the Beatrice Fontenot killing. A photo of the girl, her hair in cornrows, appeared on the right side of the screen.

The blonde anchor said, 'Police announced today that they have identified a suspected gunman in the death of sixteen-year-old Beatrice Fontenot. The man they are looking for is an alleged drug dealer who was a rival of Beatrice's older brothers, Detective Stanley Hanks said. He said the shots fired at the Fontenot house were in all probability meant for the brothers. Instead, a bullet struck Beatrice, an honor student at Grant High in the Valley, in the head. Her funeral is scheduled for later this week.'

Bosch turned off the television and looked back at Sylvia, who was propped up on two pillows against the wall. They didn't say anything.

After a room service dinner, which they ate with almost no conversation in the front room of the suite, they took turns in the shower. Bosch went second and as the coarse water stung his scalp, he decided that it was time for him to lose all his baggage, to come clean. He trusted his faith in her, in her desire to know all of him. And he knew that if he did nothing, he was risking what they had each day he kept the secrets of his life inside. Somehow, he knew facing her was facing himself. He had to accept what he was, where he had come from and what he had become if he was to be accepted by her.

They were in their bleached white bathrobes, she in the chair by the sliding door, he standing near the bed. Beyond her through the door, he could see the full moon casting a shifting reflection on the Pacific. He didn't know how to start.

She had been leafing through a hotel magazine filled with suggestions for tourists on what to do in the city. None of them were things that people who lived here ever did. She closed it and put it on the table. She looked at him and then looked away. She started before he could say a word.

'Harry, I want you to go home.'

He sat on the edge of the bed, put his elbows on his knees and ran his hands through his hair. He had no idea what was going on.

'What do you mean?'

'Too much death.'

'Sylvia?'

'Harry, I've done so much thinking this weekend that I can't think anymore. But I know this, we have to be apart for a while. I have to sort things out. Your life, it's . . .'

'Two days ago you said our problem was that I held things back from you. Now you're saying you don't want to know about me. Your –'

'I'm not talking about you. I'm talking about what you do.'

He shook his head.

'Same thing, Sylvia. You should know that.'

'Look, it's been a rough couple of days. I just need some time to decide if this is right for me. For us. Believe me, I'm thinking about you, too. I'm not sure I'm the right one for you.'

'I am, Sylvia.'

'Please don't say that. Don't make it any more difficult. I –'

'I don't want to go back to being without you, Sylvia. That's all I know right now. I don't want to be alone.'

'Harry, I don't want to hurt you and I would never ever ask you to change for me. I know you and I don't think you could change even if you wanted to. So . . . what I have to decide is whether I can live with that and live with you. . . . I do love you, Harry, but I need some time . . .'

She was crying now. Bosch could see it in the mirror. He wanted to get up to hold her but he knew it was the wrong move. He was the cause of her tears. There was a long silence, both of them sitting in private pain. She was looking down into her lap where her hands held each other. He looked out at the ocean and saw a drift-fishing boat cut across the reflected path of the moon on its way toward the Channel Islands.

'Say something to me,' she finally said.

'I'll do whatever you want,' he said. 'You know that.'

'I'll go into the bathroom until you get dressed and leave.'

'Sylvia, I want to know that you are safe. I would like to ask you to let me sleep in the other room. In the morning, we'll figure something out. I'll leave then.'

'No. We both know nothing will happen. That man, Locke, he's probably far away, running from you, Harry. I'll be safe. I'll take a taxi to school tomorrow and I'll be safe. Just give me some time.'

'Time to decide.'

'Yes. To decide.'

She got up and walked quickly by him to the bathroom. He put his arm out but she brushed by it. After the door closed he could hear her pull tissues from the dispenser. Then he could hear her crying.

'Please leave, Harry,' she said after a while. 'Please.'

He heard her turn the water on, so she wouldn't hear him if he said anything. Bosch felt like a fool to be sitting there in his luxury bathrobe. It ripped when he pulled it off.

That night he took a blanket from the trunk of the Caprice and made a bed on the sand about a hundred yards from the hotel. But he didn't sleep. He sat with his back to the ocean and his eyes on the curtained sliding door on the fourth floor balcony next to the atrium. Through the glass wall of the atrium he could also see her front door and would know if anyone approached. It was cold on the beach but he didn't need the sea wind's chill to stay awake.

THIRTY

Bosch was ten minutes late coming into the courtroom Monday morning. He had waited to make sure Sylvia got a cab and was safely off to school before going home and changing into the same suit he had worn Friday. But as he hurried in, he saw that Judge Keyes wasn't on the bench and Chandler wasn't at the plaintiff's table. Church's widow sat alone, looking straight forward in a prayerful pose.

Harry sat down next to Belk and said, 'What's up?'

'We were waiting for you and Chandler. Now we're just waiting for her. The judge was not happy about it.'

Bosch saw the judge's clerk get up from her desk and knock on the chambers door. She then poked her head in and he could hear her say, 'Detective Bosch is here. Ms Chandler's secretary still hasn't located her.'

The constricting feeling in his chest began then. Bosch felt himself immediately begin to sweat. How could he have missed it? He leaned forward and put his face into his hands.

'I gotta make a call,' he said and stood up.

Belk turned, probably to tell him not to go anywhere, but was silenced by the opening of the chambers door. Judge Keyes strode out and said, 'Remain seated.'

He took his place on the bench and told the clerk to buzz the jury in. Bosch sat down.

'We're going to go ahead and get them started again without Ms Chandler being here. We'll deal with her tardiness at a later date.'

The jury filed in and the judge asked them if anybody had anything they wanted to bring up, a scheduling problem or anything else. No one said a word.

'All right then, we're going to send you back in to continue deliberations. The marshal will come speak to you later about lunch. By the way, Ms Chandler had a scheduling conflict this morning and that's why you don't see her there at the plaintiff's table. You are to pay no mind to that. Thank you very much.'

They filed back out. The judge instructed the parties who were present to stay within fifteen minutes of the courtroom again, then told the clerk to keep trying to find Chandler. With that, he stood up and walked back to his chambers.

Bosch was up quickly and out the door of the courtroom. He went to the pay phones and dialed the communications center. After giving his name and badge number, he asked the phone clerk to run a code-three DMV search on the name Honey Chandler. He said he needed the address and would hold.

The rover would not work until he was out of the courthouse underground garage. Once he was out on Los Angeles Street he tried again and got hold of Edgar, who had his rover on. He gave him the Carmelina Street address in Brentwood he had gotten for Chandler.

'Meet me there.'

'On my way.'

He drove down to Third and took it up through the tunnel and onto the Harbor Freeway. He was just hitting the Santa Monica Freeway when his pager sounded. He looked at the number while driving and didn't recognize it. He exited the freeway and pulled over at a Korea Town grocery store with a phone on the wall out front.

'Courtroom four,' said the woman who answered his call.

'It's Detective Bosch, did someone beep me?'

365

'Yes, we did. We have a verdict. You need to get back here right away.'

'What do you mean? I was just there. How'd they —'

'It's not unusual, Detective Bosch. They probably came to an agreement Friday and decided to take the weekend to see if they wanted to change their minds. Look, it gets them out of another day of work.'

Back in the car, he picked up the rover again.

'Edgar, you there?'

'Uh, not quite. You?'

'I gotta turn around. Got a verdict. Can you check this out?'

'No problem. What am I checking out?'

'It's Chandler's house. She's blonde. She didn't show up in court today.'

'I get the picture.'

Bosch had never thought he would hope to see Honey Chandler in court at the table opposite his but he did. She wasn't there, though. A man Harry didn't recognize was sitting with the plaintiff.

As he walked to the defense table, Bosch saw that a couple of reporters, including Bremmer, were already in the courtroom.

'Who's that?' he asked Belk about the man next to the widow.

'Dan Daly. Keyes grabbed him out of the hallway to sit with the woman during the verdict. Chandler is apparently incommunicado. They can't find her.'

'Anybody go to her house?'

'I don't know. I assume they called. What do you care? You should be worried about this verdict.'

Judge Keyes came out then and took his place. He nodded to the clerk, who buzzed the jury. As the twelve filed in, none of them looked at Bosch but almost all of them eyed the man sitting next to Deborah Church.

'Again, folks,' the judge began, 'a scheduling conflict has

prevented Ms Chandler from being here. Mr Daly, a fine lawyer, has agreed to sit in her stead. I understand from the marshal that you have reached a verdict.'

Several of the twelve heads nodded. Bosch finally saw one man look at him. But then he looked away. Bosch could feel his heart pounding and he was unsure if it was because of the impending verdict or the disappearance of Honey Chandler. Or both.

'Can I have the verdict forms, please?'

The jury foreman handed a thin stack of papers to the marshal who handed them to the clerk who handed them to the judge. It was excruciating to watch. The judge had to put on a pair of reading glasses and then took his time studying the papers. Finally, he handed the papers back to the clerk and said, 'Publish the verdict.'

The clerk did a rehearsal reading in her head first and then began.

'In the above entitled matter on the question of whether defendant Hieronymus Bosch did deprive Norman Church of his civil rights to protection against unlawful search and seizure, we find for the plaintiff.'

Bosch didn't move. He looked across the room and saw that now all the jurors were looking at him. His eyes turned to Deborah Church and he saw her grab the arm of the man next to her, even though she didn't know him, and smile. She was turning that smile triumphantly toward Bosch when Belk grabbed his arm.

'Don't worry,' he whispered. 'It's the damages that count.'

The clerk continued.

'The jury hereby awards to the plaintiff in compensatory damages the amount of one dollar.'

Bosch heard Belk whisper a gleeful 'Yes!' under his breath.

'In the matter of punitive damages, the jury awards the plaintiff the amount of one dollar.'

Belk whispered it again, only this time loud enough to be

heard in the gallery. Bosch looked at Deborah Church just as the triumph dropped out of her smile and her eyes turned dead. It all seemed surrealistic to Bosch, as if he were observing a play but was actually on the stage with the actors. The verdict meant nothing to him. He just watched everybody.

Judge Keyes began his thank-you speech to the jury, telling them how they had performed their Constitutional duties and should be proud to have served and to be Americans. Bosch tuned it out and just sat there. Sylvia came to mind and he wished he could tell her.

The judge banged down the gavel and the jury filed out for the last time. Then he left the bench and Bosch thought he might have had an annoyed look on his face.

'Harry,' Belk said. 'It's a damn good verdict.'

'Is it? I don't know.'

'Well, it's a mixed verdict. But essentially the jury found what we already admitted to. We said you made mistakes going in like you did but you already had been reprimanded by your department for that. The jury found as a matter of law that you should not have kicked down the door like that. But in awarding only two dollars they were saying they believed you. Church made the furtive move. And Church was the Dollmaker.'

He patted Bosch's back. He was probably waiting for Harry to thank him but it didn't come.

'What about Chandler?'

'Well, there's the rub, so to speak. The jury found for the plaintiff so we are going to have to pick up her tab. She'll probably ask for about one-eighty, maybe two hundred. We'll probably settle it for ninety. It's not bad, Harry. Not at all.'

'I gotta go.'

Bosch stood up and waded through a clot of people and reporters to get out of the courtroom. He moved quickly to the escalator and once on started fumbling to get the last cigarette out of his pack. Bremmer jumped on the step behind him, his notebook out and ready.

368

'Congrats, Harry,' he said.

Bosch looked at him. The reporter seemed sincere.

'For what? They said I'm some kind of a Constitutional goon.'

'Yeah, but you walk away two bucks light. That ain't bad.'

'Yeah, well . . .'

'Well, any comment on the record? I take it "Constitutional goon" was off, right?'

'Yeah, I'd appreciate that. Uh, tell you what, let me think for a while. I've gotta go but I'll call you later. Why don't you go back up and talk to Belk. He needs to see his name in the paper.'

Outside he lit the cigarette and pulled the rover out of his pocket.

'Edgar, you up?'

'Here.'

'How is it?'

'Better come on out, Harry. Everybody's rolling on it.'

Bosch threw the cigarette in the ash can.

They had done a bad job of keeping it contained. By the time Bosch got to the house on Carmelina, there was already one news copter circling overhead and two other channels were there on the ground. It would not be long until it was a circus. The case would have two big draws: the Follower and Honey Chandler.

Bosch had to park two houses away because of the glut of official cars and vans lining both sides of the street. Parking control officers were just beginning to put down flares and close the street to traffic.

The property had been preserved by yellow plastic police lines. Bosch signed an attendance log held by a uniform officer at the tape and slipped underneath. It was a two-story Bauhaus-style home set on a hillside. Standing outside, Bosch knew the floor-to-ceiling windows of the upstairs rooms would offer sweeping views of the flats below. He counted two chimneys. It was a nice house in a nice neighborhood filled with nice lawyers and UCLA professors. Not anymore, he thought. He wished he had a cigarette as he headed in.

Edgar was standing just inside the door in a tiled entryway. He was talking on a mobile phone and it sounded as if he was telling the media relations unit to send people out to handle this. He saw Bosch and pointed up the stairs.

The staircase was right off the entry and Bosch went up. There was a wide hallway that passed four doorways upstairs. A group of detectives milled about outside the farthest door and occasionally they looked inside at something. Bosch walked over.

In a way, Bosch knew, he had trained his mind to be almost like that of a psychopath. He practiced the psychology of objectification when at a death scene. Dead people weren't people, they were objects. He had to look at bodies as corpses, as evidence. It was the only way to deal with it and get the job done. It was the only way to survive. But this, of course, was always easier said or thought about than done. Often Bosch stumbled.

As a member of the original Dollmaker task force, he had seen the last six of the victims attributed to the serial killer. He saw them 'in situ', as it was called – in the situation in which they were found. None of them was easy. There was something that seemed so helpless about these victims that it overwhelmed his best efforts at objectification. And knowing that they came from street backgrounds had made it all the worse. It was as if the torture visited upon each one by her killer was only the last in a life of indignities.

Now he looked down at the naked and tortured body of Honey Chandler and no manner of mental tricks or deception could prevent the horror he saw from burning into his soul. For the first time in his years as a homicide investigator, he wanted to close his eyes and just go away.

But he didn't. Instead, he stood with the other men who looked down with dead eyes and nonchalant poses. Like a gathering of serial killers. Something made him think of the bridge game at San Quentin that Locke had mentioned. A foursome of psychopaths sitting around the table, more killings to their credit than cards on the table.

Chandler was faceup, her arms outstretched at her sides. Her face was garishly painted with makeup. It hid much of the purplish discoloration which spread from her neck up. A leather strap, cut from a purse which lay spilled on the floor, was tied tightly around her neck, knotted on the right side as if pulled closed with a left hand. In keeping with the prior cases, whatever restraints and gag the killer used had been taken away with him.

But there was something outside of the program. Bosch saw that the Follower was improvising, now that he was no longer operating under the camouflage of the Dollmaker. Chandler's body was riddled with cigarette burns and bite marks. Some of them had bled and some were purplish with bruising, meaning the torture had taken place while she was still alive.

Rollenberger was in the room and was giving orders, even telling the photographer what angles he wanted. Nixon and Johnson were also in the room. Bosch realized, as probably Chandler had, that the final indignity was that her uncovered body would be left on display for hours in view of men who had despised her in life. Nixon looked up and saw Bosch in the hallway and stepped out of the room.

'Harry, what made you tumble to her?'

'She didn't show up for court today. Thought it was worth checking out. Guess she was the blonde. Too bad I didn't see it right away.'

'Yeah.'

'Got a TOD yet?'

'Yeah, an estimate. Coroner's tech says time of death was at least forty-eight hours ago.'

Bosch nodded. It meant she was dead before he even found the note. It made it a little easier.

'Hear anything on Locke?'

'Nada.'

'You and Johnson on point on this one?'

'Yeah, Hans Off put us on it. Edgar discovered it but he's primary on last week's case. I know it was your tumble but I guess Hans Off figured with court and –'

'Don't worry about it. What do you need me to do?'

'You tell me. What do you want to do?'

'I want to stay out of there. I didn't like her but I liked her, you know what I mean?'

'I think so. Yeah, this one's bad. You notice he's changing? He's biting now. Burning.'

'Yeah, I noticed. Anything else new?'

'Not that we can tell.'

'I'm going to have a look around the rest of the house. Is it clean?'

'We haven't had time to dust. Just a quick look through. Use gloves and let me know what you find.'

Bosch went to one of the equipment boxes lined along the wall in the hallway and pulled a pair of plastic gloves from a dispenser that looked like a Kleenex box.

Irving passed by him wordlessly on the staircase, their eyes barely holding each other's for a second. When he got down to the entry, he saw two deputy chiefs standing out on the front steps. They weren't doing anything, just standing where they would be sure to be seen on the TV footage looking serious and concerned. Bosch could see that a growing number of reporters and cameramen were gathering at the plastic line.

He looked around and found Chandler's home office in a small room off the living room. Two of the walls contained built-in shelves that were lined with books. The room had one window that looked out onto the commotion just beyond the front lawn. He pulled on the gloves and began looking through the drawers of the desk. He didn't find what he was looking for but he could tell the desk had been rifled by someone else. Things were scattered in the drawers, papers from files were outside of files. It wasn't as neat as Chandler had kept her things on the plaintiff's table.

He checked underneath the blotter. The note from the Follower wasn't there. There were two books on the desk, *Black's Law Dictionary* and the *California Penal Code*. He fanned the pages of both but there was no note. He leaned back in the leather desk chair and looked up at the two walls of books.

He figured it would take two hours to go through all the books and he still might not find the note. Then he noticed the cracked green spine of a book on the second-to-the-top shelf nearest the window. He recognized the book. It was the one Chandler had read from during closing arguments. *The Marble Faun*. He got up and pulled the book out of its slot.

The note was there, folded into the center of the book. So was the envelope it came in. And Bosch quickly learned he had guessed correctly about her. The note was a photocopy of the page dropped at the police station last Monday, the day of opening statements. What was different about this one was the envelope. It hadn't been dropped off. It had been mailed. The envelope was stamped and then canceled in Van Nuys on the Saturday before opening statements.

Bosch looked at the postmark and knew it would be impossible to try any kind of trace on it. There would also be numerous prints on it from the many postal employees who handled it. He decided the note would be of little evidentiary value.

He left the office, carrying the note and envelope by the corners with his gloved hands. He had to go upstairs to find a tech with plastic evidence bags to place them in. He looked through the doorway into the bedroom and saw the coroner's tech and two body movers spreading open a plastic bag on a gurney. The public display of Honey Chandler was about to end. Bosch stepped back so he did not have to watch. Edgar walked over after reading the note, which the tech was labeling.

'He sent the same note to her? How come?'

'Guess he wanted to make sure we didn't sit on the one he dropped off for us. If we did, he could count on her bringing it up.'

'If she had the note all along, how come she wanted to subpoena ours? She could've just taken this one into court.'

'I think maybe she thought she'd get more mileage out of ours. Making the police turn it over gave it more legitimacy in the eyes of the jury. If she had just presented her own, my lawyer could've gotten it shot down. I don't know. It's just a guess.'

Edgar nodded.

'By the way,' Bosch said, 'how'd you get in when you got here?'

'Front door was unlocked. No scratches on the lock or other signs of break-in.'

'The Follower came here and was let in. . . . She wasn't lured to him. Something's going on. He's changing. He's biting and burning. He's making mistakes. He's letting something get to him. Why'd he go for her, rather than stick to his pattern of ordering victims from the sex tabs?'

'Too bad Locke's the fucking suspect. It'd be nice to ask him what all this means.'

'Detective Harry Bosch!' a voice called from downstairs. 'Harry Bosch!'

Bosch walked to the top of the stairs and looked down. A young patrolman, the one who was keeping the scene attendance log at the tape, stood in the entry area looking up.

'Guy at the tape wants to come in. Said he's a shrink who's been working with you.'

Bosch looked over at Edgar. Their eyes locked. He looked back down at the patrolman.

'What's his name?'

The patrolman looked down at his clipboard and read off, 'John Locke, from USC.'

'Send him in.'

Bosch started down the stairs and beckoned to Edgar with his hand. He said, 'I'm taking him into her office. Tell Hans Off and then come down.'

Bosch told Locke to sit in the chair behind the desk while he chose to stay standing. Through the window behind the psychologist, Bosch saw the press gathering into a tight group in preparation for a briefing by someone from media relations.

'Don't touch anything,' Bosch said. 'What're you doing here?'

'I came as soon as I heard,' Locke said. 'But I thought you said you had the suspect under surveillance.'

'We did. It was the wrong guy. How did you hear?'

'It's all over the radio. I heard it while I was driving in and came right here. They didn't put out the exact address but once I got to Carmelina this wasn't hard to find. Just follow the helicopters.'

Edgar slipped into the room then and closed the door.

'Detective Jerry Edgar, meet Dr John Locke.'

Edgar nodded but made no move to shake his hand. He stayed back, leaning against the door.

'Where've you been? We've been trying to find you since yesterday.'

'Vegas.'

'Vegas? Why'd you go to Vegas?'

'Why else, to gamble. I'm also thinking about a book project on the legal prostitutes that work in the towns north of – look, aren't we wasting time here? I'd like to view the body in situ. Then I could give you a read on it.'

'Body's already moved, Doc,' Edgar said.

'It is? Shit. Maybe I could survey the scene and –'

'We've already got too many people up there right now,' Bosch said. 'Maybe later. What do you make of bite marks? Cigarette burns?'

'Are you saying that's what you've found this time?'

'Plus, it wasn't a bimbo from the sex tabs,' Edgar added. 'He came here, she didn't come to him.'

'He is changing quickly. It appears to be complete disassembling. Or some unknown force or reason compelling his actions.'

'Such as?' Bosch asked.

'I don't know.'

'We tried to call you in Vegas. You never checked in.'

'Oh, the Stardust? Well, coming in I saw the new MGM had just opened and decided to see if they had a room. They did. I was there.'

'Anyone with you?' Bosch asked.

'The whole time?' Edgar added.

A puzzled look came over Locke's face.

'What is going –'

He understood now. He shook his head.

'Harry, are you kidding?'

'No. Are you, coming here like this?'

'I think you –'

'No, don't answer that. Tell you what, it would probably be best for all of us if you know your rights before we go any further. Jerry, you got a card?'

Edgar pulled out his wallet and from it took a white plastic card with the Miranda warning printed on it. He started reading it to Locke. Both Bosch and Edgar knew the warning by heart but a departmental memo that was distributed with the plastic card said it was best practice to read directly from a card. This made it difficult for a defense attorney to later attack in court how the police administered the rights warning to a client.

As Edgar read the card, Bosch looked out the window at the huge clot of reporters standing around one of the deputy chiefs. He saw that Bremmer was there now. But the deputy chief's words must not have meant much; the reporter was not writing anything down. He was just standing to the side of the pack and smoking. He was probably waiting for the real info from the real guns, Irving and Rollenberger.

'Am I under arrest?' Locke asked when Edgar was done.

'Not yet,' said Edgar.

'We just need to clear some things up,' Bosch said.

'I resent the hell out of this.'

'I understand. Now, do you want to clear this trip to Vegas up? Was there anyone with you?'

'From six o'clock Friday until I got out of my car down the block ten minutes ago, there has been a person with me every minute of every day except when I was in the bathroom. This is ridic –'

'And that is who, this person?'

'It's a friend of mine. Her name is Melissa Mencken.'

Bosch remembered the young woman named Melissa who was in Locke's front office.

'The child-psych major? From your office? The blonde?'

'That's right,' Locke answered reluctantly.

'And she will tell us you were together the whole time? Same room, same hotel, same everything, right?'

'Yes. She'll confirm it all. We were just coming back when we heard about this on the radio. KFWB. She's out there waiting for me in the car. Go talk to her.'

'What kind of car?'

'It's the blue Jag. Look, Harry, you go talk to her and clear this up. If you don't make noise about me being with a student, I won't make a sound about this . . . this interrogation.'

'This is no interrogation, Doctor. Believe me, if we interrogate you, you'll know it.'

He nodded to Edgar, who slipped out the door to go find the Jag. When they were alone, Bosch pulled a high-backed chair away from the wall and sat down in front of the desk to wait.

'What happened to the suspect you were following, Harry?'

'We did.'

'What's that supposed to –'

'Never mind.'

They sat in silence for nearly five minutes until Edgar stuck his head in the door and signaled Bosch to come out.

'Checks out, Harry. I talked to the girl and her story is the same. There also were credit card receipts in the car. They checked into the MGM Saturday at three. There was a gas receipt in Victorville, had the time on it. Nine o'clock in the morning Saturday. Victorville's what, an hour away. Looks like they were on the road when Chandler got it. Besides, the girl says they also spent Friday night together at his house in the hills. We can do some more checking but I think he's being legit with us.'

'Well. . . ,' Bosch said, not completing the thought. 'Why don't you go up and spread the word that he looks clear. I want to take him up to look around, if he still wants to.'

'Will do.'

Bosch went back into the study. He sat in the chair that was in front of the desk. Locke studied him.

'Well?'

'She's too scared, Locke. She isn't going along. She's telling us the truth.'

'What the fuck are you talking about?' Locke yelled.

Now Bosch studied him. The surprise on his face, the utter fright, was too genuine. Bosch was sure now. He was sorry, yet felt some perverse feeling of power, having run Locke through the scam.

'You're clear, Dr Locke. Just had to be sure. I guess the criminal only comes back to the scene of the crime in movies.'

Locke took a deep breath and looked down into his lap. Bosch thought he looked like a driver who had just pulled to the side of the road to collect himself after missing a head-on collision with a truck by a matter of inches.

'Goddammit, Bosch, for a minute there, I had bad dreams, you know?'

Bosch nodded. He knew about bad dreams.

'Edgar's going up to smooth the way. He's going to ask

the lieutenant if you can go up and give a read on the scene. If you still want to.'

'Excellent,' he said, but there wasn't much excitement left in him.

They sat in silence after that. Bosch took out his cigarettes and found the pack empty. But he put the pack back in his pocket so as not to leave false evidence in the trash can.

He didn't feel like talking to Locke anymore. Instead, he looked past him and out the window at the activity on the street. The media pack had dispersed after the briefing. Now some of the TV reporters were taping their reports with the 'death house' behind them. Bosch could see Bremmer interviewing the neighbors across the street and writing feverishly in his notebook.

Edgar came in then and said, 'We're ready for him upstairs.'

Staring out the window, Bosch said, 'Jerry, can you take him up? I just thought of something I need to do.'

Locke stood up and looked at the two detectives.

'Fuck you,' he said. 'Both of you. Fuck you. . . . There, I just had to say that. Now, let's forget about it and go to work.'

He crossed the room to Edgar. Bosch stopped him at the door.

'Dr Locke?'

He turned back to Bosch.

'When we catch this guy, he'll want to gloat, won't he?'

Locke thought for a while and said, 'Yes, he'll be very pleased with himself, his accomplishments. That might be the hardest part for him, keeping quiet when he knows he should. He'll want to gloat.'

They left then and Bosch looked out the window for a few more minutes before getting up.

Some of the reporters who knew who he was pressed against the yellow tape and began shouting questions as he came out. He ducked under the tape and said he could make no comment and that Chief Irving was coming out soon. That seemed to mollify them temporarily and he started walking down the street to his car.

He knew Bremmer was the master of the anti-pack. He always let the pack move in and do their thing, then he came in after, by himself, to get what he wanted. Bosch wasn't mistaken. Bremmer showed up at the car.

'Pullin' out already, Harry?'

'No, I just need to get something.'

'Pretty bad in there?'

'Is this on or off the record?'

'Whatever you like.'

Bosch opened the car door.

'Off the record, yes, it's pretty bad in there. On the record, no comment.'

He leaned in and made a show of looking in the glove compartment and not finding what he wanted.

'What are you guys calling this one? I mean, you know, since the Dollmaker was already taken.'

Bosch got back out.

'The Follower. That's off the record, too. Ask Irving.'

'Catchy.'

'Yeah, I thought you reporters would like that.'

Bosch pulled the empty cigarette pack out of his pocket, crumpled it and threw it into the car and closed the door.

'Give me a smoke, will you?'

'Sure.'

Bremmer pulled a soft pack of Marlboros out of his sport coat and shook one out for Bosch. Then he lit it for him with a Zippo. With his left hand.

'Hell of a city we live in, Harry, isn't it.'

'Yeah. This city . . .'

THIRTY-ONE

At 7:30 that night, Bosch was sitting in the Caprice in the back parking lot of St Vibiana's in downtown. From his angle, he could look a half block up Second Street to the corner at Spring. But he couldn't see the *Times* building. That didn't matter, though. He knew that every *Times* employee without parking privileges in the executive garage would have to cross the corner of Spring and Second to get to one of the employee garages a half block down Spring. He was waiting for Bremmer.

After leaving the scene at Honey Chandler's house, Bosch had gone home and slept for two hours. The he had paced in his house on the hill, thinking about Bremmer and seeing how perfectly he fit the mold. He called Locke and asked a few more general questions about the psychology of the Follower. But he did not tell Locke about Bremmer. He told no one about this, thinking three strikes and you're out. He came up with a plan, then dropped by Hollywood Division to gas up the Caprice and get the equipment he would need.

And now he waited. He watched a steady procession of homeless people walking down Second. As if heeding a siren's call, they were heading toward the Los Angeles Mission a few blocks away for a meal and a bed. Many carried with them or pushed in shopping carts their life's belongings.

Bosch never took his eyes off the corner but his mind drifted far from there. He thought of Sylvia and wondered what she was doing at that moment and what she was thinking. He hoped she didn't take too long to decide, because he knew his mind's instinctual protective devices and responses had begun to react. He was already looking at the positives that would come if she didn't come back. He told himself she made him weak. Hadn't he thought of her immediately when he found the note from the Follower? Yes, she had made him vulnerable. He told himself she might not be good for his life's mission, let her go.

His heartbeat jacked up a notch when he saw Bremmer step onto the corner and then walk in the direction of the parking garages. A building blocked Bosch's view after that. He quickly started the car and pulled out onto Second and up to Spring.

Down the block Bremmer entered the newer garage with a card key and Bosch watched the auto door and waited. In five minutes a blue Toyota Celica came out of the garage and slowed while the driver checked for traffic on Spring. Bosch could see clearly it was Bremmer. The Celica pulled onto Spring and so did Bosch.

Bremmer headed west on Beverly and into Hollywood. He made one stop at a Vons and came out fifteen minutes later with a single bag of groceries. He then proceeded to a neighborhood of single-family homes just north of the Paramount studio. He drove down the side of a small stuccoed house and parked in the detached garage in the back. Bosch pulled to the curb one house away and waited.

All the houses in the neighborhood were one of three basic designs. It was one of the cookie-cutter victory neighborhoods that had sprung up after World War II in the city, with affordable homes for returning servicemen. Now you'd probably need to be making a general's pay to buy in. The '8os did that. The occupation army of yuppies had the place now.

Each lawn had a little tin sign planted in it. They were from three or four different home-security companies but they all said the same thing. ARMED RESPONSE. It was the epitaph of the city. Sometimes Bosch thought the Hollywood sign should be taken down off the hill and replaced with those two words.

Bosch waited for Bremmer to either come around to the front to check his mail or to put lights on inside the house. When neither happened after five minutes, he got out and approached the driveway, his hand unconsciously tapping his sport coat on the side, making sure he had his Smith & Wesson. It was there, but he kept it holstered.

The driveway was unlit and in the recessed darkness of the open garage Bosch could only see the faint reflection of the red lenses of the taillights of Bremmer's car. But there was no sign of Bremmer.

A six-foot wooden-plank fence ran along the right side of the drive, separating Bremmer's property from his neighbor's. Branches of bougainvillea in bloom hung over and Bosch could hear faint television sounds from the house next door.

As he walked between the fence and Bremmer's house toward the garage, Bosch knew he was completely vulnerable. But he also knew that drawing his weapon couldn't help him here. Favoring the side of the drive nearest the house, he walked to the garage and stopped before its darkness. Standing beneath an old basketball goal with a bent rim, he said, 'Bremmer?'

There was no sound save for the ticking of the engine of the car in the garage. Then, from behind, Bosch heard the light scraping of a shoe on concrete. He turned. Bremmer stood there, grocery bag in hand.

'What are you doing?' Bosch asked.

'That's what I should ask.'

Bosch watched his hands as he spoke.

'You never called. So I came by.'

'Called about what?'

'You wanted a comment about the verdict.'

'You were supposed to call me. Remember? Doesn't matter, the story's been put to bed now. Besides, the verdict kind of took a back seat to the other developments of the day, if you know what I mean. The story on the Follower – and Irving did use that name on the record – is going out front.'

Bosch took a few steps toward him.

'Then how come you're not at the Red Wind? I thought you said you always go for a pop when you hit the front page.'

Holding the bag in his right arm, Bremmer reached into the pocket of his coat but Bosch heard the sound of keys.

'I didn't feel like it tonight. I kind've liked Honey Chandler, you know? What are you really doing here, Harry? I saw you following me.'

'You going to ask me in? Maybe we can have that beer, toast your front-page story. One-A is what you reporters call it, right?'

'Yeah. This one's going above the fold.'

'Above the fold, I like that.'

They stared at each other in the darkness.

'Whaddaya say? About the beer.'

'Sure,' Bremmer said. He turned and went to the house's back door and unlocked it. He reached in and hit switches that turned on lights over the door and in the kitchen beyond. Then he stepped back and held out his arm for Bosch to go in first.

'After you. Go into the living room and have a seat. I'll get a couple bottles and be right there.'

Bosch walked through the kitchen and down a short hall to the living room and dining room. He didn't sit down but rather stood near the curtain drawn across one of the front windows. He parted it and looked into the street and at the houses across. There was no one. No one had seen him come here. He wondered if he had made a mistake.

He looked down at the old-style radiator beneath the window, touched it with his hand. It was cold. Its iron coils had been painted black.

He stood there for a few more moments and then turned

and looked around at the rest of the room. It was nicely furnished with blacks and grays. Bosch sat on a black leather couch. He knew if he arrested Bremmer in the house, he would be able to make a quick cursory search of the premises. If he found anything of an incriminating nature all he had to do was come back with a warrant. Bremmer, being a police and courts reporter, would know that, too. Why'd he let me in? Bosch wondered. Have I made a mistake? He began to lose confidence in his plan.

Bremmer brought out two bottles, no glasses, and sat in a matching chair to Bosch's right. Bosch studied his bottle for a long moment. There was a bubble pushing up from the top. It burst and he held the bottle up and said, 'Above the fold.'

'Above the fold,' Bremmer toasted back. He didn't smile. He took a pull from his bottle and put it down on the coffee table.

Bosch took a large gulp from his bottle and held it in his mouth. It was ice cold and hurt some of his teeth. There was no known history of the Dollmaker or the Follower using drugs on their victims. He looked at Bremmer, their eyes locked for a moment, and he swallowed. It felt good going down.

Leaning forward, elbows on his knees, he held the bottle in his right hand and looked at Bremmer looking back at him. He knew from talking with Locke that the Follower would not be driven by conscience to admit anything. He had no conscience. The only way was trickery, to play on the killer's pride. He felt his confidence coming back. He stared at Bremmer with a glare that burned right through him.

'What is it?' the reporter asked quietly.

'Tell me you did it for the stories, or the book. To get above the fold, to have a bestseller, whatever. But don't tell me you're the sick fuck the shrink says you are.'

'What are you talking about?'

'Skip the bullshit, Bremmer. It's you and you know I know it's you. Why else would I waste my time being here?'

'The Dol – the Follower? You're saying I'm the Follower? Are you crazy?'

'Are you? That's what I want to know.'

Bremmer was silent for a long time. He seemed to retreat into himself, like a computer running a long equation, the Please Wait sign flashing. The answer finally registered and his eyes focused again on Bosch.

'I think you should go, Harry.' He stood up. 'It's very plain to see you've been under a lot of pressure with this case and I think –'

'You're the one coming apart, Bremmer. You've made mistakes. A lot of them.'

Bremmer suddenly dove into Bosch, rolling so that his left shoulder slammed into Bosch's chest, pinning him to the couch. Bosch felt air burst from his lungs and sat helplessly as Bremmer worked his hands under Harry's sport coat and got to the gun. Bremmer then pulled away, switching off the safety and pointing the weapon at Bosch's face.

After nearly a minute of silence during which both men simply stared at each other, Bremmer said, 'I admit only one thing: You have me intrigued, Harry. But before we go any further with this discussion, there is something I have to do.'

A sense of relief and anticipation flooded Bosch's body. He tried not to show it. Instead he tried to put a look of terror on his face. He stared wide-eyed at the gun. Bremmer bent over him and ran his heavy hand down Bosch's chest and into his crotch, then around his sides. He found no wire.

'Sorry to get so personal,' he said. 'But you don't trust me and I don't trust you, right?'

Bremmer straightened and stepped back and sat down.

'Now, I don't need to remind you, but I will. I have the advantage here. So answer my questions. What mistakes? What mistakes have I made? Tell me what I did wrong, Harry, or I'll kneecap you with the first bullet.'

Bosch tantalized him with silence for a few moments as he thought about how to proceed.

'Well,' he finally began. 'Let's go back to the basics first. Four years ago you were all over the Dollmaker case. As a reporter. From the start. It was your stories about the early cases that made the department form the task force. As a reporter you had access to the suspect intelligence, you probably had the autopsy reports. You also had sources like me and probably half the dicks on the task force and in the coroner's office. What I am saying is you knew what the Dollmaker did. Right down to the cross on the toenail, you knew. Later, after the Dollmaker was dead, you used it in your book.'

'Yeah, I knew. It means nothing, Bosch. A lot of people knew.'

'Oh, it's Bosch now. No more Harry? Have I suddenly become contemptible in your eyes? Or does the gun give you that sense that we are no longer equals?'

'Fuck you, Bosch. You're stupid. You've got nothing. What else you got? You know, this is great. It will definitely be worth a chapter in the book I do on the Follower.'

'What else've I got? I've got the concrete blonde. And I've got the concrete. Did you know you dropped your cigarettes when you were pouring the concrete? Remember that? You were driving home, wanted a smoke and you reached into your pocket and there was nothing there.

'See, just like Becky Kaminski, they were in there waiting for us. Marlboro soft pack. That's your brand, Bremmer. That's mistake number one.'

'A lot of people smoke them. Good luck taking this to the DA.'

'A lot of people are left-handed, too, like you and the Follower. And me. But there's more. You want to hear it?'

Bremmer looked away from him, toward the window, and said nothing. Maybe it was a trick, Bosch thought, that he wanted Bosch to go for the gun.

'Hey, Bremmer!' he almost yelled. 'There's more.'

Bremmer's face snapped back into a stare at Bosch.

'Today after the verdict you said I should be happy because the verdict would leave the city only two bucks light. But when we had a drink the other night, remember, you gave me the big rundown on how Chandler would be able to charge the city a hundred grand or so if she won even a dollar judgment from the jury. Remember? So it makes me think that when you told me this morning the verdict was only going to cost two dollars, you knew it was only going to cost two dollars because you knew Chandler was dead and couldn't collect. You knew that because you killed her. Mistake number two.'

Bremmer shook his head as if he were dealing with a child. His aim with the gun drooped to Bosch's midsection.

'Look, man, I was trying to make you feel good when I said that today, okay? I didn't know if she was alive or dead. No jury is going to make that leap of faith.'

Bosch smiled brilliantly at him.

'So now at least you have me past the DA's office and to a jury. I guess my story is improving, isn't it?'

Bremmer coldly smiled back, raised the gun.

'Is that it, Bosch? Is that all you have?'

'I saved the best stuff for last.'

He lit a cigarette, never taking his eyes off Bremmer.

'You remember before you killed Chandler, how you tortured her? You must remember that. You bit her. And burned her. Well, everyone was standing around in that house today wondering why the Follower was changing, doing all this new stuff – changing the mold. Locke, the shrink, he was the most puzzled of all. You really fucked with his mind, man. I kinda like that about you, Bremmer. But, you see, he didn't know what I knew.'

He let that sit out there for a while. He knew Bremmer would bite.

'And what did you know, Sherlock?'

Bosch smiled. He was in complete control now.

'I knew why you did that to her. It was simple. You

388

wanted your note back, didn't you? But she wouldn't tell you where it was. See, she knew she was dead whether she gave it to you or not, so she took it – everything you did to her, she took – and she didn't tell you. That woman had a lot of guts and in the end she beat you, Bremmer. She's the one who got you. Not me.'

'What note?' Bremmer said weakly after a long moment.

'The one you fucked up with. You missed it. It's a big house to search, especially when you've got a dead woman lying in the bed. That'd be hard to explain if somebody happened to drop by. But don't worry, I found it. I've got it. Too bad you don't read Hawthorne. It was sitting there in his book. Too bad. But like I said, she beat you. Maybe there is justice sometimes.'

Bremmer had no snappy comeback. Bosch looked at him and thought that he was doing well. He was almost there.

'She kept the envelope, too, in case you were wondering. I found that, too. And so I started wondering, why would he torture her for this note when it was the same one he dropped off for me? It was just a photocopy. Then I figured it out. You didn't want the note. You wanted the envelope.'

Bremmer looked down at his hands.

'How am I doing? Am I losing you?'

'I have no idea,' Bremmer said, looking back up. 'You're fucking delirious as far as I'm concerned.'

'Well, I only have to worry about making sense to the DA, don't I? And what I'm going to explain to him is that the poem on the note was in response to the story you wrote that appeared in the paper on Monday, the day the trial started. But the postmark on the envelope was the Saturday before. See, there's the puzzle. How would the Follower know to write a poem making reference to the newspaper article two days before it was in the newspaper? The answer is, of course, that he, the Follower, had prior knowledge of the article. He wrote that article. That also

389

explains how you knew about the note in the next day's story. You were your own source, Bremmer. And that is mistake number three. Three strikes and you're out.'

The silence that followed was so complete that Bosch could hear the low hiss coming from Bremmer's bottle of beer.

'You're forgetting something, Bosch,' Bremmer finally said. 'I'm holding the gun. Now, who else have you told this crazy story to?'

'Just to finish the housekeeping,' Bosch said, 'the new poem you dropped off for me this past weekend was just a front. You wanted the shrink and everybody else to make it look like you killed Chandler as a favor to me or some psycho bullshit, right?'

Bremmer said nothing.

'That way nobody would see the true reason you went after her. To get the note and the envelope back. . . . Shit, you being a reporter she was familiar with, she probably invited you in when you knocked on her door. Kind of like you inviting me in here. Familiarity breeds danger, Bremmer.'

Bremmer said nothing.

'Answer a question for me, Bremmer. I'm curious why you dropped one note off and mailed the other. I know, being a reporter, you could blend in at the station, drop it on the desk and nobody would remember. But why mail it to her? Obviously, it was a mistake – that's why you went back and killed her. But why'd you make it?'

The reporter looked at Bosch for a long moment. Then he glanced down at the gun as if to reassure himself that he was in control and would get out of this. The gun was powerful bait. Bosch knew he had him.

'The story was supposed to run that Saturday, that's what it was scheduled for. But some dumb-ass editor held it, ran it Monday. I had mailed the letter before I looked at the paper that Saturday. That was my only mistake. But you're the one who made the big mistake.'

'Oh, yeah? What's that?'

'Coming here alone . . .'

Now it was Bosch who was silent.

'Why come here alone, Bosch? Is this how you did it with the Dollmaker? You went alone so you could kill him in cold blood?'

Bosch thought a moment.

'That's a good question.'

'Well, that was your second mistake. Thinking I was as unworthy an opponent as him. He was nothing. You killed him and therefore he deserved to die. But now it is you who deserve to die.'

'Give me the gun, Bremmer.'

He laughed as if Bosch had asked a crazy question.

'You think –'

'How many were there? How many women are buried out there?'

Bremmer's eyes lit with pride.

'Enough. Enough to fulfill my special needs.'

'How many? Where are they?'

'You'll never know, Bosch. That will be your pain, your last pain. Never knowing. And losing.'

Bremmer raised the gun so that its muzzle pointed to Bosch's heart. He pulled the trigger.

Bosch watched his eyes as the metallic click sounded. Bremmer pulled the trigger again and again. The same result, the growing terror in his eyes.

Bosch reached into his sock and pulled the extra clip, the one that was loaded with fifteen XTP bullets. He wrapped his fist around the cartridge and in one swift motion came off the couch and swung his fist into Bremmer's jaw. The impact of the blow knocked the reporter backward in his chair. His weight made the chair crash backward and he spilled to the floor. He dropped the Smith and Bosch quickly gathered it up, ejected the empty clip and put in the live ammunition.

'Get up! Get the fuck up!'

Bremmer did as he was told.

'Are you going to kill me now? Is that it, another kill for the gunslinger?'

'That's up to you, Bremmer.'

'What are you talking about?'

'I'm talking about how I want to blow your head off, but for me to do that you have to make the first move, Bremmer. Just like with the Dollmaker. It was his play. Now it's yours.'

'Look, Bosch, I don't want to die. Everything I said – I was just playing a game. You're making a mistake here. I just want to get it cleared up. Please, just take me to county and it will all get cleared up. Please.'

'Did they plead like that when you had the strap around their necks? Did they? Did you make them plead for their lives, or for their deaths? What about Chandler? At the end, did she beg you to kill her?'

'Take me to county. Arrest me and take me to county.'

'Then get against that wall, you fat fuck and put your hands behind your back.'

Bremmer obeyed. Bosch dropped his cigarette into an ashtray on the table and followed Bremmer to the wall. When he closed the handcuffs over the reporter's wrists, Bremmer's shoulders dropped as he apparently felt safe. He started squirming his arms, chafing his wrists on the cuffs.

'See that?' he said. 'You see that, Bosch? I'm making marks on my wrists. You kill me now, they'll see the marks and know it was an execution. I'm not some dumb fuck like Church that you can slaughter like an animal.'

'No, that's right, you know all the angles, don't you?'

'All of them. Now take me down to county. I'll be out before you wake up tomorrow. Know what all this is, what you've got? Just the wild speculation of a rogue cop. Even a federal jury agreed you go too far, Bosch. This won't work. You've got no evidence.'

Bosch turned him away from the wall so that their faces were no more than two feet apart, their beer breath mixing.

'You did it, didn't you? And you think you're going to walk, don't you?'

Bremmer stared at him and Bosch saw the gleam of pride in his eyes again. Locke had been right about him. He was gloating. And he couldn't shut up even though he knew his life might depend on it.

'Yes,' he said in a low, strange voice. 'I did it. I'm the man. And, yes, I will walk. You wait and see. And when I'm out there you'll think of me every night for the rest of your life.'

Bosch nodded.

'But I never said that, Bosch. It will be your word against mine. A rogue cop – it will never get to court. They couldn't afford to put you on the stand against me.'

Bosch leaned closer to him and smiled.

'Then I suppose it's a good thing I taped it.'

Bosch walked over to the radiator and pulled the microrecorder from between two of the iron coils. He held it up on his palm for Bremmer to see. Bremmer's eyes became enraged. He had been tricked. He had been cheated.

'Bosch, that tape is inadmissible. That's entrapment. I have not been advised. I have not been advised!'

'I'm advising you of your rights now. You weren't under arrest until now. I wasn't going to advise you until I arrested you. You know police procedure.'

Bosch was smiling at him, digging it in.

'Let's go, Bremmer,' he said when he got tired of the victory.

THIRTY-TWO

It was an irony that Bosch savored Tuesday morning when he read Bremmer's above-the-fold story on the killing of Honey Chandler. He had booked the reporter into county jail on a no-bail hold shortly before midnight and had not alerted media relations. The word had not gotten out by the last deadline and now the paper had a front-page story about a murder that was written by the murderer. Bosch liked that. He smiled as he read it.

The one person Bosch had told was Irving. He had the com center patch him through on a phone line and in a half-hour-long conversation he told the assistant chief every step he had taken and described every building block of evidence that led to the arrest. Irving said nothing congratulatory, nor did he chastise Bosch for making the arrest alone. Either or both would come later, after it was seen whether the arrest would stick. Both men knew this.

At 9 A.M. Bosch was seated in front of a filing deputy's desk at the district attorney's office in the downtown criminal courts building. For the second time in eight hours he carefully went over the details of what happened and then played the tape of his conversation with Bremmer. The deputy DA, whose name was Chap Newell, made notations on a yellow pad while listening to the tape. He often furrowed his brow or shook his head because the sound was not good. The voices in Bremmer's living room had bounced through the iron radiator coils and had a tinny echo on the tape. Still, the words that were most important were audible.

Bosch just watched without saying a word. Newell looked as if he could be no more than three years out of law school. Because the arrest had not made a splash in the papers or on TV yet, it had not received the attention of one of the senior attorneys in the filings division. It had gone to Newell on the routine rotation.

When the tape was done, Newell made a few more notes to look as if he knew what he was doing and then looked up at Bosch.

'You haven't said anything about what was in his house.'

'I didn't find anything on the quick search I made last night. There are others there now, with a warrant, doing a more thorough job.'

'Well, I hope they find something.'

'Why, you've got the case right there.'

'And it is a good case, Bosch. Really good work.'

'Coming from you, that means a lot.'

Newell looked at him and narrowed his eyes. He wasn't sure what to make of that.

'But, uh . . .'

'But what?'

'Well, there's no question we can file with this. There is a lot here.'

'But what?'

'I'm looking at it from a defense lawyer's perspective. What really do we have here? A lot of coincidences. He's left-handed, he smokes, he knew details about the Dollmaker. But those things are not hard evidence. They can apply to a lot of people.'

Bosch started lighting a cigarette.

'Please don't do –'

He exhaled and blew the smoke across the desk.

'– never mind.'

'What about the note and the postmark?'

'That's good but it is complicated and difficult to grasp. A good lawyer could make a jury see it as just another coincidence. He could confuse the issue, is what I'm trying to say.'

'What about the tape, Newell? We have him confessing on tape. What more do you –'

'But during the confession he disavows the confession.'

'Not at the end.'

'Look, I'm not planning on using the tape.'

'What are you talking about?'

'You know what I'm talking about. He confessed before you advised him. It brings up the specter of entrapment.'

'There is no entrapment. He knew I was a cop and he knew his rights whether I advised him or not. He had a fucking gun on *me*. He freely made those statements. When he was formally arrested, I advised him.'

'But he searched you for a wire. That is a clear indication of his desire not to be taped. Plus, he dropped the bomb – his most damaging statement – after you cuffed him but before you advised him. That could be dicey.'

'You're going to use the tape.'

Newell looked at him a long time. A red blotchiness appeared on his young cheeks.

'You are not in a position to tell me what I'm going to use, Bosch. Besides, if that's all we go with it will probably be up to the state court of appeals if we use it, because if Bremmer has any kind of a lawyer at all that's where he'll take it. We'll win the question here in superior because half the judges on those benches worked in the DA's office at one time or another. But when it gets up to appeals or to the state supreme court in San Francisco, it's anybody's guess. Is that what you want? To wait a couple years and have it blown out then? Or do you want to get it done correctly right from the get go?'

Bosch leaned forward and looked angrily at the young lawyer.

'Look, we're still working other angles. We're not done. There will be more evidence accumulated. But we have to charge this guy or let him go. We've got forty-eight hours from last night to file. But if we don't file right now with no bail, he'll grab a lawyer and get a bail hearing. The judge won't honor the no-bail arrest if you haven't even filed a single charge yet. So file on him now. We'll get all the evidence you need to back it up.'

Newell nodded as if he agreed but said, 'Thing is, I like to have the whole package, everything we can get, when I file a case. That way we know how we are going to work the prosecution, right from the start. We know if we are going to go with a plea bargain or go balls to the wall.'

Bosch got up and walked to the office's open door. He stepped into the hall and looked at the plastic name plate affixed to the wall outside. Then he came back in.

'Bosch, what are you doing?'

'It's funny. I thought you were a filing deputy. I didn't know you were a trial deputy, too.'

Newell dropped his pencil on his pad. His face got redder, the blotches spreading to his forehead.

'Look, I am a filing deputy. But it is part of my responsibility to make sure we have the best case possible from the get go. Every case that comes through that door I could file on, but that's not the point. The point is to have good, credible evidence and a lot of it. Cases that don't backfire. So I push, Bosch. I –'

'How old are you?'

'What?'

'How old?'

'Twenty-six. What's that got to –'

'Listen to me, you little prick. Don't you ever call me by my last name again. I was making cases like this before you cracked your first law book and I'll be making them long after you move your convertible Saab and your self-centered white-bread show to Century City. You can call me Detective or Detective Bosch, you can even call me Harry. But don't you ever call me just Bosch again, understand?'

Newell's mouth had dropped open.

'Do you understand?'

'Sure.'

'Another thing, we're going to get more evidence and we're going to get it as soon as we can. But, in the meantime, you're going to file one charge of first-degree murder on Bremmer with a no-bail hold because we are going to make sure – from the get go, Mr Newell – that this scumbag never sees the light of day again.

'Then, when we have more evidence, if you are still attached to this case, you will file multiple counts under theories of linkage between the deaths. At no time will you worry about the so-called package you will hand off to the trial attorney. The trial attorney will make those decisions. Because we both know that you are really just a clerk, a clerk who files what is brought to him. If you knew enough to even sit in court next to a trial attorney you would not be here. Do you have any questions?'

'No,' he said quickly.

'No, what?'

'No ques – No, Detective Bosch.'

Bosch went back to Irving's conference room and used the rest of the morning to work up an application for a search warrant to collect hair, blood and saliva specimens along with a dental mold from Bremmer.

Before taking it to the courthouse, he attended a brief meeting of the task force where they all reported on their respective assignments.

Edgar said he had been to Sybil Brand and had shown Georgia Stern, who was still being held there, a photo of Bremmer but she could not identify him as her attacker. She could not rule him out, either.

Sheehan said he and Opelt had shown the mug shot of Bremmer to the manager of the storage facility at Bing's and the man said Bremmer might have been one of the renters of the storage rooms two years earlier but he couldn't be sure.

He said it was too long ago to remember well enough to send a man to the gas chamber.

'The guy's a wimp,' Sheehan said. 'My feeling was he recognized Bremmer but was too scared to stick it in all the way. We're going to hit him again tomorrow.'

Rollenberger called the presidents up on the rover and they reported from Bremmer's house that there was nothing yet. No tapes, no bodies, nothing.

'I say we go for a warrant to dig up the yard, under the foundation,' Nixon said.

'We might go to that,' Rollenberger radioed back. 'Meantime, keep at it.'

Lastly, Yde reported by rover that he and Mayfield were getting the runaround from the *Times* lawyers and had not yet been able to so much as approach Bremmer's desk in the newsroom.

Rollenberger reported that Heikes and Rector were out of pocket, running down background on Bremmer. After that, he said that Irving had scheduled a five o'clock press conference to discuss the case with the media. If anything new was discovered, let Rollenberger know before then.

'That's it,' Rollenberger said.

Bosch got up to head out.

The medical clinic on the high-power floor of the county jail reminded Bosch of Frankenstein's laboratory. There were chains on every bed and rings bolted to the tile walls to tether patients to. The pull-down lights over each bed were caged in steel so patients couldn't get to the light bulbs and use them as weapons. The tile was supposed to be white but over the years had surrendered to a depressing off-yellow.

Bosch and Edgar stood in the doorway to one of the bays where there were six beds and watched as Bremmer, who was lying in the sixth bed, was given a shot of sodium pentothal to make him more cooperative, more malleable. He had refused to give the court-ordered dental mold and samples of blood, saliva and hair.

After the drug began to take effect, the doctor pulled open the reporter's mouth, put two clamps in to hold it open and pushed a little square block of clay over the front upper teeth. He then followed the same procedure with the lower front teeth. When he was done, he relaxed the clamps and Bremmer appeared to be asleep.

'If we asked him something now, he'd tell the truth, right?' Edgar asked. 'That's truth serum they're givin' him, right?'

'Supposedly,' Bosch said. 'But it'd prob'ly get the case thrown out of court.'

The little gray blocks with teeth indentations were slid into plastic cases. The doctor closed them and handed them to Edgar. He then drew blood, wiped a cotton swab in Bremmer's mouth and cut snippets of hair from the suspect's head, chest and pubic area. He put these in envelopes which went into a small cardboard box like the kind chicken nuggets come in at fast-food restaurants.

Bosch took the box and they left then, Bosch going to the coroner's office to see Amado, the analyst, and Edgar going to Cal State Northridge to see the forensic archaeologist who had helped with the concrete blonde reconstruction.

By quarter to five, everyone was back in the conference room but Edgar. They were all milling about, waiting to watch Irving's press conference. There had been no other progress since noon.

'Where do you think he stashed everything, Harry?' Nixon asked as he was pouring coffee.

'I don't know. Probably has a storage locker somewhere. If he has tapes, I doubt he'd part with them. He probably has a drop somewhere. We'll find them.'

'What about the other women?'

'They're out there somewhere, under the city. Only way they'll come up is by luck.'

'Or if Bremmer talks,' Irving said. He had just come in. There was a good feeling in the room. Despite the day's slow progress, everyone to a man had no doubt they finally had the right man. And that certainty validated what they were about. So they wanted to drink coffee and hang out. Even Irving.

At five minutes before five, when Irving was going over some of the reports typed during the day for the last time before facing the media, Edgar came up on the rover. Rollenberger quickly picked up a radio and answered back.

'What do you have, Team Five?'

'Is Harry there?'

'Yes, Team Five, Team Six is present. What have you got?'

'I've got the package. Definite match between the suspect's teeth and the impressions on the victim.'

'Roger that, Team Five.'

There was a whoop in the conference room and a lot of backslapping and high fives. 'He is going down,' Nixon exclaimed.

Irving picked up his papers and headed for the hallway door. He wanted to be on time. At the doorway he passed close to Bosch.

'We're gold, Bosch. Thanks.'

Bosch just nodded.

A few hours later Bosch was back at the county jail. It was after lock-down so the deputies wouldn't bring Bremmer out to see him. Instead, he had to go into the high-power module, the deputies watching him on remote cameras. He walked along the row of cells to 6-36 and looked through the wired one-foot-square window in the single-piece steel door.

Bremmer was on 'keep away' status, so he was in there alone. He didn't notice Bosch watching. He lay on the bottom bunk on his back, his hands laced behind his head. His eyes were open and staring straight up. Bosch recognized the withdrawal state he had seen for a moment the night before. It was as if he wasn't there. Bosch leaned his mouth to the screen.

'Bremmer, you play bridge?'

Bremmer looked over at him, only moving his eyes. 'What?'

'I said, do you play bridge? You know, the card game?'

'What the fuck do you want, Bosch?'

'I just dropped by to tell you a little while ago they added three more to the one this morning. Linkage. You just got the concrete blonde and the two from before, the ones we first gave to the Dollmaker. You also got an attempted murder on the survivor.'

'Oh, well, what's the difference? You got one, you got 'em all. All I need to do is beat the Chandler case and the others fall like dominoes.'

'Except that isn't going to happen. We got your teeth, Bremmer, just as good as fingerprints. And we got the rest. I just came from the coroner's. They matched your pubic hair to samples found on victims seven and eleven – the ones we gave the Dollmaker credit for. You ought to think about dealing, Bremmer. Tell where the others are and they'll probably let you live. That's why I asked about bridge.'

'What about it?'

'Well, I hear there's some guys up at Q play a good bridge game. They're always looking for new blood. You'll probably like 'em, have a lot in common.'

'Why don't you leave me alone, Bosch?'

'I will. I will. But just so you know it, man, they're on death row. But don't worry about that, when you get there you'll get a lot of card playing in. What's the average lead time? Eight, ten years before they gas somebody? That's not bad. Unless, of course, you talk a deal.'

'There is no deal, Bosch. Get out of here.'

'I'm going. Believe me, it's nice to be able to walk out of this place. I'll see you then, okay? You know, in eight or ten years. I'm going to be there, Bremmer. When they strap you in. I'm going to be watching through the glass when the gas comes up. And then I'll come out and tell the reporters how you died. I'll tell them you went screaming, that you weren't much of a man.'

'Fuck you, Bosch.'

'Yeah, fuck me. See you then, Bremmer.'

THIRTY-THREE

After Bremmer's arraignment Tuesday morning, Bosch got permission to take the rest of the week off in lieu of receiving all of the overtime he had built up on the case.

He spent the time hanging around the house, doing odd jobs and taking it easy. He replaced the wood railing on the back porch with new lengths of weather-treated oak. And while he was at Home Depot getting the wood, he also picked up new cushions for the chairs and the chaise lounge on the porch.

He began reading the *Times* sports pages again, noting the statistical changes in team ranks and player performances.

And, occasionally, he'd read one of the many stories the *Times* ran in the Metro section about what was becoming known nationwide as the Follower case. But it didn't really hold his fascination. He knew too much about the case already. The one interest he had in the stories was in the details about Bremmer that were coming out. The *Times* had sent a staffer to Texas, where Bremmer had been raised in an Austin suburb, and the reporter had returned with a story culled from old children's-court files and neighborhood gossip. He'd been raised by his mother in a single-parent home; his father, an itinerant blues musician, he saw once or twice a year at the most. The mother was described by former neighbors as a disciplinarian and plain mean-spirited when it came to her son.

The worst thing that the reporter came up with on Bremmer was that he was suspected but never charged in the arson of a neighbor's toolshed when he was thirteen. It was said by neighbors that his mother punished him as if he had committed the crime anyway, not allowing him to leave their tiny house the rest of the summer. The neighbors said that around the same time the neighborhood began to experience a problem with pets disappearing but this was never attributed to young Bremmer. At least until now. Now the neighbors seemed engaged in blaming Bremmer for any malady that beset their street that year.

A year after the fire Bremmer's mother died of alcoholism and the boy was raised after that on a state boys' farm, where the young charges wore white shirts and blue ties and blazers to classes, even when the thermometer went off the chart. The story said he worked as a reporter on one of the farm's student newspapers, thus beginning a journalism career that would eventually take him to Los Angeles.

His history was all grist for people like Locke to consider, to use as fuel for speculation on how the child Bremmer made the adult Bremmer do the things he did. It just made Bosch feel sad. He couldn't help, however, but stare for a long time at the photo of the mother the *Times* had dug up somewhere. In the picture she stood in front of the door to a sun-burned ranch-style house with her hand on a young Bremmer's shoulder. She had bleached-blonde hair and a provocative figure and large chest. She wore too much makeup, Bosch thought as he stared at the picture.

Aside from the Bremmer articles, the story he read and reread several times was in the Metro section of Thursday's paper. It was about the burial of Beatrice Fontenot. Sylvia was quoted in the article and it described how the Grant High teacher had read some of the girl's schoolwork at the memorial service. There was a photo from the service but Sylvia wasn't in it. It was of Beatrice's mother's stoic, tear-lined face at the funeral. Bosch kept the Metro page on the table next to the chaise lounge and read the story again every time he sat down there.

*

When he grew restless around the house he would drive. Down out of the hills, he'd head across the Valley with no place in particular to go. He'd drive forty minutes to have a hamburger at an In 'N' Out stand. Having grown up in the city, he liked to drive it, to know every one of its streets and corners. Once on Thursday and again on Friday morning his drives took him past Grant High but he never saw Sylvia through the windows of the classrooms as he went by. He felt sick at heart when he thought of her but he knew the closest he could come to her was to drive by the school. It was her move and he must wait for her to make it.

On Friday afternoon, when he came back from his drive, he saw the message light flashing on his phone machine and his hopes rushed into his throat. He thought maybe she had seen his car and was calling because she knew how his heart hurt. But when he played the message it was just Edgar asking him to call.

Eventually, he did.

'Harry, you're missing everything?'

'Yeah, what?'

'Well, we had *People* magazine in here yesterday.'

'I'll watch for you on the cover.'

'Just kidding. Actually, we've got big developments.'

'Yeah, what?'

'All this publicity was bound to do us good. Some lady over in Culver City called up and said she recognized Bremmer, that he had a storage locker at her place, but under the name Woodward. We got a warrant and popped it first thing this morning.'

'Yeah.'

'Locke was right. He videotaped. We found the tapes. His trophies.'

'Jesus.'

'Yeah. If there was ever a doubt there ain't now. Got seven tapes and the camera. He must not have taped the first two, the ones we thought were the Dollmaker's. But we

406

got tapes of seven others including Chandler and Maggie Cum Loudly. Bastard taped everything. Just horrible stuff. They're working up formal IDs on the other five victims on the tapes, but it looks like it's going to be the ones on the list Mora came up with. Gallery and the other four porno chicks.'

'What else was in the locker?'

'Everything. We've got everything. We've got cuffs, belts, gags, a knife and a Glock nine. His whole killing kit. He must've used the gun to control them. That's why there was no sign of a struggle at Chandler's. He used the gun. We figure he'd hold it on them until he could cuff 'em and gag 'em. From the tapes, it looks like all the kills took place in Bremmer's house, the rear bedroom. Except Chandler, of course. She got it at home. . . . Those tapes, Harry, I couldn't watch.'

Bosch could imagine. He envisioned the scenes and felt an unexpected flutter in his heart, as if it had torn loose inside of him and was banging against his ribs like a bird trying to break out of its cage.

'Anyway, the DA's got it and the big development is Bremmer's going to talk.'

'He is?'

'Yeah, he heard we had the tapes and everything else. I guess he told his lawyer to deal. He's going to get life without the possibility of parole in exchange for leading us to the bodies and letting the shrinks have at him, study what makes him tick. My vote is they squash him like a fly, but I guess they are considering the families and science.'

Bosch was silent. Bremmer would live. At first he didn't know what to think. Then he realized he could live with the deal. It had bothered him that those women might never be found. That was why he had visited Bremmer at the jail the day charges were first filed. Whether the victims had families who cared or not, he didn't want to leave them down there in the black chasm of the unknown.

It wasn't a bad deal, Bosch decided. Bremmer would be

alive, but he wouldn't be living. It might even be worse for him than the gas chamber. And that would be justice, he thought.

'Anyway,' Edgar said, 'thought you'd want to know.'

'Yeah.'

'It's a weird fuckin' thing, you know? It being Bremmer. It's weirder than if it was Mora, man. A reporter! And, man, I knew the guy, too.'

'Yeah, well, a lot of us did. I guess nobody knows anybody like they think.'

'Yeah. Seeya, Harry.'

Late that afternoon, he stood on the back deck, leaning forward on his new oak railing, looking out into the pass and thinking about the black heart. Its rhythm was so strong it could set the beat of a whole city. He knew it would always be the background beat, the cadence, of his own life. Bremmer would be banished now, hidden away forever, but he knew there would be another after him. And another after him. The black heart does not beat alone.

He lit a cigarette and thought about Honey Chandler, crowding his last view of her from his mind with the vision of her holding forth in court. That would always be her place in his mind. There had been something so pure and distilled about her fury – like the blue flame on a match before it burns out on its own. Even directed at him he could appreciate it.

His mind wandered to the statue at the courthouse steps. He still couldn't think of her name. A concrete blonde, Chandler had called her. Bosch wondered what Chandler had thought about justice at the end. At her end. He knew there was no justice without hope. Did she still have any hope left at the end? He believed that she did. Like the pure blue flame dimming to nothing, it was still there. Still hot. It was what allowed her to beat Bremmer.

He did not hear Sylvia until she stepped out onto the porch.

He looked up and saw her there and wanted to go to her immediately, but held back. She was wearing blue jeans and a dark blue denim shirt. He'd bought the shirt for her birthday and he took that as a good sign. He guessed she had probably come from school, it having recessed for the weekend only an hour earlier.

'I called your office and they told me you were off. I thought I would come by to see how you were. I've been reading all about the case.'

'I'm okay, Sylvia. How are you?'

'I'm fine.'

'How are we?'

She smiled a little at that.

'Sounds like one of those bumper stickers you see. "How'm I driving?". . . Harry, I don't know how we are. I guess that's why I'm here.'

There was an uneasy silence as she looked around the porch and out into the pass. Bosch crushed his cigarette out and dropped it in an old coffee can he kept by the door.

'Hey, new cushions.'

'Yeah.'

'Harry, you have to understand why I needed some time. It's –'

'I do.'

'Let me finish. I rehearsed this enough times, I'd like to get a chance to actually say it to you. I just wanted to say that it is going to be very hard for me, for us, if we go on. It is going to be hard to deal with our pasts, our secrets, and most of all what you do, what you bring home with you . . .'

Bosch waited for her to continue. He knew she wasn't done.

'I know I don't have to remind you, but I've been through it before with a man I loved. And I saw it all go bad and – you know how it ended. There was a lot of pain for both of us. So you have to understand why I needed to take a step back and take a look at this. At us.'

He nodded but she wasn't looking at him. Her not looking concerned him more than her words. He couldn't bring himself to speak, though. He didn't know what he could say.

'You live a very hard struggle, Harry. Your life, I mean. A cop. Yet with all your baggage I see and know there are still very noble things about you.'

Now she looked at him.

'I do love you, Harry. I want to try to keep that alive because it's one of the best things about my life. One of the best things I know. I know it will be hard. But that might make it all the better. Who knows?'

He went to her then.

'Who knows?' he said.

And they held each other for a long time, his face next to hers, smelling her hair and skin. He held the back of her neck as though it was as fragile as a porcelain vase.

After a while they broke apart but only long enough to get on the chaise lounge together. They sat silently, just holding each other, for the longest time – until the sky started to dim and turn red and purple over the San Gabriels. Bosch knew there were still the secrets he carried, but they would keep for now. And he would avoid that black place of loneliness for just a while longer.

'Do you want to go away this weekend?' he asked. 'Get away from the city? We could take that trip up to Lone Pine. Stay in a cabin tomorrow night.'

'That would be wonderful. I could – We could use it.'

A few minutes later she added, 'We might not be able to get a cabin, Harry. There's so few of them and they're usually booked by Friday.'

'I already have one on reserve.'

She turned around so she could face him. She smiled slyly and said, 'Oh, so you knew all the time. You were just hanging around waiting for me to come back. No sleepless nights, no surprise.'

He didn't smile. He shook his head and for a few

moments he looked out at the dying light reflected on the west wall of the San Gabriels.

'I didn't know, Sylvia,' he said. 'I hoped.'

If you have enjoyed *The Concrete Blonde*
here is a taste of another Michael Connelly
bestseller

CITY OF BONES

Published in Orion paperback
ISBN-13: 978-0-7528-4834-8
Price: £6.99

2

Bosch listened to the Lakers game on the car radio while he made his way into the canyon and then up Lookout Mountain to Wonderland Avenue. He wasn't a religious follower of professional basketball but wanted to get a sense of the situation in case he needed his partner, Jerry Edgar. Bosch was working alone because Edgar had lucked into a pair of choice seats to the game. Bosch had agreed to handle the call outs and to not bother Edgar unless a homicide or something Bosch couldn't handle alone came up. Bosch was alone also because the third member of his team, Kizmin Rider, had been promoted nearly a year earlier to Robbery-Homicide Division and still had not been replaced.

It was early third quarter, and the game with the Trail Blazers was tied. While Bosch wasn't a hardcore fan he knew enough from Edgar's constant talking about the game and begging to be left free of call-out duty that it was an important matchup with one of the Los Angeles team's top rivals. He decided not to page Edgar until he had gotten to the scene and assessed the situation. He turned the radio off when he started losing the AM station in the canyon.

The drive up was steep. Laurel Canyon was a cut in the Santa Monica Mountains. The tributary roads ranged up toward the crest of the mountains. Wonderland Avenue dead-ended in a remote spot where the half-million-dollar homes were surrounded by heavily wooded and steep terrain. Bosch instinctively knew that searching for bones in the area would be a logistical nightmare. He pulled to a stop behind a patrol car already at the address Mankiewicz had provided and checked his watch. It was 4:38, and he wrote it down on a fresh page of his legal pad. He figured he had less than an hour of daylight left.

A patrol officer he didn't recognize answered his knock. Her nameplate said Brasher. She led him back through the house to a home office where her partner, a cop whom Bosch recognized and knew was named Edgewood, was talking to a white-haired man who sat behind a cluttered desk. There was a shoe box with the top off on the desk.

Bosch stepped forward and introduced himself. The white-haired man said he was Dr. Paul Guyot, a general practitioner. Leaning forward Bosch could see that the shoe box contained the bone that had drawn them all together. It was dark brown and looked like a gnarled piece of driftwood.

He could also see a dog lying on the floor next to the doctor's desk chair. It was a large dog with a yellow coat.

"So this is it," Bosch said, looking back down into the box.

"Yes, Detective, that's your bone," Guyot said. "And as you can see . . ."

He reached to a shelf behind the desk and pulled down a heavy copy of *Gray's Anatomy*. He opened it to a previously marked spot. Bosch noticed he was wearing latex gloves.

The page showed an illustration of a bone, anterior and posterior views. In the corner of the page was a small sketch of a skeleton with the humerus bone of both arms highlighted.

"The humerus," Guyot said, tapping the page. "And then we have the recovered specimen."

He reached into the shoe box and gently lifted the bone. Holding it above the book's illustration he went through a point-by-point comparison.

"Medial epicondyle, trochlea, greater and lesser tubercle," he said. "It's all there. And I was just telling these two officers, I know my bones even without the book. This bone is human, Detective. There's no doubt."

Bosch looked at Guyot's face. There was a slight quiver, perhaps the first showing of the tremors of Parkinson's.

"Are you retired, Doctor?"

"Yes, but it doesn't mean I don't know a bone when I see —"

"I'm not challenging you, Dr. Guyot." Bosch tried to smile. "You say it is human, I believe it. Okay? I'm just trying to get the lay of the land here. You can put that back into the box now if you want."

Guyot replaced the bone in the shoe box.

"What's your dog's name?"

"Calamity."

Bosch looked down at the dog. It appeared to be sleeping.

"When she was a pup she was a lot of trouble."

Bosch nodded.

"So, if you don't mind telling it again, tell me what happened today."

Guyot reached down and ruffled the dog's collar. The dog looked up at him for a moment and then put its head back down and closed its eyes.

"I took Calamity out for her afternoon walk. Usually when I get up to the circle I take her off the leash and let her run up into the woods. She likes it."

"What kind of dog is she?" Bosch asked.

"Yellow Lab," Brasher answered quickly from behind him.

Bosch turned and looked at her. She realized she had made a mistake by intruding and nodded and stepped back toward the door of the room where her partner was.

"You guys can clear if you have other calls," Bosch said. "I can take it from here."

Edgewood nodded and signaled his partner out.

"Thank you, Doctor," he said as he went.

"Don't mention it."

Bosch thought of something.

"Hey, guys?"

Edgewood and Brasher turned back.

"Let's keep this off the air, okay?"

"You got it," said Brasher, her eyes holding on Bosch's until he looked away.

After the officers left, Bosch looked back at the doctor and noticed that the facial tremor was slightly more pronounced now.

"They didn't believe me at first either," he said.

"It's just that we get a lot of calls like this. But I believe you, Doctor, so why don't you continue with the story?"

Guyot nodded.

"Well, I was up on the circle and I took off the leash. She went up into the woods like she likes to do. She's well trained. When I whistle she comes back. Trouble is, I can't whistle very loud anymore. So if she goes where she can't hear me, then I have to wait, you see."

"What happened today when she found the bone?"

"I whistled and she didn't come back."

"So she was pretty far up there."

"Yes, exactly. I waited. I whistled a few more times, and

8

then finally she came down out of the woods next to Mr. Ulrich's house. She had the bone. In her mouth. At first I thought it was a stick, you see, and that she wanted to play fetch with it. But as she came to me I recognized the shape. I took it from her — had a fight over that — and then I called you people after I examined it here and was sure."

You people, Bosch thought. It was always said like that, as if the police were another species. The blue species which carried armor that the horrors of the world could not pierce.

"When you called you told the sergeant that the bone had a fracture."

"Absolutely."

Guyot picked up the bone again, handling it gently. He turned it and ran his finger along a vertical striation along the bone's surface.

"That's a break line, Detective. It's a healed fracture."

"Okay."

Bosch pointed to the box, and the doctor returned the bone.

"Doctor, do you mind putting your dog on a leash and taking a walk up to the circle with me?"

"Not at all. I just need to change my shoes."

"I need to change, too. How about if I meet you out front?"

"Right away."

"I'm going to take this now."

Bosch put the top back on the shoe box and then carried it with two hands, making sure not to turn the box or jostle its contents in any way.

Outside, Bosch noticed the patrol car was still in front of the house. The two officers sat inside it, apparently writing out reports. He went to his car and placed the shoe box on the front passenger seat.

Since he had been on call out he had not dressed in a suit. He had on a sport coat with blue jeans and a white oxford shirt. He stripped off his coat, folded it inside out and put it on the backseat. He noticed that the trigger from the weapon he kept holstered on his hip had worn a hole in the lining and the jacket wasn't even a year old. Soon it would work its way into the pocket and then all the way through. More often than not he wore out his coats from the inside.

He took his shirt off next, revealing a white T-shirt beneath. He then opened the trunk to get out the pair of work boots from his crime scene equipment box. As he leaned against the rear bumper and changed his shoes he saw Brasher get out of the patrol car and come back toward him.

"So it looks legit, huh?"

"Think so. Somebody at the ME's office will have to confirm, though."

"You going to go up and look?"

"I'm going to try to. Not much light left, though. Probably be back out here tomorrow."

"By the way, I'm Julia Brasher. I'm new in the division."

"Harry Bosch."

"I know. I've heard of you."

"I deny everything."

She smiled at the line and put her hand out but Bosch was right in the middle of tying one of the boots. He stopped and shook her hand.

"Sorry," she said. "My timing is off today."

"Don't worry about it."

He finished tying the boot and stood up off the bumper.

"When I blurted out the answer in there, about the dog,

I immediately realized you were trying to establish a rapport with the doctor. That was wrong. I'm sorry."

Bosch studied her for a moment. She was mid-thirties with dark hair in a tight braid that left a short tail going over the back of her collar. Her eyes were dark brown. He guessed she liked the outdoors. Her skin had an even tan.

"Like I said, don't worry about it."

"You're alone?"

Bosch hesitated.

"My partner's working on something else while I check this out."

He saw the doctor coming out the front door of the house with the dog on a leash. He decided not to get out his crime scene jumpsuit and put it on. He glanced over at Julia Brasher, who was now watching the approaching dog.

"You guys don't have calls?"

"No, it's slow."

Bosch looked down at the MagLite in his equipment box. He looked at her and then reached into the trunk and grabbed an oil rag, which he threw over the flashlight. He took out a roll of yellow crime scene tape and the Polaroid camera, then closed the trunk and turned to Brasher.

"Then do you mind if I borrow your Mag? I, uh, forgot mine."

"No problem."

She slid the flashlight out of the ring on her equipment belt and handed it to him.

The doctor and his dog came up then.

"Ready."

"Okay, Doctor, I want you to take us up to the spot where you let the dog go and we'll see where she goes."

"I'm not sure you'll be able to stay with her."

"I'll worry about that, Doctor."

"This way then."

They walked up the incline toward the small turn-around circle where Wonderland reached a dead end. Brasher made a hand signal to her partner in the car and walked along with them.

"You know, we had a little excitement up this way a few years ago," Guyot said. "A man was followed home from the Hollywood Bowl and then killed in a robbery."

"I remember," Bosch said.

He knew the investigation was still open but didn't mention it. It wasn't his case.

Dr. Guyot walked with a strong step that belied his age and apparent condition. He let the dog set the pace and soon moved several paces ahead of Bosch and Brasher.

"So where were you before?" Bosch asked Brasher.

"What do you mean?"

"You said you were new in Hollywood Division. What about before?"

"Oh. The academy."

He was surprised. He looked over at her, thinking he might need to reassess his age estimate.

She nodded and said, "I know, I'm old."

Bosch got embarrassed.

"No, I wasn't saying that. I just thought that you had been somewhere else. You don't seem like a rookie."

"I didn't go in until I was thirty-four."

"Really? Wow."

"Yeah. Got the bug a little late."

"What were you doing before?"

"Oh, a bunch of different things. Travel mostly. Took me a while to figure out what I wanted to do. And you want to know what I want to do the most?"

Bosch looked at her.

"What?"

"What you do. Homicide."

He didn't know what to say, whether to encourage her or dissuade her.

"Well, good luck," he said.

"I mean, don't you just find it to be the most fulfilling job ever? Look at what you do, you take the most evil people out of the mix."

"The mix?"

"Society."

"Yeah, I guess so. When we get lucky."

They caught up to Dr. Guyot, who had stopped with the dog at the turnaround circle.

"This the place?"

"Yes. I let her go here. She went up through there."

He pointed to an empty and overgrown lot that started level with the street but then quickly rose into a steep incline toward the crest of the hills. There was a large concrete drainage culvert, which explained why the lot had never been built on. It was city property, used to funnel storm water runoff away from the homes on the street. Many of the streets in the canyon were former creek and river beds. When it rained they would return to their original purpose if not for the drainage system.

"Are you going up there?" the doctor asked.

"I'm going to try."

"I'll go with you," Brasher said.

Bosch looked at her and then turned at the sound of a car. It was the patrol car. It pulled up and Edgewood put down the window.

"We got a hot shot, partner. Double D."

He nodded toward the empty passenger seat. Brasher frowned and looked at Bosch.

"I hate domestic disputes."

Bosch smiled. He hated them too, especially when they turned into homicides.

"Sorry about that."

"Well, maybe next time."

She started around the front of the car.

"Here," Bosch said, holding out the MagLite.

"I've got an extra in the car," she said. "You can just get that back to me."

"You sure?"

He was tempted to ask for a phone number but didn't.

"I'm sure. Good luck."

"You too. Be careful."

She smiled at him and then hurried around the front of the car. She got in and the car pulled away. Bosch turned his attention back to Guyot and the dog.

"An attractive woman," Guyot said.

Bosch ignored it, wondering if the doctor had made the comment based on seeing Bosch's reaction to Brasher. He hoped he hadn't been that obvious.

"Okay, Doctor," he said, "let the dog go and I'll try to keep up."

Guyot unhooked the leash while patting the dog's chest.

"Go get the bone, girl. Get a bone! Go!"

The dog took off into the lot and was gone from sight before Bosch had taken a step. He almost laughed.

"Well, I guess you were right about that, Doc."

He turned to make sure the patrol car was gone and Brasher hadn't seen the dog take off.

"You want me to whistle?"

"Nah. I'll just go in and take a look around, see if I can catch up to her."

He turned the flashlight on.